A Queen's Traitor

by Sam Burnell

All rights reserved. No part of this publication may be reproduced, stored in or introduced into a retrieval system, or transmitted, in any form, or by any means (electronic, mechanical, photocopying, recording or otherwise) without the prior written permission of the writer. Any person who does any unauthorized act in relation to this publication may be liable to criminal prosecution and civil claims for damages.

Thank you for respecting the hard work of this author.

A Queen's Traitor is written in British English.

Dedication

For Clive Andy Lomas and Elmidena

CHARARACTER LIST

Fitzwarren Household

William Fitzwarren - Father of Richard, Robert and Jack
Eleanor Fitzwarren - William Fitzwarren's wife
Robert Fitzwarren – William's son
Jack Fitzwarren – William's son
Richard Fitzwarren – William's son
Harry – Cousin to the Fitzwarren brothers
Ronan – William's steward
Edwin – Servant
Charles – Servant
Hal – Stablehand
Walt – Stablehand
Garth – Walt's brother

The English Court

Stephen Gardiner – Bishop of Winchester
Alberto – One of Phillip's Spanish Courtiers
Anne Bouchier – Mary's Lady in waiting
Anne Bassett – Mary's Lady in waiting
Jane Hardwich – Mary's Lady in waiting
Wriothesley – Privy Councillor
Kate Ashley – Elizabeth's governess
Travers – Controller of Elizabeth's household

York Pilgrims

Father Andrew – Group leader
Paul – Pilgrim
Annie – Paul's wife
Sim & Giles – Robbers
Roger Clement – York resident
Oswald – Roger Clement's son

Geoffrey Clement (lawyer)

Geoffrey Clement – Lawyer
Marcus Drover – Employee of Clement
Bartholomew – Debt collector
Brom & Stan – Bartholomew's men

Marshalsea

Master Kettering – Controller of Marshalsea
Ross – A gaoler

Richard's Mercenary Band

Dan – Also a family servant
Mat
Froggy Tate

Conspirators

Cuthbert Fairfax
George Sewell
Thomas Cressworth

Other Characters

Francis Ayscough – Sheriff of Lincoln
Jamie – Priest at Burton Village
Lizbet – A London prostitute
Daisy – A London prostitute
Roddy – Inn keeper
Master Drew – London shop keeper
Lucy Sharpe – Apothecary
Nonny – Brothel owner
Colan – One of Lizbet's customers
Hugo Drego – Captain of the Dutch Flower
Christian Carter – Richard's friend
Anne Carter – Christian's wife
Coleman- Christian Carter's steward
Cuddy – Christian Carter's servant

Prologue
Summer 1554

'Jack is leaving.'

It was known by a few, but rumour soon courted everyone's ears, until they all were aware that they were about to be abandoned, leaderless. Some cared, some sneered, some worried about the future, but most were indifferent.

Since Richard's death Jack had existed in a state of melancholy. His nerves were raw; a passionate and pleasant nature had now twisted into a temper fuelled with incoherent rage. His was a palpable grief, worsened by the feeling of utter rejection that had been his brother's final gift. That he had left Jack - and the world - for another was too abhorrent to consider. Whilst the men at Burton felt leaderless and looked to the future with concern, Jack was adrift. The only person who could have reached out to still his destructive passage was dead. Jack listened to no-one.

'Jack is going today.'

It was said amongst the men, quietly and they considered the news. Would he pay them? Would he come back? Would he say anything at all? They pressed the only person who had any link at all with Jack, and they hoped for some answers. Dan, however, was reluctant to face him again. He was only too well aware of his state of mind and didn't at all relish yet another confrontation. He'd tried; there was little more he could do. But they pressed him further, and eventually he gave in and went in search of Jack.

†

He knocked, opened the door and received the reply he expected. "Get out."

Breathing deeply, Dan squared his shoulders and strode into the room with purpose.

"Not this time Jack. The men have sent me. They have a right to know what is going to happen," he said bluntly.

Jack sat in the window embrasure in his room, ignoring him, his eyes unfocussed, lost in the distance. He didn't want to talk to Dan or to anyone.

"You need to let them know what we are going to do. You can't sit in here forever." Dan crossed the room and placed a hard, sinewy grip on Jack's shoulder, forcing him to look at him. This time he'd get an answer.

Jack twisted away. Springing to his feet he faced Dan; his eyes cold and mouth set in a hard line. "Get out."

"You owe them an answer. Jack, you know you do." Dan was prepared for a fight now and watched the other man carefully.

"I don't have the contacts Richard had, what do you want me to do?" Jack was breathing deeply. "Just get out."

"Not this time. There must be something you can do? You can't just throw it all away for nothing!" Dan argued, keeping his eyes firmly on Jack. He could sense that the man's temper was about to break.

"If we stay, they will drag us before the next Assize as sure as anything: we were Richard's men. He was a bloody traitor Dan, a traitor to the Crown! Like it or not he was, and we are tarred with it as well. Do you really think they are going to leave a little nest of treasonous sinners to their own devices? Do you?" Jack was shouting now.

"You'll just have to think of something," Dan was not having any of it, his next words adding to Jack's misery, "The Master would have."

They were merely words, but the blow they delivered was a physical one. "Christ Dan," Jack had gone pale, "I'm not him am I? As you keep reminding me. I don't have his connections, I was not privy to his thoughts, and I don't know what he would have done any more than you do. I am going to get my backside out of here before it gets dragged out for me and I get my neck stretched. And if you don't want to end up swinging from a rope you'll do the bloody same."

"He left you all this," Dan flung his arms wide. "you can't just throw it all away for nothing."

Jack's temper snapped. A moment later he had a poniard in his hand, "He threw it away, he didn't care what happened to any of this, or any of us."

Dan's eyes moved between the blade and Jack's face, and he took a precautionary step back before he deliberately delivered the words he knew Jack didn't want to hear, "He didn't care about you? Is that what you think?"

The blade was still, July sun sparking from the tempered steel.

"He cared for her more than any of us. More even, than he cared for himself," Jack swallowed hard. He'd not meant to vocalise that thought.

"He cared more for her than for you, that's the crux of it isn't it?" Dan accused.

Jack didn't reply: faced with the truth he couldn't.

"Put that away Jack, for God's sake, there's been enough bloodshed already. You need to decide what we are going to do next," Dan advised. He watched Jack's face and saw the anger turning to pain. A moment later, Jack slammed the knife back into its sheath.

"Damn you, I'm leaving here. I'll not stay for more of this. Get out of my way," raged Jack his voice hoarse.

"You can't just leave!" Dan continued to argue, bringing the argument right back to the start again.

"Just watch me, you can stop here and do what the hell you like." Blood was pounding in his head, his throat was tight, he knew he couldn't take any more of this and, as it was, his decision had been made for him when Mat suddenly burst through the door.

"There are three men here from Lincoln," Mat glanced between the two men. He could sense the tension in the room, "they want you, Jack."

"Are they at the gates?" Dan questioned, his attention drawn by necessity to the newcomer.

"No, they are in the hall," Mat blurted, still holding the door open behind him.

"What!" Jack exclaimed in disbelief, pausing in the act of reaching for his sword belt. "When did we stop bothering with closed gates?"

"Sorry, the men didn't think," Mat apologised.

Jack swore. This was his fault. The gates would never have been left to stand open while Richard was alive. The leather belt tight, he rammed a short blade into a wrist guard and pulled his sleeve back down to conceal it.

It seemed an end had come and Jack welcomed it. "Right then, shall we greet our guests?" Jack squared his shoulders and pushed brutally past Mat and Dan, leaving them to catch up with him. It was a short corridor that led onto the open stairs to the hall. He dropped down the steps easily, and as Mat had said, there were indeed three of them watching his approach carefully.

Jack smiled broadly, "Gentlemen, how can I help?"

"I'm Nicholas Norton. We've come from the Sheriff, he'd like for you to come with us," it was the tallest man who spoke. His face was impassive and his voice calm, which was at odds with the nervous expressions of his companions.

"That's good," Jack replied quickly, still smiling. "I had a mind to see Sir Ayscough as it happens." Then, calling over his shoulder. "Dan, get my horse ready."

"We can ride to Lincoln together," Norton suggested. He had been told that he'd know Jack Fitzwarren when he found him and they had not been wrong. The man's hair marked him out. Bright burnished yellow, falling to his shoulders, it framed a fair-skinned face with ice cold blue eyes. Ayscough had branded the man a fool. Norton looking at Jack Fitzwarren doubted very much that this was the case. Confident, well built and wearing a sword-belt that spoke of use; Norton knew he should not underestimate the man.

The incumbent Sheriff of Lincoln was one Sir Francis Ayscough. Jack had already met him when he had negotiated the deal to trade his brother for the manor and the liberty of himself and the men. Ayscough had made promises that Jack could retain Burton, but he knew perfectly well that this was likely to be reneged upon.

Had he known it, Ayscough actually owned land that bordered onto the woodland surrounding the small manor at Burton and he had every intention of extending his Lincolnshire landholding. With Jack gone he could easily and legally, disperse his men to procure the place for himself. What information he had about Jack came mainly from Robert and he cast the man as a simpleton who had inherited Burton upon the death of Richard: he seemed to think the man had neither wit nor sense. So it had been with little worry that Ayscough had sent three of his men to summon Jack to his office in Lincoln.

†

'Think! Damn you, think!' Jack silently cursed himself. It was only half an hour's ride to Lincoln and once there he knew he'd lose his liberty or worse. If he had acted against Ayscough's men at Burton, every one of his men there would have been branded with the crime. At least this way there would only be himself, and Jack cared little anymore. Analysing it he supposed he would prefer a quicker end, rather than a filthy one entombed in Lincoln's gaol until the day arrived to have his death delivered at the end of a choking rope.

There were three of them and all looked more than capable. These were poor odds but Jack was going to take them. He drew his horse a pace or so back so she neared the back of the pack: he knew there was meadow on the left soon and a break in the trees. There was little chance he could outrun Ayscough's men, but if he could put a little space between them he could turn back and bring the fight to them on his own terms. At the moment he was too close: if he drew his sword now he would easily be hacked from his mount.

At this point the road to Lincoln was still enclosed on both sides by trees. The three riders waiting impatiently on the road ahead were obscured from view until Jack rode around the bend. One of Ayscough's men riding on the outside saw them first and stiffened in the saddle, shouting, "This looks like trouble."

Trouble it was. Dan, Mat and Froggy Tate sat astride sweating horses blocking the road. Jack could not hide his smile. The officer who had spoken wheeled his horse round to cut Jack off from his men, the other two closed ranks as well. There was a resonating hiss as the men drew their swords. Jack also had steel in his hand but his route was blocked.

"What do we do?" Mat asked, holding his horse next to Dan's. "If we ride in they'll kill him."

"And if we don't they will anyway," Dan shot back. "Jack can look after himself. He'll have to, come on." He pressed his heels into the horse's side and asked the panting mare for one last short gallop.

They saw them coming and it split the group. Nicholas Norton hauled on his reins, pulling his mount next to Jack. Instinctively Jack heeled the mare round. She spun and her hindquarters crashed into the side of the other horse, momentarily pinning Norton's leg between the two horses. It was long enough for Jack to grab a handful of the man's jacket.

Pushing his horse further back he sought to pull him from his saddle. If the other rider's horse had not at that moment reared he would have succeeded. Unseated from the vertical horse and dragged as well by the man behind him, Norton cannoned into Jack dismounting them both.

Training, kept both men's blades in their hands as they fell.

"Jesus!" Jack swore. As he landed heavily on his left shoulder, his right leg took a glancing blow from one of his mare's rear hooves as she swung to bite the rearing horse. In the moment of the fight his mind ignored the pain. Before he had stopped falling he was already trying to get to his feet. His assailant fared little better and rolled over twice from the force of the fall. Jack was righted and on his feet a second before him.

Jack offered Norton no quarter, his blade aimed to kill, the leading edge set on a path for the other's head. A defensive up thrust forced it away, the lethal blade only inches above the exposed head. Breathing hard and using his body's weight to add speed to the sword, the point of the other's weapon made for Jack's exposed chest. Jack easily forced the blade away, but as he stepped back his right foot found a hole in the road. His balance was hopelessly lost.

Nicholas Norton sneered and took the opportunity he had been given, all of his strength behind a killing blow aimed at Jack's exposed left side. To stop the blade Jack was forced to hold his sword level, using it two-handed to block the attack. The impact forced his own blade to slice into his left hand where it held the edge. But it gave him an opening. For a moment his Norton's sword was stopped dead, all the man's weight held on Jack's blade. Removing the support meant it was Norton's turn to stagger.

You fool, thought Jack. An effective back swing of the blade cut neatly through leather and on into the fleshy shoulder, only to stop when the blade nicked the bone. Within him all the hopeless anger pooled. Withdrawing his blade, the second cut had twice the force behind it and met its mark: the broad blade first sliced neatly away the top of the Norton's ear, and then buried itself halfway through his skull. Before the dead man's weight could draw his blade down, a brutal kick sent the body reeling backward, sliding off the blade, to land prone in the road.

Jack spun around, the noise of the mêlée behind him. Dan and Mat's blades were engaged and Froggy was heading towards him, his hand wrapped around the reins of Jack's horse. Drawing level, he threw them at Jack who, without a moment's hesitation, flung himself back in the saddle.

"Come on," Jack yelled to Dan and Mat. The odds were now four to two and it was not likely the remaining men would want to continue the fight, especially with their leader laid flat in a spreading pond of blood behind them.

They rode hard for five minutes and pulled up when they felt they were a safe distance from the fight, all of them breathing hard. Jack, on the other hand, felt he was breathing more easily than he had in days, the brutal exacting fight and the hard ride had appeased his need for violence. For the moment his anger was satisfied.

"My thanks," Jack pulled the mare to a halt and held her tight on the reins. "Now we surely all have to leave. We must go back to Burton warn the men, tell them to scatter and we do the same."

Dan regarded him bitterly, but kept his counsel. This time he had to agree with Jack. Now they did have no choice but to leave: Jack had indeed thrown everything back in his brother's face.

Within half an hour of leaving them, Jack was on the road north, his belongings behind him and going God only knew where. He'd told them in no uncertain terms to all go their own way, to stay together would be to attract attention and they would be the easier to find.

The girl grasped another handful of horsetail stems and began again her vigorous scouring of the wooden chopping boards in the kitchens. Her hands were sore, her soul even more so. It seemed to Catherine De Bernay that she had now lost everything. Richard had tried to help her and she in turn had tried to save his life, but that had gone wrong, so very, very wrong. He was dead and like some inherited chattel, Catherine had become the possession of his brother, Robert.

The memories came back to her of the journey from Burton to London with Robert; she scrubbed harder trying not to think about them. It was only a few weeks ago. The bruises were gone now, but the feelings, the memories and the violence he'd delivered to her as he'd raped her still made her stomach retch. Twice, she'd fought back as hard as she could, using fists and feet, teeth and nails and he let her kick and scream and hit him while he laughed. Then, when he'd had enough, a blow to the head would make her senses reel and he would begin his rape.

The third time though, she didn't fight back: she'd just let him get on with the foul act. He'd shaken her badly then and Catherine realised he wanted her to fight, needed her to resist him. That time he'd left her with both her eyes closed with bruises and a split mouth that took days to heal, but he had not raped her and he didn't bother with her again on the journey to London. It was a bitter victory.

The bloody Fitzwarren family had a lot to damn well answer for. Robert she hated. Last week, he had received the report back from his lawyer about her property at Assingham. Her father, he told her, had been quite astute. Before he died, he had added extensive woodland to his holdings and it was this that was worth money indeed. Her poor father: he had bought that for his family, for her and her poor mother. She had cried then and Robert had laughed.

But it did give her hope. She'd told Robert he could keep it if she could have Assingham back and he had agreed. Even she knew how valuable good mature timber was. The woodlands around the manor had been stocked with the building blocks of England: chestnut, hazel and oak, lots of mature oak. It might as well have been a pile of coins, so valuable was this commodity and it was one Robert intended to obtain and harvest into his own coffers. Old Henry's war against France had raped the countryside of mature timber and Assingham's untouched tract of woodland was a golden bounty indeed.

For now she was trapped as servant in the Fitzwarren household. The steward, Ronan, kept her on a short leash for only a few weeks, until it became obvious that she was not likely to leave. Then his cold gaze and prying eyes left her alone. Catherine was now just another servant to work for the family: a mender, a baby minder, a cleaner, a cook, whatever they needed her to be. All she could hope was that Robert would be able to persuade her father's family to hand back Assingham. At least then she could be the Lady of her own household again.

The next blood she had seen was her own and the tears this time had been ones of relief. If Robert had saddled her with his bastard she knew that would have been more than she could have borne. In the darkness of night, alone and scared she'd choked back tears as she contemplated her own death.

Catherine sniffed loudly; she hated thinking of her family. They were gone and all that was left were painful memories. Her last hope had been Richard: not an easy man to gauge, but he had tried to help her and asked for nothing in return. And she missed Jack; she missed his easy manner and his quick smile. But she missed his presence the most; she had not realised how safe he had made her feel.

Catherine didn't know where he was, but she looked for him in every stranger's face she saw. Jack wouldn't have let Robert abuse her like he had; of that she was sure.

†

Jamie heard the movement from the truckle bed in the corner as the man rolled over and he knew he was awake then.

"Jamie... what day is it?" The voice that spoke was weak and broke as he tried to form the words.

"It'd be a Tuesday...not that that will be much good to you." Jamie chuckled moving over to kneel near the bed.

"Tuesday...that means I've been here for nearly a week." The voice spoke again in a hoarse murmur.

"Like I said knowing it's a Tuesday would be no good to you lad! You've been there for nearly three. And as like to stop there another couple I would guess." Jamie mused. "God has saved you. He didn't have to, but he most assuredly did."

"So long...but it can't..."

"Aye it was and it is. You bled a lot and by the time I got you here, I thought I'd be digging a grave the next morning I surely did, or at least the morning after. I prayed for your soul and I saw that there was nothing that could be done. But you didn't die. Every day I thought 'he'll be gone soon,' but you weren't. After three days I sent for Mistress Crill in the village and she's been tending to you since."

"A drink..." the voice managed.

Jamie poured one from the pitcher on the table and handed it to the prone man. A hand behind his head, he helped him raise himself so he could sip from the cup. Sweat beaded on his forehead and he fell back, spent by the effort of sitting up. Jamie sat back on his heels. Maybe he would be digging that grave after all he thought.

"Where's Jack?" Richard spoke with apparent effort.

"He's gone. Took himself off two weeks back, the men have left and the manor is in the keeping of Sir Ayscough until they decide what to do with it," Jamie supplied, shaking his head.

"Where did he go?"

"I don't know where he went. He wasn't left with much choice to be fair. The Sheriff would have taken him by force if he'd not fled, so hopefully he's gone far away from here." Jamie poured himself a cup of water and took a draught.

"Does he know I'm here?"

"He thinks you are dead, lad. I thought you were."

"Maybe I am dead," Richard's voice almost sounded amused. What was it they said about Hades, he pondered. It was easy getting in - the tricky bit was getting back out again. God he hurt. Richard's mind felt detached; he was aware of the pain in his left shoulder but somehow it seemed a long way away. There seemed to be no connection between his thoughts and his physical form.

"Maybe," agreed Jamie, "we'll have to wait and see won't we?"

Richard's mind drifted back into unconsciousness once more. Sweat darkened his hair to the colour of a raven's wing and illness had accentuated the angular cheekbones, the mouth, often so cruel, was softened in sleep. The grey, cold searching eyes, lidded, couldn't see Jamie watching him closely. The priest's thumb pulled the rosary beads through his fingers, slowly and in time with the laboured breathing from the man on the bed.

Chapter One

It was a slow journey and it was three days before he even had a sense of his surroundings. The sword injury to his left hand was deep and painful, searing like a burn, but the agony of the cut flesh stopped his mind from wandering. It was bound tight to help the wound heal, and his mind was preoccupied with the pain, sometimes it helped to banish the sense of loss which would not leave him.

It had been a poor summer, the temperatures cool and the rain heavy, leaving the roads mired, the fields flattened and the trees dripping. Alone, trying to take shelter from the weather against a tree trunk in the dark, he was finally reduced to tears. In the morning he awoke, soaked, half frozen and with his brother's scornful voice ringing in his ears. It was then that he realised just how much a part Richard had played in his life. He had constantly craved Richard's approval; he'd worked for it, strived for it and, on rare occasions, even gained it. If he'd never met him Jack was forced to admit, he would still be a servant in Harry's household, and he would have been there his whole life.

Richard had known the truth, but that had not mattered to him, he knew Jack could never claim his inheritance. It was only on that lonely journey that he finally realised what he had been given by his brother. It had been gifted to him slowly, sometimes brutally, often reluctantly, but in the end, Richard had shown him that he could be his equal.

And then... Jack swore inwardly... and then he'd given his life for some futile cause, some woman who would probably not even miss a heartbeat at his passing. It was not likely that he'd ever meet her, but if he did, God help her.

Jack reached into his jacket and pulled out the ring that had been Richard's. It sparkled even in the dull summer's light. The crest was his, he knew that now. Pushing it onto his finger, he considered it for a few moments before he reversed the ring so only the gold band showed.

†

At Pontefract, he had come across a group of pilgrims from the west-country bound for York to pay homage at the tomb of St William. They were, to Jack, the most wholly inadequately organised group of travellers he had ever come across. How they had made it so far was a complete mystery, he was sure God must also be shaking His head in disbelief. They were under-provisioned, had little to no equipment with them and relied on charity and

God to provide. Their blind faith, however, seemed to be working.

The group consisted of a Catholic priest, Father Andrew and four families, with an elderly couple riding in a flatbed wagon pulled by the family horse. The wagon provided the accommodation for the stops, under or on top, depending on the weather; mostly this journey so far it had been under. The group was in high spirits, Father Andrew told a good story and when he'd stopped to help them with a loosened wheel he had accepted their invitation to join them. After all, they were all going north.

Jack glared at the second rabbit caught in the snares he had set and swore under his breath. The young rabbit, fur soaked and matted by the incessant drizzle was barely worth skinning. He used his knife quickly and tucked the lifeless bundle into the bag with the other he had caught. The snares and pegs he pulled free of the meadow.

He'd had four snares: two had been embedded tightly in the furry legs, the third he had found un-tripped, and the fourth he could not find. Jack cursed the Almighty for the second time. Tell-tale black loam marked the spot where the pegs anchoring the snare had been torn free. It was now probably adorning the hind leg of a hare, for it was nowhere to be seen. Six was the best number to set, and he'd already lost two, so now he was going to have to craft some more. With only three he was likely to go hungry.

Trudging back to the makeshift campsite Jack handed the catch bag apologetically to Annie, "They are poor rabbits, sorry."

"Thank you, Jack, they'll do us just fine," Annie smiled. She was always smiling, continually thanking the Lord, and held a firm conviction that all would be well. Jack, who liked often to dwell on the bleaker aspects of his existence, found her tiresome.

"We'll soon be at York. So what takes you to the city?" Paul, Annie's husband, was poking the fire back to life while his wife settled down next to him, humming happily, as she set to skinning the two small rabbits Jack had brought back.

"Work," was an automatic response. Jack sat cross-legged, laying out the thin strips of elder bark he had collected to make up a new set of snares.

"Aye, I'm sure there's a wealth of that there, what's your trade lad?" Father Andrew joined the group and seated himself in the companionable circle.

"Marshal, farrier, stablehand, anything working with horses," Jack supplied, his head bent to his task, hoping it was obvious he didn't want to continue the conversation.

"Really?" Paul cast a sideways glance at Jack's horse.

"Well, it's been a long journey," Jack sounded defensive. Corracha had belonged to his brother. The horse's coat was mired in mud, mane tangled, tail clogged and wet, but despite all this the horse's beauty was still evident. The chiseled head and dished face set on the long arching neck marked the stallion as an Arabian. Possessing a confident manner, the way he moved announced to the world his proud, powerful and energetic nature.

Guilt flooded through him, he knew the time Richard had spent on the beast. He was worth ten, no maybe even twenty times the cost of any horse Jack had ever owned. It was the reason he'd taken him from the stables in place of his own palfrey. Corracha was worth gold should he need it.

"That's a fine beast you got there," Father Andrew, lay a hand on his shoulder, "why not give the boys over there a coin or two, they'll have him cleaned and brushed out for you in a trice." He added, "It'll do them some good, they have had little to entertain them these past few weeks."

"Aye, I might," Jack conceded a little grumpily, not enjoying the unwanted attention.

Father Andrew smiled; he knew when to leave a man alone. Clapping Jack on the shoulder he settled beside him, watching Jack's skilful hands fashion the cord for a new set of snares. Jack used a knife to split the bark lengths into narrow strips. Then ran the back of the knife down each to straighten them and remove the damp spongy material from the side. He twisted a peg into the ground and used it to secure the first of the elder strips and then began to twist them into a tough and durable cord.

"It makes you wonder, doesn't it? Who was the first man who looked at a tree and thought he could make something as delicate as that?" Father

Andrew picked up one of the finely twisted lengths Jack had finished making from the elder bark. "You'd not connect the two would you?" he mused, rolling it between his fingers.

Jack was about to speak, but it was Paul who commented first, "God provides us with all manner of wondrous opportunities, Father."

Jack rolled his eyes: it never took this lot long to drag the Almighty into the conversation.

"Indeed, where do any of our notions come from?" Father Andrew continued. "All that comes to us that is good is from God's bounty, even our wisdom. Our skills are all His to give and take away as He wishes."

"So you believe every skill is God-given?" Jack couldn't help himself.

"Of course," Father Andrew continued, with a twinkle in his eyes. "go on lad, I can see you don't believe me."

Jack had just finished using his knife to neatly trim the ends of the elder bark string; he flipped the poniard in his hand, holding it out, hilt first for Father Andrew to take. "Hit the centre of the wheel," Jack gestured at the cart that stood a good ten paces away.

Father Andrew laughed, "I can barely see that far these days, let alone throw a knife that far."

"Surely though, God - seeing you are hungry - will give you the skills you need to throw a knife so you'll not starve?" Jack pressed.

"Indeed he might if there was that need," Father Andrew replied, then added, "can you hit the wheel?"

In a smooth movement, Jack reversed the knife and sent it spinning to embed itself neatly in the wheel hub.

"There then. There's no need for me to throw, God has provided you, has He not?" Father Andrew spoke triumphantly.

"It doesn't just happen, that's borne of practice," Jack's patience was wearing thin.

"Yes, and God gave you the time to do that, just as He gave us the eyes to see that this," Father Andrew held out the fine cord, "could be made from the bark. He put the thoughts into a man's head that he could make this and he did."

"Or maybe, someone was just hungry and wanted to catch a rabbit," Jack said under his breath.

The next day, the cart trundled on. The background to the day was always the same: the low chatter of voices and the creak from the cart as the wooden back board twisted when the wheels negotiated the uneven road. Jack liked to ride at the back: here the voices were just sounds, he couldn't hear the words, and more importantly, they wouldn't try to include him. Corracha was happy to follow, and it was some moments before he realised that the horse had pulled to a halt behind the wagon.

'If the wheel pin has come out again, they can bloody well put it back in themselves,' Jack thought. He had no desire to crawl in the mud again and kept to his saddle; the reins loosely folded in his good right hand and waited.

The tug on his leg made him jump. It was one of the boys, "Help! There's three men arguing with Father Andrew."

"Shhh lad," Jack held his hand out to silence the boy, "you stay here."

The horse had sensed the change in it's rider instantly: Corracha's head was up, the muscled withers tensed, liquid black eyes alert and nostrils wide. Jack saw three men ahead of the cart, arguing with Father Andrew. The cleric seemed as if he was trying to appease them. But, as Jack watched, one of them thumped him hard in the shoulder sending him reeling over backward to land in the road. Jack heeled the stallion round, riding him away from the road.

"Where are you going?" wailed the boy as he watched Jack disappear into the forest.

Father Andrew was trying to struggle to his feet and Annie, a hand under one of his arms, was trying to help him.

"Stay down there!" one of them shouted. All of them wore the pinched look of hunger, and that made them dangerous. From where Father Andrew sat, uncomfortably aware of the water seeping through his clothing, he saw on two of their doublets where the soldier's badges had been pulled from them, leaving loose stitches. Turned off, or deserters, it didn't matter which, they were still a real threat.

Then Annie started to plead with them.

"We've nothing to give, we are just poor folk..." there was a loud smack and a choked scream; Annie fell to her knees clutching her face.

"We'll be the judge of that love," one of them laughed. Paul ran towards his wife, but the knife in the man's hand stopped him dead.

"Now, some coins, some food and that horse, and we'll let you be on your way," the shortest of the group demanded. He addressed Andrew, as the undoubted highest ranking member of the group.

"We beseech you, please have some kindness, these are simple folk who would gladly share a meal with you..." A rough kick in the leg stilled Father Andrew's words. "I said, I want what coins you have, food and that," he pointed directly at the pony tethered to the cart, "horse. Now get to it, or you'll be getting a bit more than a few bruises."

"In the name of the Lord please Sir..." Andrew tried again.

The man grabbed Annie by the hair and hauled her to her knees, a dirty knife in his hand pressed under her ear. "Get me what I ask for or I'll cut her ear off and that'll be just the start."

"Wait, wait, I've some money, not much but you can have it all, please let her go." Paul, Annie's husband started to reach into his jacket for what little he had and then stopped abruptly.

"Get on with it or her ear comes off," the man realised a little too late that Paul was no longer staring at him but at the mounted man some paces behind them who sat quietly on his horse; a sword unsheathed resting on his shoulder.

"Let her go," Jack stated simply, and then he added, "or don't, it's your choice." He dropped lightly from the saddle and crossed the short distance to the group.

"You should have stopped up there: now it's three against one. Get him, Sim!"

Sim, the largest of the three, already had a blade in his hand: a professional soldier, he was trained and hardened for a fight. The man standing before him, in torn clothes, with the filth of rough living on him and a sword stupidly balanced on his shoulder wasn't a threat. He rolled the hilt of his own sword in his hand, and then set the blade to whistle through the air in two quick flashing cuts. Jack just stood unmoving.

"Come on then," Sim goaded, moving the sword point threateningly toward Jack. "This'll not take me long; you just keep hold of that woman Giles."

"Anytime you like," Jack sounded unimpressed. He was a big man he'd fight on power, not skill. His attack would aim true, but it would be slow, he was sure.

"Go on Sim," the leader, Giles, called from where he still held the whimpering woman.

Sim growled, and grasping his sword a little firmer, stepped forward to strike. The grim and capable face was replaced by wide eyed surprise, as the blade cut only through air: his target had moved faster than he could have thought possible. The only impact was Jack's blade slicing up over and taking the blade out of his hand to send it spinning end over end into the mud.

"Let her go," Jack demanded, the point of his weapon now levelled, unmoving, at Sim's chest.

"Sim, you useless idiot!" Giles shouted back. He'd dropped the blade from Annie's ear to her neck and the woman could not contain her scream. "Now let Sim get his blade back or I'll let her next breath out for her."

Jack glanced between them. Sim unarmed before him, the leader with Annie's hair wound round his fist and the third man who'd yet to join in. He appeared as nervous as Annie's husband did, and Jack guessed rightly that he'd not act unless he was pressed to. Jack lowered his blade and nodded to Sim to go and collect his from where it lay on the black mud. As he stooped to pick it up, his back was to Jack for an instant and it was long enough to flick the knife from his wrist guard and send it on a fast and accurate flight.

Sim, hearing the scream turned; the wet muddy blade now in his hand.

"You're not bloody well touching me with that," Jack announced and took the fight to Sim. Jack on a good day was dangerous, but on a day when he neither cared whether he lived nor died was formidable. His reckless abandon added an edge that soon marked itself in terror on Sim's face, as he realised that he was badly matched to fight the man in front of him.

Jack let their blades touch seven times, smiling as they did, and then with a finality that Sim's bowels recognised, he shook his head. The first cut went through Sim's exposed throat and the second, vicious, unnecessary slice, unzipped his stomach. The wide gaping wound spewed forth visceral innards to the mud in a steaming grey, and bleeding heap.

Annie was crawling away. Giles was on his knees now, his face pale, with the knife's hilt protruding from his chest. Jack made a quick move towards the third man and he ran backward, taking quick flight away from the road into the trees.

Jack advanced on Giles. The man tried to move backward, but bleeding and with a knife between his ribs, it was a hollow gesture. Jack grabbed him under one arm, his other on the hilt and lifted him back upright. Giles screamed, bubbles of blood running down his chin. Jack's breathing was even, his eyes were wide, and he could smell the blood. When his fist hit Giles it felt good. The bone of his nose splintering beneath his knuckles, the man landed prone on the road, and Jack went with him, fists intent on inflicting as much hurt as Jack had within him.

"Stop," Father Andrew had hold of one of Jack's arms, "stop lad."

Jack delivered one more blow, a choking gasp catching in his throat.

"Stop, come away, he's dead," Father Andrew tightened his hold on Jack, feeling the tremors run through his body.

"I know he's dead, I know it, but I still want to hit him, why did he do it?" Jack rocked back on his heels and covered his face with his blooded fists. *God Richard why did you leave me?*

It was Father Andrew who took charge then. He rallied the group and before long the bodies were consigned to the bracken cover of the forest floor. The cart trundled once more back along the muddy path. Jack, still in a daze, had been helped back into the saddle and one of the boys led his horse. Jack's crusted blades lay under the cover on the wagon. They were a silent and reticent group that moved towards York that afternoon, the woman and men casting wary glances at their saviour.

That night's meal around the fire in the dampened woodland was set to be a quiet and strained one. Jack sat apart, aware of the suspicious glances he was attracting. His knuckles were raw; the skin torn and red, Giles's dried blood on his hands, and the cut in his palm had opened up again and was bleeding steadily. It was Annie who came over eventually and kneeling near him, held out a cup.

"I was saving this, but I think we've all a need of it tonight." Annie smiled. He took the offered cup and she poured him a good measure of aqua vitae. "Go on, try it."

Jack did: it burnt his lips, and he attempted a smile.

Annie smiled back. "Thank you for what you did. Paul and the others, they're just farming folk. They feel ashamed, that's all. We were lucky the

Lord set you to join us." Jack, for once, kept his thoughts on the Divine to himself.

"Come on, join us I've a good supper for you," Annie stood, hands on hips and waited for him to get up, which he reluctantly did. Shoving her arm through his she set their course back to the fire and the waiting group. Jack let her lead him.

"Come on you lot, make room for the lad," Annie gave Paul a nudge with one of her feet.

She had not lied: it was a good supper. There was pottage with meat, and warm and filling unleavened bread, baked on a stone near the fire. Father Andrew produced a second bottle to supplement Annie's and he found a few new stories which even had Jack smiling quietly. That night, Jack's sleep was not wracked by haunting memories and he awoke feeling guilty that for a time, he had forgotten.

†

When Mary took the throne, like her father before her, she enjoyed the finery of her position. That she would be remembered as a dark and restrained figure would have been consternation to the keeper of the royal wardrobe who kept the accounts for her lavish expenditure. Henry's final year had seen a disbursement of funds on his wardrobe of eight thousand pounds, Mary had spent double that figure in her first year.

Mary, elegant in deeply pleated dark velvet, extravagantly embellished with delicate Flemish lace with a hemline picked out in finely stitched roses, waited impatiently for the Bishop of Winchester to arrive. Mary had inherited her father's small dark piercing eyes and ridged nose, her thin disapproving lips were set in a perpetual hard line; there was little soft beauty to be found in her face.

The desk before her was heaped with paperwork, all in neat piles, all awaiting her attention and all of it relating to the repeal of her half brother's religious legislation. Mary scowled now at the physical manifestation of her wishes.

"Lawyers are making this difficult just to justify their own profession," Mary lifted one of the sheaves of documents from the table and then dropping it back with a thud, "I am sure they are in league with the parchment vendors. Look at all this."

Mary glowered at the two Annes; though both knew better than to comment and both dropped their eyes to their needlework. Anne Bourchier was Countess of Essex and the other, Anne Bassett, a Tudor courtier from a bygone age. It was rumoured that Mary's father had turned to Bouchier after the death of his one true love, Jane Seymour. That Mary kept around her such women was a constant irritation to Stephen Gardiner, Bishop of Winchester. They appeared to be part of the framework of the Court. Bouchier had later eloped with her lover and borne two illegitimate offspring in Mary's mother's time. Gardiner supposed she liked neither of these women and it was true that in return for their places at Court they had to put up with Mary's tempers, irritations and tirades. Both women had outlived two previous Tudor sovereigns and a host of wives. One could only suppose they were by now well acquainted with the Tudor temperament and knew how to deal with it.

"My Lord Bishop of Winchester," announced the page at the door to Mary's presence chamber. He bowed low, always sure of his place. His were the hands that had placed, confidently and with purpose Edward the Confessor's crown on Mary's head. For him it had been symbolic, a coronation that returned England to Rome and to the Catholic state. The true way.

Monarch's were traditionally crowned by the Archbishop of Canterbury. Thomas Cranmer, who held that post, was a reformer and Mary would not have him preside over her coronation. Instead, it had been Gardiner, Bishop of Winchester and her soon-to-be Lord Chancellor that had the honour. He was prepared to overlook that he had to bow to a woman as Monarch, for this stern and unfriendly female was a tool, a willing tool, of the Catholic faith.

Mary's joyous match to Phillip of Spain had been one of the more repugnant tasks that had been his to carry out; England was not a country that liked the idea of a foreign wedding. For Mary, it was the perfect marriage; Philip was already set to rule Spain, a country she felt close links with through her mother Catherine of Aragon and he was Catholic. Mary truly believed the people supported her choice and her inability to judge public sentiment would be a characteristic of her reign.

"Look at this." She waved imperiously at the paperwork.

"Your Majesty, I can assure you all is in order," Gardiner came to stand near the table.

"It has taken months, and now I know why." Mary was annoyed: her first act after her coronation had been to reinstate the Catholic Mass. This had meant suspending the Act of Uniformity. However, from a legal point this had been reasonably easy and left Mary thinking that reversing all of Edward's reformist measures would be as simple.

"The Statute of Repeal is a difficult matter, Your Majesty. There are so many affected, the legislation was complicated and so many property issues were implicated as well that..."

Mary cut him off. "You assured me that this would be an easy matter. I know we cannot take the land back from the nobles, there would be an outcry, but surely we can bring England back to the Catholic faith a little quicker than this?" When Henry had dissolved the monastic institutions, he had not only enriched his own coffers but the ruling elite had also benefited from his sale of Church land. This redistribution of wealth was not an easy issue to face. Mary would have returned all the monastic lands and reinstated all the religious houses Henry had torn down. However, she was a realist and recognised that without the support of England's nobility her reign might prove to be a difficult one.

"Your Majesty," Gardiner said, as calmly as possible, "we do need to make sure that this is correctly done. You do not want to leave the reformist rabble with a legal loophole for them to attach their cause to."

"You came to me months ago and told me the easiest and surest way forward was to return the land to the legal position as it was in 1547, before my brother was led astray by Edward Seymour's Reformist ambition. So, surely, why can it not state that anything after this date is no longer effective? Why does this have to be such a complicated matter?" 1547 was the year her brother had taken the throne after Henry's death and recognition of this year was an important demonstration that anything enacted during Edward's brief reign no longer applied. "The slate should be clean, his reforms were removed. I cannot wipe them from history but we can negate their effects."

"I understand, Your Majesty, but the Reformist policies took the Church a long way from Rome. The clergy were allowed to marry; and many had families; Latin was no longer the voice of the Church. There is much change in many lives and we need England to be with you, Your Majesty."

Once the coronation had been completed, Mary had seen for herself the countrywide support her reign had attracted. It became apparent she had a powerful weapon on her side: the people were loyal to the legal ruling monarch despite the fact that the new legal succession was vested in a woman. Devoutly Catholic, she had quickly decided that it would be an easy task to unravel the religious reforms of Edward and return England to the true religion.

Religious upheaval had been the tone in England since the 1520s. Mary's father took the first steps away from Rome when he appointed himself head of the Church in a bid to rid himself of his first wife, Mary's mother, Catherine of Aragon. Since then it had been accepted in England that the Monarchy, not Rome, ruled supreme. To move England back under the control of Papal authority was another thing entirely.

"Look at this," Mary picked up the top manuscript and read from it; "*whereof hath ensured amongst us in very short time numbers of divers and strange opinions and diversities of sects, and thereby grown great unquietness and much discord, to the disturbance of the commonwealth of this realm, and in very short time like to grow to extreme peril and utter confusion of the same, unless some remedy be in that behalf provided...*" Mary threw the document back down. "Did you hear that? Short time it says, not once but twice!"

"Your Majesty, everything has now been given the royal seal and very soon you will have returned the realm to Rome."

"My people wish this to be so, I will deliver them back to the protection of the faith," Mary glowered at the documents. "This was not, however, what you wished to speak to me about," Mary spoke through thin lips. A ringed hand waved the two Anne's away and Gardiner seated himself where she indicated.

"Indeed, Your Majesty, it is with great pain that I have to report what is happening within your royal sister's household," Gardiner made himself comfortable on the velvet perch.

"You have staff within her household?" Mary enquired. She knew he did, indeed she herself had suggested that her sister was closely watched.

"For the Lady's good guidance and for her salvation, I have indeed made sure that goodly souls attend her. Lady Travers and her husband have been part of her household whilst she is at Durham Place, Your Majesty." Little did he know that Travers was a man with two masters, reporting not only to Gardiner but also to Mary.

"And what does Lady Travers have to tell us then?" Mary asked, her fingers twisting the crested heavy ring that sat on her right hand.

"Lady Elizabeth still adheres to her Protestant ways, and so do her household. She has a copy of John Knox's latest writing; Lady Travers has seen her reading it." Gardiner was sure that linking Elizabeth and Knox would finally be her undoing.

"Have they found a copy of it?" Mary asked. Then when Gardiner did not instantly reply, "Well? Did you find it?"

"Kate Ashley believes she has security over Elizabeth's possessions but when they have been absent from Durham Place, Travers had Elizabeth's private coffer opened. He has not found the book yet: Kate guards the key and takes great pains to keep everyone out, so Travers is sure it is there somewhere; he has just not found it yet." Gardener was nervous, his hands fidgeting in his lap, and then he added, "She has her mother's Book of Hours; Lady Travers has found that in the coffer. It is an affront to the Lord, the book is defaced by her own hand with so many scurrilous lines in it she even wrote..."

Mary cut Gardiner off, "The whore wrote in it, not Elizabeth, and however much we dislike it I can understand why she would keep something belonging her mother."

"It is Reformist propaganda, Boleyn's book should not be in her keeping," Gardiner protested.

"And what is in it that is to be kept secret?" Mary already knew what the pages contained; Travers had already sent her copies of the added scripts. Anne Boleyn's Book of Hours contained nothing more than love notes between her and Henry. Mary hated it, striking as it did at the marriage which had at that time still stood between her father and mother, but she accepted that it had nothing to do with Elizabeth.

"Anything she wrote would be held up and flaunted by the Protestant cause."

"They are love letters! My father's addled love-struck words and his whore's replies. There is nothing, *nothing*, in there that the Reformist cause could use." Mary's temper flared.

"Your Majesty, Knox's works are..."

"These you have not found, and maybe it does not exist at all? Kate is right to protect her mistress's possessions, that does not mean in itself that she colludes to keep secret such things does it?" Mary snapped at him.

"Your Majesty, if I may just have a little more time..."

"More time? You've been hunting for months, Gardiner. First, you told me she had secret communications with Courtney, then you tell me that Knox had been writing to her, and now you tell me that she is openly within her household, reading aloud his latest heresy? What proof is there? None and I fear you begin to make a fool of me."

"Your Majesty, I just want to keep your royal sister safe, there are many who would collude against her." Gardiner insisted, perspiration starting to form on his brow.

"So you keep telling me," Mary sounded weary. "Do not continue with this, Gardiner, unless there are some grounds. The Lady is our royal sister, do not bring me mere hearsay."

"Indeed, Your Majesty." Gardiner's resolve hardened. He knew that to return England fully to Rome he had to remove Elizabeth. She was a figurehead for the disaffected and – worse - for the Protestant cause. However much Mary tried to tell herself this was not so, and that she could bring Elizabeth to the Catholic Church and let her see the joy of the Mass as Mary did, Gardiner knew that this would never be the case. Even if Elizabeth herself eschewed Protestantism and became outwardly devoutly Catholic, they would still flock to her as Anne's daughter; as a sister who was closer to her dead Protestant brother Edward VI than Mary had ever been.

Knox's latest pamphlet which had been printed outside England was a direct assault on Mary. Titled, "The First Blast of the Trumpet Against the Monstrous Regiment of Women," it was aimed directly at Catholic Mary. Knox saw it as an affront to God that a woman could in any way rule over men, and that she was a Catholic made it an abomination. However, his polemical treatise against female sovereigns and their policies was gaining popular support.

Chapter Two

Used to the South, and to London, York made Jack feel a little more at home. A city of some ten thousand souls, it had a strong heart, the noise and odour comforting and familiar. At York, for the moment, his weary northern trudge was halted. You could smell York the closer you got: a knot of a city, wound in a tight ball around the bend in the river, walled and secure. Although he'd never been here before, there was a feeling of homecoming as he rode towards the City.

The towering walls were punctuated by four main entrances and as his horse plodded down Holgate Road, Micklegate Bar came into view. Two round towers gilded with arrow slits stood either side of the darkened opening. Between them, supported on a thick oiled chain, was a raised portcullis. The lower walls were blanketed in shadow but the top of the towers shone white in the sun's rays, the heraldic shields fastened there glinted like gold. In front of the gate were the first set of defences, lower stone walls and wooden palisades, with a first gate house where visitors, into and out of the city, had to queue before being allowed to enter through Micklegate Bar.

They passed easily through the security at the gates, being as they were a small pilgrimage group. Jack led his horse and stood amongst the group unnoticed, then made his way into the city.

"Stay with us, Jack," Paul asked, still a little nervous around him after the violent incident on the road. "Annie has family near Bootham Bar and we're to stop with them a few days. I doubt as one more will make a difference."

"That would be most appreciated, I've not been to York before, and it would be good while I find my way around," Jack accepted as he walked next to Paul leading Corracha.

"We'll be going to the shrine tomorrow, come with us lad." Father Andrew added his own invitation.

Jack gave him a black look. He had no liking for religion, priests or churches. He would have thought Father Andrew would have understood that by now.

"Don't be so bleak," Father Andrew continued, and he leaned a little closer, "You seem to me, lad, like you could use some help. And it comes from strange places sometimes, come and join us. Paul there, he'd not tell you, but he has a little one at home. Fair ill the boy is, and he hopes his namesake will help the boy's cause."

"I might," conceded Jack gruffly.

"This way, this way," Father Andrew herded his followers through the gate and onward into the northern stronghold. They followed the crowds under the raised portcullis and onto Micklegate towards the river. The way was narrow, the black and white buildings on either side crowding in towards the road, diamond glass panes twinkling in the sunshine.

"There, look," Father Andrew was acting as their guide, "the tower came down in a great storm in 1551." On their right the road opened up as they drew level with the Priory Church of the Holy Trinity. Indeed one end of the church resembled a masonry yard rather than a monastic building. Stacks of stones stood around the church yard and makeshift wooden props held up the end of the nave that the storm had not taken down.

"Was a terrible storm," Father Andrew continued, "the parish folk hereabout were sheltering in the Priory Church with the monks when a single bolt of lightning lit the sky and blew the tower apart. And mark this, not a soul in the church was hurt."

Annie crossed herself, awe on her face, "A Godly miracle, Father."

The cleric nodded sagely in agreement, "Indeed, indeed. We are in a place now oft touched by God."

The group continued further on down Micklegate. The way narrowed even more, and those coming and leaving the city jostled for space on the busy street. The road swung gently to the right and when they rounded the bend, the grand structure of St Martin's Church stood on their right.

Beautiful arched windows seemed to reach to the very tops of the walls. The tower was graced with a magnificent clock-face and as they passed, the bells began to toll. The group smiled at each other and the boys put their fingers in their ears and received a belt round the back of the head from Father Andrew.

"They're God's bells, boys!" he admonished harshly. Jack agreed with the boys. He winked at them mouthing that he too would like to put his fingers in his ears.

The buildings on both sides stopped abruptly. Jack realised they had reached the bridge over the River Ouse which took travellers into the very heart of the city. Much to the annoyance of the passing traffic, Father Andrew brought his group to a halt and bid them kneel while he recounted the tale of Archbishop William's return to York.

William had come back in triumph to take up his Godly position once again, after being wrongly outcast by a misinformed monarch. Many had lined the streets cheering at his return to the city. So mighty had been the weight of the faithful that the bridge had collapsed and over two hundred souls had been cast into the cold folds of the River Ouse. Archbishop William had fallen to his knees and begged God to save the citizens of York and not one life was lost on that day.

Jack saved his knees and, despite a hard stare from Father Andrew, he remained standing. With his weight against the side of the bridge he stared about him. To his right, further down river, was another crossing over the Ouse, a myriad of small boats made their way up and down the river carrying every kind of cargo: men, beasts, barrels, timber. York was a busy place.

Finally the group rose from their knees and continued into York's centre. Once off the bridge, the street became narrow and tightly packed again. They continued up Micklegate, turning left into the even narrower High Ousegate. Progress became even slower as Paul carefully manoeuvred the cart past shop fronts and the displays of wares for sale piled in front them.

They turned twice more in the narrow streets. At one corner the wagon got completely stuck with the wooden flatbed hooking into the frame of another wagon going in the opposite direction. Only with the strength of four men did they manage to untangle the wagons, the boys holding the startled pony still while they heaved and jostled the cart round.

Jack was sure that Father Andrew had no idea where they were going as he led them into Davygate, another busy little street. The smell of ale wafted to his nose along with that of roasted meat, Jack was sure everyone heard his stomach rumble in complaint. They pressed on, and it was with relief when they turned into Stonegate which was wider and a lot easier to navigate.

"Soon we will be there. Look forwards," Father Andrew's voice was excited as he urged them all on to their final destination. The group carried on down Stonegate and already they could all see, towering behind the streets of York, the great edifice that was York Minster. Even Jack was impressed as they emerged from the narrow, dark street to stand in the sunlight in front of the great Cathedral. The sun picked out all the tiny facets that made up the enormous rose window; jewelled glass held secure in the exquisitely carved stone: stone that appeared like it was carved like clay to form the beautiful sweeping forms and shapes that decorated every part of the towering building. So many windows. Jack had never seen a building like it.

Everywhere were towering, arched frames; each one paned with glass; each one pointing to the heavens, and all bounded by carved pillars, hundreds of them all leading the eye up to the top of the Minster. Every point on the roof, every corner, was finished with a towering pinnacle reaching even further towards the sky. The roof line was embellished with a fretwork in stone as delicate as ladies' lace. While Jack gazed in wonder at the Minster, Father Andrew was offering a prayer. All his pilgrims were on their knees, humbled by the majesty of Gods house, a house where Saint William had been laid to rest centuries before.

They left York centre. Paul's wife's sister lived near the walls and they began to retrace their steps back through the narrow streets. Jack, as he helped heft the cart bed round yet another bend, asked himself for the umpteenth time why the hell they hadn't left the bloody thing wherever it was they were going to stop rather than jamming up most of York with it. They were not popular.

Finally, the light poured in and Jack recognised the break in the buildings where the road led on to the bridge. On the other side, the road was twice as wide and the flat bed of the cart would not get rammed up constantly against the sides of the narrow streets and the rest of the crammed traffic could at least get past them.

Jack had just remounted Corracha to lead him over the bridge when there was a scream from behind him followed by the hammer of pounding hooves as a horse drew level and overtook him making straight for the bridge. Hanging on for dear life, round its neck, was a child.

Without thinking, he kicked Corracha hard and took off straight after the fleeing horse. It didn't seem like he would be able to reach the beast, but Corracha's stride lengthened and he drew level with the small mare. Jack pressed his heels into the horse's side and forced him over so the saddle on the mare was within arm's reach. Swinging one leg over, he judged his moment before he loosed Corracha's reins and jumped. He caught the pommel on the mare's saddle in both hands, legs hanging freely, the toes of his boot sliding along the bridge. Bending his knees, he brought his legs forward in a practiced move. As his heels contacted with the wooden boards they provided the momentum he needed to swing back upwards and into the mare's saddle.

One hand wound around the reins to slow the horse and the other none too gently, grabbed at the cloth and skin of the rider who was still clinging screaming to the horse's neck. The boy would have fallen had one foot not still been tangled in a stirrup. Before the horse had made it across the river, the mare began to slow. Recognising the feel of a controlling rider on her back she responded as she had been taught, slowing her gait steadily to a bouncing trot, the screaming child in front of him balanced uncomfortably on the pommel of his own saddle.

"Steady there, girl," Jack slowed her to a halt, and helping hands appeared instantly to lower the boy from the horse and hold the mare still on the bridge. Corracha had been brought to a halt some way in front of him and a large man with a leather apron was leading him back towards Jack across the bridge.

The boy was still crying loudly, taking in great big, gulped mouthfuls of air between wails, snot and tears pouring down his red face. He couldn't be more than six or seven, Jack thought.

"Oswald...Oswald." There came a shout from behind, "Lord be praised, Oh, Oswald, are you alright?" The man who appeared was well dressed, and he dropped to his knees in front of the bawling boy taking him into his arms. Jack presumed it was the boy's father and stood back, a little embarrassed. He still had hold of the mare's reins and a second man in livery held out his hand for them.

"That was a feat: I'd thought for sure the horse and boy were going to end in the river." Jack handed the reins over. Everything was just moving too quickly; just moments before, he had been trying to slow the speeding mare.

"Aye. Is the lad alright? What happened?" Jack asked of the kneeling man.

"He'll be fine, thanks kindly to you. Some stupid fool just before the bridge was taking chickens out of a cage and let the lot out. They ran across the street and the horse took off." As he spoke he used an expensive sleeve to wipe the worst of the mess from the boy's face.

"It's a big mare for such a little lad," Jack observed. "He'll not stop her if she'd a mind to go."

"I agree, sir." The man rose, a protective arm still around the boy, "I was against it, but his tutor insisted the boy have a new horse and I'll be having a few words, I can tell you, after this."

"How old is he?" Jack asked, pointing to the child who had stopped crying and was now wrapping his arms around his father's leg.

"Five, just gone."

"Five! No wonder he ended up round its neck. He needs a little, sturdy mare, something about ten hands, no bigger," Jack exclaimed.

"You seem to know your horses, judging by what I've just seen," he grinned, "I'm Roger Clement, and this is my son Oswald. What do you say, Oswald."

"Thank you, sir." Oswald complied quietly.

Jack dropped down onto his haunches at the boy's level. "Don't let her scare you, lad. Get back on now, and take her over the bridge. She's calm now and with someone leading her she'll not take off with you again."

"No, don't want to." Oswald pressed his face against his father's leg.

"It's always best to get back on, I'm sure you've been told that." Jack tried.

"Will you come with me?" The boy asked, turning to observe Jack with tear reddened eyes.

"I could, or I could lift you up and lead her for you. Should I do that? I'll not let go of her, she'll walk nice and quietly for you I'm sure." The boy smiled weakly as Jack lifted him back into the mare's saddle.

"I'll lead him over the bridge for you, if that's fine with you?" Jack asked, taking a tight hold on the mare's bridle.

"I'll walk over with you," Roger turned to the liveried servant.

"Callum, go and get my horse and bring..." he looked at Jack, who supplied his name, "...Jack's horse as well and we'll meet you on the other side of the river."

Jack spent some minutes chatting with the grateful Roger until Callum arrived with Corracha and Roger's own mount. Jack turned down the offer of a meal, very much wanting to be elsewhere, not enjoying at all the attention he was getting. Father Andrew and his group stared on, waiting for Jack to re-join them which, with some relief, he did and they continued on to Paul's in-laws.

✝

York was the end of a long journey; Jack, seeking solitude, declined the invitation to stop with Annie's family. The Black Sheep's rooms offered travellers good fare and for those who could afford it, better than average food. The ale was expensive as well, half a shilling for a tankard, and the room on the creaking floor above him had cost him two shillings a night. Jack knew he could have found another inn, less central, and could have halved his spend, but right now he didn't care too much. The Black Sheep had been close and the smell of cooked food too inviting to resist. Famous locally for a pie stuffed with game and herbs, he'd fed well and was, on the whole, feeling much better. A night in a dry bed with a roof over his head and tomorrow would be a better day. Jack resolved to ponder the future in the morning. When he'd slept well surely then he'd be able to think a little clearer?

Jack wanted to be alone. There were few patrons inside and he'd easily found a table in a peaceable corner. The door to the inn swung open, lighting the inside. Jack, feeling the cold draught, instinctively turned to the doorway. There, framed by the light, was Father Andrew closely followed by Roger Clement. For God's sake, what were they after now? Quickly he looked away, hoping that they'd not seen him. It was a dark corner if he was lucky... but he was not.

"There you are, lad. Annie said she'd seen you come in here, what a place to be in after our travels." Father Andrew, without invitation, hooked a stool out from under the table and pulled another one over for Roger, and the pair sat down opposite Jack.

Leaning back, Father Andrew settled his shoulders comfortably against the wooden boards behind him, it was obvious he meant to stay. "So Jack, what will you do now?"

"I'll think of something," Jack replied tersely, interested not at all in talking with either of them, and hoping very much that his unwanted companions would realise this and leave.

"You told me that a week back. Have you not made any plans from here?" Father Andrew persisted. He had caught the eye of one of the serving girls, "Ale for three, lass, please." Jack groaned inwardly, Father Andrew turned back to his companions, "You must have some notions about where you go next?"

"No, I haven't," Jack's eyes were full of fury, and Roger Clement, looking between the pair of them, was feeling less than comfortable.

"Maybe we can help." Father Andrew leaned across the table. "Often the paths are there, it just takes a little while to truly see what choices we have that God has laid before us."

"I haven't got any bloody choices, and I told you before, I've no plans," Jack took a long draught of ale and when he spoke, his voice was carefully controlled. "Just let it be. I just want to sit in here, on my own, and enjoy an evening of peace."

"I can see you are one in need of help, Jack, and I'm not going to leave you until I know you are set on a path chosen by the Lord."

"You're just another nosey bastard," Jack set his drink down hard on the table; the other patrons glanced in his direction as the cups on the table danced. "I'll not sit here and be your bloody evening's entertainment, that's for sure."

Father Andrew was not in the least put off. "Now settle that temper; I'll bet it's been one that's got you in trouble more than once."

"If you don't shut up, it'll be getting me in trouble again very soon," Jack retorted, wondering just how far Father Andrew was going to push him, and why on earth he'd dragged Roger Clement in here with him.

"You'd surely not hit a man of God?" Father Andrew admonished his eyes bright and a smile on his face.

"Try me," Jack spoke through clenched teeth.

"Now there's a challenge," Father Andrew laughed and reached over to fill Jack's cup from the pitcher, not at all unsettled by the mood of his companion. "Help comes sometimes to us when we least expect it so settle yourself, lad, and prepare to be helped."

The chair behind Jack toppled, banging loudly on the wooden floor as he stood suddenly, "If you won't leave, I will."

"I think perhaps..." Roger Clement started to rise from his seat when Father Andrew's hand stopped him.

"Will you *sit* down." The command was aimed at Jack; the voice loud and steady was one used to being obeyed. "Now."

Jack drew a loud breath. *Damn the man.*

"Pick that chair up and put your backside on it," Father Andrew continued, pointing at the fallen furniture. Roger also reluctantly settled himself back into his seat.

Without taking his eyes from the cleric's face, Jack leant down, and in one smooth movement, righted the chair and sat down, arms on the table in front of him, temper barely contained. "Is this going to take long?"

"That depends on how hard you decide to make it doesn't it?" Father Andrew countered.

"I'm not the one making it hard, I don't want to talk to you! I don't want to tell you anything and I don't need your help," Jack was exasperated.

"You need God's help, and I'm His instrument here to guide you, and guide you I will."

"You'll be guiding without any bloody teeth in a minute," Jack growled. "My life's my own business and none of yours, and it's enough of a mess without having the likes of you picking over the corpse for your entertainment."

"That bad, is it?" Father Andrew was not going to be put off and Jack had unwittingly given him an opening.

"Yes, it is," Jack retrieved his cup and he drained the pale ale.

"So tell me something of your family then; every man has a place where..."

Jack cut him off. "My family! We might share the same blood, but family I do not have."

"So a falling out then? Go on lad, tell me what happened." Father Andrew persisted.

"I wouldn't know where to start, the tale's too long and I've no stomach for it anymore." Father Andrew saw Jack's shoulders slump and knew that he was going to get the confession he wanted, in a little time, with a little patience.

"At the beginning, that's always the place to start." Father Andrew encouraged.

Jack rubbed his rough hands over his face; it made the cut on his hand sting, reminding him painful of the past. "In the beginning...." Jack told his tale, haltingly at first. The truth of the story had not been his for very long, he was still trying to get used to the reality of it.

"In the beginning, my mother was Lady Fitzwarren. She berated her husband, William, for taking her waiting lady to his bed while she was pregnant with me. The servant, who I always thought was my mother, gave birth to another son a few months or so after I was born. William Fitzwarren liked the child well and kept him in the castle. His wife told him she would never be well or able to leave her room while his bastard was under their roof. So, he got rid of the child to his brother's household where it was raised." Jack paused, all the air leaving his lungs in a rush.

"Go on lad...the child, left then what happened?"

"The child who went to his brother's household was me William switched the babes to spite his scolding wife. The child of her servant was Robert, who he kept in my place. I'd heard that he'd meant to undo the wrong but he never did. His wife, Eleanor, accepted the child in the crib as hers. The servant was sent to an Abbey and life went on. No-one, it seemed, knew the truth and the few that did cared little."

"That's certainly a beginning, Jack, I'll give you that. So then what happened? How did you find out?" Roger Clement was now an extremely attentive listener.

"A long time later. I worked as a servant in Fitzwarren's brother's house all my life serving those bastards, cleaning up their mess, being made to feel grateful for the food in my mouth and the roof over my head even if most of the time it was the stable roof. William Fitzwarren had another son, Richard, and there was some great enmity between him and Robert. Robert tried to kill Richard during a hunt. I was there and I know not why, but I helped him and gave him a horse to escape. I left England after that and I stayed with him. He knew I was his father's child raised in his brother's house and he also knew the full truth of it as well: that I was his full true brother, not just a bastard by-blow. However, he didn't choose to share it until the end." Jack stopped suddenly, his expression distant.

"The end? What end? Jack, a moment ago we were at the beginning. You can't just jump to the end." Father Andrew snapped his fingers in front of

Jack's face when he didn't get a reply. "Come on, lad."

"What?" Jack pulled back from his thoughts focused his eyes on his audience opposite him.

"We want the middle of the tale." Father Andrew pressed, leaning forward.

"The middle is an even worse mess," Jack said, both men could hear the pain in his voice.

"Well then, get started and let's see if we can smooth the past out for you," Roger Clement smiled encouragingly.

"We came back to England. Richard had connections, he'd spent time working for Thomas Seymour," Jack smiled when he saw that the name he'd dropped had raised both men's eyebrows by a degree. "He had connections and after King Edward died he lent the Lady Mary some help to secure the throne and we were rewarded with a manor at Burton. Not a big place, but enough, a start," Jack paused reflectively.

"Well, you're not there now so what happened?" Father Andrew prompted.

Jack placed his hands palms down on the table and met Father Andrew's steady gaze. "When we were helping Northumberland, a young lassie lost her home and her family. To keep her safe Richard had confirmed that she too had died; it was safer at the time and later it was too late to do anything about it."

"Ah," Roger Clement nodded, considering the facts, "A little like your own problem?"

"Exactly like mine; the girl should have had a Manor, lands, servants. Her father was Mary's man, but, when her family thought her dead, her uncle took over Assingham and nobody wanted a dead child resurrecting to change his recent inheritance."

"I can see what you are meaning, lad, now. So where is the girl? Still with your brother?" Father Andrew asked.

Jack laughed harshly, "She's with my brother alright, just the wrong one. She's with Robert Fitzwarren, my bastard brother, who thought he'd seek himself a profit from her. Robert tracked down Richard to Burton and on a charge, he had him arrested. He'd helped Mary to the throne and he was involved with powerful people." Jack knew exactly which powerful people he was involved with, but even though Richard was dead he couldn't bring himself to say.

"They didn't want him on the scaffold where he could publicly condemn them; they wanted him dead, quickly and quietly. They turned some of his men against him and arranged a trial by combat. But, with their own rules. There were an unlimited number of combatants and they just wore him down until one was lucky enough to get through his guard."

"And you were there?" Roger sounded surprised; this was a tale indeed.

"Aye, I was there. I tried to help, but there was so little I could do, you see. He did make an escape, but not for long. It was a bad wound, and he was found dead, bled out." Jack's breath shuddered as he released it. "There was nothing I could do. Richard was dead. Robert came to see me before he left with Catherine and told me our father had died some months past and that he was now the head of the household."

Jack rocked back in the chair, his eyes downcast. "So there you have it. I couldn't stay; they had got rid of Richard on some false charges and it would have been only a matter of time before they came back and arrested me. Richard's dead; Catherine, I know not where they took her, and although I've got the proof of my father's crime against me who's going to believe me? Do I look like a Lord's son?" Jack was now thoroughly depressed.

"No, you don't, I agree. What you do look like is someone who's feeling right sorry for himself." Father Andrew's tone was not particularly kind. Sympathy he decided, was not what the man before him needed.

"What would you do, eh?" Jack snapped back, "Richard left me the proof of it, but who would believe me? He might be dead but he left me with the curse of it."

"Oh please. The man's dead and you're blaming him for your sorry situation?"

Jack didn't answer.

"You've got choices; you've got a brain between those loppy, great ears of yours, so why don't you use it?" Andrew continued sternly.

"He had the connections, he was the one with the plan. Me, I just followed him and..."

Father Andrew cut him off tersely "I can see that very well, you just followed him and now that he's not here to lead you by the hand, that's his fault as well." He drew a long breath and folded his arms. "It seems to me you've got two clear paths: two choices, two roads to travel down."

"Really?" Jack's voice was resigned.

"Go and find this lass, the one who's lost everything. Help her to regain her land and home, and, in doing that, you may gain her gratitude and a place for yourself. If she had a Manor and wealth perhaps she'll look kindly on you if you could help her."

"Assingham wasn't exactly a wealthy place, you know?" Jack pointed out.

"Oh, and you've got gold pouring out of your backside, have you?" Father Andrew scoffed. "I'm betting it'd be more than the likes of you could ever dream of earning, even if it wasn't a royal palace."

"I suppose so," Jack conceded grumpily. He lifted his eyes to meet the older man's. "And the second path?"

"Go and claim your place. You say you have proof? Use it and bring a suit against this man who calls himself Robert Fitzwarren!" Father Andrew proclaimed.

Jack straightened his shoulders. "I've met the bastard; he'd run me through and throw me in the gutter. I've not got the money for a law suit I don't have Richard's connections; he would have known what to do."

"There you go again - the man is dead will you leave him be!" Father Andrew admonished again.

It was Roger Clement then who spoke, thoughtfully, "I know a little of the law: my brother, Geoffrey practices in London and has his own firm with lawyers working for him," Roger spoke proudly. "Your case could be a lucrative one for you if you won, and any lawyer worth his calling would be able to see, that if they aided you in this, they would benefit mightily if they could place your inheritance in your hands, do you not think?"

"I suppose so," Jack admitted a little sulkily.

"My brother, he was always father's favourite and went off to the law and he's done well, very well for himself. I can write you a personal letter of recommendation that you could take to Geoffrey and he could listen to your facts, as I am sure he would and advise you."

Jack was silent for a moment, then, "You'd do that for me?" He sounded shocked.

"Yes, I would," Roger Clement stated solemnly, "You risked your life to save my child today, I believe God means for me to help you on the right road. And I would like to help," Roger leaned across the table and clapped the other man on the arm.

✝

Why Jack went, he never really knew. Maybe it was just because it was somehow the end of the journey? Maybe like Paul he wanted help? Or perhaps it was just curiosity? Saint William was interred before the high alter in a shrine that towered above him. Wooden framework, adorned with winged angels and glossed with gold, was built over the entombed bones inside. Forever attended, William would never be alone: at each corner of the shrine, a kneeling monk watched over his final sleep.

A rope across the middle of the Minster separated the main crowd from the shrine. Waiting his turn, finally, Jack reached the barrier and saw before him the majesty of the Saint's final resting place. Here, he did kneel. Jack was weary, so tired. Beyond the shrine, he could see the huge gilt cross standing on the high altar, smell the incense.

The candles, in gold and silver holders, burned into the back of his eyes; shafts of light falling from the painted windows were highlighted in the smoky air. There was noise and silence all at the same time and Jack's head spun. If there was a power in the world, if there was a God, then He would be here.

Jack felt his throat tighten. *Why did you kill him? Why did you? Why did you let this happen?*

There was nothing. No answer. Just the silence of the Church.

Jack breathed in heavily, the sickly smell of the incense almost too much.

Then it happened.

The words he heard were too clear to have not been spoken aloud.

"Pity is a man's downfall. For your sake, Jack, let it not be yours,"

The voice mocking him was his brother's.

He glanced wildly about him looking for the speaker. A woman kneeling, hands tightly clasped, to his left, jumped in fright as he spun around. Jack mumbled something in apology and using the carved pillar to his right, pulled himself up and stumbled from the Minster.

Sitting on the paving outside, it took some minutes for his senses to begin to re-order themselves; the thick and sickly smell of the incense clearing from his head. His palms flat on the cold stone steadied him as he fought to regain a sense of the world. Swallowing hard, he rubbed his shaking hands over his face and felt an acute sting on his right cheek. His brother's ring, that he wore reversed, had carved a livid line from the corner of his mouth up to his eye. He needed a drink!

✝

Elizabeth took the prayer book she was passed and stowed it beneath the one she already carried. She didn't want it: at the earliest opportunity it would be discarded on the church pew or on the floor. For now, though, she had them both. She sat on the embroidered, cushioned bench in the chapel, her eyes downcast and expression demure, as she knew she must appear when Lady Travers was near. Elizabeth realised she was staring fixedly at the book that had been forced upon her.

It was a simple book of common prayer: the cover was of calf skin and the pages crisp and creamy. What caught her attention though, was the green point of a dry leaf just slightly poking out from between the pages. She couldn't see all of it and knew she couldn't open the book while she sat in the chapel. Later, alone in her room, she opened it and watched as a green fingered chestnut leaf, dried and crisp from last summer, lay there tucked between the pages.

Taking the leaf from the hiding place revealed four words underlined on the two facing pages – *oh thou goodly sinner*. She quickly checked the smile that lit her face. The chestnut leaf, she lay out on the top of a coffer. Smoothing the leaf flat, she laid her hand on it, so much bigger than the span of her own fingers. She pocketed the psalm book until she could find the opportunity later to remove the telltale marks from the pages. Once done she left the book where she knew it would be found and inspected.

The message was no message at all, merely a reminder that she was not alone and to be of brave heart a state of mind that was not easy to accomplish. In her few years, she had found out all too well what it meant to be a Tudor and – worse - a member of her father's terrible household. Her own mother had ended her life with her long Boleyn neck slit by a sword when Elizabeth was only three. Her thoughts on that were her most private: whether from a deep sense of self-preservation or from a childhood terror, she never shared them.

From there, she had been welcomed, mothered and cosseted by Henry's most loved and treasured wife, Jane Seymour. Jane, after fulfilling her royal duty to give him an heir, had perished, and Elizabeth was once again forgotten in the turmoil that ensued. As a young girl, Henry's fifth wife had once again brought her back into the royal fold. Elizabeth and Catherine Howard had been close. The pain could not even be imagined when her friend, confidant, and ear to her father was taken from this world to the next on the block on Tower Green. Katherine Parr, Henry's last wife, outlived the Tudor tyrant and married her childhood love, Thomas Seymour. The pair took over guardianship of the Lady Elizabeth until poor Katherine had perished soon after giving Thomas a daughter. She had been fourteen.

The Elizabeth now, aged twenty two, was wise beyond her years. However, she had inherited from Henry a temper and a stubbornness that would not be checked. The message bolstered her flagging spirit to the point of recklessness.

Two days later it was Sunday. Elizabeth was to attend Mass, as she did every week, with Mary. All morning she had clutched at her stomach and wailed bitterly, but her illness would not stop her attending her sister.

Mary stood with her ladies. The morning was icy, the air still pinched with cold. They were waiting to enter the Royal Chapel and Elizabeth was late. Mary was furious.

"Your Majesty, she comes now. Mistress Kate says she has been unwell." Anne Bouchier bobbed a curtsey in front of Mary before taking up a safer position behind the glowering Monarch.

"Ill? Really?" Mary spat.

Elizabeth appeared, leaning so heavily on the lady at her side the small girl was forced to weave under the heavy burden, her eyes filled with terror as she fought to hold the Princess up.

"Forgive me," Elizabeth performed the curtsey due to Mary clumsily, clutching her rosary tightly to her breast as she did.

"It is not me you need to beg forgiveness from." Mary snapped, her lips a thin hard line.

The royal party entered the Chapel and Mary's scratched and raw nerves under the presence of her sibling bled anew as she had to sit and listen to the other retch behind her.

†

"She should not have come," Kate was kneeling in front of Mary after she had been summoned for an explanation. "Elizabeth is most wholly unwell and we had begged her to remain in bed and send word to Your Majesty, but she would not hear of it, and said it was her dearest wish to attend you in the chapel."

Mary turned abruptly away. A skirt hem, heavy and jewelled, caught Kate harshly across her cheek, but she kept her place, eyes downcast staring at the cold marble flagging.

"You are too familiar with our sister, she needs a firmer guiding hand," Mary spoke as she stared from the window. "I shall have Gardiner see to her household arrangements in future." Mary's hand waved behind her and Kate, sickened, left. There was no doubt in Kate's mind what was about to happen, indeed, before the day was out her employment - ten years with Elizabeth - was terminated.

✝

The change in Elizabeth's household took place seamlessly. Kate was removed from her rooms, her belongings packed, and she was out of Durham Place and out of Elizabeth's company before the day grew to a close. There wasn't time for appeal or reproach, no time was afforded for tears or temper. Kate was rewarded for her dutiful service with a small supply of coins and her servants had already found her suitable lodging within the city. Kate had taken rooms at an inn on the Strand, close to her mistress, should she be needed, there she waited.

Richard left it for three days before he went to see Kate.

She rose as the uninvited man stepped into the room and closed the door quickly behind him.

"Richard!" Kate let the needlework slide from her lap to the floor, the shock plain on her face. "What's happened to you?"

"Ah, do I still look that bad?" he smiled back and came to stand a little way in front of her.

"You seem like you've been..." she signalled for him to sit opposite her, and added tactfully, "unwell."

Chapter Three

October 1554

It had taken Jack another four weeks to retrace his steps and make his way back to London, though this time with a sense of purpose and even hope. Near his skin, under his jacket, he kept the papers Richard had bequeathed to him proving his place in the world. Nestled next to them was a letter written in Roger Clement's close-clipped characters: a note of introduction requesting that his brother Geoffrey hear his case.

Roger Clement's words to him had been well-reasoned ones. If he could prove his claim then it was indeed worth a considerable amount. His father had a manor outside London, extensive lands and also a London residence as well. More than that, he did not know of, but he assumed there would be other assets in the Fitzwarren name all adding up to a princely sum.

Roger Clement had insisted that if he could assert a right over the titles then the lawyer who helped him would probably never need to open the door to a client again, such would be the reward Jack could offer. There was indeed much sense in it, and Jack was for once not only hopeful but optimistic that the truth would be the easy victor in the face of the evidence he held.

The lawyer's chambers he had not found easily. Geoffrey Clement chose not to keep company with his fellows and his office was some way out of Lincoln's Fields where all the main legal firms clustered. A handsome and costly façade had been allowed to crumble, paint curled away like lichen from the sun-bleached woodwork. Moldering daub, weather softened, fertile and damp, husbanded the weeds, roots secured behind slatted panelling. Clement's sign hung creaking on un-oiled brackets. The letters on the sign, once a neatly gilded calligrapher's testament to the skills and services on offer, were now a pale barely readable grey.

Jack took in the setting and groaned inwardly. Hopefully, the lawyer within was successful and too busy to deal with such trifles as the appearance of his premises. He didn't really have any other choices.

Approaching the door a sniping woman's voice, argumentative and hostile, could be heard. The words became clearly audible as the front door opened, a woman backed out, her finger wagging menacingly in the face of a man firmly trying to expel her onto the street.

"The Devil take you! Five weeks I've been coming here and for five weeks you've been taking coins from me. I'll be back, mark it, next week, Master Lawyer and you had better have what I need." The woman was still issuing threats through the open door and backed into Jack as he was walking up the path.

"Don't you be going in there unless you've money to waste, a fine tongue he has on him. But results? Ha! You'll never be seeing any of those," she spat in the road to emphasise her point and with a last shout of, "Next week!" over her shoulder, she marched off into the street.

The door was still open when Jack reached it and standing on the other side was a very distressed-looking servant.

"Mistress Taylor has high expectations and little patience, I am afraid," he said, by way of apology.

Jack grinned, "That would make her very much like most women I've ever met."

His smile was returned. "Indeed it would; they do not appreciate that there are procedures, practices and timescales. All that the lady wishes is being done, but the law is not as speedy as Mistress Taylor would like. Woman are such foolish creatures, they lack the capacity to appreciate even simple processes. Why the law allows them a presence, I have no idea." Jack, nodding in sympathy, let him finish, "Anyway, how can I help?"

"I have this for Master Clement; I would very much appreciate it if you could pass this to him. I have a matter that I would like him to advise me upon." Jack saw the other assessing his worth as a client. Hastily he added, "This letter is from his brother."

"Certainly I'm Marcus Drover, and you are?" Marcus reached over and took the offered letter.

"John Fitzwarren," This was the first time Jack had ever spoken his given name and he regretted it; it felt like theft.

"Please wait in there, I will see if Master Clement is free," Marcus gestured to a dusty room with a few sticks of poor furniture. He doubted very much that his Master would want to meet him. Only last year they had received two similar letters from Clement's clerical brother, this charity case looked, and very much smelt, like another waste of his Master's time.

Pleased with his preparation, backed with written facts and bolstered by words from the lawyer's own brother, Jack felt confident. It was a confidence, however, which decreased with time. Jack waited. Silently, he rehearsed the lines he would use, words he had composed on the slow journey south.

The story was, he knew, a hard one to believe. Aware of a need to convince, he'd made a tally of the facts and mentally prepared what he hoped was a believable and convincing summary. He paced the room, then waited, then paced some more. Eventually Jack convinced himself that, whilst his letter may have been delivered, Marcus Drover had failed to inform his employer that his newest client was waiting to be seen. He left the room, intent on tracking down the lawyer.

The building on the inside reflected the exterior. It was dusty, with an air of disuse and another odour Jack didn't care too much for: the smell of rot, but with a little too much edge, making it unpleasant on the nose. There were two doors leading off the passageway near the front door. A knock on the first brought no response, but a knock on the second gained him a reply.

"What is it, Marcus?" Jack chose to ignore the mistake, and impatiently stalked in like a hungry dog.

The door gave onto a large room filled with tables and shelves, upon every surface were piled sheaves of paper, all tied neatly. Even the floor had been employed to house the files; some in stacks had given way, the top bundles having slithered into untidy heaps at the foot of the mountainous piles. Jack stared about him open-mouthed: how anyone could find anything in here was a mystery.

"Who are you?" shouted the small hunched man from where he sat in the middle of the vast paper island.

"Fitzwarren, I passed a letter..."

The lawyer cut him off. "From my brother, the kindly simpleton of the family. Yours is not the first worthless case he's passed my way. He seems to think I have nothing better to do than waste my life on God's lost causes. I've read your letter and your hard luck story. So what do you want me to do about it?" He barked.

Jack was shocked, "You're a lawyer, I'd hoped..."

"Yes, I am a lawyer. And a good one. And I cost money. Do you have any?"

"No, sorry, no..." Jack was lost for words, this was not the reception he had expected.

"Sorry! Indeed! Well sorry is not going to get you very far. You need to place a suit in Chancery, and that costs money. Lots of money. From the look of you, that's not something you have, is it? What proof do you have? It says here -" Clement picked up the letter from his brother and scanned it briefly, "- a signed confession from your father. Really?" Clement scoffed.

"Yes, I do."

"Sure it's not something you've had written, eh? Let me see it," snapped Clement, holding out his hand.

Jack reached automatically to the pocket where he kept the document, then he stopped. "No. I'll thank you for that letter you hold there and I'll trouble you no more. Your brother was sadly mistaken in his recommendation."

The little man's hand went to grasp the letter from Roger Clement but Jack was by far the quicker and before the elderly man could secure a tight hold on the sheet, it was snapped neatly from his grasp.

"I'll say good day to you, sir." Jack turned on his heel and left, slamming the door behind him, the dust billowing from the walls and ceiling in a silent explosion in his wake.

✝

The filth and unwanted contents of London sailed by under the bridge as he watched. Bloated and rotten, the distorted corpse of a dog rolled under the bridge. The pull of the current turning the canine over made it seem alive, the gas-filled stomach struggling to stay above the black surface of the river.

At least the dog is going somewhere – the mocking voice in his head was a familiar one.

What do you want me to do? Damn you.

Pressing fingers into his temples he tried to push away the pain that was starting to become a familiar companion.

The dog's brown, slick furred back bared itself for a moment before the grotesquely stretched pink barrel of its belly beneath it spun it over once more. Further down the bank two boys, armed with stones, had the fetid animal as their mark. Even in death, the desperate creature had no peace.

I've been dragged along as well by this for far too long. I need an end.

Jack pushed himself away from the rail and set his steps on a dangerous path.

The Fitzwarren's had a house in the Newgate area of London in addition to manorial lands outside the city. With no idea why, and with nowhere else to go, Jack headed to it as dusk approached.

The house was a sizeable triple fronted, wooden framed structure and on the end, a large gated arch led to the stables and yard at the rear. Upper floors protruded out over the ground floor and all were filled with neat square glass panes. Black timbers outlined the front, great oak beams framing the white-washed wattle and daub. On the ground floor, at street level, herringbone brickwork neatly flanked the diamond-paned windows, telling the visitor of the Fitzwarren wealth.

The house was in darkness on the lower floors; the only lights showing were through a few scattered windows on the second and third floors. As he watched, three men came out of the postern gate and set off down the street. Jack stepped back into the shadows.

"Come on Edwin, hurry up, my throat's parched," the men were within earshot of Jack.

"I'm coming, wait up. The old Master's had me running round him all day, I'm footsore I tell you. Move that over there, pick that up, stoke the fire, wipe my arse," the others all laughed at his parody of their Master's voice.

"I'd like to say the old devil would not see the year out, but cantankerous, nasty, evil bastards like him seem to go on forever," his companion quipped back.

"Nah, he's a lot worse than he was at Easter, he can barely walk at all now. It takes me and Jon together to lift him onto the close stool." Edwin laughed. "If I ever, *ever*, need to be picked up and put on to the jakes, please Lord, strike me down with shame."

"That's as might be, but his lordship there has no shame has he? If you ask me he just does it to make us poor buggers suffer. Oh and the smell of it as well, it's enough to make a pig gag," the other man replied.

They passed Jack who loosened himself from the darkened door and began to follow them down the street, close enough to hear them still and yet far enough away to be masked by the gloom of the London night.

"Well lads, there are worse ways to make a living. At least these days he can't catch us at his favourite malmsey, stuck as he is upstairs."

"Can you imagine it when he goes? It'll take half a dozen of us to carry his rotting carcass down two flights of stairs."

"Maybe that's why he smells so bad, he's already putrid on the inside," Edwin grimaced. "Come on, I need to get the smell of him out of my nose."

Jack let their strides lengthen in front of him. He made no move to follow them: he'd learned what he needed to know. His father was still alive. Robert had lied. This did indeed change everything.

Retracing his steps he returned to the house. It didn't take long to make his way to the back where the stables were and learn what he wanted to know. They were practically empty; none of the fine beasts Robert would have ridden were housed within, which meant his brother was elsewhere.

Two flights of stairs they had said, so that meant he needed to be on the second floor. It was an easy climb up the back of the house. The timbers and daub wore ivy at the rear, the tendrils fast around the wooden frame, the main branches thick, bearing his weight with ease. When he reached the first windows, he glanced carefully around the stone embrasure.

There was a corridor with rooms on both sides and, in the end farthest from him, a stairway leading downwards. The corridor, lit by tapers, illuminated a makeshift bed and upon it a man curled in sleep beneath a blanket. Could this be one of his father's watchful servants waiting for the bellow of orders from within?

Pressing his face close to the thick diamond panes, Jack peered into the room. Although the imperfect glass distorted the scene within, the view was still enough. A well-lit room, candles flickered in holders and sconces, the fire casting an orange steady light and it all illuminated the man who watched the flames. Resplendent with rugged knees, his father sat immobile but alive.

God's bones! This is all your fault, everything is down to you. You've ruined my bloody life, Richard is dead because of the churl you raised in my place.

Jack's ragged breath frosted the panes and his father was lost from view.

†

William Fitzwarren did indeed still live. He remained in his London house in isolation in his rooms, despised by his son, Robert, and hated by his household servants. There would be few, if any, to mourn his death when it came. He was a man who knew his time was passed and he grieved for the loss.

Fitzwarren had sat on the Privy Council, he had hunted with the King, his lack of personal morals and selfish ambition had made him many friends in the courtly circle. Fitzwarren was one who could be counted on to provide pressure when and where it was needed and with a band of trained, well-skilled men on his staff, he had force to back up his words. All this was lost to him now: the muscles in his legs had failed him and now, trapped on the top floor of his own house, he was nothing but a prisoner to old age.

Robert stood in his place now, but he was a man with little ambition and saw all of William's possessions only as toys for his own amusement. It grieved him greatly that his son would never take over the positions he had held at Court, that the Fitzwarren name would no longer be one spoken when there was a time of need. When Henry had died, the old Court, the old ways, which William understood, had gone to the grave with the old King. Under the Lord Protector, the Duke of Somerset, he had received only a passing acceptance at Court. Somerset had seen him for what he was: an enforcer from a bygone age, a man who would act out the King's will without thought, a powerful tool, but one that, in the times of Edward's young sovereignty, needed to be curbed.

When Henry died, his final will had listed the names of those to sit on the Privy Council, William Fitzwarren was not one of those penned in the neat addendum to the lengthy document. Somerset, an ardent Protestant, had made sure of that. He wanted Reformers and in particular, Protestant Reformers who sided with the claim he would make to be Lord Protector during Edward's minority; William was no such man. He had worked for Henry, indeed he had been key to the fall of Wolsey and later More. He was a man treated courteously, but suspiciously.

However, Fitzwarren had powerful friends; thirty years in and out of Court circles meant he knew many and he was willing to trade just about anything to sit once more on the Privy Council, that rare organisation that indeed steered England. He'd won his place back but it had been a fleeting reinstatement; like Henry age had taken hold of his once powerful and athletic frame.

William's legs had begun to wither and thin. His physicians bled him constantly to balance the humors, yet their strength continued to fail. He had sent them from his rooms when he realised their efforts were futile. Fate indeed had a cruel hand. Now he just waited. Sometimes his mind ran over and over the great events that had brought him power and influence; but now, seated alone, it was difficult to gauge their success. He had finally realised that never again would anyone call at his door to seek his advice or services. The only thing that lived within him that had any force, any power, any real presence, was rage.

The old man had old man's senses. Once keen eyesight was blurred, faces indistinct unless he peered at them through the glasses that perpetually graced his veined nose. His hearing had fared worse; there was nothing to help reverse it's decay. So he didn't hear Jack's knife as it scraped along the window casement to lift the latch from the outside, he missed the creak as it swung back on unoiled hinges, and his ears didn't register the light pad of feet as they dropped on to the wooden floor.

The first he became aware of his visitor was when a filthy hand from behind clamped across his mouth silencing him, a blade glinting menacingly in the firelight. A voice said quietly, "One noise and it will most certainly be your last." The hand remained in place until Jack felt the almost imperceptible nod of acceptance from the man in the chair.

Jack kept the knife where William Fitzwarren could see it and walked round the chair to stand between the man and the fire, staring down for the first time at his father.

William was old, but a coward not at all. He gave the knife not a second glance but settled back in his chair and gazed up intently at the face of the man before him. It was he who broke the silence first.

"So is it silverware or money, then?" William leered at Jack, "Or was it rape? If it was, you've bloody got that wrong, the bitches are on the ground floor."

The man chuckled and smiled, the firelight lit his blond hair and the candlelight twinkled in pool blue eyes. "Silverware or money. Well then, there's a thought I hadn't had until just now."

Jack was rewarded for the briefest of moments as the seated man stiffened slightly, sensing that this might be more than a burglary.

"You have me...." William paused and opened empty hands, "at somewhat of a disadvantage."

Jack's face darkened. Those words, the voice, all held a memory of his brother, the gesture so like Richard's arrogant nature it made him start.

William saw the emotions play across Jack's face. '*Well here's a man with a problem,*' William thought watching him now very carefully.

"Speak up. So, if it's not silver, then who sent you?" William demanded quietly. The blade was still only a foot from his throat.

"Thirty pieces of silver I believe would be the reckoning." Jack replied a little too hastily.

"Thirty pieces?" William repeated quietly and thoughtfully, his eyes fastened on the man's face.

"Aye, that's the price for betrayal, isn't it?" Jack's words were bitter.

William could sense the barely contained anger behind his words. Pushing the glasses up his nose, he carefully considered the man before him. *Could it be?* William proceeded carefully, still unsure. "Do you think I have betrayed you?"

"Aye, you have," Jack spat, "and my mother. You have no idea what you bloody well did to me, and you couldn't care bloody less, I have no doubt."

So Robert had been right, Richard had found Eleanor's son.

Robert had not spared his father the details of the lengths he had personally had to go to, to protect both his own inheritance and his father's reputation. Robert had assured William that they'd as like hear nothing more from Jack; he was nothing but a churl and now that Richard was no longer alive he would pose no danger.

A thick skinned forefinger pushed his glasses a degree further up his nose, he observed the other man closely. Smell had remained when the other senses had retreated; the common odour of the street mixed with the smell of smoke and sweat met his nose. His clothes had once been good, certainly above the man's station, William would wager they were probably not his own. Now they were tired, worn and dirty; it was obvious this was probably all he owned.

That this was his wife's son, his eyes could not deny. Eleanor's hair, a sun-bleached river of fine flowing white gold, was the same bright icy colour as the man's who stood before him. On Jack's face he saw her mark, her bright summer blue eyes, deep and intense observing him coldly, her disapproving mouth, down-turned at one corner, waiting for him to speak first. It was Eleanor, annoyed, angry, hot-tempered Eleanor who stared at him.

"You look like her," William's voice was hoarse. The resemblance to his long dead, beautiful wife, had more of an effect on him than he liked. William dragged his gaze back from Jack's face and took in the rest of his sorry state. This gutter whelp was a disgrace to her memory. William kept that thought from his face.

Jack's guard dropped, he'd not expected recognition.

William saw the shock on Jack's face and he pressed on. "She was the most beautiful woman I had ever seen, hot-tempered but she was worth it. You should blame her for what happened. I had to teach her a lesson. For all her ways I loved her and..." Jack's hand holding the knife had dropped. William saw the move and carried on. "She had your eyes, as blue as summer sky and brighter than any gems." William was smiling now, "she was always smiling and her hair was like gold, same as yours, but it ran like a river down to her waist. I always wanted a girl, another beautiful Eleanor."

When Jack did speak his voice was shaking, "Why did you do it to me? Why?"

"I told you, I needed to teach my wife to be a little more submissive."

"You kicked me from your door. You never thought once again about me just because you'd argued with your wife!" Jack's voice was incredulous.

"It was done. I saw you, maybe four or five years after at my brother's house. Mired in filth and even then sounding like a gutter whelp. You had your place and there's no coming back from it." William countered.

Jack just shook his head in disbelief. "He told me I'd get nothing from you, and God, he was right."

"Richard? I heard he'd found you. He might have dressed you in finery, lad, and promised you gold and gifts, but believe me, he lied. He kept you at hand to throw in my face when the time came. It didn't, thanks to Robert. Look at you! What did he tell you? You fool, you look and sound like what you are, a common churl, you could never be anything else." William scoffed.

Jack had not seen William's hand as it reached for and insistently pulled on the cord attached to the table near his chair.

The sleeper in the hall opened the door to the bedroom and stepped inside.

"Robber, robber, robber," William's thin, reedy voice screeched.

The man who had entered was not armed and stopped in fright when he saw the knife in Jack's hand. Their eyes met for a second before Jack dived past him and out into the corridor, taking the steps three at a time downwards and out of the house.

✝

Richard leaned back in his chair and surveyed the group before him. He'd listened to them now for nearly two hours, recognising them for what they were: dangerous zealots. Worse, in fact: dangerous zealots with a bad plan. Mary's reforms had forced Protestants underground; many had even left for Europe and were waiting to return if Elizabeth took the throne, or if Elizabeth and a new husband took the throne. She would pave the way for reform and a Protestant England once more.

Their fear, and Richard conceded that they were correct at least on this point, was that Mary would permanently remove Elizabeth from the running for the throne. A quick meeting with the headsman on Tower Green would make a terrible mess of their dynastic plans. With this in mind, the loosely formed group hatched a plan. It was simple, highly likely to fail, and even if it did succeed, the outcome was not certain.

They intended, for her own safety, to kidnap Princess Elizabeth and transport her to Holland. There, she would be out of Mary's reach and could wait until she could safely return to England. So far, they had little in the way of a plan to acquire her from the close guard Mary and Gardiner had on her household, and no real plan for her once in Holland. Among their number was a merchant called Fairfax who owned a house that was close to where the Lady Elizabeth lived at Durham Place. So far the plan was to start a fire on the adjacent property and somehow, in the confusion and chaos that would ensue as her household was evacuated, they would seize her and guide her to Holland.

"Do you know how many guards there are?" Richard asked of Fairfax.

"There are a few, but as soon as the fire starts we will have dozens of people on site. My steward reduced the size of my orchard last year. We wanted to expand the lawned area; it's useful for entertaining and now that I'm head of the guild, my wife..."

"Yes, yes. Enough of your wife's social ambitions, Cuthbert," another of the plotters cut in, George Sewell was in the same Guild as Fairfax and had been its head three years before Fairfax took over the position.

Cuthbert Fairfax gave him a withering glance. "As I was saying. He cut the orchard back and burned the boughs. The smoke went through the adjacent house and they were forced to flee to a man. This time we'll do the same but we'll let them believe it's not just smoke, but a fire. The smoke will fair persuade them to leave."

"What," continued Richard, in the same deceptively mild voice, "if the wind blows in the opposite direction?"

The other five seated men all turned and stared at him.

"Sir, everyone in London fears fire, even if the smoke blows south away from the Lady Elizabeth's house they will still want to take the precaution of seeing her safe." Fairfax snapped.

"Her stewards, the men guarding the house, will not all be fools and Durham Place is a sizeable manor. Are you sure that smoke alone...?"

Fairfax cut him off, "We saw what happened last year and there is no reason to doubt it will not work a second time." Richard, exasperated, at last decided to venture no further comment and sat, a quiet listener, for the rest of the meeting.

"Do we have a date set?" Thomas Cressworth, a small man with a perpetually worried expression, asked.

"The Lady has moved back into Durham Place, her London house. If we look at what happened last year we can guess that she will be summoned to Court by Mary for the Christmas celebrations. So ideally we need to plan on a date before then." George Sewell contributed.

"Well, that gives us hardly any time, it's already the start of December," Fairfax said, "She will as like move back to her own lodgings after Christmas. The New Year would be a better time surely?"

"The Queen is due to deliver a child in May, though no-one seems to know if it will be the start or the end of that month," George provided.

"Phillip will gather all the Court around him, and that will include Elizabeth, as soon as Mary goes into confinement."

Mary was expected to spend the last month of her pregnancy alone with her ladies. An elaborate church service would be held and after that, she would close herself off from the world until the child was born.

"So if we take a date then of the first of April for Mary to go into confinement, and if Elizabeth is going to be summoned to Court it will be before this date: surely Mary will want to see her before she leaves the world?" Thomas Cresswell questioned, adding, "So that means really, to be safe, our plan needs execution before the middle of March?"

"Elizabeth will be back at her own house, Durham Place, by the end of January, so we have six weeks, really, to work with," Fairfax took control of the conversation again. "What we need to find is a ship to Holland. Once we know we can get passage for the Lady out of England then we can set a date for her rescue. Richard, you are always pressing your contacts, can we leave this task to you?"

Richard didn't speak but instead inclined his head in acceptance of the task.

"Good, good, then we can meet again in, say, two weeks, and that should give us enough time to get everything in place. Richard, is two weeks enough time for you?"

"Two weeks," Richard agreed.

✝

The news towards the end of 1554 was all that Mary could have hoped for. A child was to be born, her child, long prayed for and most wholly desired. An heir for Phillip, a child for her husband, a baby for Mary, but most importantly an heir for England. In this child, the succession would lodge. Elizabeth's position had changed yet again; she was no longer the contender for the throne she once was, not now that Mary was to give England a new heir. Elizabeth could breathe a little freer and a little easier, her sister had other, more pressing concerns. And for the moment at least Elizabeth was not one of them.

✝

Elizabeth, Richard was sure, would not want to be a part of this badly ordered plan. Granted, her position under Mary's reign was uncertain. Already she had been questioned in the Tower and had quite properly feared for her life. Exile on European soil would, he knew, hold a certain appeal. He was sure the uneasiness Elizabeth felt would be lessened when Mary no longer cast her dark, cold shadow over the lady's life: to speak more easily, to have her own household, to know she was not watched and spied upon from morning until night. Elizabeth was indeed a prisoner even if the cage was a large and varied one. That she lived was because Mary willed it. Escape to Europe could offer her relief, but the price would not be cheap. He needed to speak to the Lady; it wasn't his decision to make.

✝

In the end, the meeting came sooner than he could have imagined possible. Elizabeth had toothache. The Lady had cried, shouted and screamed for two days. A barber-surgeon had been brought but she had flung plates at his head. Another had been summoned as the Lady continued to cry and sob. He had not been so lucky, a hot poker from the fire spinning end-over-end had left it's print on his arm. The noise continued. A wad of wet cloth clamped to the side of her face, Elizabeth continued to howl in agony. The ache, which came and went, was so much worse at night and by the end of the second night of sleeplessness, her erstwhile gaolor, Travers, had taken about as much as his nerves could stand. He'd penned a note to Gardiner outlining the Lady's medical emergency, begging leave to summon Kate Ashley back to the house to help the Princess. He suspected that this was the only person who could exert any level of control over the Tudor temper.

Gardiner had taken too long to reply and a third night of sleeplessness was delivered to the household. Elizabeth, unable to contain herself in her rooms, had taken to roaming around the house that night, moaning, exclaiming loudly and slamming doors.

A terse note was received back the following day in Gardiner's secretary's neat hand. Informing Travers that the day-to-day arrangements for Elizabeth's household were not the concern of the Lord Chancellor and if there was a need to consult with her former governess then that was Master Travers' business. Travers balled the paper and sent it to the back of the fire, cursing. One minute, the bloody Bishop wouldn't allow so much as a change of linen without his damned say-so and now, it seemed, he cared not at all. Travers wished they'd make their bloody minds up and stomped off to summon Mistress Ashley.

Travers' man delivered the note to the Lady's hand personally as he had been instructed to do.

"The Master bid me take you there now if you will?" He instructed before she'd even finished reading the note.

"Did he indeed now? Well I'm not his to order about, am I?" replied Kate, pushing the note into her pocket.

"He said you'd say as much and I was to remind you that it is not him, but the Lady

Elizabeth, that needs you and she is in much pain," he replied.

A black look descended on Kate's face. "Very well, toothache is it?" she asked, "wait downstairs. I need some of my things and I shall be as quick as I can."

In the end, Kate was nearly an hour and when she emerged, a man followed her carrying two huge boxes.

"I was told to just bring yourself to her Lady," Travers' servant complained.

"Fine then," Kate spat, "you carry those boxes."

He took one look at them from where he sat on top of his horse, then gestured the servant to follow them. They rode on side-by-side, back along the Strand to Durham Place with Kate's servant walking slowly behind carrying her medicine boxes. It was a short distance, but she could only guess at how much Richard's arms were burning under their load by the time they arrived.

Kate entered Durham Place, her servant staggering slightly behind her under the burden, "I'll need those in the kitchen. Can you show him where it is please, I'll go and see Elizabeth straight away?"

A servant bobbed in front of Kate. "We are right pleased to see you, Mistress Kate, there's no-one can get near her and she's in frightful pain."

Kate began briskly pulling her gloves from her hands, "Take me straight up to her now. Is she in the solar?"

"No, she's in her own room and she's blocked the door." Lilly supplied.

"We shall soon have that open. Now take me up." Kate bustled her way up the stairs.

From the kitchen where Kate's servant sat with her boxes, they heard the hollow, deep scrape of wood on wood as something large was dragged across the floor. Elizabeth's door, it seemed, was no longer barricaded.

†

"Now scream like you mean it," advised Kate heeling the door shut behind her.

"I bloody well do have tooth-ache," Elizabeth replied petulantly, but she wailed loudly anyway for the audience's ears' sake.

"Let me see," Kate took hold of her jaw and set to pull her into the light.

"Will you leave me be, woman," Elizabeth wrenched herself free.

"Three night's apparently you've kept them awake, now let me look," Kate admonished. "Will you hold still," Kate pulled her round so the light from the window fell on Elizabeth's face. "I can't see anything inflamed. Which side? Point with your tongue."

Elizabeth pulled back and started laughing, "I even had you fooled!" Kate's face broke into a sudden smile and she flung her arms around Elizabeth, "I have missed you sorely, have they been looking after you well?"

"Well enough, but a little too closely," Elizabeth replied.

"I'm afraid we are going to have to put on a little show for Travers. He thinks you are beyond the pale with pain; we can't just give you a cup of spiced wine and expect him to swallow it. I'll tell him you need a tooth out."

"What! You're not coming anywhere near me to pull a tooth!" Elizabeth backed away.

"Oh hush will you, all you need to do is provide the noises, I'll do the rest. And we all know what a fair pair of lungs the Lord blessed you with," Kate was headed for the door. "Wait here while I get my things and let Travers know what the problem is."

Kate descended quickly into the kitchen, addressing the servant who'd carried her supplies, "You there: bring those boxes up, follow me,"

Travers asked, "What can you do for her?"

"She needs a tooth taken out. I can do it but I'll need to get it over quickly before she realises what I mean to do. Paul there can hold her while I pull it, unless you want to?" Kate asked.

Travers was quite sure he wanted to be no part of this and moved aside to let Kate and her servant set foot on the steps back to Elizabeth's rooms above.

"It'll be Kate that'll be getting her teeth knocked out, not the Lady Elizabeth, you mark my words," Traver's wife pointed out.

✝

"Put them on the table," Kate instructed, it was with relief, Richard banged down the two heavy chests and backed to put his weight against the closed door to ensure their privacy.

"Elizabeth, talk to him, you have but a few minutes." Kate advised quickly.

Elizabeth's brow furrowed as she realised who it was standing with his back to the door; she'd not seen him in months. "Richard, I thought you'd deserted my cause."

"Elizabeth, there is much to tell, I will talk to you later. Let him talk to you now, we do not have long," Kate urged, as she began pulling bottles from her medicine chests.

"This can't be good news. One day, maybe you will come on the heels of good news but not in these dire days," Elizabeth give him her close attention. He seemed changed. Thinner than she remembered, his face tired and drawn; but she did not say so.

"I am afraid you are right," Richard spoke quickly. Elizabeth was about to speak but Richard raised his hand to silence her. "Kate's right, we have moments only. The Guilds are planning to free you from Durham Place in the coming weeks and secure you a passage to Holland."

"Holland!" Elizabeth gasped.

"The Protestant cause is strong there and they believe your supporters there will be sufficient to protect you until you can return to England as heir."

"They'll raise me up a puppet Queen without a kingdom. Mary would never stand for that, or the nobles," Elizabeth was thoughtful, then added, "or Parliament either."

"That's the risk, it doesn't matter what you say, it is unlikely that, once they have your person secure on foreign soil, they will be able to remain quiet about it. They will raise you up, I would expect, as England's Protestant Queen in waiting."

"No, no, no." Elizabeth's tiny fist beat on the table. "If they do this I will lose everything. Have I not made my nerves of steel and braved out all that has been cast towards me. Can I not continue here to outwit them?"

"My lady," Richard continued calmly, "that was all the answer I needed."

Kate handed Elizabeth a reddened linen square which she recoiled from.

"What's that?"

"Your blood, and the tooth I am about to pull out. Well, actually, it's a piece of horse tooth and ox dye, you have to admit looks fairly well like blood," Kate had been busy in her chests while the pair had their brief exchange. "Now, count to five and scream while we get this tooth pulled."

Elizabeth screamed, Richard threw over a heavy table and added the smashing of a hand basin.

Kate held up her hand for silence; she spoke in a quiet voice designed not to carry. "They will be up in a moment. And indeed, as Kate descended the stairs with Richard burdened once more behind her, Travers and his wife passed them on the way to Elizabeth's room.

His Reformist contacts had bought his way into Fairfax's group. Richard's loyalty though was not to the cause; it was to Elizabeth, always Elizabeth. He had very much doubted that she would want to leave England, indeed she had not for a moment even been tempted. That took courage; to slam the door on what very well might be her only escape route. Elizabeth had spent time in the Tower, closely questioned and she must have feared for her life. One wrong word, one inappropriate action, one harsh accusation and he had no doubt she would be taken back again. He knew his role now had changed, no longer would he aid Fairfax, now his goal was to frustrate their plans, to ensure Elizabeth stayed in England and out of the hands of Fairfax's Reformist mob.

Chapter Four

"There, put it there," the old man barked from the chair near the fire.

The servant put down the wine glass on the table.

"Not there, man. God's wounds. Put it where I can reach it, man."

Without meeting his Master's eyes he picked the glass up and placed it on the side of the table nearest to William Fitzwarren.

"Now, push the table closer," William barked.

The wood of the table legs grated on the oak floor as it edged closer to the elderly man, the wine vibrating and swilling in the glass, dangerously close to the rim.

"Please don't spill," prayed Edwin, his eyes on the ruby liquid.

William reached out and satisfied himself that the wine was near enough.

"Now the fire; I don't want to sit here and freeze. Put those two logs on," William pointed with age bent fingers. "Push them to the back. I don't want to sit here and roast like a pig," Edwin dutifully obeyed the old man's commands.

"Leave me, but stay outside in the hall, listen for me tonight, not like last week when that dolt left me," William's voice commanded.

Edwin, breathing a sigh of relief, backed to the door. For the moment his duties were done and he'd escaped the old goat's presence. Quietly he closed the door behind him and left the Master bathed in firelight. The flames flickered orange making the wine in the glass glow. William reached and took the goblet into his gnarled keeping; the arthritic, lumpy knuckled figures could no longer bend to hold the rounded form evenly. Too full, it tipped and spilled, wine pouring over the rim to the table.

Before William could shout for Edwin, a hand caught the stem righting the glass. Taking it from him, William's visitor placed it down carefully on the table.

"I don't think Edwin needs to share the moment, do you?" Richard voice was soft, speaking to his father for the first time in five years.

The shock left the old man and he dropped back in his chair, his shoulders straight, his face set and hard. "I'd expect little less from you."

"Little less?" Richard sounded amused.

"So what is it that you want then? I'm hardly thinking you've finally come to see me out of a sense of duty, have you?"

"Duty! How could you ever imagine I'd ever owe you anything?" Richard used in the same deceptively mild voice. Stepping back he propped himself against the fireplace to better observe his father.

"I'm still your father," the aged, rough voice barked.

"Aye, you are and I think you're looking a little cold back there. Come here and warm yourself nearer the fire." Before William had a chance to move, Richard moved around the back of his chair and pushed it a foot forwards. William's right hand, outstretched, was inches short of the bell chain he'd been reaching for. His face was furious.

"Why should you have anything to fear from me?" Richard asked conversationally, "especially after we parted on such good terms?"

"You dragged our family name, my name, into the gutter. My only regret is that I was too soft on you; I should never have let you live."

"Oh come now, let's not dance around the lies. We both know perfectly well that I had no blame to bear. And I think you fairly well left me for dead. Has senility made your conscience clearer by deciding otherwise?" Richard was beginning to laugh.

"People still blamed you, powerful people. And it might not have been you on that one occasion but I've been fairly well assured that you'd made the Lady Elizabeth your whore well before Seymour got his hands on the bitch. She was, by then, well soiled..."

He didn't see the blow coming: the back of Richard's hand smashed into his cheek, a ring tearing a strip from the heavy jowls. His son's hand clamped quickly over the dribbling mouth to muffle any noise William made.

"A step too far," Richard growled in his ear. He removed his hand cautiously from his father's mouth. "Now, I think I'd like to know who these 'powerful' people were."

"It's done. Does it matter?" William replied angrily wiping blood from his mouth with the back of his hand.

"It does, to me. Tell me who and tell me why?"

"Why should I?" growled William, "You've no name to clear, it's too late. You're a treasonous, untrustworthy whelp."

"Untrustworthy?" still his voice remained calm and level. "I think we can both agree that any lessons I learned in that came to me from your hand, did they not?"

"Any lessons you got, boy, were well-earned and well-deserved." William spat back.

"Let us not digress down that route again," Richard warned.

William closed his mouth and returned the hard stare.

"So who? And why?" enquired Richard, his mild level tone had returned.

"And if you knew, would it matter? There's nothing, *nothing*, you can do about it."

"Let me worry about that..."

William cut him off. "Too powerful...you've no idea have you?" He laughed. William glanced quickly at Richard's right hand and the laugh choked in his throat. He didn't want another crack across the face.

"Maybe not, so why don't you tell me?" Richard folded his arms and leaned with his back against the side of the fireplace.

William said nothing; Richard's eyes never left his face.

"Oh, so this was no accident of fate then?" Richard asked.

William laughed, "Fate had nothing to do with it, nor did accident or coincidence. It was all by design."

"Now we are getting to the heart of it. Whose design?"

"Think, you bloody idiot. Who'd want to hold something like that over Boleyn's whelp, eh?" William spat.

"I don't know, the list could be fairly long. How about you tell me?" Richard's voice sounded dangerously quiet now.

"You're nothing but a clod-head."

Richard pushed his shoulders from the marble carved fire surround. "That maybe, so help me to understand. What did you do?" Richard hissed, reading his father's thoughts.

"I gave them you. I didn't care,"

"You didn't care," Richard echoed quietly. "Giving away sons has become quite a habit with you, hasn't it?"

"No. It was a bargain. Clear and simple. They get to hold you to account, should they ever need to bring Elizabeth to heel, and I got a place on the Council." William was chuckling now. "It was a security, that was all; they were unlikely to ever use it. What they had could ruin any prospect she ever had for a good marriage and bar her from the succession. Only if they wanted to."

"Oh, and I would have been where, then, if that game had played out?" Richard said coldly.

"I'll tell you where lad: on your knees with your head on a block, that's where."

"Very concise. I can see that. But for whom? Who wanted to bar her from the succession?"

William did laugh this time, Richard even glanced at the door expecting to see Edwin summoned by the unexpected noise from within.

"For God's sake who do you think?" barked William.

Richard had more than a good idea, but still, he wanted to hear it.

"Thomas Seymour, of course." William spat. "Henry Wriothesley worked for him, but he was also working for the Privy Council and between them they tried to control the Crown. Lot of good it did them."

"Seymour lost his head on the block and Henry Wriothesley, he's been dead now at least three years," Richard spoke more to himself.

"More like four," mumbled his father. "That's bloody stopped you, hasn't it? You idiot. Wriothesley and the Council wanted to control the succession, you were just part of their control over

Elizabeth, should they need it. You are lucky they haven't used it. Yet."

"So he had a testimony?" Richard asked acidly.

"Of course, it wouldn't be any good without it, now would it?" William replied, raising his bushy eyebrows.

"So who's in Wriothesley's place now?" Richard asked.

"How the Hell should I know? Do I look like I go to Court often? Eh? No, my days are spent in this eternal room, and I know there won't be many more of them."

"Spare me the self-pity, please," Richard admonished an edge in his voice, his elegant face hard.

"There's nothing you can do about it. As you say, Seymour and Wriothesley are dead, but you can be sure that there'll be a packet somewhere with those bawdy tales all tied up and ready to tell their story if someone on the Privy Council feels they need to use them."

"Yes, quite, I can't see the benefit in indulging in conjecture at the moment, can you?" Richard had retaken his place, leaning once more against the fire surround. "This has all been very pleasant. However, this is not the only reason I wished to see you again."

The old man's eyes narrowed.

"There's the small matter of my inheritance," Richard said cheerfully.

"Your inheritance?" William laughed out loud, "Is that what you are after? That idiot you call a brother couldn't get you anything, so now you've come to see what you can press out of an old man. You are pitiful."

Richard was silent, he was staring at William.

William's eyes widened and his face cracked into an ugly smile, "Oh, that is funny. You didn't know he'd been to see me?"

"When?" Richard demanded.

"Find out yourself," William spat.

"No, I'll find out now, or you'll have no need of Edwin any longer." Richard threatened, moving from the fire to stand close to William, a little too close.

William could sense his power. Seated, he was forced to tilt his head back a long way to meet those cold eyes. There was nothing of his wife in the face before him, Richard was made in William's image and he knew just how much strength he would have. It felt savagely unfair; all the power of youth, all the virility, all the strength of maturity that had deserted him by some cruel twist, he saw it all now vested in another. How he hated him. "A few weeks ago," was all William conceded, then added, a sneer on his face, "He left empty-handed."

Richard was quiet for a long time. "Did you feel nothing? He's your son? He'd done you no wrong."

"He's a piece of gutter filth, bred in the byre..."

"He wasn't bred in a byre, he was born to your wife, in your home," Richard stopped William's words.

"What does it matter? He's a common churl, and if he's not, then he does a bloody job of looking and acting like one," William said hotly. "Robert told me you'd kept him with you. What did you expect to do with him? Eh? Did you keep him to taunt me with, a threat, was that it?"

Richard just shook his head.

"Robert had the chance to get rid of him and the fool didn't take it, so it's his problem now." William continued.

"Yes, Robert did a bad job, did he not, of getting rid of me as well," Richard agreed. "Such a shame. Anyway, we digress. I did tell him he'd get nothing from you. Where did he go?"

"How should I know? I raised the alarm, Edwin chased him from the house. If you want to find him go and start turning over every muck heap in London, I'm sure you'll find him under one."

Richard let out a long breath and pushed himself from the fireplace, "I would find him. If you hear from him would you get a message to me?"

"Why would I want to do that?" William's eyes were wide and he leaned forward in his chair. "Why the hell do you think I would ever help you?"

"You have no idea just how bloody lucky you are." There was disbelief in his voice. "I came here wholly expecting to leave with your blood on my hands." William's face drained of colour. "Now I have a use for you, that moment, it seems, has been postponed," Richard continued patiently. "So, will you send me a message?"

"Why would I? If you are set to murder me, why would I hasten that end?" William asked carefully.

"Well maybe I'll just leave your end to the natural course of things, you don't look like you will live that long anyway. That would be my bargain. I'll let you die the rotting death of old age, rather than offer to end your suffering quickly," Richard flipped a knife in his hand, "and only a little sooner. Or, if you choose a swifter end, I would only be too happy to help. Send your message to Christian Carter, I'm sure you remember him, he'll pass it on to me."

"How do I know I can trust you?" William asked quickly, watching the knife flicker in the firelight.

"Simple," Richard smiled malevolently, "you don't."

☦

Clement opened the letter; a smile flashed across his face revealing a row of stumped and rotting teeth. Robert Fitzwarren had expressed his gratitude and confirmed that he would, indeed, not only be continuing to use the lawyer's services, but would be engaging his firm in some additional matters. He promised soon that he would visit and discuss these in person with the lawyer.

Clement's clients varied. What his offices lacked in prestige the lawyer made up for in sheer animal cunning. You paid, and you got your result. The prices were often high, but Clement was very helpful in finding a missing witness or unearthing some critical written testimony. His services were highly valued by his clients, even if his methods were questionable.

Robert Fitzwarren had used Clement twice in the past. Once to help him prove that the debts he had accumulated, which he had neither the means nor inclination to pay, had indeed been discharged. Clement produced evidence of payment and receipts. The poor silversmith had been hard pressed to refute these and had left the Court with nothing. Fitzwarren's legal bill had been considerable, but it was still a lot less than he had owed to the silversmith.

The second time he had need of his services Clement had proved superbly efficient in proving, without a shadow of doubt, that Robert Fitzwarren had indeed been absent from London at the time a man was beaten to death in Crane Street, despite there being several compelling witnesses stating that he had indeed delivered the fatal blow.

Robert Fitzwarren was a client worth keeping and when Jack had turned up with the letter from his bumbling brother and a tale of a lost inheritance Clement had wasted no time. After reading the letter from his brother he had quickly sent word for two men he used regularly for the collection of his client's debts and had engaged them to follow Jack. When Jack had left Clement's dank offices, he suspected not at all that he was followed.

They had reported directly back on Jack's visit to his father's house and also supplied Clement with details of the inn that Jack was stopping in. That was enough for Clement, and he passed what information he had on to Robert Fitzwarren for a reward he hoped to receive sooner rather than later. Not averse to a little blackmail, there was more than a slight hint in his letter to Robert that, of course, his silence on the matter could be guaranteed.

Clement did not know when he sent the letter that Robert was currently out of London at his father's manor, hunting along with his cousin Harry, and it was another three days before Robert returned and read the note.

✝

Jack ran his hands through his untidy hair and tried not to cast his mind back to the confrontation with his father. Could it have really gone so badly wrong? After all this time how could he have made such a mess of it? He knew the answer to this, unfortunately. The visit he made was an impulsive one: he had entered his father's room with not a plan in his head. That's why it had gone so wrong: no planning. Why was he such an idiot, could he not for once have learned from Richard?

Jack was trying now to fathom a path through the mire, asking himself what possibilities there were and what he could do with them. He'd been chased from William Fitzwarren's house as a robber; he'd been outwitted in a few minutes by his aged father, that's all it had taken. The lawyer was not going to offer him any help unless he had money and that was something that he had very little of, so that path was closed. He rocked back in the chair. *Think, damn you, think. What would Richard do?*

It was of little use, his tired brain came back constantly to the same conclusion – *Richard would not have got himself into this mess in the first place.*

The lawyer was not his fault. He'd been given assurances that this was his path to help. How was he to have known that the lawyer was a penny-pinching uncharitable dog? But his father? He could have handled that so much better.

What if he went back? Tried again?

Think, damn you, think!

✝

Kate was back with Elizabeth. Even if the measure was only temporary, both women felt a marked upturn in their spirits. Even Travers was a happier man now that his household was no longer being tormented by the Lady Elizabeth. Kate, he had assured Elizabeth when she had enquired, could remain to tend to her over the next few days in case the toothache returned. Elizabeth, too sensible to press the case left it at that and contented herself with the small victory she had achieved.

Kate shared Elizabeth's concerns over the plan to steal her, like some gilded plate, and take her to Holland.

"You would think they would have thought, at some point, to ask if this course would be acceptable to me," Elizabeth stated again, the needlework forgotten in her lap. She'd been working on it for weeks but, agitated and easily distracted, her progress was painfully slow.

"They want a champion for their Protestant cause, naught else; to them you are just a trophy. If they did secure you from here, mark my words -" Kate put down the book she had been staring at but not reading. "- you'd be no freer than you are now."

"I agree, no freer and no safer," Elizabeth accepted. She tucked the needle into the fabric and discarded the material on the table. "I am safer here for the moment, and my protector is an unborn child it seems."

"Aye, for the coming months Mary's attention is going to be elsewhere and if she is brought to bed of a child then you'll be safer still." Kate agreed. She reached over and squeezed Elizabeth's knee, recognising the tension building in the other again.

"A little safer, we will wait and see." Elizabeth smiled maliciously, "remember Kate, the birthing chamber is a perilous place."

"Especially for a woman of her years. If she thinks she will get some special dispensation from on high when it comes to birthing the babe, then she'll be sadly mistaken," agreed Kate.

Elizabeth's face darkened as she remembered another loss. "Poor Katherine, she was thirty-six when her first child came." Elizabeth's stepmother had been Katherine Parr, Queen to Henry VIII, who had married her childhood love Thomas Seymour shortly after the old Kings death. She had lived only long enough to see her baby four days old before she died.

"She was a good woman and it was grievously unfair what happened." Kate shook her head.

"I know," Elizabeth sounded sad, "women ever seem to bear the burden men cannot carry."

"Mary is older than Katherine, so you never know. I can't see her having an easy time of it." Kate agreed, hoping it would be the case.

"I do hope not," Elizabeth mused, "but in the meantime the last thing I need is to be turned into the new Protestant torch bearer."

"We are well warned, we know their plan even if we do not know the date, and if it comes into play we can at least take matters into our own hands to avoid them" Kate reassured.

"Indeed, it is well that we know." Elizabeth laughed, "every time I smell smoke I think to run to find you!"

Elizabeth had been held for two months in the Tower in 1554 and knew she owed her present reinstatement of liberty to Spain. A political pawn, and a popular one with the people, Phillip realised early on that he could ill-afford for his wife to anger her populace by harming her sister, Elizabeth. The thoughts that ran through Elizabeth's head about Mary's troubled birthing were also thoughts not far from the minds of Phillip and his advisors. He could always, they had suggested, marry the sister; she may be a Protestant, but it would keep England from

France's hands. So they all waited. No decision, no plan, no firm course of action could be taken or laid out until Mary emerged from her confinement with, or without, a child.

Chapter Five

"Why didn't you tell me he'd been here?" Robert Fitzwarren demanded. He waved Clement's letter in his father's face and the old man sank back in his chair. "He's a bloody risk. Look at this, he's been to see a lawyer. My bloody lawyer at that! God's wounds, he needs to be brought to account and quickly. I knew I should not have let him live when I left him at Burton, but I thought such a snivelling underling would never amount to anything, let alone a threat. Now the gutter whelp has got a lawyer!"

"No, he tried to get a lawyer, not quite the same thing is it?" his father offered in a conciliatory tone.

"Oh, don't bloody well sit there and correct me! This is all your fault anyway, you and your bloody conscience. If you hadn't felt the need to unburden your soul like some whining woman this would never have happened. Now this snivelling clod has your confession, God only knows where it and he will turn up next."

William stared at him from his chair and wished again that his strength would return, for he would have knocked Robert to the floor and made him eat that bloody letter while he grovelled at his feet.

"Did he say nothing else? Is there anything else I need to know?" Robert brought his face close to William's and a brutal hand dug into the flesh of his shoulder making the old man wince in pain. "Well, is there?"

"No, nothing. Robert, leave me be." William begged.

"God curse you, can you not do anything right? You can't even die and let me take on the Fitzwarren name in full, can you?" Robert turned, yelling full in William's face "CAN YOU?"

William was quiet, he was well acquainted with Robert's rages; once upon a time, it had been his own temper he'd turned on the boy. Now that time was past, he knew all too well what Robert was capable of and how much he was counting on his death when he could then fully control the wealth that, at the moment, still rested in his frail hands. William knew it would not take too much to push Robert too far, then he would bear what might be the final brunt of his anger. William kept his mouth shut and spoke not a word about the visit he had endured from Robert's other brother, the supposedly dead Richard.

Robert smoothed out again the letter from Clement that he had balled in his fist, his breathing calming as he started to think of a way forward. "He says here he has taken rooms at The Golden Swan."

"He'll be no match for you, Robert. Why don't you take a few of the men...?" William ventured helpfully.

"For God's sake, I sometimes do think you want rid of me! Is that the best you can think of? I take myself there and kill him in cold blood. He might not have those papers on him anymore. What if he has persuaded some other lawyer who'll work without a retainer to take his case? Any number of people could know of this by now."

William gritted his teeth and waited for his son's temper to settle itself.

"No, I need to be a little cleverer here; I need him and anything he might have that could harm us."

William's eyebrows raised at the use of the word "us." Robert didn't give a damn about him. Why had he protected the worthless wretch? Didn't he realise that without him he would be shovelling horse shit, or worse, for the rest of his life?

"I'll have a word with Clement. He knows how to keep his mouth shut when it counts and he knows how to get rid of people," Robert was talking to himself.

Go on, shirk off your problems onto the backs of others, then howl with pain when they fail you - again, William thought. Instead he said, "Aye, Clement. A good idea, Robert, indeed."

✝

William sat staring at the fire for an age after Robert left. It took a long time to make his mind up, but make his mind up he did. He reached for the chain attached to the side table and pulled it angrily.

"Edwin, Edwin, get in here."

Edwin arrived breathlessly a few moments later.

"I want you to deliver a message for me," William barked.

"Certainly my lord, I shall fetch pen..."

William cut Edwin off, "No you dolt. Remember my words and deliver them."

Edwin was confused.

"Christian Carter, he lives near Blackfriars; you'll find him easily enough. Go and tell him you have a message for him from William Fitzwarren, tell him...are you listening?

"Yes, yes my lord," Edwin replied quickly wringing his hands together.

"Tell him I wish for Richard..." William thought for a moment before he continued. "No, tell him I wish for my son to visit me."

William sat back satisfied. "Now, tell me what is the message you will deliver and to whom?"

"My lord, I shall deliver it to Christian Carter and tell him you wish for your son to visit you," Edwin dutifully recited.

"Good, good. Now what day is it today?" William barked.

"It's Wednesday, my lord," Edwin supplied hastily.

"Remember my message well and I want you to deliver it on Friday, Friday do you hear?" William instructed. Hopefully, by then, Robert would have disposed of Jack, but William would appear to have fulfilled the bargain he had struck with Richard.

"Friday, my lord, I will remember," Edwin replied, eager to be out of his Master's presence.

"Aye, now be gone, and let me know when it's done," William closed his eyes, a smile settling on his face. Old he might be, trapped in a spare and withered frame he was, but his mind was still a match for any of them; he'd show them all. Christian Carter had been a close friend of Richard's. Indeed they had attended Cambridge together until Richard was thrown out. Carter had taken over his father's business and was a wealthy merchant now, by all accounts.

†

Bartholomew stooped low to enter the tap room of The Golden Swan. He'd already been there earlier in the day and, as was his way, he had spoken quietly with the landlord about the man he sought. The landlord knew his trade as a debt collector and Bartholomew also told him as much. The landlord cared little; the man's bill was paid and if Bartholomew wanted to return later and lay hands on him for an unpaid debt, then that was fine by him, as long as his fixtures remained intact and his patrons undisturbed. He had also helpfully pointed out that the man they sought had a horse in the inn stables that would fetch a goodly price and might indeed discharge a debt or two. Bartholomew had thanked him and as he returned now, one of his men was indeed in the stables collecting Jack's horse.

Jack had done little that day and now sat alone in the inn, his back to the wall, an untouched plate of food before him. Jack was dragged back from his reverie as a man blocked the light from the open doorway and he looked up. The rest of the inn was fairly empty, his new companion who had dropped onto a trestle opposite him had not joined him due to a shortage of seating.

"Hello," he ventured conversationally, loosening his hand from the cup and sliding it away, "Join me for a cup or two." Jack's voice bore the edge of inebriation and, as he sat back to rest against the wooden wall, he misjudged the distance and his shoulders banged heavily against the panelling. "Whoops," he said, smiling a little lopsidedly.

Bartholomew relaxed; this was going to be easy. He planted his big hands on his elbows and leant across the table so only Jack heard his words.

"Well, me good fellow, I'm sorry to spoil your afternoon but it seems my Master has an argument with you for not paying a bill or two." Bartholomew held up his hand to silence Jack's protest, "It's all here in black and white," he continued, pulling a paper from his jacket, "in the lawyer's hand, if you could read, which I'm damned sure you can't, it says either you pay, or you get delivered to debtor's gaol for them to deal with. Ah now, I'm a reasonable man," Bartholomew raised his hand again, "and I'll let you finish your ale. It'll be a long time before you smell another one." Jack did not pose much of a threat and he also wanted to give his companion a head start in retrieving the horse from the inn stable.

"Maybe I can pay," Jack slurred, reaching for the paper. Bartholomew let him take it and smiled broadly as Jack unfolded it and held it upside down, purporting to read it. "It's too dark in here, where's the amount?"

"Here, you dolt," Bartholomew took the paper from him and laid it down, pointing one blunt, meaty finger at the paper, "a hundred pounds, owed by Master Kilpatrick and that's you."

Jack wasn't reading the amount, his eyes instead were fastened on the name of the lawyer affirming the debt: Clement. The name Kilpatrick might be a false one, but the name of the lawyer certainly wasn't.

"A hundred pounds," he slurred, "I've never even seen a hundred pounds in my life! There's a mistake."

"You don't look like you have, I agree, but if there's a mistake you can put it before Master Kettering at Marshalsea. Come on, sup up, and we'll be on our way."

Jack slumped back against the wall muttering, his eyes raised to the ceiling. His hands though, palms up, grasped the edge of the table tightly.

Bartholomew never saw it coming. The table smashed up into his nose, splintering bone and tearing sinew. Jack continued forcing the table onto the man until it took him over backward and onto the floor. Over it, as nimble and as sober as a child went Jack, making his way straight to the door before the big man even realised what had happened. His escape was neat and quick, he did not stop until he was four streets away and was fully assured that he was not being followed. Coming to a halt, he stood with his back to a wall trying to catch his breath, eyes on the street he had just come down.

Jack let out a cry of utter frustration. Now he truly had nothing. His cloak was back at the inn, his sword was in the room and his horse in the stable. All he had were the few coins he allotted himself for his evening's ale and a name: Clement. There could be only one explanation: the lawyer had gone to his family, this had to be their doing. He didn't owe anyone any money, someone was trying to set him up using a false name. Fuming still, he set his feet back to the street and headed once more in the direction of Clement's offices.

Jack knew London fairly well, but not as well as his pursuers did and they had not given up easily on their prey. Bartholomew was furious. He had four men with him who he sent out to try and find the bastard. When he found him he intended to make his displeasure known only too well.

Rounding the next corner, hands holding his jacket closed against the cold, Jack did not see the man approaching until he gave a piercing whistle to alert his fellows. Jack quickly turned and attempted to double back the way he had come but found the route blocked by another man with an evil grin.

"He's here Brom, we've got him!" the grinning man yelled and that brought the third pursuer to the street.

Jack knew he would stand little chance, but he'd be damned if was going to go down easily. A lucky punch as Brom was moving in broke the man's jaw and he reeled backward from the fight screaming. But the other two were on him at the same time: a choking hold around the neck held him fast while repeated punches to the stomach and head rendered him immobile.

"Stop, lads," it was the quiet but muffled voice of Bartholomew, walking up the street, his face partly hidden behind a bloody cloth, disguising what was left of a nose that never would again point forwards.

The man behind Jack still held him tight whilst the one in front stepped back to allow Bartholomew space. Pulling his feet back together, Jack braced himself for what he knew was coming. He was, as it happened, luckier than he could have guessed. Bartholomew knew only too well that he could, with a single punch, send Jack's mind spiralling into blackness but that had, on occasion, ended with the rather messy situation of a dead bad debtor and a dead debtor was no good to anyone. Instead, he snarled into Jack's face, "you bathtard, we could have gone eathy on you, but now we'll drag you there on your arth."

Jack laughed at Bartholomew's new lisp; he'd lost a tooth or two to the table, it seemed. He didn't mean to, but the gurgle of laughter escaped his throat nonetheless. Bartholomew's fist, when it came, sank into the ill-prepared stomach and sent him to his knees, retching. His hands wouldn't support him and he ended face down in the dirt and vomit.

"Pick him up" Bartholomew commanded.

"Oh for God's sake, he's been sick on me now," one of his attackers complained, wiping his hand on Jack's jerkin. "I only just got these boots and now bloody look at them," He slapped Jack hard across the face but Jack didn't care anymore. Between them, they dragged him back to the inn where Bartholomew had a waiting wagon, neatly tied him and hoisted him onto the back.

They took him south of the river to the Marshalsea prison in Southwark. He was pushed, kicked and beaten until finally they opened a door to a large room where he swore there was no light at all and thrust him inside. Jack landed on his knees, his hands went to his face and he wept tears of pure frustration.

†

The day was closing when Catherine started her evening ritual: bringing in firewood for the various rooms that would be heated during the night. Today there were only four, as Robert was away, so wood was needed only for the fire in the lord's room, Ronan's room, the one in the kitchen and the one in the room that the servants all shared at the back of the house.

The wood for the lord's room was the worst, as several baskets of wood needed to be hefted up to the top of the house where William lived. If she was lucky, Edwin would be on duty. He was kindly and would let her leave the firewood outside and he would take it in. William Fitzwarren hated everyone, it seemed, especially serving wenches who were too slow, or too clumsy, or too useless.

There was snow on the woodpile the icy crystals had frozen on the wood. Her fingers were numb by the time she had carried in enough wood to keep the upstairs fire fuelled for the evening. The only solace was that it was pine and the smell, that pungent green aroma, reminded her of home.

Pulling her shawl tightly around her shoulders and lifting the heavy basket she was heading back to the yard at the back of the house when she heard the commotion.

"Will you get its bloody bridle and hold it still," Hal, one of the stable lads was struggling with a horse that was dragging him backward and his companion was no help as he clutched his sides, laughing.

"Go on Walt, give Hal a hand and stop laughing at him, how would you like it?" Catherine scolded Walter, good naturedly.

"I will in a minute, I just wanted to see if the beast would drag him all the way to the street; look, his breeches are coming down!" Walt was doubled up in mirth. Catherine could not resist a giggle, for indeed the unfortunate Hal's clothing was descending and he dared not leave hold of the horse to retrieve them.

"Oh come on, help me you bastard," shouted Hal, a fair portion of white backside now plainly visible.

"I can't, I can't," Walt managed between howls of laughter.

Catherine dropped the pail and, laughing, went to help. "Whoo there, come on." Reaching up, she caught the horse's bridle and added her steadying hold to that of Hal's. "I thought the Master was away?" she said to Hal.

"This isn't his horse, it's just been brung in for me to look after and it doesn't like the stables. I got it halfway in, then it started to drag me back out again," Hal provided.

"It looks like it's got a right evil temper on it as well," Walt added.

"I don't know what kind of horse it is, it looks really strange, look at it's face. I've not seen one like it before." Hal still had one hand holding his breeches up.

Catherine looked, the horse was so distinctive, could it be Richard's Arab Corrache? "Where did it come from?" she asked, her heart in her mouth.

"I dunno, someone working for the Master brought it. Said we were to look after it, that's all I know," Walt answered.

"When?"

"Just now, I was out here and they handed it over," Hal said helpfully.

"Which way did they go, I must see them. Hal show me, I know who owns the horse, I have to see him, please." She had hold of his jacket and was pulling him to the open gate.

"There, Mistress, look," Hal pointed at two men walking away.

"Those two, are you sure?" Catherine asked, and Hal told her he was sure. Hoisting her skirts, she set off after them.

"Please sir, wait," She called.

Both men turned, "Well, hello to you, this one's fair throwing herself at me, come on here darling," he opened his arms wide, grinning.

"I'm with Lord Fitzwarren's household," she said tersely, coming to a halt.

"Well you dinna look like it, sorry," He replied, disappointment evident in his voice.

"You brought a horse, I know it's owner," Catherine spoke quickly.

"That bloody wild thing, we are glad to get rid of that. Bit Stan on the backside and I've got a bruise or two I didn't need."

"The owner though, where is he?" Catherine pressed, her hands together nervously twisting her apron.

"Sorry, love, if you knew him, but he'll not be coming a-calling on you anytime soon, he's in Marshalsea." Stan smiled, apologetically.

"The debtor's prison?" Catherine exclaimed.

"Shut up, Stan. Bart will have our hides."

Stan gave Pete an angry look. "It's only a lassie for God's sake, quiet your noise, Pete."

Catherine had learned well. "No, he never told me he owed money, he was to take me to the fair near the river on Sunday. We've been walking out for weeks."

"Aye, he'll not be coming for you again, sweetheart," Stan said with some compassion.

"Oh no," wailed Catherine, "he was to take me to meet his mother after."

"Ah, now you're better off finding this out now, rather than later on when he's led you a dance," Stan said. "I've a girl about your age and I'd show my fists to the fellow who led her along."

"How much did he owe?" Catherine sniffed, her apron to her wet eyes.

"I can't rightly say, sweetheart, but it must have been a lot to get Bart…"

"Will you shut up," Pete's teeth were clenched, "Lassie or no, it's not her business."

"Aye, he's right, I'm sorry for you, but I can't help." The men retreated from the distraught girl quickly.

After a moment she raised her dry eyes from the apron and watched them go. This was news indeed. But who was in Marshalsea. Was it Richard? Was it Jack? Or had someone else bought Corracha, Richard's horse? How on earth was she going to find out? Catherine turned her step back to the house.

"Walt, where are you?" Catherine shouted as she entered the yard.

"Here Mistress," replied Walt from the stables.

"I caught them, but they were not much help," Catherine watched as Walt, with some satisfaction, slammed the bolt home on the stable housing the Arab.

"Thank the Lord for that," Walt said with feeling. "I'm not sure what we are going to do with that beast."

"Master will most like sell him, he'll be worth a bit in gold, a horse like that." Hal replied inspecting the horse from over the safety of the stable door.

"Good, as long as we don't have to look after him that will be fine with me," Walt agreed. "Life is hard enough without having to deal with the likes of him every day."

"I'll put his tack and saddle on the stand," Hal spoke to Walt.

"He didn't have a saddle on," Catherine, looked but couldn't see one anywhere.

"No, it's outside along with a saddle bag I'll pass that on to Ronan," Hal replied.

Catherine would swear she had never moved quicker in her life. The saddle was dumped in the wet yard and next to it was a bedding roll. It took but a second to release the knot on the roll; the blanket unfurled to reveal Jack's sword. He'd never be parted from it. The family motto stared at her from the quillons.

Catherine gasped. Jack must have kept Richard's horse and now he was in Marshalsea and his possessions were here. She'd travelled with him.

He had little more than the clothes on his back, and... she stooped and shook out the blanket. The sword clanked heavily on the cobbles and a small bag followed it. The sword she left, the bag disappeared into the folds of her skirts.

☦

It took Edwin most of Friday morning to track down Christian Carter. He had easily found his house, a well-appointed one indeed and had asked for the Master. The Master, he had been informed, was at the docks; a cargo had come in and it was his custom to be on hand. Master Carter, he was told, had a head for figures and facts and liked to make sure all that arrived was in agreement. If there was a message, Edwin was told he was more than welcome to leave it with Coleman, who was Christian Carter's steward.

Edwin kindly turned the offer down and smoothly told him it was an urgent message he was to deliver, his Master would much prefer to know it had indeed been delivered in person: there may, after all, be a reply to return. Coleman agreed and summoned one of the kitchen lads to take Edwin down to where the Master was likely to be.

"Cuddy here will show you where Master Carter is. He works with him sometimes too so he's acquainted with the docks and he'll find him for you easily," Coleman pointed to a small boy standing behind him.

Edwin thanked him and in the company of Cuddy, set off to the docks.

"I'm in the kitchen, sir, but soon I'll be workin' for Master Carter proper like. He needs people who can count and I," Cuddy pronounced proudly, "can count."

"Really!" Edwin was genuinely surprised. The boy could be not more than ten or eleven, but he was good humoured and Edwin had warmed to him as they walked along.

"Aye, let me show you." Cuddy held up the fingers on his left hand. "You see," he began seriously. "There are five fingers on this hand and five on the other hand and Master Carter says the key to everything is ten, which is this hand and this hand together." He held out all his digits and wiggled them expressively. "So they could be ten, or if needed, they could be a hundred, or even a thousand. Each finger," he waved them up and down again to emphasise the point, "having a different number."

"Get away with you," Edwin grinned, "A boy with a thousand fingers! Are you trying to tell me a tale."

"No, sir, not at all, this is how it works Master told me. This finger here," he wiggled a little finger, "could be one hundred, and this finger here could be another hundred."

Edwin aimed a good natured blow at the boys head. "I don't know how all that works but you have fair baffled me."

"It's easy, sir, let me show you," Cuddy continued, not easily put off. He had a genuine desire to share his knowledge. By the time they got to the docks Edwin was fairly impressed by the lad who had indeed taught him to reckon up to one hundred.

"Master Carter is down there," Cuddy pointed, "I can see him easily."

Edwin strained to see and there, through the debris of the quayside, was indeed a well-dressed man arguing loudly with another.

"We'd best wait," suggested Cuddy, "Master's not one who likes to be interrupted."

Wait they did and for some time until Christian Carter reached something close to satisfaction with the answers he was receiving. There was much doffing of caps and hand shaking, the two seemed to have got over their earlier argument.

"It's always the way," Cuddy sounded confused, "they start out hating each other, then end like brothers."

"This is how men are, Cuddy, when they are seeking to strike a bargain; you'll learn," Edwin said. "Now go and fetch your Master, please tell him I have a message for him."

Christian Carter, receiving Cuddy's message, reached out and ruffled the youngster's hair before heading in Edwin's direction.

"He's a bright lad, that one," Edwin smiled at Cuddy and Christian beamed broadly, "he's taught me a thing or two I didn't know on the way here."

"Indeed, as bright as a pin. A few more years and he'll be working for me once he has all his letters," Christian agreed. "You have a message?"

"Indeed My Master, William Fitzwarren, bid me to tell you that he wishes for his son to visit," Edwin hoped that these obscure words would mean something, and that he could adequately report back to the old goat that he had done as he was bid.

If Christian Carter was surprised he didn't show it. "I will pass on your message, thank you. Now, Cuddy, do you want to guide Edwin back, and on the way, you can teach him to count to ten thousand?"

"Why would anyone need to count so high?" Edwin laughed.

"You'd be surprised," replied Christian Carter, smiling.

Cuddy did indeed attempt the feat on the return journey but Edwin's brain could not accept the fact that his thumb, in Cuddy's new game, was worth now a number as high as a thousand.

Christian Carter watched them go and thought for a few moments before deciding what to do. He wrote the briefest of notes on a square of paper and calling over one of the men unloading the cargo, sent him instead to deliver his message. No doubt he would find out soon enough what was happening and he returned his thoughts to the cargo of the Lavant and his check sheets.

✝

The note from Christian Carter was delivered to Richard's lodgings. The words were few, inviting him simply to call at his own convenience. Sending the paper into the fire, he set off. Edward had offered to help him locate a safe passage to Holland; a wealthy merchant with a booming business importing wares from Europe, he was well placed to find a vessel to engage for Fairfax's plan. Or it could be that his father had seen fit to contact him. Long standing friends, they had studied together at Trinity College in Cambridge for a year before Richard's father saw the folly of his ways and withdrew his funding.

☦

"So, father wishes to see me?" Richard was sitting on a barrel in the dimly lit warehouse.

"That was the message," Christian replied. Richard had little of his attention, occupied as he was on finishing the inventory of the Levant. The cargo was accounted for and stored safely in his warehouse. Now his mind was on the task he loved: of numbering and arranging the boxes, barrels, and bales in ordered stacks. Each row had a number, each stack a letter and numbers and letters were matched to quantities and entered neatly into Christian's inventory records. Empty columns would be completed as sales were made and the stocks diminished. Christian was very proud of his system: oldest went out first, waste was minimal. He knew he was ahead of his competitors and his love of detail turned him a high profit.

He didn't look up from the column he was completing, "It would seem so." He paused, then satisfied with what he had written, added, "How long is it since you saw him?"

"Not as long ago as you'd imagine," Richard replied, "I went to see him about a week ago."

Richard received only a grunt in reply from Christian. So he said, "There is a snake on that cask behind you. If you stay still, it might not strike."

"What!"

"You are busy, I'm sorry," Richard apologised folding his arms.

"I was listening; the only snake in here is the one sat in front of me. I have to get this finished whilst it's fresh in my mind," Christian tapped his head with the pen. "Otherwise I make mistakes, and mistakes..."

"Cost money," finished Richard, "tell me what I need to do."

Christian smiled and threw a wood board through the air. Richard snatched it before it sailed past him. On the board were white sheets with neatly marked columns, all awaiting new entries.

"It'll be quicker if I call out the quantities and you note them in the columns, and for God's sake make sure I can read it, and if you make a mistake..."

Richard didn't reply, but the look he gave his friend was enough.

"Sorry, but some of the clod-heads I've had working for me in the past you would not believe. It's taken twice as long to undo their work as it took to mark it down in the first place. That's why I do this myself now; a mistake at this stage is costly indeed. Only last year we showed six kegs left of English wine. I sold the lot at a goodly price and then found the idiot should have marked it as Rhenish wine. Cost me a penny or two, that one."

"Can we get on with it before I open this keg I'm sat on and drown my sorrows," Richard said testily.

It took three hours. Christian hunched over his piles of neatly penned sheets showing the shipping quantities, called out numbers, letters and amounts. They transferred all the information into a neat and workable inventory. Christian took the board from Richard and inspected the sheets with approval.

"If ever you need work," Christian grinned mischievously.

"When my fortunes run so low, I'll let you know," Richard stretched straightening his back.

"Pass that other board here," Christian gestured towards another laid next to Richard, covered with more neat tally marks.

Richard examined the board before passing it over, "You haven't lost your love of details, I see."

"Don't mock," Christian received the board, "it keeps me at the top of the heap, and that's not an easy position to retain these days, I can tell you."

"I wasn't mocking, although when we studied together it did have it's advantages," Richard laughed.

"I know - I read all the books, made all the notes and shared them with you. I remember it well, Why did I do that?" Christian asked.

"Because you felt sorry for me?" Richard ventured.

"Hardly!" Christian exclaimed.

"There wasn't time for everything and I had to take advantage of what opportunities there were and you, my dear Christian, were one of those," Richard replied stretching to ease his aching back.

"I've been called a lot of things, but never before an opportunity," Christian replied grumpily.

"It was a fair trade, do you not think?" Richard smiled and Christian inclined his head in agreement. Tying himself, as he had, to the charismatic Richard had gained him entry to groups he could never have got close to; many of the men he had met would be lifelong friends and more than a few had been pivotal in advancing his business when he took over from his father.

"That coin I was keeping for you isn't going to last forever you know," Christian replied. A year ago, Richard had extorted money from his cousin Harry and, by what could only be judged very fortuitous foresight, he had left a portion of it with Christian.

"I shall temper my spending, worry not. It will be enough," Then Richard added, "I could always ask my father for money, could I not?"

"Aye, you could. So he wants to see you, are you reconciled? After all these years, after what he did?" Christian asked sounding doubtful.

"Not at all. I went to see him about a week ago and we struck a bargain," Richard supplied, jumping down from the barrel.

"A bargain? Go on, tell me the whole tale," Christian gave Richard for the first time his full attention.

"He told me a tale of how he'd got a fair price for me. At least he'll not be able to say how worthless second sons are," Richard mused as he hitched himself up onto the end of Christian's desk.

"Sold to whom?" Christian asked, his brows furrowed, absently pushing an ink pot away from Richard.

"Oh, it's the same family scandal, but up until now I hadn't realised he'd actually profited from the arrangement. He got a place on the Privy Council." Richard supplied.

"That's terrible I knew he was a mean bastard and never had much liking for anyone save himself, but to do that is beyond belief. Are you sure?" Christian's hand was still pushing the ink pot and Richard leant and grabbed it a moment before it fell from the desk.

"As sure as I need to be. He got himself on the Council in return for pledging my neck," Richard placed the glass ink bottle down with a solid bang.

"There's more to this," Christian observed. "Go on, tell me."

"I cannot say more." Then seeing the look on his friend's face, he added, "Christian, it's not safe, you don't need to know."

Christian grumbled under his breath, "I've also got those other details you wanted." He delved into his pocket and pulled out a few loose squares of paper. "No, not that one, or that one, ah - here it is." He passed it over. "The ship you want would probably be the Dutch Flower. She's back and forth pretty often on a fairly regular run. It's a sturdy vessel as well and her Captain is Hugo Drego. His name is on there; he's honest and reliable. We used him last year to get two families over to Holland before the Crown caught up with them. If you wanted to get a passage to Holland, that's the ship I'd be taking."

"Thank you. Do you know when the ship is due back in London?" Richard asked.

"I can do better than that," Christian smiled. "They are berthed down at the dock now and due to set sail in two days when she is re-loaded."

Richard smiled, "As always you are thorough to a point."

"I know that's why you like me," Christian replied a little grumpily.

Richard dropped from the barrel and moved swiftly over and clapped the other man on the arm. "You know that is not true."

"Well, I don't see you often, and when I do..." his words trailed away.

"I am straining our friendship," Richard replied, sorrow on his face. After a moment's silence, he sat back down heavily on the barrel. "There is much I cannot tell you; much I would have you know."

"I know, I know and then I would understand," a bitter edge in Christian's voice. "You can trust me, you know. How long have we known each other?"

"Too long," Richard reflected. The square of paper Christian had given him he had folded length ways until it made a neat spill. Leaning forwards he fed it to the flame from the candle on Christian's desk. Both men watched the smoke until the paper was gone.

"Will you dine with me at my house tonight?" Christian asked changing the subject. "Anne and I would enjoy your company."

"Thank you, but another night, Christian. Soon though," Richard replied, too quickly.

"Damn you, Richard! You test our friendship too far!" Christian's voice was raised and the look he gave Richard was a cold one.

Richard ran his hands through his hair. "Alright, alright. I need to see my father soon that is all."

"You've spoken to him once in five years and now he demands your immediate attention? Really?" Christian snapped, angrily, "Can it not wait until tomorrow?"

"No, it can't," Richard spoke with finality, and dropped from the desk back to his feet.

"We are friends. Bloody well tell me what's going on?" Christian demanded.

"I'll not bare my soul, Christian, not even to you," Richard voice was once more calm.

"I'm not asking for your soul on a platter. Just why such haste to see a man you've not spoken to for years?" Christian asked reasonably.

"He might have news of someone I am trying to trace, that is all," Richard conceded. "It's important I reach him before Robert does."

"So who is so important to you? I'm feeling quite hurt." Christian asked, sounding not at all upset.

"You never give up, do you?" Richard smiled.

"Not usually, it's a talent. So, tell me, who is this person that has fallen into an unlucky hole between yourself, Robert and your father? What poor bastard could deserve that fate?" Christian mused. He was closer to the truth than he knew and he sensed it from the look on his friend's face.

Richard smiled. "A poor bastard indeed, he's my brother." Then he added, "Half-brother, one of my father's by-blows. We have been together sometime and I owe him a debt. I'd not see him ruined by my family." Christian listened in silence until Richard had finished. He told him of Jack, not all the story, but up to a point. He stopped short of telling Christian that Jack was indeed the Fitzwarren heir.

"Alright, as always you have me I am sorry for doubting you. Where is he now? Is he still in the city?" Christian asked, wondering why he'd never heard of Jack before.

"Knowing him as I do, I would think that after his recent failure he's sitting in an inn somewhere trying to find the solution at the bottom of an ale jug," Richard sounded troubled.

"If he's such a man as that is he worth helping?" Christian asked, "I can understand you feeling obliged to help him, he is kin, but still..."

"He's... I need to find him, Christian, before Robert does," Richard explained. Christian was right – no-one deserved to be in the situation Jack had found himself in. He knew that there was only one way Jack would deal with the situation: badly.

"That isn't going to be easy. There are hundreds of places he could be staying in London. He'll not be using his own name, where do you begin looking?" Christian asked, sitting back and folding his arms, a thoughtful look his face.

"My father told me Jack had been to see him. I was full of hate and I wanted retribution when I went to see him. I'll accept that there was a good chance I'd leave with his blood on my hands. I let him be and the bargain was, if he heard of Jack he'd let me know and send a message to me through you," Richard stretched like a cat. "So I will off and find out what he has for me."

"Are you sure that's such a good idea? Be careful," Christian meant it.

"He's hardly able to move these days: the onset of age is upon him. If he has indeed news of Jack, I need to find out quickly before Robert."

"Your father might be old and withered but you can bet that Robert isn't. Be bloody careful Richard." Christian warned.

"Always," Richard grinned.

"You are many things, but I don't rank careful amongst them," Christian shook his head. Then he added, "Like you said, it is all in the details," and his voice this time was quietly serious. "I know you well. I can tell you have been unwell and I know you use your left hand as well as your right, when I threw the board for you to catch with your left hand you caught it badly in your right. You've the look of sickness still about you. I know you're not going to tell me what has happened, I can read that from the look on your face."

"At least you know you'll not get an answer," replied Richard quietly, then smiled. "I learned a valuable and somewhat painful lesson in loyalty, that's all. Atropos controls our lifespan, does she not? Only she knows how long the mortal thread is, where she chooses to cut it, we are blessedly ignorant."

"Atropos! You don't believe in fate any more than I do!" Christian scoffed, hands on the desk as he pushed himself up from his chair.

Richard rubbed his hand over eyes that suddenly seemed very tired. "It would be a comfort though, would it not?"

"Perhaps. However, we both know it's just an excuse." Christian's voice was stern. "And you are just trying to divert me from my questions, more to the point."

Richard smiled, "Yes, well, I forget you are not as easily diverted as some." Rising, he squeezed Christian's shoulder. "I will make an honest account of all my humble deeds. Give me time."

Richard bid his friend goodnight and slipped quietly from the warehouse into the dark of the early evening. Christian watched him leave. He wished him well.

†

"Madam, for the child, please you must not spend hours like this," pleaded Anne Bouchant.

Mary, on her knees in front of the small shrine in her room, rosary in hand, pretended not to listen. Always devout, her Catholicism her defining characteristic, it was no surprise that now in her real time of need she was leaning heavily on the crutch.

The child was heavy within her: she felt it's weight like a stone, a cold hard rock deep inside. Although never before with child, she had spent her whole life surrounded by pregnant women. They smiled, they caressed their broadening stomachs, their faces bloomed and they pulsed with the vigour of a double life. Mary felt none of this joy.

Her ladies asked her if she felt the baby turn yet, assured her that when she did she would know it; there was no feeling quite like it in the world they said. They reassured her that it would happen and it was most likely that she carried a lazy boy, who had not yet woken within her. Their comments and reassurances calmed her a little, but never for long.

Soon the dragging weight would return, she'd pray to the Virgin for some sign from within her, some movement to show her that there was a living son, safe and warm within her womb.

They had resorted eventually to an intervention that even Mary would not ignore. They had sent for Phillip.

"My lady," he spoke in Spanish, "the Lord will hear you, whether you are on your knees or in a chair. We must think of the child, and your health, my love." Kneeling next to her he smiled and reached over to take her hand. "The day is warm and bright, come walk with me, and let a consort show off his pretty Queen."

Mary blushed and allowed him to raise her from the cushion she knelt on. Trapping her hand in the crook of his arm he guided her from the room.

"Now come with me, and let me show you what has just come to us from Spain," Phillip implored. "I am tired of English entertainment, and tonight we shall have proper Spanish dancing and singing: my father has sent over the De Fablio troop from the Spanish Court to entertain us."

Phillip took her to see the wagons, all filled with the costumes and stages and instruments they had brought with them and to meet the esteemed leader of the troop, one Monsignor De Fablio.

Eventually, he returned Mary to her ladies, and bid her not to overtire herself, and he would escort her that evening to the entertainment. Then he returned to his own rooms, surrounded as always by his Spanish nobles.

"How long must we endure?" Phillip pulled the gloves from his hands and slapped them on the table. "The very damp of this country is between my bones, and my nose, it drips. How do they put up with it?" Phillip pulled a silk square from his sleeve and delicately dabbed his nose. "It is so sore! This is why the English sniff so much Alberto: they fear to dab their noses, they know it makes them so painful, so the revolting creatures suck it all back up."

"Quite so," Alberto laughed. "Have you heard the Earl of Winchester? Every third word is punctuated by a great rattling sniff. His head must be packed with snot."

Phillip smiled, amused, "To be fair, it is not packed with much else. And Arundel and Gardiner have just given up entirely and let their noses drip. I can hardly look them in the face now the winter is upon us."

"How fares the Queen today?" Alberto enquired, changing the subject. It was well known in Phillip's Spanish camp that whilst Mary was devoted to her new husband, he, on the other hand, saw her merely as a part of the necessary process of obtaining England. If she produced him an heir then the realm was secure for him and England would be firmly tied to Spain.

"She is well, as well as a Lady of her years can be, I expect, in her condition," Phillip's voice was resigned, he hated his inability to have any control over the situation.

"We shall trust in our Lord, and hope for a son for you," Alberto replied, a poor reply, but there was little else he could say, Phillip acknowledged his words with a weary smile.

It was December, the Queen was due to give birth in May and the Court was preparing itself for Christmas. Phillip hoped fervently that this would help him pass another month of his own confinement in England a little quicker than was the norm.

✝

They met in a room above The Sheep's Wool, a smart inn near Blackfriars. Richard arrived early and took a place at the table towards the back, sitting in the shadows to better observe the rest. Inn staff brought up cups, ale and wine in readiness for Fairfax's meeting. Richard look skyward; he might as well have put a sign outside the place advertising the fact. The word 'secret' was something entirely alien to Fairfax and he was treating the whole venture like one of his guild events: a grand affair with himself at the centre.

Some arrived and seated themselves at the table and enjoyed the wine and talk. There were eight of them all present when finally the guild master, predictably late, finally arrived.

"Gentlemen, gentlemen, I am so sorry. Pressing business at the guild hall I am afraid. Nothing I could avoid. Lord Hadley called by to discuss the coming Christmas feasts we are supplying and I simply could not get away." The guild always provided the Court with meat and wine for the Christmas celebrations and Fairfax could not resist reminding everyone of his close Court links. A pity, thought Richard that the stupid man was plotting against the current Court!

The talk covered little of any interest to Richard. It seemed that no significant progress had really been made since their last meeting which at least boded well. They were all in agreement on one thing: that any action should be put off until after the New Year. January or February were the preferred months.

"Richard, did you get any information on passage to Holland?" Fairfax asked at last.

"Indeed, there is a ship which makes a regular crossing with a sympathetic captain," Richard replied.

"And how much would his sympathies cost?" George Sewell asked ever the ventures treasurer.

"I have not asked him yet," Richard replied shortly.

"Why not? We need to know. His fees could be extortionate and our coffers are not bottomless man!" Thomas Cresswell retorted hotly.

"It seemed," Richard spoke patiently, "prudent to leave those inquiries until we indeed had a date in mind, in case careless words are spoken and our intent revealed."

"Hmmphh," was the reply from Fairfax

"I will call to see the captain when the ship next comes into London and I will find out as well what his sailing plans are for the early part of the year," Richard offered.

"Good man, good man," Fairfax's voice was loud bringing the attention back to where he liked it. "On my side, we are all set, the orchard has been cut back, and the wood all set ready to light. If we get the sailing dates for the ship then we can agree on a date at our next meeting,"

"Please remember that the weather in that month can play havoc with well-laid plans. A bad storm and a ship could remain in port at either side of the North Sea for weeks," Richard warned sensibly.

"Always on the black side," Fairfax countered, "I am sure that we could find a safe refuge for the Lady for a few days if the weather does change our plans. We are nothing if not resourceful and the Lord is most certainly on our side with this venture."

Richard sat back and in the darkness, the look of incredulity that sat on his face was invisible.

Chapter Six

Robert dropped easily from his horse in the street outside Clement's house and flipped the reins at one of the men who rode with him.

"Wait here, I'll not be long," he commanded and strode with the confidence of the rich up the path to Clement's moldering office door. Robert didn't consider knocking and let himself straight in, calling for the lawyer.

"Master Fitzwarren," Marcus attempted to intercept him as he stepped towards Clement's office, "I'll let Master Clement know straight away you are here."

"Do that," Robert commanded, pulling his riding gloves a finger at a time from his hands.

"Please sir, if you would like to wait in the…"

Robert didn't allow him to finish. "Get to your Master, man, now. Tell him I'm here and I wish to see him" Robert was not for moving.

Marcus knocked and let himself into the lawyer's office. Even from outside Robert heard the raised high-pitched voice of his legal advisor.

Marcus, his face reddened, returned a moment later. "Sir, he is with a client and asks that you wait please, he will see you shortly."

"Go back and tell him I'm not one of his flea-bitten clients. And no, I will not damn well wait," Robert spat. Marcus wrung his hands together, stuck as he was between an angry client and an even angrier master.

"I will try, sir..." Marcus ventured, backing towards the door.

"Oh God's bones, out of the way." Robert shoved the man aside and advanced towards the door he knew to be Clement's, wrenching it open.

"Marcus, I told you I was not...Master Fitzwarren, it's a pleasure as always," Clement's voice sounding not all in agreement with his words.

"Hurry up Clement, I've not got all day. I'll not sit in your waiting room like a commoner," Robert barked.

"I'll come back," the small man sitting in the client's chair opposite Clement offered.

"You stay there Master Green," Clement commanded. "We will finish our business, then I will attend to this gentleman."

Robert banged a fist on the panelling releasing a torrent of dust from the niches.

"I can come back Friday, it's not a problem for me," Green was rising now from the chair.

"Sit down. We'll finish our business. Master Fitzwarren will wait his turn," Clement almost shouted across the desk.

It was too much for Green. He continued to rise, bobbed a half bow at Fitzwarren and was out of the door in an instant.

Fitzwarren dropped into Green's seat and smiled at the lawyer. "There then, it looks as if you have time to talk to me now."

"Every time you come here you put the very fear of God into my clients: Mistress Murrow never came back you know? You, sir, are not good for business," Clement complained.

"I, sir, am very good for your business and you know it. So how is the De Bernay case coming on?" Robert asked, hitching his feet up onto Clement's desk.

"I told you last time this would not be quick. I'm waiting for letters back from his lawyers and I have lodged a case with Chancery Court, but all this will take time," Clement supplied wearily.

"Time, time. Yes, so you keep telling me. And the other matter?" Robert asked; this was the real reason for his visit.

"The papers are in order and your friend is stuck in Marshalsea until someone can come up with the amount, and of course the interest. Prison isn't cheap," mused Clement. "He'll not last long, they never do. It's a big debt so they'll have some interest in him at first, a goodly fee would attach to it's recovery, but very soon they will realise that no-one is coming for him or going to redeem his debt, and then why give him food and water? He's just a waste of resources."

"Are you sure?" Robert regarded him closely. "I don't want him back out of there again."

"I'm sure. The only way for him to get out of Marshalsea is if someone pays them a hundred pounds, plus interest, and as you say he has no-one. He'll die soon enough and rot in a common pit."

"And none of this will be traced back to me?" Robert pressed.

"Not at all. The creditor is fictitious and, under client privilege, no-one can see the papers. As if they would care to even ask anyway," Clement scoffed.

Robert seemed satisfied. "Good, send me a note when he's dead then. How long does that usually take by the way?"

"Good God, man, I can't be exact," Clement was exasperated.

"Aye, but I bet this is something you've done before for your clients, isn't it?" Robert replied slyly.

Clement reddened. "Two or three weeks, once they realise no-one will pay; then no one can last long without food or water. He'll have to pay for whatever he wants, and he has no money, no means and no sponsors."

"Good, two weeks then. I'll expect your note." Robert rose and left the lawyer.

Clement cursed his retreating back. Fitzwarren should be grateful for all the work he had put in. It wasn't easy, there were risks, he could at least show some gratitude. Clement resolved to raise his fee.

✝

It was the following day before they came for Jack. He was dragged out of the cell and into another one opposite. Manacles were clamped round both his wrists, the chain linking them was no more than a foot long.

"There you go," his gaoler rattled the chains between his two wrists, "you're a properly dressed debtor now."

Jack didn't retaliate. He knew where he was and he was more than aware that survival was going to need every ounce of strength he had. He was wise enough to waste none of it on them. The only change they could make to his circumstances would be one for the worse. So he took their shoves and pushes and their insults and kept his head bent, his eyes down and his focus on a place deep inside himself.

"Right then, take him down to see the keeper. You'll get assessed and we shall see how you fare. I hope for your sake you've a family that loves you well," one of them laughed.

He walked between them and entered the keeper's rooms. Jack was shivering and he could feel the heat from the fire in the room and was glad of it.

"For the Lord's sake, Ross, you've done it again. How many times have I told you not to put them in there before you bring them to me? Why do you have to subject me to the smell of piss and filth first thing in the morning? Don't bloody well do it again, do you hear, or you'll be spending a night in there yourself." Then addressing Jack, "You, yes you, shift yourself near the door and come no nearer," the keeper of Marshalsea, one Mark Kettering, instructed.

Jack dutifully backed three steps towards the door.

"I'm sorry, sir, but I wasn't on duty last night when they brought him in. It was late like, and the lads just put him in there for safe keeping," Ross apologised, giving Jack an accusing sideways glance as if it was his fault.

"See it doesn't happen again. It fair turns my stomach. Right then, we have your papers here." Kettering found the correct sheet. "So you owe one hundred pounds: quite a sum, quite a sum indeed," he raised his eyes and looked at Jack over the spectacles. The man before him did not look like a gentleman. Many passed through here that were of a noble birth and Kettering could spot them from a mile away: this was, after all his trade. Gambling debts usually, and their families would be pressed to save the wretches from Marshalsea, either by paying in full and freeing them or by contributing weekly amounts to cover the debtor's board and lodge and to reduce the balance of the debt. "Mmm, so who shall we apply to for cancellation of this debt, Master Kilpatrick?"

Kilpatrick was the name Jack had seen on the papers Bartholomew had shown him. He knew enough to know that arguing they had the wrong man would do him no good.

Jack met Kettering's eye. "No one, sir, there is nobody to press for this debt."

"Nobody? Are you sure?" asked Kettering. "You do realise where you are don't you?"

"Marshalsea," Jack replied.

"And you do realise that if there is nobody to discharge this debt for you," Kettering flapped the sheets of paper in front of him, "then you have no chance of setting foot outside of these walls again?"

"I do know that," Jack accepted. "There is no-one to pay that debt. I have no family."

"Oh well, that's not good is it?" Kettering was looking quite disappointed, a hundred pound debtor did not come his way every day. This man should have proved quite lucrative. You didn't get into this kind of debt if you were a nobody, and Kettering was quite sure that out there somewhere would be family, a friend, even an employer or a business partner he could press for Jack's release. It happened often. They came to him full of bravado, but he had his methods. A few days in the pit usually persuaded them to divulge the names of family and friends who might be able to help with their release.

"Well then, Ross, how much did he come to us with?" Kettering shifted his attention to the gaoler.

"Four shillings and an angel, Sir," Ross replied.

"Four Shillings and an angel," Kettering repeated. "That's not a lot: that is going to buy you four meals and pay for a roof over your sorry head for a week. Are you sure there is no one can save you from this sorry state?"

"No-one, sir." Jack's voice was firm.

Kettering was finished with him, "Go then Ross, put him back where you found him," he waved them from the room, "and leave the door open for a few moments and let some of that stench escape."

They led Jack back to the room he had spent the night in and opened the door. "Last chance, matey. Is there anyone to help you?" Ross asked. Jack didn't reply and Ross pushed him hard in the small of the back sending him sprawling on the filthy floor.

"Bloody idiot," Ross turned the key locking the door.

There wasn't any light in the room at all. The only variation came from a narrow slice of grey marking the bottom of the door where some light from the gloomy passageway outside leaked in. Jack crawled on his knees until he found the wall. There he sat, back to the wall, knees pulled up to his chest, head bent; alone in the silence and cold of Marshalsea.

✝

Richard broke the seal on the letter. He'd written to Jamie at Burton, using Christian Carter as his name. There wasn't any news of Dan and the other men; they had left and not returned. To be fair he had not expected them to. Burton was a dangerous place, but he had needed to start looking somewhere.

Sliding the letter away, he pulled the open book towards him. After half an hour he heard the bells ringing. Pulled back from his reverie he realised the same unread page still sat before him. Snapping the book shut, he accepted that his tired mind had reached the point where it would work no more. Reluctantly he went to his bed. His was always an uneasy sleep, and he knew tonight would be no kinder to him.

†

A sense of time had finally left him and Jack had no idea how many days he had been there. The dark was absolute, the cold complete, the isolation final. Sometimes he was unsure whether his eyes were open or closed. The fire in his wrists from the crushing manacles felt almost like warmth, pain no longer felt like pain.

Then the terror attacks started, and Jack's misery was complete. He didn't know where they came from, but he had begun to recognise the onset of the terrible, paralysing fear.

"No, no, please, please, no, please," escaped his lips on an anguished sob. Nobody listened, no-one heard and even less cared. Fear, his only companion, crawled from within him and spread, clamping his heart in a hard fist so it hammered in his chest. It pressed his lungs flat so the air wouldn't fill them and it caught painfully in his throat. Then his body shook; he had no control. The chains on the manacles clanked. Pulling his knees to his chest

Jack clamped his arms around them, his head sagged and he begged for it to stop.

✝

The door onto the living world opened. The air that flooded in smelt fresh and wholesome. Breathing it in was almost like food for his lungs, unlike the poisoned rank air that filled the room to which they had abandoned him.

"Where are you?" called the voice at the door.

"Water," Jack's voice cracked.

"Master Kettering wants to know if you've got something to tell him. If you've had a change of heart?" Ross asked.

"Yes, I have, I need water," Jack closed his eyes against the sudden light.

"Good lad. Why didn't you do that before? I tell'd you there was no need to suffer in here, didn't I. Right get over here and I'll take you up to see Master Kettering," Ross was pleased that he would have good news for his Master.

Jack pulled himself up the wall and walked to the door, breathing deeply the pure, cleaner air.

"Lord, you do stink," Ross had a hand over his nose. "You'd think I'd get used to it, but I don't." Ross rattled on, but Jack wasn't listening anymore. He was out, out of the dark for the moment and that was all he cared about.

"Right then, here we are. Now you just wait at the doorway: you right upset Master Kettering last time." Ross knocked on the door and opened it when he heard Kettering's voice on the other side.

"Master Kettering, I've brung him up, he's had a change of heart," Ross said triumphantly.

"That's most fortunate," Kettering sounded pleased. "Well then," he looked back down at the record book in front of him, "Mr Kilpatrick, who can we contact to help relieve you from your sorry state?"

"Water, if I may, please, sir," Jack begged.

"Let us sort this, then water and food you can have," Kettering readied a pen.

"I can't speak, sir, please," croaked Jack.

"Oh very well. Ross, get him a drink," Kettering waved his hand impatiently.

A cup was brought and Jack raised it with two shaking hands. "More," he pleaded finishing it.

"Here, and that's all you're getting." Ross slopped more water into the cup.

Jack drank the second cup slower, grateful for every mouthful.

"Now then, let's get this sorted out," Kettering tapped the pen on the desk. "Names please."

Jack held the cup up and let the last drops run into his mouth.

"Come on, man, I haven't got all day," Kettering barked impatiently, Ross gave him a shove in the arm, making Jack drop the cup to the floor.

"I can't think properly. If I could have some food please, some..." Jack's voice was quiet, his eyes downcast.

"I said after we sort this out, now come on..." Kettering insisted.

Jack shook his head, "I can't remember."

Kettering slammed down the pen. "Ross take him back. I'm a busy man, and if you are not going to help yourself, then how can I help you?" he finished angrily.

Jack just shrugged.

"Go on, Ross, you know where to put him," Kettering turned angry eyes on the gaoler.

Ross shoved Jack down the passages of Marshalsea again, complaining bitterly that he, meaning Jack, had made a fool out of him, and he was in trouble with his master on Jack's account for the second time.

"Right you, in there," Ross opened a door and stepped back, the smell that rolled out was pure evil.

Jack then did fight back. He could already feel the fear starting to clamp a cold fist around his heart, the blood starting to stop in his veins. He stood little chance, being as he was half-frozen and chained, the gaoler made short work of propelling him through the door.

The room had a high grilled window onto the world letting in a little light, enough light for Jack to be able to see his new companions. He was no longer alone, no longer by himself: now he shared his confinement with the lifeless debtors of Marshalsea. Their rotting corpses, awaiting final disposal were left to decay in the cold cellar until there were enough to warrant an efficient collection.

Jack screamed in the dark. He screamed until his throat hurt. Finally taking a long shuddering breath he realised, with relief, that the fear was passing. A second breath opened his tight lungs further and he let it out noisily.

"God, will there be no end to this?" he spoke to the darkness.

Jack had hated and despised the Church all his life. They had branded him a bastard, and that put him on the same societal rung as thieves, prostitutes and beggars. His birth meant that in a priests eye's he should not exist. He couldn't inherit, his final resting place would be a common pit outside the church ground and not interred beneath the hallowed sanctified soil. On the whole he'd not overly cared much. His death, he had decided, would be an occasion long distant and one he could do little about. Jack very much dealt with the here and now, the physicality of existence. His soul, if he had such an ethereal presence, he found it hard to consider.

Sitting in Marshalsea, alone, in the dark, his only companions pain and a hammering in his chest that felt like his very life was trying to escape, was something he couldn't bear. He wasn't a bastard, but who knew that? Who cared? If God had a face, Jack had never looked for him before. If he could have bought anything at all, he was forced to admit, what he wanted the most now was faith.

He'd seen men go to their deaths well, murmuring the words of a prayer, offering their souls to God, before the axe fell or the rope, if it was merciful, snapped their necks. As a boy he'd watching the hangings and he'd laugh and jeer with the other boys when the rope delivered a choking death, the faces contorted, purple tongues distended, piss pouring down their legs as the bodies convulsed. "God doesn't love you," they'd shout at the dying faces, and they'd call it Lucifer's end: for surely the Devil was taking them straight to Hell and starting their eternal torment on the rope.

Jack didn't think he would live long. Once, when he was a child, there'd been a lamb rejected by the ewe and it had been brought to the stables and put into a byre. He could never remember why he forgot about it; probably he'd not listened to the instructions he'd been given. But after three days it was dead and he got his backside lashed for the waste of it. So just three days. It was not long he decided.

There was water in the room, but he ignored it to start with. Later the icy droplets running down the slimy walls became too tempting. An animal urge from within made him crawl along the walls until he found the dampest point. The putrid water made him gag but it offered some relief. He cursed himself over and over but he couldn't stop, despite knowing that three days now would become four and then five and then more. After two days, he knew that if there'd been a knife, he would have used it. On his hands and knees, he felt over the whole floor hoping to find something he could have used.

There was a presence in the room with him. No longer did he find himself afraid of the dark and the loneliness; now it was his companion who delivered terror to his nights and days. The malevolence was not always there, mostly the cold lacked a presence. It was just cold and he knew he was alone. When it was there, the first he would become aware of it was with a kind of warming on his skin, as if one side of him was turned towards a fire. The feeling of warmth gained his attention, turning his mind towards the creeping evil he knew was back in the corner of the room with him. A black and unholy presence, inescapable and wholly terrifying.

In the back of his mind he heard the laughter, felt its touch he and knew that it meant to torment him beyond his endurance. There was no defence against it. He'd tried to block it out, tried to focus his thoughts deep within himself, to turn himself away. But the laughter would just increase and he couldn't keep his thoughts from the sordid, putrid evil that stalked his mind. He'd even found his knees, and humbled himself to the Lord, begged for salvation, for help, for redemption, for his soul; the laughter in his mind had cackled and gurgled and hiccupped with glee at his efforts.

Then they'd given him a plate of food. The bread was so stale he'd had to gnaw at it like a rodent and the cheese, if it was cheese, was harder than a stone. But they did give him a small, blunt knife on the plate. He'd sharpened it on the stone floor until, even in the gloom, the new exposed sharpened edge glinted and then he'd set it at the veins under the manacles. He couldn't get the angle right: the clasps were in the way and there was little room to slide the knife in and even less room to twist it into the skin.

Jack let out a desperate breath of relief as he felt the blade slice into his flesh. It was the deep cut he knew he needed to make. It was then he realised the laughter had stopped; there was just a sense of anticipation. On the verge of ripping the knife through the veins, he stopped. "Go on," he heard the words clearly, "finish it."

Jack felt the tears on his face, they ran down his cheek and dripped onto his wrist, the sting of salt more of a jolt to his senses than the knife blade buried in his flesh. This was what it wanted: for him to bleed out and take his soul. This wasn't an end, it was a beginning. He flung the knife across the room into it's face and heard the howl of anger from it as he did, exploding and reverberating around the inside of his head. Pressing his fingers over the hole he'd torn in his wrist, he sought to stop the flow of blood. Crying freely, he knew the only way to outwit the creature in the corner was to survive. To keep himself from Hell he needed to live.

†

Catherine didn't know what to do, she'd agonised over the problem for days. Jack was in London, but helpless and locked up in Marshalsea. He owed a hundred pounds. A hundred bloody pounds; she couldn't get hold of that amount of money.

Everyone knew how debtor's prison worked: if he didn't get help from outside soon he'd die, starve to death. Pulling the small bag out of her pocket, she looked again at the contents: five angels, a crested ring that she knew had belonged to his brother and a large jewelled cross, not at all of the current fashion but the metal was gold so it would probably fetch a good price.

She needed to get this to Jack, but how? No one watched her closely anymore but that said, Catherine had never set foot outside of the house since Robert had brought her there. Ronan would soon notice her missing and Marshalsea was on the other side of London, too far for her to make the journey there and back without being missed.

Catherine wrestled with the problem for another hour before finalising what she admitted to herself was indeed a poor plan. She would set out for Marshalsea as soon as the house went to bed. That would give her enough time to make it across the city without being missed. She was sorry but she'd need to use some of Jack's money to get her across London. She didn't know the way and a woman alone at night was not going to stand a good chance of arriving where she needed to be.

She'd ask Walt: the boy was kind and he seemed to know a lot of people; maybe he would know someone who could take her and bring her back. If she got back early enough in the morning then all well and good and she would not have been missed. And if she was missed, she'd say she had decided to go for a walk and had got herself lost. It was poor, but it was all she could come up with.

Walt was indeed helpful. She told him of a sick relative and her desire to visit. His brother Garth worked at the Black Swan, an inn a few streets away, and the boy soon confirmed that he would be willing to take her and bring her back for the extortionate sum of two angels. Catherine agreed, and three days later she was on her way to meet Garth as soon as the house slept.

†

"Put your arm over my shoulders," the voice told him. "Listen to me. Do it...right I've got you, now on three we stand. One...two...three...there we go now you're up."

Jack obeyed; he didn't know why he didn't know anything anymore. His arm over the man's shoulder, his helper grasped his wrist firmly and he stood albeit unsteadily.

"Good, now walk with me," the voice spoke again.

The journey was short, thankfully short. Jack didn't know how far he could walk but he guessed it wasn't far.

"Is this the one then?" Ross asked.

"My God! What have you done to him?" Catherine blurted. It was Jack, or at least what was left of him. He was filthy: his hair, skin and clothing all blackened with dirt; his left arm seemed covered in dried and cracking blood; the manacles at his wrists seemed to drag him towards the floor with their weight. His eyes were open, just, but unfocussed and his stare was a distant one. It was not likely, Catherine thought, that he would be able to stand on his own.

"So, you know him then," Ross sounded pleased, "lucky bastard he is an' all. Right then, Mistress, we'll take you to see Master Kettering and he can sort out what's to do next."

"Where are you taking him? Jack, can you hear me, Jack?" Catherine moved across the room to the door where two men stood with the filthy form of Jack hanging between them.

"He'll be fine, Mistress. Now you go and see Master Kettering and maybe he will be in a better room soon," Ross chuckled.

"Please, please don't put him back," Catherine touched the skin on his face. "He's frozen and soaked. You'll not put him back. Here take this." She pushed a shilling into Ross's hand. "Surely that will buy him some minutes by the fire while I see your Master?"

Ross smiled and inclined his head towards the men holding Jack. "Lads, come in here and you can all get warm by the fire while I take Mistress here to see Master Kettering."

Ross ushered Catherine into Kettering's room.

"Looks like your man has led you a merry dance. We have him down as a Jack Kilpatrick, but it sounds as if you know him by another name," Kettering looked up from his paperwork.

"Indeed, sir, but it is of little matter. We have found him, and I have brought with me some of his belongings, which I am sure will ease his time here," Catherine pulled the purse out from her pocket.

"Good, come on then, I do not have all morning," Kettering snapped holding his hand out across the desk. Catherine handed over three angels, the ring, and the cross.

Kettering slid the angels to one side. "They will keep him well and fed, and these," Kettering examined both items with a practiced eye, "will bring you ten pounds off his debt. Will there be more to come?"

"Indeed Sir. His family are wealthy and live in the North. As soon as I can get word to them they will, I am sure, pay for his release." Catherine had practiced the lie, hoping it would buy Jack a little more time. Kettering would know they would have to wait a while for a message to make it north and for help to come all the way back down to London.

"Whereabouts do they hale from?" Kettering asked.

"Newcastle, Sir. They are in the shipping business," Catherine continued to lie.

"And you?" Kettering asked peering at her closely.

"His wife, Sir," she replied and added a quick curtsey.

"You've not made yourself a good choice, have you? Been married long?" He asked harshly.

"Two months, sir, not so very long." Catherine could not believe the lies she was telling.

"Nothing on the way, I hope, for your sake?" Kettering asked, reaching for a pen.

Catherine blushed.

Kettering looked her over, "Can you write?"

"Aye, sir, I can,"

"Good, well, fill this in; name here, address here, and leave these parts blank. I will fill those in for you." Kettering indicated where with the end of the quill.

Catherine gave the address of Garth's inn, which she knew, and quoted her name as Catherine Kilpatrick.

"Right then, all done. Ross here will see you out."

"Can I not see him for a moment please?" Catherine pleaded.

"Oh, very well. Ross, give her a moment with him and put him up on the second floor in Caltrice's old room. The lad's wife has bought him a better room."

"Will do, sir," Ross nodded, then to Catherine, "Mistress, follow me."

They had indeed not taken Jack back, but that said he wasn't faring much better. His clothes were still soaked and stuck to his icy skin and he was laid on his side holding his knees and shivering uncontrollably. Catherine knelt on the floor in front of him, but his eyes did not focus on her.

"Jack, can you hear me, Jack?" Catherine put her hand out and laid it on his arm. There was no spark of recognition. Wherever Jack was, he was alone there. Catherine dropped the cloak from her shoulders and wrapped it around him, enclosing him within the black folds. "If you can hear me, Jack, I'll be back, I don't know how, or when, but I will get back to you."

"Come on, lassie, he can't hear you anyway," Ross opened the door for her.

Catherine made it back to Fitzwarren's house. Nobody had noticed she had not been there that morning; she'd never made to venture out and so no-one had even thought to look for her. She had brought Jack some help, but after seeing the state he was in she wondered if it was too late. Another ninety pounds she needed. There was nothing for it, she was just going to have to steal it somehow. Catherine looked with new eyes at the Fitzwarren household. There must be something she could get hold of that she could sell for Jack.

Chapter Seven

William didn't know how he'd got in or even how long he had been there.

"You wanted to see me?" The voice came from behind his chair and William couldn't see the speaker. "So, do you have news?"

"I wondered when you'd come," William chuckled. "I think perhaps we can both help each other."

"Help each other?" The voice sounded incredulous.

"Come round here where I can see you, damn you," William barked.

The speaker moved soundlessly to stand in front of William. "Well?" was the only word Richard spoke.

"I know you want to find the man you call your brother and I can help you. In return though I want something from you."

"Firstly, let's get something quite clear, he is my brother and he is your son. Let's not trifle with the facts," Richard's voice bore a hard edge. "We already had a bargain. You tell me where he is and I will spare your neck my knife."

"Aye, I do remember. However, Robert's wings need a clip and I thought that maybe you would like..."

Richard cut him off. "So he's not just making my life hell, he's started to make yours a little uncomfortable as well, has he?"

William scowled.

"You sit alone too long old man. If you think I'll ever help you then you have made a sorry mistake," Richard was shaking his head.

"Well then you'll never find him, will you?" William smiled unpleasantly, his gnarled hands gripping the chair arms fiercely.

"Are you really so stupid?" Richard's voice was incredulous. "If I wish for you to tell me then you most assuredly..."

There was a light knock at the door and a woman's voice spoke, "My lord, I have your firewood."

William smiled triumphantly. "Come in, come in, girl."

Richard moved into the shadows at the back of the room as the door opened.

"Put it over there girl and be off with you," William snapped.

Richard watched as she filled the wood box next to the fire. Her job done, she turned to William. "Will that be all, my lord?"

"Yes, yes. Get out," William waved her away.

Rising from a rapid curtsey, her eyes met those of the man who had come to stand behind William's chair, her mouth open in silent surprise.

"Get out, I said. Go on," William ordered pointing towards the door,

"You're dead!" was all Catherine could manage.

"Actually, no I'm not," Richard found himself smiling, "And it seems that you too are safe and well."

"What are you talking about? I'll shout for Edwin," William threatened trying to turn to face the man behind him.

"You'll shout for no-one tonight," Richard told him as he rounded the chair and ran his knife down the front of William's shirt, the blade clicking menacingly off the buttons. "Who's outside the door?" the question was directed at Catherine.

"No-one yet, they don't come up here until after supper, then someone always sleeps in the hall outside," Catherine supplied, then, "I've found Jack, he needs help."

Richard put his fingers to his lips, only Catherine saw the silencing gesture.

"Right let us not waste the visit, my father owes me plenty," Richard began swiftly and efficiently to open drawers, cupboards, boxes and taking things out he deposited them on a desk top. "Find something to put that lot in Catherine." Then turning to William, "Those are trinkets, where is the rest?"

William just stared at him defiantly from his chair.

"I told you I would have my way," Richard pulled the knife from his belt once more. "Once you showed me no mercy, why should I show you any?" Tell me or I am going to cut your thumbs off. And believe me, that's not a threat." Richard took a vicious hold on his wrist and laid the blade across the base of the thumb on William's right hand; blood welled from the small cut.

"The box, the box, in the candle box, in the coffer," Richard released his hold and William dragged his hand away; there was fear in his eyes.

"Aye, old man that is what you have done to others your whole life. How does it feel to be afraid?" Richard's face was close to his fathers. William didn't reply, he just turned his head away from the steady malicious gaze.

"It's locked." Catherine said, trying to lift the lid.

"The key?" Richard demanded.

"I can't, it's round my neck," William whimpered.

Richard's hand ripped open the shirt front and, sure enough, there was a key on a chain. He neatly flipped it over William's head and tossed it to Catherine, never taking his eyes from his father.

Trembling, she managed to open the lock and lift the lid of the oak coffer, propping it against the wall behind, The candle box inside did not contain candles but neatly tied bags of coins, four of them.

She lifted them out and dropped them with the pile on the desk.

"Anything else?" Richard called over his shoulder.

"Just letters," Catherine answered, shuffling through them to see if there was anything else of value.

"Just letters," Richard repeated smiling, "take them as well." From the look of horror on William's face, Richard knew he had won. "Lock it back up, and give me the key."

She did and Richard put it back around his father's neck, "we wouldn't like Robert to think anything is missing now would we?" Richard was smiling still. "I'll take this as a down payment on my inheritance." Richard was laughing now. "Remember old man, your safety depends on your silence, so don't shout for help."

"Come with me," he held his hand out to Catherine.

"I can't," she blurted.

"After helping rob the house, I hardly think you can stop here," Richard laughed.

"Your horse is in the stable," Catherine suddenly remembered the Arab.

"Corracha?" Richard sounded shocked.

"The same, I helped put him in there, that's how I found..." Richard's look silenced her.

He held out his hand again, "Trust me."

They fled down the stairs. At the bottom he motioned her to be still and he disappeared. Her heart in her mouth, she waited. The house was quiet: the servants rarely came into the main hall during the evening and even if they did they would expect to see her there anyway filling the fire boxes as she did every night.

Catherine was about to take a step to look for him when he came back and took her hand again. With a finger to her lips, he bid her be quiet. The hold on her hand was hard and firm as he guided her out of the back of the house and through the gate which now stood open and led out into the street. He took her a little way along the road and stopped outside a shoe-makers. The shop was shut and the doorway dark.

"Wait here, there's about to be some noise." With that he was gone.

Noise there was indeed. Catherine realised he was getting Corracha from the stables. The horse was stamping and neighing as he led him out. Then she heard Walt's voice shouting. Catherine nearly ran back to stop him from being foolish but then she heard the horses hoof-beats as Richard set him to leave the stable yard, Walt safe and in pointless pursuit.

He pulled the horse up and gave Catherine his arm so she could mount behind him. Eyes tight shut, one arm around the rider and another holding the bag with William Fitzwarren's belongings in she held on as best as she could. Soon she was forced to shout for him to slow down before she either lost the bag or herself off the back of the horse.

Richard took the bag and tied it to the pommel. "Better?" he asked as the agitated horse circled below them. Her silence was enough and he pushed the horse on again until they were a safe distance from the house.

From the turns he made Richard had a destination in mind, and very soon they found themselves in the Bankside area where Richard had taken lodgings within the city.

He dropped Catherine without ceremony in the yard and took the horse into the stables where she heard a brief exchange of voices. Emerging a moment later, he took her elbow and guided her into the house, up two flights of stairs and into his rooms.

Depositing the pillowcase on a table, she spoke for the first time. "Jack's in Marshalsea, we need to get him out. He was nigh on dead when I saw him," she blurted.

"Marshalsea? How?" Richard questioned, shaking his head.

"I don't know. They want another ninety pounds, or was it a hundred, I don't know, I can't remember," Catherine wailed.

"Right, let us start at the beginning," Richard calmed his voice. Standing, he took a hold of both her arms and reversed her towards a seat.

"No, I'll not sit, we need to go," Catherine protested pulling her arms free.

"A few more minutes will not make a difference. Now tell me from the beginning, I need to know everything," Richard pushed her into the seat.

"He's in Marshalsea..."

"I think I've got that fact now," Richard spoke patiently, "Let's start with how you found out he was there."

Catherine looked up. "The horse, your horse, it was brought to the stables and they told me the man who'd had it was in the debtor's gaol. His possessions were still with it: I recognised them as Jack's. Walt helped me and his brother took me across London to go and see him. He's under the name of Kilpatrick and he owes a hundred pounds. He had no money and when I saw him he was so cold I swear he was close to death. I paid them over the money I'd found and gave them his belongings, and Master Kettering said they would be worth ten pounds, but I can't remember if he needs another ninety or another hundred." Catherine had tears on her cheeks and her nose was running.

"And why did they let you see him?" Richard asked.

"I told them I was his wife, and that he came from a good family in Newcastle who would surely pay his fines and debts," Catherine sniffed loudly. "I thought to buy him a little time."

"I'm sure you did." Richard tipped the pillowcase out and the bags of coins thumped dully on the wooden table top. "Let's see if we have enough."

They did.

✝

"Mistress Kilpatrick, how nice to see you again, and with you is..." Kettering asked gesturing towards the man at her side.

"James Kilpatrick, sir, at your service. I've come as soon as possible, his poor wife was quite sorry to find out what had happened to him," Richard spoke in an accent that placed him firmly from the North of England and not far from the Tyne.

Kettering didn't fully understand Richard's strong accent that much was quite clear. "Yes well, Mistress Kilpatrick came to see us and assured us his family would be willing to help. It is a fair sum that is owing."

"I'll be taking it back out of his pocket, you can be sure I will. I'm fed up of helping the lazy idiot." Richard shook his head sadly. Kettering nodded in acceptance of the man's words even though he could make little sense of them.

"How much, Sir?" Catherine asked, and Kettering looked at her, thankful to be able to understand at least one of them.

"One hundred pounds plus," he ran his finger down a column of neat numbers, "six shillings. You are looking to pay in full?" Kettering looked very pleased at the prospect.

"We are, yes," Catherine smiled.

"My idiot brother can get out of here and get back to work the sooner the better, and pay me back for my kindness," Richard pronounced and Kettering stared at him with a total lack of comprehension.

Catherine elbowed Richard hard in the arm. "The money for Master Kettering, if you please, sir."

"I'd like to see my brother," Richard asked. Then, when he didn't get a reply, he persisted, "My brother, you understand? I'd like to see him first before I part with any money."

Kettering stared, totally baffled by Richard's heavily accented words. Catherine quickly translated. "He'd like to see his brother first, if he may, sir."

"Of course, of course," Kettering's voice was filled with relief, "I'll have him brought up now."

Jack was dutifully presented at the doorway to Kettering's office, no longer manacled but still leaning heavily on Ross. The look on his face one of sheer disbelief as he stared into the room.

Richard marched up to his brother, saying loudly. "You useless idiot. If our poor mother ever got to hear of this she would turn in her grave. I'm only here for the sake of your poor wife. If it was not for her I'd leave you this time to rot. Mind you it's still good to see you." With that he flung his arms around Jack and spoke softly in his ear, "Keep quiet, say nothing."

Richard stood back, a hand still on each of Jack's shoulders. "Have you got nothing at all to say for yourself then?"

Jack just hung his head and sagged a little more against the gaoler.

"Yes well, if we can sort out the paperwork we can get you all out of here this morning," Kettering spoke, regaining Richard's attention.

It took no more than twenty minutes to complete the transaction. Richard paid and redeemed Jack's belongings that Catherine had left. Richard and Kettering parted on good terms and even though Kettering only understood one word in three it was enough, and he found Richard to be a likeable enough fellow. Catherine waited quietly, eyes downcast, while the payment was completed and recorded, money counted and stowed, receipts issued.

"Right, that's all I need from you," Kettering closed his account book.

"Thank you for your time, sir, and I will take no more of it from you. I'll collect my brother and get him home to his wife and back on the straight and narrow. I'll make sure you'll not be seeing him again," Richard turned and neatly swapped places with Ross, adding a supporting arm around Jack's body and they headed out of Marshalsea.

"Thirty more steps brother, and we are out," Richard spoke quietly in Jack's ear. His arm around him, he felt the convulsive shakes that ran through Jack's body every few moments.

They came to the first door and paused while Ross fumbled with his keys before finding the right one. Jack leaned even more heavily on his brother and Richard pulled the other's arm tighter around his own shoulders.

"Count in your head, Jack, just twenty paces," Richard uttered under his breath. Ross finally got the door open, "Nineteen."

Ross held the door open so they could make their way into the winter December sun.

"Sixteen."

"Thank you, sir, you have been most kind," Catherine was saying to Ross.

"Twelve," Richard was now bearing most of Jack's weight; one leg had buckled and the other gave him little support.

"Eight, come on!"

Catherine ducked her head under Jack's other arm and pulled his hand down round her neck so he could use her as support.

"Four."

The horse and cart fortuitously hired by Richard, was almost in reach.

"No, Jack, no," but Jack had lost consciousness before he could make the last steps.

Getting him into the cart was no easy task. With his collapsed body slumped on the end of the cart bed, they had no option but to drag him in by his arms. His face and chest gained a goodly number of splinters from the rough sawn boards, but there was little else they could do. Richard was intent only on getting all three of them outside of the confines of the gaol and back to the relative safety of London as quickly as possible.

†

Back in his hired rooms Richard stripped off the filthy clothes and surveyed the damage they'd done to Jack. His wrists, where the manacles had been set, were bloody, the skin gone and the flesh beneath red and weeping. All of his body was mired in the stench and filth of Marshalsea; he looked and smelt like he had just been pulled from the gutter. Richard gently rolled him onto his side to inspect his back where a row of ugly cuts twinkled at him through the filth.

"Where the hell did you get that accent from? It's bloody terrible," Jack murmured as Richard let his body roll back on the bed.

Richard smiled broadly and said in the same thick accent he had used with Kettering. "It is indeed fair good to see you."

Jack laughed but it ended in a choking cough that rattled his lungs.

"Rest, be warm, and I will look after you," Richard's voice was sincere.

Jack closed his eyes and turned his head away. "You can't. You're dead." Were he last words he spoke.

†

Catherine didn't seem to matter she concluded. Richard had been in the room with Jack for an age before he emerged, when he did come out he announced briskly that he was going out and that she should keep an ear open in case Jack woke up. She was advised not to go into the room and to leave him alone should he remain asleep.

Annoyed, Catherine pulled a face at his retreating back. She knew Jack as well as anyone, she'd be damned if she'd leave him alone when she could offer him comfort.

The man she found on the other side of the door was not one she knew. Stripped of his clothes every cut, every mark, every hurt that had been inflicted upon him was visible; sores covered every part of his body from where he had lain on the ice cold floor of the gaol. Tears rolled from her eyes, she had her hand over her nose, the smell in the room was almost unbearable. Backing towards the door, she was closing it when a voice spoke behind her.

"I said, did I not fair lady, do not go in unless he calls?" Richard spoke from the doorway. "This is Lizbet," he inclined his head to a woman stood at his shoulder, hands on her hips smiling broadly. Her painted face and a bodice barely covering her breasts betrayed her profession.

"Well then, where is he?" Lizbet asked loudly. Richard motioned towards the door and Lizbet sailed through. Her head emerged round the door a moment later. "Bloody hell, I'm charging more, I can tell you that for a start. That's going to cost you double, and I want half up front. You alright with that?"

"Not double, no," Richard shook his head. "I've offered a fair price."

"You didn't tell me he stunk like a Billingsgate gutter, did you?" Lizbet countered.

"I'm sure you've had worse," Richard replied. "If it is not to your liking I'm sure I can find another."

Lizbet wasn't prepared to lose such lucrative work. "An extra sixpence for today then, and I'll have him fit for a visit to the Pope in an hour."

"We have a bargain," Richard agreed.

"Right then, I'll get myself started and you sort out some coin for when I get back," Lizbet flounced between Catherine and Richard to the door.

"Who the hell is that?" Catherine's eyes were wide.

"I heard that," laughed Lizbet as she descended the stairs.

"That, as I said," Richard replied, "is Lizbet."

"You told me that, she looks like a..." Catherine couldn't finish the sentence.

"A whore? Undoubtedly, and she's well acquainted with men's bodies. I'm sure and she's seen worse than Jack so she's going to help me to look after him. Unless of course, you want to go in there and give him a wash?" The look on Catherine's face was answer enough. "I thought not. Lizbet would, I am sure, rather spend her days here looking after one man, than her nights on her back looking to the needs of many."

Catherine was horrified. "She's a whore. You can't just leave him with her."

Richard laughed. "I've left him with plenty of them before. Why? What's she going to do to him?"

"I don't know, but she's a whore, she's..." Catherine was stuck for words, "she's unclean."

"I think he's a bit worse than her at the moment don't you?" Richard stepped aside to let

Lizbet passed with a basin, water, and cloths. "Even Aquinas said do not be too moral, you may find you have cheated yourself out of much life."

"Did he indeed?" retorted Catherine, "I doubt very much that he was talking about whores."

"She still moaning about me is she?" Lizbet elbowed her way between them to go back to Jack's room. "Who is she anyway? Can't be his wife. Under all that dirt I think I'm going to find a man, and I can't say as he looks the type to tie himself to a church mouse. Excuse me."

Catherine watched the door close and turned to Richard open-mouthed. Richard was laughing silently.

†

Lizbet insisted Richard send for Lucy Sharp, a lady revered locally for her curative powers. Women in London were barred from practicing as apothecaries; Lucy's late husband had been appointed one and no-one had seemed to mind when his shop continued to trade after his demise. Lucy, his more-than-capable widow, provided an efficient service much more to the liking of the ladies of the borough.

Lucy pulled the blanket back over Jack and sat back on her heels. "So your Master has coin has he?" Lucy asked Lizbet.

"Lucy, he's got money, he's paying me a good sum to tend him. He can pay you, don't you worry. It'll be good for both of us," Lizbet supplied confidentially. She needed Lucy's help, without it she didn't think the man on the bed would last overly long.

"Tell him it will be five angels for what he needs and for me to come every day this week." Lucy said; it was a high price.

"Five angels!" Lizbet exclaimed, "That's too much and you know it."

"That's what it is," Lucy declared shortly.

The door opened. "It is five and you'll come twice a day," Richard's voice was firm.

The women looked at each other.

"I will," accepted Lucy, her eyes narrow. "Upfront mind you."

Lucy was back in a half-hour, a basket laden with pots, creams, and salves. She held out a small bottle to Lizbet. "One spoonful of this in some wine, no more you hear me? Or he'll be sleeping the sleep of the dead," Lucy pushed the stopper back into an earthenware bottle.

"I hear you, one spoonful in some wine." Lizbet accepted.

"This dwale is potent I make it for Chiswell, the sawbones, and it'll put a man to sleep while you watch. So one spoonful no more." Lucy's warning was not idly made. Her concoction was indeed a potent mixture. Byrony root and vinegar gave it an acidic tang but the damage to a man's senses came from the henbane, opium and hemlock.

Lizbet smiled. "I ought to buy a bottle of this from you, Lucy. I can slip it to the lads and they'll never know whether they've had me or not."

"Aye, and you will be known as a murdering whore and be in Billingsgate waiting to have your heels warmed before you know it. This lad is likely to die anyway. If he does it'll be no fault of ours," Lucy gave Lizbet a serious look.

"He might, but it's yours and my job to make him last as long as possible," Lizbet advised, then added, "Do you really think he'll die on me?"

Lucy, her hands on her hips nodded. "That's why I want my coin now, and make sure he pays you. He'll not be so willing to settle his bills when he has a corpse to get rid of. Look at him," Lucy gestured to the man on the bed. "That's just the rags of a man, if the Lord hasn't carried him off by tomorrow I will be surprised. Now remember, no more than a spoonful and I'll be back in the morning."

Lizbet looked down at the man on the bed. "You better not bloody well die on me, you hear?"

✝

The women were with his brother, and Richard sought the peace of the stables at the back of the inn. Corracha sensed his presence before he spoke and the noble angular head appeared over the stable door looking for him. Agitated the horse stamped and snorted as it saw him approach

"I never thought to see you again," Richard spoke softly to the horse and let himself into the stable. The Arab nuzzled his open hand and Richard rested his forehead against the strong muscular neck. The minutes passed and the stallion calmed and stood quietly, both of them enjoying the shared silence.

"It does not look like anyone has cared for you overly," Richard said running his hands over the horse. The steel grey coat was full of shed hair; he'd not been brushed out properly for a long time.

Corracha was the best horse he had ever had. He had bought him when he had been in France. Arabian horses were rare in Europe and in England he doubted very much that there were any at all. The Ottoman Turks had ridden against Vienna in 1529 and when their cavalry were defeated their prized horses had been the first pure-blooded Arabian's in Europe. From these ancestors Corracha had been bred. He'd paid far too much for the animal, and he knew it. Jack had choked in disbelief when he found out Richard had parted with twenty pounds for him, almost double the price of some of the best horses on the market.

He was thankful Jack had taken him from Burton. Riding the agitated and delighted beast out of the stable yard at his father's house and through London with Catherine would forever be a memory that would make him smile; the horse's excitement had been matched by his own.

☦

"It's not what you can see that's harming him," Lizbet reported to Richard later on when she'd done as much as she could for him. "Lucy Sharp has been and given me drinks he has to have. When he coughs it makes you want to cry for the pain he's in. His skin is as hot as an oven," she continued. "Lucy said to bathe him with cool water to lessen the burning, but he shivers and shakes so that I feel I'm being cruel."

"You're not Lizbet, just follow what Lucy says and hopefully the fever will break." Richard directed.

"I hope so, for my sake. I'll not be looking after him for long if it doesn't," Lizbet sounded morose.

"You are all heart," Richard accused.

"Well it's true," Lizbet replied reproachfully, "and you had better not be going blaming me if he dies neither, it'll be nothing I've done. He's in a bad state, what happened to him?"

"I'm not sure, yet," replied Richard. "I'll not hold you to account Lizbet, but see to his comfort with some kindness."

Lizbet knew he meant this and smiled. "You can trust me."

They both knew that a fever like the one raging through Jack's body and the sound coming from his chest when he breathed was enough to put him in the ground. Marshalsea might win out even yet.

The room was dark and smelt now of herbs tinged with the slightly sickly aroma of some concoction Lucy Sharp had instructed Lizbet to give him. A cup of it stood still on the table next to Jack. Richard picked it up and sniffed deeply; aqua vitae he recognised, but there was something else as well. He tipped the cup and recognised the laudanum in the mixture.

Jack was asleep, well maybe not asleep after drinking Lucy Sharp's remedy, but blessedly unaware nevertheless. The only injuries that were more than superficial were around his wrists where the manacles had ripped away the flesh. Jack coughed and Richard held his own breath as he listened to the rasping rattle within the other man.

Sitting on the edge of the bed, he laid his hand on Jack's shoulder. It seemed a long time since that final day at Burton. Jack had tried to keep him safe, and he'd heard later from Jamie how Jack had frustrated their pursuit. He knew Jack had been to see their father and it was likely that he laid here now as a result of that.

He squeezed Jack's shoulder. "Sleep well."

†

Ronan cursed under his breath. He'd already incurred his Master, Robert Fitzwarren's wrath once this week when he'd had to tell him of the theft from the stables of the horse. Now he was going to have to report that Catherine was gone. He'd waited two days before he broke the news, hoping the stupid girl would appear. In the end she hadn't been found, and he had little choice but to tell Robert. It was a small lie, but he told Robert that she'd not been seen since the morning; he had servants looking for her, but as yet there was no news.

Ronan had received another belt round the head for his carelessness, and he had to stand and silently endure one of Robert's screaming rages. Every servant in the house made themselves scarce when they heard Fitzwarren's angry voice. Ronan's delay in telling him about Catherine meant Robert did not connect the disappearance of the horse and the girl. His father, also fearing Robert's rage, had kept his own counsel about his visit from Richard and the loss of most of his portable wealth from his own rooms.

✝

"I'm not in charge of the household here anymore, Richard, I don't know if I can help," Kate apologised. "I might be able to say she is my niece. I don't suppose they would turn down one more pair of free hands in the kitchen."

"If you could, I would be grateful," Richard's eyes met Kate's. "I indeed owe the girl my life as it happens."

Kate quickly reached for paper and pen. "This is my sister's name, and her daughter is about the right age, she is called Eugene. Send me a letter tomorrow that she is coming to visit and I will tell Travers that she'll be joining me for a few weeks. Once she's here it's not likely they will send her away again, and if anyone checks the names will be right. My sister lives in Chester so there's no risk of anyone meeting her."

Richard smiled, "Kate, as always, I am indebted to you."

"Any other news?" She asked, handing him the folded paper.

"Fairfax still has not decided on a firm date. As soon as I know more I will let you know," Richard supplied.

"They still intend to go ahead with it then; Elizabeth is totally against it," Kate was shaking her head. "As am I."

"They do indeed. It is a poor plan, and I fear it will be poorly executed as well. Be assured, though, I will ensure Elizabeth's safety." Richard replied.

"Renard, the Spanish Ambassador has been in touch again, and Phillip has ensured that Elizabeth will take part in all the main Christmas celebrations at Court. One cannot tell whether they feel secure that Mary will deliver an heir, or whether they are keeping Elizabeth close as they fear Mary's ability." Kate concluded.

"Probably both," laughed Richard. "Only God can know the outcome. We will have to wait until May is here to find out the answers."

"It seems a painfully long time in coming," Kate grumbled. "Elizabeth's nerves are raw with it, and another five months will make her no better."

"I wish I could offer you some hope, but they would be but empty words I am afraid," Richard sympathised.

"Yes, and we have all had enough of empty words over the last few years," Kate agreed. "We shall trust in God and hope he gives us the strength to walk tall."

"You always walk tall," Richard drew her so close she felt his breath on her skin.

Kate blushed and pulled away. "Send me the letter tomorrow and I will gladly take care of your lady."

So Catherine went from servant in the Fitzwarren household to servant in another. There was little she could do, and Richard assured her it would be safer and he hoped, a temporary solution only. Catherine didn't believe him but faced with few other choices she agreed.

✝

"Yeeouch," Lizbet let out a screech; Richard had a tight hold of her. "What's that bloody well for? Let go you're hurting me."

Richard released her, "Sit down."

"Bloody won't," Lizbet rubbed the bruised flesh on her arm.

"Sit down, I'm not asking," Richard commanded.

Richard had sat back down at the table and she slid onto the bench opposite him eyeing him warily. They were in the crowded inn beneath Richard's rented rooms.

"What do I pay you for?" he asked conversationally.

Lizbet was careful. "To look after him upstairs. I was just getting myself a bit of supper, sir, Lucy is with him now." Then she added, lowering her voice, "An' I'm doing you a good job, he's..."

Richard held a hand up to silence her. "Indeed, I've no complaints, if I did you would know about them," he said coldly.

Lizbet wisely kept her mouth shut and waited.

"So, who do you work for now?" he asked.

Lizbet was unsure where this was going, "You," she replied.

"Yes, and do I pay enough? I would venture that in fact, you are better paid than when you were in your previous trade," Richard surmised.

Lizbet's eyes narrowed; what he said was true. "Aye, Master, I can't complain."

"However it seems you do complain," Richard sounded angry.

"I've said nowt to anyone Master, an' I'll take to task any who says that I have and ..."

Richard held up his hand, stilling her words again. "It's not your voice Lizbet, it's not your words. But that man over there in the green jacket no longer has coin in his pockets, does he?"

Lizbet's face turned scarlet.

"Put it back. Now. Without him knowing and then come back here." It wasn't a request, it was an order, and Lizbet knew it.

It was easy enough. Richard quashed a smile as he watched Lizbet bump into him, exchange a few words and slide the coins back where she had found them. Lizbet sidled back over and took her place on the bench again.

Richard, smiling, held his hand out across the table. "Give me your hand, I'm going to read your fortune."

Lizbet nervously held her hand out and he took it in both of his as a palm reader would. His brow furrowed as he silently concentrated on her palm, his fingers tracing the lines that lay there.

"It seems," his eyes held hers, "that your lifeline is tied to mine. If you keep me happy then I will endeavour to keep you so as well."

Richard abruptly turned her hand palm down on the table, his own covering it and holding it still.

"Did you know that each of your fingers has three bones, and, if you use them against me to fill your pockets again I'll break them all."

Lizbet dropped her gaze from his first. "Sorry Master, old habits."

"Old habits," he agreed, then smiling he turned her palm over again and studied it carefully. "Here..." he traced a line, "is life and it's a long life. Look how far the line goes beyond the base of the thumb, and see these four lines that intersect it, here, here, here and here," Richard pointed to each one. "These are your children, and all will grow to be healthy and strong. You will marry," he paused and twisted her hand to the light, "twice. Your first marriage dies out, see the line here, but your second runs well and he will be the one to give you your sons. Now money." Richard bent his head closer to her hand. "Well I am surprised." His eyes met hers. "You'll have silks, stockings, and petticoats a plenty."

Lizbet held his gaze. "And you are a lying bastard," she pulled her hand back.

"Not about the broken bones," came the reply, and Lizbet believed him.

☦

The noise was finally too much. Damn Lizbet, where the hell was the woman? Richard opened the door to Jack's room, formerly his own, and the volume of his brother's cries increased. Hell, if he kept this up people were going to think there was a murder in progress.

On the table was a pitcher of wine next to the bottles and pots Lucy Sharp had brought. Pulling the first stopper from a pot revealed a buttery cream. He pushed the lid home again and opened another. In the third he found what he was looking for: the drink Lucy had brought for him to quieten his ravings. Locating a cup, he slopped half the brown liquid into it. He wrinkled his nose against the fumes; the familiar acrid smell told him he had the right bottle.

"Jack, Jack." Richard sat on the edge of the bed, cup in hand. Where Jack was, he could only guess at. The noise was terrible. Sometimes there was a word but generally without any context. Jack was laid flat, naked beneath the sheet, swaddled in Lucy's wrappings. Richard was unsure where to grasp him to sit him up.

"For God's sake, Jack, help me!" His arm under the other's shoulders, he hoisted him a degree and jammed pillows behind him. Satisfied at last with the angle, he planted a firm hand on Jack's head to hold him still and lifted the cup to his blistered lips.

"No!" Lizbet screeched. Taking in the scene, she cannoned into him. The cup bounced off the bed frame, the contents splattering over the wall. The blow to the side of Lizbet's head sent her across the room, slamming her painfully against the door.

"You bastard, that'll kill him," she spat at him, eyes blazing, readying herself for the next assault.

"It's what you give him," Richard retorted grabbing the dwale and holding it in her face.

"A spoonful only, neat and it'd kill a cow in five minutes, you fool," Lizbet raised herself back up and eyed him warily.

"You should have told me," Richard retaliated, slamming down the earthenware bottle.

"I just did," Lizbet opened the door behind her, preparing her escape.

There came a scream from the bed; Lizbet jumped.

"Give him what he needs," Richard said. Lizbet stood transfixed. "Now," Richard commanded, roughly grabbing her arm and pushing her towards Jack before he left the room.

Lizbet swore under her breath as she eased the drink past Jack's dry and bleeding lips. She sat back and watched. Even before the cup was finished he'd calmed and within a few more moments he was, again, asleep.

Lizbet left him alone and opening the door, she found Richard watching her. "You should have told me," he repeated again, his cold grey eyes holding hers.

"I hardly thought you'd be tending him now, did I?" she replied, her anger barely contained, her eye on the door to the stairs. Her face still stung and she had no intention of taking another beating.

"Neither did I, that's why I am paying you. Where were you?" Richard demanded.

"Lucy had some salve prepared; she asked me to collect it," Lizbet said defensively, it was indeed true. "I was not gone for long."

"Why didn't she bring it?" Richard said; she could tell from his tone he didn't trust her.

"She had another to see this morning, she's coming this evening she said." Lizbet still watched her employer warily, her left eye now surrounded by a purple spreading stain where he had hit her.

"Don't leave him again," Richard pushed himself up from the table and left, leaving Lizbet staring after his retreating back.

"Aye, you bastard," and she spat in his direction.

✝

Lizbet watched Jack's chest, her own breath held as she waited to see if the prone man would breathe again. There was, eventually, an almost imperceptible rise, and Lizbet let out her own breath loudly.

"I can't stand this anymore, do you hear me?" Lizbet scolded. "Me stuck in here with you, watching your every breath, and wondering if I should be sending for Lucy Sharp or a priest."

She had spent nearly a week with him. At the start he'd been troublesome, shouting, delirious, throwing the blankets off. He'd quietened down after a day or so, and Lizbet had been thankful until Lucy told her that his body was preparing to die, that the stillness that was upon him was the start of the veil of death. Lizbet had lost her temper then with Lucy. Richard had stormed in from the other room commanding them to still their tongues and reluctantly they called a truce.

Pouring wine into a cup, Lizbet started the long and tedious process of getting Lucy's concoctions into Jack. He could no longer drink; all she could do now was pour small amounts onto his lips and hope some of it made it into his mouth and that he'd not choke. Lizbet's nose wrinkled as she pulled the stopper from the dwale; for something that cost as much as it did, Lizbet thought Lucy could at least make it smell nice. It gave off noxious fumes that caught in the back of your throat. Lucy reached for the spoon then looked at the man on the bed.

"I'm not so sure you need this anymore, laddie," Lizbet smiled. She might as well get something worth having out of this. Pushing the stopper home, she dropped the bottle into her pocket and resolved to ask Lucy to prepare more when she came that evening, if the poor beggar still lived.

Three long, painful hours passed and Lizbet was sure he had died. There was total silence in the room. The man's body was pale and bathed in a sheen of fine sweat and the small tell-tale movements that would betray his breathing had stopped.

"You miserable bastard, you could have lasted at least a few more days. I've done me best for you..." Lizbet groaned. Well, Lucy had warned her he was likely to die, at least she'd be getting seven days good money. Then a thought occurred to Lizbet. It was late, she could just as well sit in here until tomorrow, no-one would know, and then she'd get another days pay for her pains. Another hour passed before she heard Lucy Sharp letting herself noisily into the room. Lizbet held up a finger to bid her be quiet and quickly closed the door behind her.

"Be quiet Lucy, he's dead, but let's keep that to ourselves for another day, eh?" Lizbet suggested quickly.

Lucy looked between the man on the bed and Lizbet. "Until the morning only, mind. After that you'll not get away with it," Lucy warned quietly.

"Aye, that's another day, and you can make up another bottle of dwale as well and charge him for it," Lizbet smiled, glad Lucy was agreeing with her plan.

"What did you do with the bottle I already brung? If you gave it all to him then no bloody wonder he's breathed his last," Lucy hissed, her eyes wide.

"I spilt it. Just bring another bottle and come early tomorrow," Lizbet replied, a little too quickly.

Lucy eyed Lizbet, clearly she didn't believe her. "Until the morning only, mind you."

"Just till then. Come on Lucy what harm is there in it?" Lizbet smiled.

"None that'll touch him anymore that's for sure," Lucy looked at the man on the bed. "Right lass I'll see you in the morning."

Lizbet found the night a long one. She had blankets in the corner of the room but found herself unable to lie down and close her eyes in the presence of a corpse. Her conscience was pricked as well by not having got him a priest to help with his passing. Jack dead, in the dark, was altogether different from Jack alive. When Lucy came in the morning, ending Lizbet's lonely vigil, she was relieved to have another living presence in the room with her.

"Right lass, here's the dwale you wanted and I'll put that on his bill," Lucy's voice was loud enough for Richard in the other room to hear, then she put down another small earthenware bottle beside all the other medicines Lizbet had on hand. Then quietly for Lizbet's ears only, "Right I'll leave you soon, but you must tell him in an hour or so lass or he'll know by looking at him you've led him a dance."

"Are you sure? It's cold in here, I've not had the fire on, maybe another day..." Lizbet ventured hopefully.

Lucy was exasperated, her hands on her broad hips. "In a few hours he'll be as stiff as a board, woman and he'll stay like that for a day and a half. You'll not be telling anyone then that he's just died on you, will you?" Lucy moved passed Lizbet and, leaning down, grasped Jack's jaw pulling his mouth open. "It's not set in yet, it starts with the neck and the jaw, but once it gets hold it spreads really fast. The man you are working for is no fool Lizbet, I can see the bruises on your face, lass, are you looking to get some more?"

"Alright, I'll leave it for an hour then after you are gone and I'll tell him," Lizbet conceded, folding her arms and looking particularly unhappy about it.

Lucy relented and squeezed her arm. "It was a good job Lizbet, we both tried. Some things are just not meant to be."

Lizbet waited an hour and soon after hearing the bells strike, splashed water on her eyes, adopted a suitably mournful expression and bolted from the room.

"Master...Master," Lucy stopped. Richard was not in the room outside Jack's.

Well now, what am I going to do!

Lizbet heeded well Lucy's warning and so she sent for both a Priest and Lucy to confirm the recent demise of her charge.

When Richard returned he found the door to Jack's room opened, a sullen Lizbet standing in one corner and a Priest kneeling beside the bed, muttering in Latin the words of the last rites. "Per istam sanctan unctionem et suam pissimam misericordiam, indulgeat tibi Dominus quidquid..."

Richard stopped listening. The feeling was as if he'd taken a physical blow to the chest and he reached out a hand for the wall to steady himself. Lizbet saw him sway and quickly grabbed his arm. "Master, here," she helped him to where a chair was. "I'm sorry sir, he was very ill, I did try my best for him."

Richard waved her away and she was glad to step back. Jack was no longer hers to worry about and she liked not at all being within striking distance of Richard.

Lucy Sharp bustled up the stairs. From the threshold she observed the scene within. "It doesn't look like I'm needed anymore," she concluded, holding Lizbet's gaze until the other looked away.

"Lucy, come in, please. I would thank you for the care you showed my brother," Richard had his hands over his eyes and his voice was strained.

Both women looked at each other; his brother? Neither had known of the bond between the two men.

Lucy softened immediately. "You've had a shock, it'd be a good thing for you to sit a while and we'll look after him for you." Then to Lizbet, "Get him a drink will you?" Lucy squeezed Richard's arm, adding quietly. "When the Priest is done with him we'll get him ready, sir."

The Priest took an age; he'd do a good job and expect Richard to show his gratitude in coin. Lucy and Lizbet both wished he would cease his Latin mumblings, pack up his Popeish trappings and get himself gone. The man was dead, a priest wasn't much use to him anymore. Lucy, very much in charge, spoke quietly and kindly to Richard. He gave her the coins she asked for and she despatched Lizbet to go and buy a two-shilling shroud to sew him up in. When Lizbet returned with it nearly an hour later the Priest was just leaving and as she passed him on the stairs, he gave her a sympathetic smile.

"Right then lass, bring that here and fetch a needle and thread," Lucy instructed. Kneeling down next to the low bed, she prepared to roll the body on to one side so the two women would be able to wrap the linen cloth around him. She laid a hand on his chest; it felt cold, as it should, but the flesh was still soft. Using a thumb, she lifted his eyelids - the skin still peeled back, malleable to the touch. It was usual for the eyelids to succumb first to the rigidity of death, often refusing to close, leaving the living to deal with the stares of the dead.

"What are you doing?"

Lucy ignored the voice in the doorway.

The jaw was also slack still. Lucy counted on her fingers; this meant he wasn't dead last night when she'd called, the rigor should be setting in properly by now.

"I said, what are you doing, woman?"

Lucy reached over and pinched Jack's nose closed between her fingers.

"Will you..."

"Hush, still your words," hissed Lucy, intent on listening to something else. Then she heard it, faintly, the movement slight, but the mouth opened to take air into his lungs. Richard had dropped to his knees beside her, "Watch carefully," and both of them saw the frail intake of breath.

Lucy was on her feet in a moment. "Lizbet, get that fire lit, it's as cold as a church in here."

Lizbet, wide eyed, hesitated on the threshold.

"Girl, he's not dead, but he soon will be if you don't get a fire lit," Lucy smiled triumphantly.

"Are you sure? The Priest said..." Lizbet's words trailed away her eyes flicking between Jack's inert form and Lucy.

"What do they know; he's not very much alive, but a little, so are you going to stand there or help him lass?" Lucy reprimanded.

Chapter Eight

Lizbet was getting a shilling a week for laundry and that, on top of what she had already negotiated for looking after Jack, amounted to a fair sum indeed. With coins in her pocket, a free roof over her head, Lizbet was indeed happy. She didn't want to think about how long it would last, that just soured the feeling.

Standing in front of the fruit seller, Lizbet eyed the apples. She wanted the biggest, rosiest, crispest one – but which was it? Her hand hovered over one, then another caught her eye. Smiling, she made her decision and bought the reddest apple she had ever seen in her life. The skin was shiny; its cool, hard feel told her of the sweetness within. Turning the apple over in her hand, Lizbet decided to eat it later - not wanting to bite into it in the street - and set off to walk back to the inn.

Lizbet gasped. The apple left her hand, her eyes followed it, watching as it bounced first off the wall and then rolled onto the dirty street.

"Well, lass, and where've you been this last week?" it was a voice she recognised, one that filled her with hate. Lizbet's eyes, though, were still on her apple; it had come to rest near the wall and it looked un-spoilt.

His eyes followed hers and saw what she was looking at. "Ah, you've even bought me dinner." The man leant down, scooped up the apple and without a moment's hesitation bit a huge chunk from the ripe fruit.

"You bastard, Colan, that was mine," Lizbet was genuinely upset.

"Well then, lass, come and take it," Colan waved the apple in front of her.

"I don't want it any more," Lizbet's eyes were wet as she looked at the remains of her apple. She continued, "That was mine, why did you do that?"

"Ah come on, Lizbet." Colan threw the half eaten apple in the gutter. "Put a smile on my face again, and I'll buy you another apple." Reaching out, he wrapped his arms around her.

Lizbet tried to wriggle out of the unwanted embrace. "Get off, you oaf, let me be."

"Ah now, come on, Lizbet, that's not how you are with me," Colan tightened his hold.

"Colan, I need to go somewhere, now let me be," Lizbet said, trying even harder to push him away.

"I don't care where you need to be, this'll not delay you very long," Colan replied slyly. A hand in the centre of her chest, he rammed her back against the wall.

"No!" Lizbet wailed, she dug her nails into his face until a hand to her throat persuaded her to stop.

"Let her go!" It was Richard's cold voice.

Lizbet tried to look round but Colan's hold was so firm she couldn't move. Colan though had a fine view of the newcomer and he smiled maliciously. "This is mine. If you want it when I'm finished, then you can just wait your turn." Colan looked at the man. He was slightly built compared to Colan's bulk and he doubted very much that he'd want to risk his fine clothes in a fight over a whore.

"That wasn't a request. Now, let her go." Richard repeated calmly.

"She's yours?" Colan said incredulously. "She's a bloody whore. When did anyone want to claim a right there?"

Richard stopped looking at Colan and switched his gaze to Lizbet. "She looks likely to faint."

Lizbet took the instruction and dropped like a leaden weight; Colan's hold was tight but not enough to support an unconscious woman. He looked at her for a moment then he dropped her and turned to face Richard. "What bloody problem do you have?"

Richard ignored him and instead spoke to Lizbet, "Get behind me."

Colan heard the words and realised the trick. "So you think you'll take the whore from me for your own use, do you?"

Richard regarded him coldly, waiting until Lizbet was behind him. "I do."

Colan's advance was quick, his fists were balled and it was obvious he meant to use them. He stopped suddenly when he saw the blade flash in Richard's hand, a guttural growl escaping from his throat. "Next time - and there will be a next time." Colan stepped back warily before turning and leaving them.

Richard grabbed Lizbet's arm. His fingers bruised her through the linen sleeve and he didn't let go until they had returned to the rooms, where he roughly shoved her inside. Lizbet could sense his rage and backed to the wall rubbing her arm. She'd been on the wrong side of his temper twice before and wasn't about to do that again if she could help it.

His words were light when they came and his voice didn't betray the temper of a moment ago. "Don't do that again."

Lizbet was silent for a moment. His eyes stared into hers demanding an answer. "I didn't do anything. I only bought an apple."

Richard rubbed the back of his hand across his face. "Your clothes declare your trade," he told her quietly, then, "how old are you, Lizbet?"

She hesitated, then, "Twenty, Master, last Easter."

Richard's eyes still held hers, "The truth."

Lizbet dropped her eyes from his, then quietly, "fifteen last Easter."

Richard closed his eyes and pushed his hands into his hair. Fifteen. "Just leave me. Go and see to Jack." He should have known: her painted face with the whore's ruby cheeks and red inviting lips disguised her age.

As she made to leave he asked, "Why did you just lie to me?"

Lizbet sniffed loudly, "You'd get rid of me if you knew my age. I'm doing a good job for you and for him, I am."

"Is that your only dress," Richard asked, pointing at the one she wore.

Lizbet pulled the sleeves straight, "Yes, Master."

Richard fished in his purse and put two coins on the table. "Get yourself another. One that does not proclaim your trade."

Lizbet's eyes lit up at the sight of the two coins, "Really, for me?"

"No, it's for me, so I don't have to come between you and your bloody customers again," he said with a little less anger in his voice. "Now see to my brother and get me some wine."

When he saw Lizbet again a day later she did indeed look changed. The loose dress she had worn was two sizes too big and the slack bodice was now replaced by a linen shift with an over dress of dark brown wool. It was simple, laced at the front with a white apron tied at the back.

Her hair, which habitually coiled long and loose over her shoulders, was pulled back and tied, and her head was crowned with a linen cap. She'd surprised him even further when she told him that the dress was one sewn by Lilly Tate, who was a friend and he received into his hand change in the form of two dark pennies. A day later, when she had turned down the blanket on her makeshift bed she had shouted out loud to the room in delight. There, red, cold and perfect, sitting beneath the blanket, was an apple.

✝

It was ten days before Jack - with Lizbet's help - sat up in bed and demanded something more than soup. In those days, Lizbet had watched his breathing strengthen and his senses begin to return. After four days his eyes were open and after six more he was sitting up and, with help, drinking and taking the soup Lucy was bringing for him.

"Look at that," Jack held out his right hand and watched it tremble, "Do you think that will ever stop?"

"I'm sure it will; if you could have seen yourself a week ago, a shaking hand would have been the least of your worries, my lad," Lizbet chided, as she sent another spoonful of soup towards his mouth.

"Watch out, woman, it's hot! You're pouring it down my chest!" Jack protested, trying to get his mouth round the spoon she was holding just too far away.

"I think, my bonny boy, you are well enough to do that yourself now." She dumped the soup bowl and spoon in his lap.

"But it tastes so much nicer when you do it," Jack smiled. "Come here and give me a taste of you."

"Ah now no, Master's told me I'm not to lay my hands on you," Lizbet moved down the bed out of arm's reach.

"Why not?" Jack snorted.

Lizbet leant forward, a serious look on her face. "Jack, there's parts of you that are not that well held together. Give yourself time." She brightened, "I don't want you bleeding all over me."

"Where's Richard anyway? I want to talk to him." Jack changed the subject away from his injuries.

"He's gone to visit that sour-faced cow, said he'd not be long," Lizbet supplied, smoothing out his blankets.

"Sour-faced cow?" Jack asked confused.

"Aye, every time I see her she looks down her nose at me. He said she's a cousin of his; all I can say is, I'm glad she's lodging somewhere else. No man's type if you ask me. She'll not keep a man that one," Lizbet concluded, an edge of animosity in her voice.

"Oh, Catherine," Jack said, realising who she was talking about, "She is not too bad when you get to know her."

"She needs to learn a thing or two about life and men, is all I can say," Lizbet countered haughtily.

"I think she might have learnt a few hard lessons already, Lizbet. Leave the girl alone," Jack losing interest in the soup, pushed the bowl from him.

A few minutes later he'd fallen back to sleep and Lizbet, pulling the piled pillows out, gently laid him back down. Lucy told her she wasn't to use any more dwale, unless she herself personally said so. Instead she had crushed feverfew mixed with saffron and laudanum to make into a hot drink for him, should he need it. Lizbet was sorry her patient was asleep again; in his lucid moments she was starting to get to like him. The body she was helping to heal would be a very nice one when she was finished and if anyone was going to get some enjoyment from it, Lizbet was. Behind the paling bruises, underneath the reddened and scabbed skin, Lizbet was starting to see quite a beautiful face emerging.

Quietly she cleared away the pots and jars. Taking out the soiled bandages, she walked straight into Richard as she left Jack's room. The pair had reached a stable relationship of Master and servant. Lizbet, most of the time, kept her tongue civil, and Richard, recognising the good care she was giving his brother, kept his temper in check. That Lizbet's care of Jack was motivated by reward did not bother him. For the moment he was happy with the arrangement.

"Master, he's all asleep and needs me not at all at the moment, so if I can do anything for you," Lizbet swayed passed him, banging him with one hip as she drew level, "you just let me know."

Richard ignored her, "How is he?"

"Much better." Lizbet dumped the bandages on the fire and watched them sizzle. "Even tried to get me in his bed."

"Are you sure the fever is not returning?" Richard remarked sarcastically.

Lizbet ignored his comment. "A couple more days and I think he'll be getting out of bed," Lizbet put another log to the top of the fire to keep it alive. "He wants to talk with you," she added, remembering Jack's request.

Richard spoke quietly to himself, "I want to talk with him as well."

"Any madness has left him now, he's quiet, and I told him I'd ask you to come and speak with him."

"There is something else I need you to do. We burnt his clothes, can you arrange to get him some new ones made?" Richard asked, then added, "there is a good Mercer's in Proudgate, do you know it?"

"Aye I know it well, Master Drew's, can't say as I've been in there much myself," Lizbet said sarcastically.

"You can order everything from there and use this to open the account, tell them a Master Garrett will call and settle the bill later." Richard said holding out five shillings. Cloth merchants in London, the good ones, had attached to them tailors and if you had money, clothes could be fashioned from the chosen cloth overnight if need be.

Lizbet's eyes lit up at the sight of the coins and Richard's hand snapped shut around them before she could take them. "I'll know if you bought yourself something."

"I would never do that," she held out an open hand for the money.

"Yes you would." Richard opened his hand and loosed the coins into Lizbet's palm. "Remember I'll be settling the account so I will know whether you paid this money to Master Drew."

"And what would you have me buy him? I know nothing about him." Lizbet said; it was a reasonable enough question.

"You only need to know one thing." Richard said. "He's my brother."

Lizbet smiled broadly. She looked at Richard's clothes, squealed with delight and dived past him to the door.

"The woman is truly mad!" Richard said to no-one in particular.

Richard got a full hour's peace before his landlord stamped up the stairs.

"It's Lizbet. She's been arrested!" Roddy gasped as he came spinning through the door.

"And that's my concern, why?" Richard asked, looking up from the book he was trying to read.

"She said to send for you," Roddy said, then added, "are you coming?"

"If I must," Richard replied, wearily closing the book with a thud.

✝

Outside the cloth merchant's shop there was a good sized audience gathered all peering through the windows. Ignoring them Richard pushed his way passed them, opened the door gently and applied himself to the door frame, taking in the scene inside.

Lizbet sat on top of a packing box, on her shoulder the hand of a soldier was pressing her down to keep her seated. The shop keeper stood in front of her and by turns, they traded abuse.

Richard took two steps, allowing the door to swing closed with a loud bang behind him. All eyes turned towards the noise.

"There, he'll tell you!" Lizbet shrieked, her eyes bright.

Richard raised his eyebrows and looked at them all in turn. It was the soldier who addressed him first. "Master Drew here says she's trying to steal from his shop, that's the pile there she's being trying to help herself to. Do you know her?"

Richard walked to the pile and lifted two shirts from it to reveal the fabric bales below and then started shaking his head.

"Blue. Really!" turning to Lizbet he looked at her in disbelief. "You can't imagine I'd wear blue could you? My eyes, my sweet, are grey; such a contrast would never work, what were you thinking? Blue is..." he paused, pulling a linen square from his sleeve and gently dabbed his face. "Blue is harsh..." He walked straight past Lizbet to a pile of folded bales of fabrics, "...Now this would make me look fine. He pulled a golden russet bolt of cloth to his chest and then turned so they could all admire the fabric. "See, this would be right: golden brown with grey, not too dark a brown, but just bright enough.

What do you think?" he asked of his audience, generally.

"I think," said the soldier, eyeing Master Drew, "that I've been wasting my time. You must be Master Garrett and do you know this... good lady?"

"I do," Richard was now wrapping the russet cloth around his arm in a makeshift sleeve. "Trimmed maybe with a cream lace. Master Drew, do you sell lace?"

"We do, it's upstairs," the shop owner replied, not really knowing what else to say.

"Good, you can show me," Richard pitched the brown bale onto the top of the pile of Lizbet's purchases, pushed his arm through Master Drew's, and started to steer him towards the stairs.

"Sir," the soldier protested, halting Richard's exit, "does this mean you can vouch for the lady?"

"Sir," Richard sounded offended. "Surely you can tell I'd vouch for no lady." His eyes raked the soldier's body from top to bottom before coming to rest again on his face, a slight invitation playing on his lips. "However, if you'd care to join me and Master Drew..." The Soldier didn't move. Richard releasing Master Drew and took a step towards him.

That was enough for the soldier. "I'll bid you good day," he said, hastily retreating to the door.

Richard winked at Lizbet. "So little time and so many soldiers." Then, returning his attention to Master Drew. "Right, Sir, lace. Show me lace."

Lizbet sat still and watched, open mouthed, as Richard ascended the steps in the middle of the shop. She listened to him talking with Master Drew for five minutes before he found what he was looking for, exclaiming loudly, "It is, as you say, Sir, as delicate as a petal and as soft as snow! I'll take it."

Richard descended the steps with the shopkeeper following carrying the lace.

"Shall we have them delivered, sir?" Drew said, laying the purchases down on a counter top.

"No need," Richard was now distracted by yet more gilt cloth. "I'll settle the account now. Can you recommend a tailor Master Drew?"

Drew smiled; this was going to add up to a good day's sales. "I can indeed; Master Jessop next door, there's no better tailor in London. Shall I have your cloth delivered there?"

"Indeed, please send it to Master Jessop, and..." he waved a hand absently in Lizbet's direction, "will come and make an appointment for measurements. And don't put the blue in that the hideous creature chose, mark me," Richard called over.

"No, sir," Drew agreed, giving Lizbet a sideways glance.

Settling the account, Richard made for the door then stopped abruptly. "Master Drew, I'd rather not have an audience follow me down the street," He waved a hand at the crowd that was still peering through the windows.

"Aye, I'm sure you would rather not. If you'd be so kind as to follow me we have another way out; leads on to the next street and if you take a right and then another right it'll bring you back to the top of the lane." They left, quietly avoiding the stares of the onlookers and made their way back to the rooms over the inn.

"What was all that about?" Lizbet demanded, hands on her hips as the door closed behind them.

"All what?" Richard's voice once more bore its usual edge.

"That soldier fled from you. You looked like you were about to have him on the floor of the shop." Lizbet was confused.

Richard smiled, "And who do you think they'll be talking about?"

"A bloody sodomite with a loud mouth who likes soldier boys." Lizbet catching his eye laughed. "You had me, for a moment you did."

†

Richard opened the door to Jack's room and, for the first time in over a week, met his brother's focused steady stare and smiled. Richard had seen his brother little. Lucy's remedies had rendered him mostly insensible and he preferred to leave his care to Lizbet. Today was different. The crystal blue eyes that held his own were clear, steady and sentient. Jack was propped up in bed but he was very much awake. The voice was also unmistakably Jack's, even if its tone was a little quieted by illness and roughened by a throat reddened and painful with coughing.

Jack's smile, though, was warm and like some conspiratorial schoolboy, Richard found himself returning it, saying, "God, it's so good to see you looking better, Jack."

Jack pushed down on one elbow and painfully hoisted himself up on the pillows. "Christ." Jack looked down at his bandaged, bruised and grazed body and grinned, "How bad did I look before, then?"

"You cheated the Devil, Jack. Shift your feet over," Richard sat down on the end of the bed, his back against the wall.

There was much to say; too much. The silence between them was not awkward or tinged with any kind of anticipation or need, it was a simple one borne of pure relief. Jack closed his eyes and rested his head back. He could sense his brother's presence, hear his breathing, feel the weight of him on the bed resting against his feet. It was enough. Richard, his eyes closed sat quietly, propped against the wall, his head forward, fallen locks obscuring his face from view, his thoughts his own.

Outside the coldest month of winter held London in an icy caress and both men listened to the uneven sound of her dull kisses as the rain met the shutters. The light noise ran on, a background to their thoughts, if they had any. Jack, breathing deeply, felt as if his lungs were able to fill freely with air for the first time in months. The choking pressure in his chest restricting his breathing had gone and Jack let out a long and easy breath.

Both men heard the noise at the same time: Lizbet's step on the stairs up to the rooms. Jack opened his eyes and Richard raised his head and met his brother's steady gaze. But it was Jack who broke the silence first. Smiling he quietly said, "save me from that scold."

"How would you have me do that?" Richard replied.

"Stay a while," Jack requested, a serious tone to his voice. "Tell me what happened?" He closed his eyes again. "How are you here? Jamie said you were dead, then I heard your voice. I couldn't see you, just hear you, I thought maybe I was dying."

Richard considered his reply for a few moments. "Jamie thought I was going to die as well, but I didn't and neither did you. It seems we shall both endure, despite both of us having received the last rites."

Jack paled and looked seriously at Richard. "I was that bad?"

"I did say both of us. Thanks for the concern," Richard said sarcastically.

"So when I left Burton, where were you?" Jack was just starting to realise that a chain of events, all starting with Richard's death and leading to the cells in Marshalsea, might have all been wrongly founded.

Richard detected the note in Jack's voice; he couldn't tell if it was anger or disbelief. His brother though, was entitled to both emotions. "I didn't know where I was. Like you I was fastened to a bed and stripped of my senses, I couldn't have helped you and I am sorry for that."

"There was no fault, I know you could not have helped me," Jack's hands tightened on the blanket. "So, how did you find me?"

"I didn't know where you'd gone and I needed to come to London anyway. I made the fortuitous decision to visit our father. He told me you had visited and there I found Catherine. The lass had seen them bring Corracha and your belongings to the house. They told her that the owner had gone to Marshalsea. You are lucky she had the nerve to go, Jack - she took money and it was enough to get you a room and food; otherwise I am sure we would not be talking now." Richard told him how they had got him from Marshalsea.

Jack listened quietly, then, when Richard had finished he said, "Christ, I owe her a debt. I'd heard her voice while I was ill and wondered how she'd come to be here."

"We both owe her a debt," Richard corrected, "I've found her a safe place in a large household. If I can help her I will." Then to Jack, "Was Marshalsea bad?"

Jack's face went white again. "Richard, it was terrible, I felt as if I had been delivered to Hell. I shall never in my life say I feel cold again, for that was cold the likes of which no-one should face."

Richard reached a hand out and put it on Jack's shoulder. "I have something to finish in London and then I'll take you somewhere warmer. Until then, little brother, stop in here and get well."

Jack smiled: it was what he wanted to hear. Despite everything, his brother was keeping him at his side.

"I'll not let you down," he managed hoarsely.

"I know you won't," Richard changed the subject, "Anyway, how do you like Lizbet?"

"Where on earth did you find her?" Jack asked, settling back against the piled pillows.

"You needed tending and I thought you'd like her," Richard smiled simply, adding, "I think she likes you."

"I think you'll find it's your money she likes," Jack yawned and lay back, closing his eyes. "This tiredness just won't leave me."

Richard waited patiently and watched quietly until Jack was again asleep. His skin at last had some colour and the bruises were fading. The sores and torn skin under the bandages were healing well. Richard hoped the man who would come back to him would be the Jack he'd known. Jack wasn't the only one to have endured the savage trial of loss.

✝

After nearly two weeks in close company with Lizbet, Richard had grudgingly admitted that the woman had indeed a sharp wit and even sharper senses. She had run away when she was twelve, escaping from a father who beat her and a mother who made her work until she dropped. Her parents had a laundry business and made black soap; their eleven children were their unwilling slaves. Lizbet, never one to miss an opportunity, had already taken over Richard's laundry work. That had caused quite an argument. Bessy Todd, the street laundress, more than a little upset at the loss of a customer, had taken it as a personal slur that Richard's washing was now in the hands of a whore. Bessy had come up to him in the taproom and informed him in detail of the personal illnesses he was likely to contract now that he had let a whore handle his linen. The laundress was curtly told that he had let them handle a lot more than his shirts in the past and so far he had lived to talk about it, so he was willing to take the risk.

When she had changed her dress for a simple servant's one, Lizbet had also stopped painting her face. London whores marked their trade on their faces in the most unnatural fashion and the eyes that were watching him now were thankfully no longer outlined with smudged charcoal.

Lizbet glanced quickly at him over the cards - if she hoped to catch the other player unawares she was sadly mistaken; steel grey eyes and an impassive gaze met her own. Lizbet huffed audibly. Her hand was good: four cards, including a six of clubs, a seven of clubs and an ace of hearts. Not the highest hand you could get in Primero, but not far away. There were two pennies on the table: it was a difficult call. Previous experience warned her not to underestimate the other player. She peeked quickly, back from the hand to the other player and met again the cold enquiring eyes.

"Well," Lizbet smiling laid her cards down one at a time. "A six, a seven, both clubs and," she paused for effect, "an ace of hearts."

The other player gave her the slightest of nods then laid his cards down quickly, neatly and next to hers.

"God's bones!" Lizbet exclaimed loudly. Four cards, all different suits and all following on stared at her. "Primero again. If you were playing in the taproom downstairs, I swear one of the lads would have slipped a knife between your ribs by now."

"And you really think they could manage that?" Richard slid the pennies towards him with the edge of the cards.

"Nah, probably not now, they'll all be too drunk by this hour," Lizbet conceded.

Richard reunited the deck. "Another?" he enquired.

"Aye, I'll deal if you don't mind." Lizbet reached over and claimed the deck from his hands.

"You're as gracious at losing as Jack is," Richard remarked.

He didn't often speak of Jack. Lizbet looked up from her card-shuffling. "I'd wager he's easy to read."

"That's a bet you would win," Richard agreed. "Jack thinks he plays well and it comes as a continual surprise to him that he keeps on losing."

"Does he ever beat you?" Lizbet started to deal the cards out on the table between them.

"Not often." Richard collected his cards, "Unless I want him to."

There was a scream from the other room; Lizbet jumped. "Lord, here we go, don't you dare look at them while I'm gone," she warned, "If I lose I'll know you took a peak."

"I'll go," Richard started to rise from his chair.

"No, please, you let me go," Lizbet was on her way already. "He'd be shamed if you went, it's not so bad if I go."

There was much sense in her words and Richard dropped back into his seat to wait. He was thankful for her compassion. This was good work for her and Lizbet was trying her best to impress. Sleeping on the floor outside Jack's room had meant she had given up the room she shared with the other girls. Now she had regular pay with no fee to pay for her nightly roof; she fervently hoped it would continue.

"I didn't look," Richard assured her when Lizbet returned.

"I believe you," Lizbet retrieved her cards, but her mood was sombre.

"Here." Richard poured her a drink from the flagon on the table. "I can read your face now and I know this isn't easy."

Lizbet met his gaze, "What happened that could frighten a man so much?"

"I don't know," admitted Richard. "I honestly don't know and I am afraid to ask."

"I can guess from his wrists he's been in gaol, that's the only place you get marks on you like that..."

Richard's hard stare stopped her words.

"It's not my business, sorry Master, I shouldn't have said that." Lizbet cursed herself, she'd already been on the wrong side of his temper too many times and she didn't want to be there again.

"Just keep your counsel," Richard warned.

"I will." Feeling the need to change the subject she murmured, "He'll be well again soon, I'm sure of it." Lizbet paused momentarily before continuing, "the fevers only been gone a few days and he's not much strength back yet. Lucy says he'll need quite a bit of tending."

"I can still read you," Richard smiled. "I'll be needing you for a few more weeks, don't you worry."

Lizbet's smile widened. "Thank you, sir." She discarded a four of clubs and drew another from the top of the pack. Then she loosed the cards, letting them fall onto the table. "Maybe I should learn when I'm beat and not let you take another penny from me."

"Maybe indeed." Richard folded his cards and put them back on the top of the pack.

Lizbet stood. "I'll bid you a good night. Is there anything I can get for you before I go?"

Richard didn't look up from the table. "Some peace perhaps."

Lizbet misunderstood his remark. "I'm sure he'll be quiet now. I gave him some of that drink Lucy left and he'll sleep like a babe, don't you worry."

"I wasn't thinking about him," Richard replied.

Five minutes later Lizbet was back and set a steaming cup before him. "It's nothing bad," she assured him, suddenly more than a little nervous at her presumptuousness. "Just feverfew, honey and chamomile."

He didn't say anything. Later, when he'd left to go to his own room, Lizbet saw the cup on the table was empty and smiled.

✝

Jack awoke; for a moment he didn't know where he was.

"Oh God," he whimpered while running his hands through his hair as he sat on the edge of the bed. His mind began to order itself; he knew where he was, he was safe. The candle he always asked Lizbet to leave to burn had blown out. In the wintery gloom from the window, he spotted the wax stick and the tinder box next to it. Jack took a long breath and steadied himself. Lizbet would have left the fire set, he just needed to light it.

Standing on shaking legs, he reached for the tinderbox and slid the lid open. Inside he found the sharp flint and cold steel by touch, as well as the soft cloth he needed to catch the spark. Jack was sure there were shavings in a box near the fire. The steel slid over the fingers of his left hand so he could strike it with the flint in his right. The first stroke connected and the shower of orange sparks lit the table for a moment while they lived, however none caught on the cloth and the darkness resumed. Jack swallowed hard, fighting to focus on the task. Again a strike and a shower of vivid brief pinpricks of light. Now his hands shook so badly he missed the steel with the flint and felt it cut the backs of his fingers. He knew he didn't have long and tried again. It was too late: the trembling hands would not obey him. The final agony came when he dropped the flint somewhere on the dark floor. The shadowy presence in the corner near the firewood laughed.

"Have mercy, please, no!" Jack begged, the laughter increasing, ringing maliciously in his ears.

Lizbet flung the door open, her eyes wide when she did not find her charge in the bed. She thought he'd fallen and went to his aid where he lay on his side on the floor. His knees caught by his arms and his head bent down, curled tight as kitten in the cold.

"Jack, Jack, tell me what's happened." Placing her hands on him, she felt tremors running through his body. "Oh no, it's the fever come back."

Lizbet was alone and she stood no chance of getting Jack back in bed, so she brought the bed to Jack. Pillowed and blanketed, he nestled on the floor. Soon the fire was lit and the room glowed with the orange from the flames.

"The candle," Jack's voice was a quiet, shaky plea.

Lizbet saw the look on his face and understood. Nimble fingers nipped the wick straight and she lit it quickly with a spill from the fire. Kneeling, she set it close to Jack on the floor, watching the yellow flame dance in his eyes as he stared at it.

†

The only thing within reach was a wine flagon. Clement grasped it and hurled it at the wall where it smashed into a hundred pieces and spread a wet, red stain across the wood panelling.

"How can everything go this badly wrong?" Clement shouted. "Damned Kettering has ruined my plan; too bloody clever for his own good. They've lost that bastard at Marshalsea by the look of it."

"Lost him?" Marcus asked, stooping to collect the largest pottery shards from the floor.

"He went in: Bartholomew's men took him in, the paperwork was correct and he should be rotting in their cells right now, but he's not." Clement dropped back heavily in his chair.

"How, sir?" asked Marcus his hands full of pottery. He looked at the mess; he'd need to get a cloth before the wine soaked into the files and set the ink to run as well.

"How should I know? Kettering said his debt was redeemed! Nobody was going to pay it, it was a false name and a false debt, so who on earth could know about it? Now Fitzwarren wants to know what's happened - he's hoping the man has perished as I promised he would. How can I tell him he's vanished?" Clement flustered hotly, "He's got the worst temper on him of any man I've ever come across."

Marcus glanced up at that remark: Clement's temper was not much better. "Master he's not likely to go to Marshalsea and check, why not just tell him what he wants to know?"

"What, tell him that the wretch is dead? What if he turns up?" Clement flung his arms wide.

"It could be he is still in Marshalsea. As you said Master, no-one knew he was in there so who could have paid his debts off?" Marcus suggested. He'd collected all the broken pieces now and was picking up files and letting the wine run from them to the floor to limit the damage.

"True, true," Clement thinking it over, tapped his chin with his forefinger. "And if he does turn up then we can deal with that problem later. Pass me paper and pen - I'll write to Fitzwarren now. Maybe it will put him in a good mood and we can go forward on the other legal matters he's been looking to set in motion."

Clement finished the letter to Robert Fitzwarren and put it aside, Marcus would arrange for it to be delivered later. The letter from Kettering he opened again and spread before him. He had been going to burn it and leave the matter well alone, but Clement was a greedy man and he could not resist. Kettering's letter detailed the discharge of the debt owed by Master Kilpatrick of one hundred pounds, after the fees payable to Marshalsea, there remained an amount for collection of eighty one pounds. That was a lot of money. As the fictitious debtors lawyer Clement was entitled to collect this on behalf of his client, deduct from it his own fees and pass the remainder on. If he did not collect it then the money would remain to line Kettering's pockets. Clement reasoned that he had to collect it, if he didn't it would look more than suspicious that such a large sum remained unclaimed; he had indeed little choice but to take it himself.

✝

Elizabeth and Kate sat together in a window seat. Kate was sewing and Elizabeth stared at the grey winter beyond the window. She felt the cold coming through the glass; so far that winter, the snow had stayed away but the rain and sleet had barely stopped. The weather matched her mood

"So, she saved his life? Richard told you that?" Elizabeth asked.

"Yes, he didn't tell me how, or what happened, but he said that this was the debt he owed her," Kate replied, looking up from her needlework.

"It's a cold afternoon and I could use a fiery tale to warm me. Bring her up to my room and she can regale me with how she managed to save a man who I know needs no saviour," Elizabeth said, her eyes still fixed on the cold vista outside.

"Are you sure this is wise?" Kate asked, now regretting now having mentioned it. "We know nothing about her."

"Well then let's change that, shall we?" Elizabeth returned her gaze to the room and met Kate's eyes. "She can bring me a drink in my room."

Kate bobbed a curtsey, wishing she'd kept her mouth shut about the newly-arrived Catherine and her acquaintance with Elizabeth's friend Richard. It was her own fault, but the days were long and tensions high so any distraction was one to be seized upon and followed to its final conclusion. Anything at all that would help to pass the excruciating hours was welcome.

☦

"Now take this in," Kate instructed Catherine, straightening the glass and jug on the tray.

Catherine opened the door with one hand and manoeuvred through, carefully closing it behind her. When she turned to enter the room, she was bought up short by the expression on the face of the woman standing near the fire. Catherine dropped her eyes to the floor, fervently wishing herself elsewhere.

"Bring it over here." Elizabeth indicated a table for her to deposit the tray.

Catherine brought it over and, placing the tray down, began to pour wine into the glass.

"I don't want any," Elizabeth stepped back and seated herself neatly in the chair behind her.

Catherine stood, paralysed, in the act of pouring the wine.

Elizabeth settled back in the chair and turned her father's hard gaze on the girl before her. "So, a tale has come to me that you are acquainted with Richard Fitzwarren?"

"I am, my lady," Catherine replied quietly, lowering the jug and putting it down quietly on the tray.

"Tell me how?" demanded Elizabeth. Her hands folded in her lap, she looked supremely relaxed and very much in control.

"How?' my lady?" Catherine stammered.

"Yes how girl, it's not a hard question is it?" Elizabeth demanded.

"I met him..."

"I can't hear a damn word, come and stand here." Elizabeth pointed imperiously to a spot on the carpet just in front of her chair.

Catherine stood where she was bid. "My lady, he led a troop of men who took over my father's house," then she added, "my home."

"When was this?" Elizabeth demanded.

"Nearly two years ago, my lady, in the summer of 1554," Catherine supplied, her confidence returning as her breathing evened out again.

"And he's kept you with him since?" Elizabeth sounded quite shocked. "Why would he do that?"

"I don't know, my lady," Catherine replied honestly.

"So I am told he owes you a debt, am I to believe you saved his life?" Elizabeth asked, looking the child before her up and down, a poor mousey brown creature indeed.

"I tried to help when he needed it, my lady," Catherine was unsure of what she should or should not relate of the final events at the manor at Burton.

"And how did you render this help?" Elizabeth asked, now quite interested.

Catherine cleared her throat: she'd had enough of this. "There was a warrant for his arrest my lady, but they did not wish for him to stand trial. Instead, they arranged for a trial by combat for their own sport. He had little chance to escape and I offered myself as a hostage so that he could escape from them."

"Oh a victim? Yes, you do look like you would fit such a role," Elizabeth sounded smug. "And so he feels duty bound to discharge the debt. How very like Richard. And now you are indebted to me."

"How so, my lady?" Catherine immediately wished she could take back the words.

Elizabeth's cold eyes met her own, "You are now hiding in the very last place anyone would ever look for you, are you not?" Elizabeth told her. "You will of course mention his name to no-one, the association could be a dangerous one for you."

"I have already been told, my lady," Catherine replied.

"I am reminding you of your duty. Not a word," said Elizabeth sternly.

Catherine was waved from her presence, regaining the proper use of her legs once she was on the other side of the door and it was closed behind her. Outside she found Kate, whose gaze was no less harsh than that of her Mistress.

"This is a strict house and these are difficult times. Make sure you keep your counsel close," she warned.

"Yes, my lady," Kate disappeared to join her mistress and Catherine made a hasty retreat.

†

Jack was confused. No, Jack was confused and angry. So many thoughts fought in his mind for his attention. He'd pick up one thread, follow it for a while until either it became too painful to dwell on anymore, or another distracted his attention. When he'd left Burton, his brother was alive. He should have known, someone should have told him. Did Dan know? Did Mat know? Jamie had known and the bastard had just let Jack tear himself apart. He'd ended up with nothing, in the pit at Marshalsea, facing a devil in the dark and two bloody words, 'He's alive,' would have stopped that. He would not have ended up there, of that he was sure.

He would have taken Richard somewhere, helped him recover and then the two of them, together, could have begun again. Being with Richard offered safety and shelter from the world, he'd have known where they would go next; he would not have led Jack to the hell he had ended up in.

It had been chance that Richard had found out that he was in Marshalsea. Jack couldn't face that thought for very long; the hard claw seemed to force its way into his chest and clamp his heart in a sickening grasp. The knowledge that he owed his escape to luck was too fearful to contemplate and he moved away from those thoughts very quickly. He feared Fate would shake her fickle finger at him and send him back.

Richard had been alive. Worse, he'd recovered and come to London. He had not gone looking for Jack. The rejection left him feeling cold. If the roles were reversed Jack knew he would have moved anything in his path to find his brother. Richard had come to London and Jack had an awful feeling that he knew why.

Sitting alone, with little to do, pain a constant reminder of Marshalsea, his tired mind convinced himself he'd been driven there and that part of that fault lay in his brother's hands. If Richard had set himself to look for Jack then that course would have changed. If someone had told him his brother was alive it would have all been so different.

Jack was in the middle of his own gloomy nightmare when the door opened and Lizbet came in, a smile on her face. "And how's my lad this morning then?" Her brow furrowed when she saw his eyes drop from hers and he failed to return her smile. "What's the matter?" She came and sat on the edge of the bed, reached her hand out and stroked his forehead and he pulled away from her touch. "This is not like you, tell me what's wrong." Lizbet had found him in his sentient moments both likeable and charming, with a quick smile, sparkling blue eyes and, now the bruises were diminishing, a fair face that would please any girl.

"Just leave me be, Lizbet," Jack tried to turn away from her.

"You've not scratched those bandages off again have you?" Lizbet was having none of it and pulling the blanket down started to inspect the dressings on his wrists. When the fever had been upon him he'd clawed at them constantly, setting them to bleeding again.

"Leave me be woman!" His voice this time had an edge that stopped Lizbet and she dropped the blanket back on him.

Recovering, he was no longer docile and compliant. Lizbet persisted and held out a cup for him. "I'll leave your..."

Jack batted the cup from her hand and sent it to clank against the door. Lizbet leapt back startled, her fingers stinging from the blow.

"Just get out! Get out now!" Jack's shouted, his head turned towards the wall.

Lizbet slammed the door to his room. Rubbing her fingers and muttering under her breath. She met Richard's enquiring eyes.

"What's the matter with him?" Richard sounded worried – there was no way he could have missed the commotion. "Has the fever come back?"

"It's not fever, he's got a temper on him and it's nothing I've done. He'll not let me see to him, he's shouting and I can't force him can I?" Lizbet was truly upset.

"I'll go and talk to him," Richard conceded, squeezing her arm as he passed her. "It's not your fault." He knew he should have done this earlier, he shouldn't have left it so long.

✝

Richard sat on the chair in the room Jack occupied, his feet up on the end of the bed. Jack, propped up on pillows and still swaddled in Lucy's linen wraps was feeling less than comfortable. It was one thing having to sit helplessly while the woman fussed about him, but it was quite another to have to sit in a bed in the presence of his brother. Especially now Richard asked questions about how Jack had ended up in gaol. Jack knew the answers he gave sounded poor. He wanted to get up, desperately wanted to see what lay outside of the four walls he was forced to stare at, but so far neither Richard nor Lizbet were prepared to let him leave the bed. Jack's mood was still belligerent and he was having difficulty dealing with the fact that Richard had left him, abandoned him to his own devices and had taken himself to London without him.

"What happened, Jack, for you to end up in Marshalsea?" Richard asked again.

Jack looked up from the bed into Richard's face. "Oh I see, you actually think I owed that bloody money do you?"

"I didn't say that..."

"You don't have to! It's written all over your bloody face." Jack retorted hotly.

"Give me patience," Richard spoke through clenched teeth.

"Patience? I've run out of patience. Have you any idea what it was like in there?" Jack retorted angrily.

"I can imagine," Richard spoke in a voice aimed to calm the other. "I don't think this was through your own fault Jack, this was by design but I'm not sure how. My horse, Corracha, was taken to our father's house after they took you to Marshalsea and that didn't happen by accident did it?"

"No, it didn't," Jack accepted grudgingly. "I was taken there and left to die, Richard, that is the truth of it. I'd thought a lawyer would help me. I had a letter from his brother recommending my case, but he wanted nothing to do with me and showed me the door. Aye, and it was his bloody name on the debtor's papers."

"A lawyer. Who was that?" Richard asked, truly interested now.

Jack told him briefly of his trip north to York and the letter of recommendation Roger Clement had given him to present to his brother. "...I gave him the letter but he wasn't interested and practically threw me from the door. The letter and the family papers I had were taken from me at Marshalsea."

Richard pushed himself from the bed. "I got what papers you had on you back from Kettering." He returned a moment later with them in his hand. "We both know what that one is," and he discarded the sheet containing their father's confession on the bed; the other he opened and read thoughtfully as he sat back down.

"I did truly believe he was going to help me," Jack then added defensively, "I couldn't have known of the connection to Robert or William, how could I?"

Richard folded the sheet and sent it spinning to land on top of the other folded paper. "You couldn't, maybe you should have found out a little more about his clientele before you opened his door. I am guessing Clement will have the answers as to why you were in Marshalsea. Shall I pay him a visit?"

"No. Don't," Jack responded quickly, "I'd like to do that myself. I'll not be laid on my back in here forever you know. And believe me, I have a score to settle there."

"I got this back as well." Richard delved into a pocket and threw over the black crested ring Catherine had given to Master Kettering. It landed near Jack's hand; he looked at it but didn't reach out and take it.

"I've told you before, the only person who will help you is yourself," Richard watched his brother carefully.

"There's a truth in that, isn't there?" Jack muttered, his blue eye's holding those of his brother.

Richard matched his gaze; he could read the question on Jack's face and after a moment he answered it. "I would have found you, Jack. When I came to London I could barely sit on a horse, I had little money. What would you have had me do?"

Jack dropped his eyes first and rubbed his face with the back of his hand. "Would you have looked for me?"

"You've sat in here too long on your own, you idiot. Of course I would have tried to find you. As it is fortune smiled did it not?"

"Fortunate I ended in Marshalsea?" Jack countered.

"No, fortunate that Catherine found out. I got you out, Jack, remember that," Richard reminded him firmly; he knew Jack well enough to know he dealt in facts. Changing the subject, he added, "and then you went to see our father?"

"Aye, after I'd seen that damned lawyer." Jack, sounded depressed, "I was at an end, I truly did not know what to do next. I don't have your..."

"Sense of purpose?" Richard supplied, unhelpfully when Jack's words trailed off.

"Aye, go on, there's the sheep and the shepherd and we both know I'm one of those woolly beggars." Jack lamented.

Richard ignored his brother's self-pity. "So William, did he welcome you with open arms?"

"No; he tricked me and shouted robber and I only just got out of the place before they grabbed me," Jack sounded gloomy. "It wasn't one of my best moments."

"Well, we will go and see Clement soon and I'm sure he will be forthcoming when we put a few questions to him," Richard reassured.

"If that snivelling lawyer had anything to do with putting me into Marshalsea, he'll be more than forthcoming, believe me," growled Jack.

"Let him answer our questions first before you take your anger out on him," Richard suggested evenly.

"Richard, in Marshalsea there was someone else with you," Jack spoke hesitantly. "I cannot really remember, but I heard the voice, my head was fair spinning with pain. I remember very little, just that voice. Who was there with you?"

"The lass, Catherine, was with me. They thought her your wife," Richard replied, taking both documents back into his keeping but leaving the ring near Jack's hand.

"No, another. Someone from the north," Jack looked up into his brother's face. "Or was I just losing my mind?"

Richard smiled, then supplied in an accent which resonated from just south of the Scottish border, "Aye, that might have been myself."

"You! I thought it was a dream. Or worse. I thought the realms of Hell were full of Northerners," Jack shook his head.

"Catherine told Kettering your family came from the North, so I invented James Kilpatrick from Newcastle. That's the name and the address in the records at Marshalsea settling your debt," Richard explained.

"And where did you pick up such an accent?" Jack asked.

"Chester Neephouse: I studied with him at university, he came from Newcastle. I was the only one who could ever understand a word he said. Even the inn horses he hired hadn't a clue what he was talking about," Richard grinned. "I remember once, at Crofts Tavern, I had to translate his every desire to a whore who, 'wor a fair canny lass,' but she had not a clue what he wanted her to do."

Jack laughed, "And did he get his way then?"

"No, not at all. I'm telling her all the things he wants to do to her and her to him and all the time she's looking straight into my eyes and then she stands up, declares that she'll not bed a foreigner, takes me by the hand and off I am dragged. What could I do?" Richard smiled at the memory. "I fair enjoyed Chester Neephouse's suggestions as it happens."

"I'll have to get you to pass on those ideas to Lizbet then, so I can try them out," Jack laughed.

"I doubt there's anything you are shy of doing with a woman," said Richard, then, "She's been kind to you Jack, it's not been the nicest of tasks looking after you. Don't be cruel to her. From the look of you she's doing a good job." Richard pointed to the bandages on his arms and round his torso, clean and neat and any of the smell that had dogged his arrival was gone. Lizbet even had a posy of holly with berries and fragrant sage on the table.

Jack's face reddened as he took the rebuke: he knew Richard was right. "Aye, I'm sorry for that, tell her I am."

"Next time you've a mind to lose your temper send for me," Richard added, a cold note in his voice.

"Send the lass in. I'm sorry, I'll tell her so," He genuinely did regret his treatment of her.

Richard sat a while, the silence companionable. A loud snore from the other man told him Jack had succumbed to sleep again. Richard was more than a little jealous.

Chapter Nine

It was nearly a month into the New Year and Jack was now bored, prowling the rooms like a caged dog. Neither Richard nor Lizbet would let him out and his temper was sour. Blisters on his hands and ribs were now only pale scars, a fading reminder of the cold floor at Marshalsea. The only lasting memory his body would carry for the rest of his life were the brutally scarred wrists.

Richard was often absent which made Jack's mood worse. Why was he allowed out? Where he went he rarely shared with Jack; time, it seemed, had not changed things that much. Neither Lizbet nor Richard sympathised overly with his dark moods. Richard was firmly of the opinion that if they humoured him they would make him worse, something Lizbet, getting to know her charge, was inclined to agree with.

Jack looked at his wrists; the right was worse than the left by far. The skin was puckered, pitted and twisted where it had grown back, as well as pale and painful to the touch, even more so when he bent his wrist back and stretched the new skin.

Standing, he pulled the sword from its sheath and smiled as he hefted the familiar weight in his hand. Not his own blade - that had been lost to Bartholomew - but a good replacement supplied, along with a poniard, by Richard. He loosened his grasp on the hilt, letting it roll over in his palm then catching it quickly again to halt the spinning sword.

He held the blade out level in front of him - a move he'd practised thousands of times - and this was when he saw it. The blade was not still: the point which should be stationary was moving in an arc. He couldn't see his hand moving but it must be. Jack dropped the blade to his left hand and held out his right flat in front of him. It shook. Jack balled it into a fist and held it out again. No - it trembled and there was nothing his mind could do to will it to stop.

What was he going to do?

That was how Lizbet found him, sitting on the edge of his bed, his head in his hands. The sword lay discarded on the floor in front of him, the steel glinting in the fire light.

"And what's the matter with you now then?" Lizbet groaned, seeing his downcast head.

"Oh Lizbet, sorry," Jack instinctively picked the sword up and slid it back into the sheath.

The harsh metallic sound made Lizbet wince, "I hate those bloody things."

"Aye, I don't think I'll be using one again for a while," he said gloomily.

"And why's that then?" Lizbet heard the self-pity in his voice and ignored it.

"Look." Jack held out the offending right hand.

Lizbet took it and turned it over. "What's wrong with it? Looks alright to me," she released it and pushing it back at him.

"Look woman, it still shakes like a leaf in a gale," Jack held the trembling hand just under her nose for her to observe.

Lizbet took hold of his hand again. "It's not that bad, not as bad as it was. Turn it over." Jack complied and the shaking worsened when he held it palm-up.

"Bloody hell," Jack cursed harshly, pulling his hand away from her grasp. "What use is that to me?"

Lizbet thumped him on the chest with the flat of her hand. "Stop being a bleedin' child. It'll take time, it's not long ago you were in that bed and we were not sure if you'd ever come off it again alive. Give it here again." Lizbet extended her hand for his, "Come on! I haven't all day."

Jack complied and held his hand out. She pushed his sleeve up and turned his hand over, examining the scars on his wrist. "These were bad, Jack." She ran her hands over them and he winced, her eyes quickly meeting his. "Do they still hurt?"

"Not hurt so much as ache," he explained. "And when I do this," he bent his wrist to demonstrate, "then I can feel it pulling the skin."

"The answer's simple, don't do it," Lizbet was still studying the scars. "Look, the skin is chafing on your jacket. If you cover it that might help," Lizbet suggested, as she wrapped her small hand around his wrist.

"Squeeze tighter," Jack said suddenly. Lizbet increased her hold. "Look, it shakes less." Jack smiled.

"Oh well, that's going to work, isn't it?" Lizbet laughed, letting go. "Every time you need your sword arm just call me over to hold your hand." Jack couldn't help but laugh.

Jack held his own wrist with his other hand. "Maybe if I brace it with a wrist guard, see." He held his right wrist tight with his left hand and the trembling subsided. Their eyes met. "That's better, much better," Lizbet agreed with a smile.

Before she could retreat, he'd caught her in his arms. "Now then Mistress, you've promised me entertainment, so entertain me. I have been in here for weeks and if I stay in here any longer it will turn me into the village idiot."

"Turn you into one, Jack? I think you are a good way there already," Lizbet teased, slipping her arms around his neck.

"Richard's away and I'm going out tonight and you are coming with me." Jack decreed.

"Ah now, no Jack. The Master said you were to stay in here until he returned and you agreed. Don't go getting me into trouble," Lizbet chastised, sliding from his embrace.

Jack wasn't so easily put off and pulled her back, an arm round her waist, holding her firmly against him. "I see only one Master here and I'm going out. You're not likely to stop me lass are you?

So either come with me, or sit in here and worry about where I've got to; those are the choices."

"No Jack, he'll kill me. He's a right temper on him and I'm not getting on the wrong side of it again," Lizbet had two hands now on his chest as she tried half-heartedly to push him away.

"I'll tell him I gave you no choice." Jack buried his face in her hair and finding an ear nibbled it playfully. "I'll tell him I forced you to come with me."

"You promise?" Lizbet had stopped pushing him away.

"I promise," murmured Jack, intent now on exposing Lizbet's white smooth shoulder from under her linen.

Lizbet smiled and let him slide his hands where he would. She liked the idea of going out and if he would say it wasn't her fault then that should keep her out of trouble. "When the girls see you, they are going to have to take back their words. They tease me rotten that I am caged up here all day with an old clod in his dotage."

"An old clod in his dotage," Jack repeated, his mouth seeking the place on her neck he knew would make her press against him harder with delight. "I hope you set them straight."

"When I take you out with me tonight that will certainly stop their tongues from wagging," Lizbet's voice was hoarse, his touch sending tendrils of fire through her veins.

"And now I'm going to still yours," Jack stated, planting a kiss on her open mouth; it left her breathless. Smiling he felt her weight increase in his arms.

"Jack, you'll not be cruel to me in front of them, please?" Lizbet said, for once her confidence absent, leaning heavily against him. "I've not seen the girls much since I've been tending you and..."

Spinning her round and then bowing low to her, he made Lizbet squeal with laughter and clap her hands together. "Tonight I shall extol your virtues, sing your praises and let no other shine in your presence."

"No idea what you are talking about, but if that means you'll be nice to me then I'd be very pleased," Lizbet eagerly returned to his embrace.

Jack released her, smiling and slapped her backside. "Well then lass, get me some clothes and we'll go and find out."

Lizbet laughed then, as she realised he'd very much been intent on getting his own way. She smoothed out the clothes that had been made for him - his brother had been right to choose russet, it would suit him well. A cream snug-fitting doublet with silver buttons, fashionably slashed to show the linen shirt beneath; a velvet jerkin with a low collar; Matching hose and stockings with calf skin boots; a felt cap trimmed with feather and a cloak: fur trimmed with a silken lining. Next to all this was a pile of fresh white linen. Lizbet was sure she had never been so excited.

So Jack, in russet, a colour he had only just found out existed and Lizbet in her best and only dress, went to the Kings Arms on the opposite side of the street.

Richard discovered them both absent and tracked them to the tavern across the road. Opening the door, his eyes soon found the bright blond head of his brother, surrounded by women, with Lizbet balanced proprietarily on one of his knees. Jack was beaming broadly, happy and a little drunk: Richard resolved not to spoil his mood.

Lizbet, feeling the cold draught on her back from the opened door, turned and found her eyes locked with those of the Master. Her cheeks flushed. She'd fervently hoped they would be back in the room before he returned, then he would have been none the wiser that Jack had been outside. She gave Jack's arm a warning squeeze.

Jack, on the other hand, was happy to see him. "Come and join me," Jack stated, "I'm outnumbered and I need help."

Richard dropped onto an empty trestle opposite his brother and looped his cloak over one of the partitions. "Since when did you need any help with women?"

"I have six! Four would be fine, five I could manage but it would be a long night, but six would be the death of me to be sure," Jack pronounced a little drunkenly. Lizbet looked at him darkly and Richard hid a smile.

Blond, fair and with a smile born to charm, Jack was cast in his mother's image. Sometimes, when the light was right and he caught sight of Jack out of the corner of his eye for a brief instant he'd be aware of a sense of her bright, shining presence. It would have been a help if Jack had inherited just her looks and not her irrational and terrible temper. He supposed though, that the traits went together hand in hand: looks married to temperament.

"How did you end up here?" Richard asked.

"Lizbet wanted to show them what 'russet' was," Jack laughed.

Lizbet shot him another accusing look; it hadn't been her idea to come to the inn.

"As we are here I might as well join you for a drink." Richard's expression conveyed to Lizbet that he wasn't holding her responsible for Jack's escape; Lizbet's relief was palpable. A whore, with a jug of wine, a bodice on the way to her waistline and an invitation written on her face, settled, unbidden, on Richard's knee.

"Get your backside off him Saster. If he wants such as you, I'll let you know." Lizbet leant over and whacked the girl hard with the back of her hand.

"Get you with your graces!" Saster rose from her seat and shot Lizbet an evil look.

Lizbet hurriedly justified her action to Richard. "She's not good enough for you, I'll not have them taking advantage, just because I know you."

Richard shook his head and laughed, "Lizbet, I can look after myself."

"Aye, I'm sure you can, but I'm looking after you now and I have standards and she isn't one of them," Lizbet replied tartly. This time Richard laughed so hard Jack had to hit him on the back after the ale went down the wrong way.

It was much later, when Lizbet was seated with her friends, that the brothers finally found themselves alone. "So what are you planning for us next? I'm sure you've got something in your head," Jack was now pleasantly drunk and enjoying his new freedom.

"What or who?" Richard replied.

"I'll stand by you, brother, and by whatever cause you commit us to," Jack slurred his words a little, then clanked his cup noisily against Richard's, spilling a quantity of ale over the table. "As long as it gets me out of that room. I'm fair tired of being inside."

"Are you sure?" Richard asked.

"Yes, I've had enough of Lizbet's company and those four walls," Jack stated.

"That's not what I meant," Richard said.

"I know, I'm not that drunk. Whatever you decide, anything is better than being inside. I'd work for the Devil himself if it got me away from the fireside and Lizbet."

Richard raised his glass and brought his head close to Jack's, "To the Lady Elizabeth."

Jack's blood stilled in his veins. That was a name he never wanted to hear again: that bitch was the cause of a lot of sorrow. Richard's face clouded as he read Jack's expression, "That is where my loyalty lies."

Aye, thought Jack and to hell with anyone else. Jack had already had a quantity to drink and an argument was not something he wished for. He stated simply, "It nearly killed you last time," and then added, "and me."

"Join me or not. It's your choice," Richard stated bluntly.

Jack sighed resignedly, "I'll join you, as it happens. I've little better to do. So tell me then, what is it we are about to get involved with this time?"

From where they were sat Richard knew they could not be overheard and he told Jack of Fairfax's plot to steal Elizabeth away from England and hold her in Holland.

"And that's the plan?" Jack sat back, an incredulous look on his face.

"That is the plan, yes," Richard conceded, palms spread in an expression of helplessness.

"Do they truly think it will work?" Jack shook his head as he considered the ludicrousness of it.

"God, they feel, will be taking care of the details," Richard's words were loaded with sarcasm.

"I usually find God sticks to grand plans and leaves us mere mortals to make a bloody and unholy mess of the details," Jack said equally sarcastically. "So they will just have a melée of men in the area, no coordination. They just hope that in the confusion they will be able to acquire the lady and get her away under the cover of a bit of smoke?" Jack asked, tapping his cup on the table, thoughtfully.

"Do they not know how well Elizabeth's household will be organised? The men in there will be the Queen's men. They will be well-trained and they are not going to be duped by a child's plan such at this."

"Actually her household is being run by Gardiner and Travers. Elizabeth does not have her own money. Her expenses are being met, for the moment, by Mary who has not allocated a lot of funds, so what there is has been used to support quite a small household. There are a few servants, grooms and only two men at arms in the house," Richard ticked them off on his fingers.

"And you know all this because..." Jack then held his hand up. "No don't tell me, I'm not sure I want to know."

Richard just shot him a black look.

"And the Lady Elizabeth, does she want to go to Holland?" Jack asked.

"Ah now, you have asked the right question - one Fairfax and his associates have never entertained. No, the lady does certainly not want to go, for many reasons. And our task is to ensure she stays in England and out of the hands of this Protestant mob," Richard concluded.

"Shouldn't be too hard," Jack replied. "So what's our plan?"

Richard smiled. "Our plan?"

"Tell me what it is. If I like it, then it can be our plan." Jack produced a loud hiccup before continuing, "And if I don't, then it can be your plan."

"How gracious of you," Richard said, more than a little caustically.

"Remember." Jack pointed his finger accusingly at Richard, "I've been on the wrong end of some of your plans in the past."

"Agreed." Richard accepted the truth of Jack's remark. "At the moment we are waiting for them to decide on *when*. There is another meeting tomorrow and if their nerve has held then I suspect they will finalise a date," Richard surmised. "Once we have a date we can put some measures in place. There didn't seem to be much point in starting to act unless I know for certain that they mean to carry it out. A large pile of cut green wood is not exactly evidence that they will go ahead. Fairfax likes the sound of his own voice; when it actually comes to it, I'm not so sure they will press ahead. The longer they take the better, it will give you a little more time to recover. How are you faring anyway?"

"Another week and I'll be as good as I was. It's just this." Jack held out his hand, Richard saw it tremble. "If I held a sword with that I'd be as likely trip over it as make a strike."

"Well if you'd not drunk quite as much I'm sure it would be as steady as a rock." Richard reached over and took his hand; he felt it shake even when he held it. "What about the other one?"

Jack held out his left. "It's just as bad. And sometimes..." Jack wanted to tell him about the nights, the terrors, but in the bright reality of day they somehow didn't seem that real.

"Give it time, Jack," Richard released his hand.

"Aye, and in the meantime don't fill my cups so full. If Lizbet sees me spill any more on this bloody russet, shaky hands will be the least of my worries," he laughed.

✝

Christian didn't hear the man come into the warehouse. He was far too absorbed by the figures on the sheets before him.

"You shouldn't be alone at night here: anyone could get in." It was a familiar voice, but still Christian jumped.

"Richard! Christ! Was there really a need to try and scare me half to death?" Christian exclaimed, then, "How did you get in? I locked the doors from the inside."

"Ah, now your precious chattels are in danger you are interested," Richard laughed.

Christian was not to be put off. "Tell me how?"

Richard looked upwards. "Through the roof; the timbers at that end are rotten where the thatch has come away."

"Good God, I'll have to get that fixed," Christian sounded worried. "I have men in here at night, but they don't come for another hour, I dare not leave this place at night unattended. We live in sad times. Only two weeks ago Mercher, a good friend, lost half a warehouse full of brandy. It must have taken them half the night to carry it out. And can you believe it, not a soul saw a thing."

"Sad times," echoed Richard, smiling.

"Stop laughing at me. I know that tone," Christian chided.

"I'm not, there is much in here that you would not want to lose," Richard had wandered down one of the closely packed aisles. He reached a pile of long wooden crates, wrapped in linen and sat himself down on the top one.

Christian's eyes narrowed but he said nothing.

"What did you say to me when I was here last?" Richard mused. "Oh yes, I remember, attention to detail."

"You didn't say much last time you were here," Christian countered defensively.

"I was, if you remember, in a hurry. Now I'm not, so satisfy my curiosity, if you will; tell me why a wine merchant would have nine boxes of flintlocks in his warehouse?"

"Ten actually," Christian corrected him smiling, "I will tell you, but only if you'll come to dinner."

☦

Christian's wife never quite knew how to take her husband's friend. Charming, attentive: as a guest he was perfect always taking the time to include her in the conversation. Regardless, she just wanted the evening to reach that point when the meal was done so she could retire. There came from him an air of danger, of recklessness. She knew from Christian some of the antics they had been involved in before he had wed her. She was quite sure she did not want her respectable merchant husband involved in anything less than legal.

This time was worse. Christian had even told her before their guest arrived not to use his name in front of any of the servants, also not to mention his visit either, in passing, to any of her women friends. It seemed that Christian's charming guest was, at the moment, wanted for some crime, as yet she could not persuade her husband to reveal what it was. Closing the door on the two men, she left them, feeling for the first time that evening able to breathe easily.

The latch on the door clicked loudly and the pair were alone, the only noise for the moment the crackle of the fire and sound of wine pouring as Christian filled their glasses.

"This is very nice," Richard said, genuinely appreciative swilling the wine around the inside of the glass.

"One of the benefits of my trade: my house shall not want for good wine," Christian sounded pleased.

"Or flintlocks," Richard added. "Everyone's house should be well supplied with those, don't you think?"

"You don't waste any time do you?" Christian responded reproachfully.

"I'm genuinely interested. Come on, tell me." Richard pressed; Christian had his full attention.

"It's not as exciting as you might think," Christian said, knowing that in fact the tale would be one Richard would find most interesting, it was also one Christian was going to most wholeheartedly enjoy telling. His anticipation was heightened because, as yet, it was a story he had been forced to keep very much to himself.

"I'll take the risk," Richard leant back comfortably in his chair. "Come on, begin. I can see you are bursting to entertain me."

Christian smiled. It was a tale he wanted to tell. "Alright. It's quite simple really. They were purchased for the King's army by Northumberland when Edward was King. He ordered flintlocks and crossbows. Northumberland was preparing to bolster himself and his cause should Edward fail..."

"As he assuredly did and Northumberland had plans of his own, had he only known where they would lead him," Richard mused.

"Who is telling this tale?" Christian reprimanded him.

"Sorry, you were saying?" Richard replied, apologetically.

"As I said, Northumberland, allied to the Grey's was trying to consolidate his position. A force well-supplied with Italian arms would have been an asset when Edward died. So he had ordered the arms, the purchase had Edward's backing and the royal seal approved by the Council. A part-payment was made, with the balance due upon satisfactory delivery of the order, a common enough transaction. They came in from Italy by ship all the way, but by the time the whole order had arrived here, Edward was dead. Not long after Northumberland was dispatched to the hereafter by Mary, and the current

Crown wanted nothing to do with an expensive arms order from Italy."

"Right, so what happened next?" Richard was leaning forward now, elbows on the table, all his attention on Christian.

"The order arrived and a part-payment had been made, as I said, with the balance due on delivery. The shipment was accompanied by a Frederico Monsinetto. He arrived here with the order and hoped to take back payment with him; however, when he landed England was in turmoil and he didn't know who to press for the balance. Northumberland was trying to secure the throne for the Grey's and Mary was gathering her supporters and setting out for London. Monsinetto did not know where to turn and he had a need to find somewhere to store the order until he could find out who the buyer would be."

"Ah, so you offered your warehouse and stored it for him? How kind of you Christian," Richard interjected smiling.

"I didn't do it for free. So I have Monsinetto's cargo, and he waits until Mary has taken the throne and tries to complete the deal and get payment for the order. But they want none of it, telling him that the order was placed by Northumberland and Mary will not honour it. So poor Monsinetto can't take it all back to Italy; he hasn't the money to secure a ship to return the cargo. So he sets off back to Italy, alone, and leaves his cargo secure in my warehouse."

"This is what, two and half years ago?" Richard commented.

"Will you leave me to tell the tale?" Christian admonished again. "So, he sets off back to Italy, and after about six months I hear his boat floundered off the Spanish coast and all lives were lost. The ship sank about two and half years ago and his cargo has been sitting in there ever since. I'm sure that people have been looking for it, but obviously Monsinetto was the only person who knew where he had left the cargo. So far no-one has knocked on my door to ask me about it. If the truth be known and they did come looking for it, everything is there, I would be handing them a large bill for storage, I can tell you. There are forty-two boxes in total."

Richard choked on his wine. "Forty-two?"

"Aye, that stopped you in your tracks didn't it," Christian smiled with some satisfaction.

"This time you have amazed me. I only saw ten, though," Richard was puzzled.

"I've had the rest repacked, so they looked like wine casks, just in case anyone took too much of a close look," Christian supplied.

"Do you know how much it must be worth?" Richard asked.

"Not much; I can't sell it. If I start trading in Italian flintlocks and crossbows, then it won't take too long before someone finds out where Monsinetto left his cargo. There are forty-two cases Richard, all full. You need an army to take that kind of a consignment. It also needs to be one that is not going to ask too many questions about where they came from. So as you can see, it's not the gift it looked like it could be," Christian concluded sadly.

"I do see your problem." Richard agreed. "I'm assuming, because I know you so well, that you indeed know exactly what you have?"

Christian feigned a hurt expression. "Of course."

"Do you want to show me?" Richard asked.

"I might," Christian accepted. "And I know you so well, that I can practically hear your mind working even from the other side of the table."

Richard smiled. "Well then, perhaps between us we can find a new home for Monsinetto's cargo."

"I have records; I'll share them with you later. Anyway, tell me, the meeting with your father; did it go well? Did you find your brother?"

"I did, or at least what's left of him. They had got him into Marshalsea on some charge. He has had a fairly rough time," Richard didn't want to speak of Jack's torment.

Christian grimaced. "Marshalsea is indeed a Hell-on-earth, especially for those with no coin. Did you get him out?"

"I did. I thought him likely to die, but it seems he is made of stubborn stuff and isn't finished with life just yet." Richard changed the subject as he did not want to dwell on recent events. "Now stop trying to divert me, tell me more about this cargo. I want to know everything."

Christian relented producing the inventory of Monsinetto's cargo and Richard committed it to memory. It was indeed a huge opportunity.

Christian smiled. It was not often that he had the opportunity to impress his friend; it was usually the other way around. Richard was still staring at the neatly-penned inventory.

"Two and half years! In that time no-one has come to look for them?" Richard was shaking his head in disbelief.

"No-one. Where would they look? I've been very careful - I've sold none. Save yourself, no-one else knows. They are all, bar two, safely in the warehouse," Christian had a wide, pleased smile on his face.

"Bar two?" Richard repeated carefully.

Christian, hands on the table, pushed himself up from his seat. "As beautiful as my ledgers are, they cannot compare with these," he gestured at the coffer behind him. Lifting the lid, he reached in and removed a long, cloth-wrapped flintlock. He lay it on the table in front of Richard, then next to it he placed another, shorter bundle.

Richard smiled and set his fingers to the wrappings. "Christian, you know me too well."

"I knew you would want to see them." Christian watched with undisguised pleasure as Richard unpacked the weapons. The careful knots holding the cloth in place undid neatly, soon Richard had set the long flintlock musket and its matching pistol on the table. Christian stared at them; to him they were beautiful in their own right. Innovative and heralding a new era, their power and supremacy, proclaimed by the craftsmanship were etched into every aspect of the guns.

"Do you know how it works?" Christian couldn't help himself from asking, "I've seen them before, of course, but never in action."

Richard stopped turning over the musket he held. "Sometimes, something simple can be very effective. This is the hammer." Richard showed him the intricately carved 'S'-shaped lever on the side. "In the clamp at the end would be a thin sharpened flint; this screw here holds it fast. You half-cock this," Richard clicked back the hammer until the lever stood proud of the barrel, "then a set amount of gunpowder goes into the barrel. After that you push down a lead ball wrapped in paper. The paper makes sure the bullet holds tight and the charge remains fixed behind it."

Richard pushed up a second lever next to the hammer. "This is the frizzen. Push this and the pan is open and in there you pour a small amount of gunpowder and then put the frizzen back down to keep it contained in the pan." Christian watched closely.

Richard hoisted the musket to his shoulder. "Now you fully cock the hammer" - there was a metallic click as the flintlock armed - "then press the trigger." With a loud clunk the hammer sprang forward. "The flint would strike down the frizzen and spark as a fire steel does, then it forces open the pan and the sparks light the powder. The powder in the pan ignites the charge in the barrel and fires the shot."

"How does lighting the charge in the pan on the side fire the powder in the barrel though?"

Christian tipped the gun towards him to view the mechanism more closely.

"Here, look." Richard pushed the frizzen back. "The pan is made like a dish, and if you look carefully there is small hole at the back leading to the inside of the barrel. When the flint ignites the powder it flashes through this hole." Richard pointed and Christian peered closely at the metal workings. "Can you see it?" Christian nodded. "Then it lights the larger charge in the barrel."

"When you explain it like that, there's very little to go wrong with it." Christian picked up the pistol. "And does this works the same?" He half-cocked the hammer and pushed the frizzen forward as Richard had.

"Much the same, though I believe this" - he hefted the musket in his hand - "is quite a bit more accurate than the pistol."

"Stands to reason, I suppose, as that one has the longer barrel," Christian fully-cocked the hammer. Trapping his thumb behind the mechanism, he swore loudly.

Richard laughed, "Remind me, what was it we used to call you?"

"I remember well." Christian sucked at his thumb where a blood blister was forming. "Clumsy Carter, I suppose not without reason."

"These are extremely fine; are they all the same?" Richard asked, running his hands over the beautifully polished wood stock.

"All the same," Christian confirmed, holding his thumb out so he could examine the damage, "and there are two cases with what I take to be spare parts in as well."

"You do know there are enough here to outfit a small army?" Richard ventured, gauging Christian's reaction.

"That is what they were ordered for. Northumberland pledged the Crown's money; these weapons were to have been decisive in keeping him in power. Not that they did him a lot of good." Christian mused. "The problem is they are so distinctive: if they could speak it would be in Italian."

"They are, you're right," Richard ran his hands over the elaborately decorated mechanism on the pistol, "Venete e lasciatemi fare l'amore con te."

"They speak to you of money, that's why you love them," Christian scoffed.

"They might be the closest I shall ever get to a wealthy wife. We need to find a buyer, there must be one," Richard said thoughtfully.

Christian leaned across the table, a serious note in his voice, "Now be careful Richard. I've kept this quiet a long time, I don't want the wolves at my door."

Richard met his eyes. "Trust me, I would do nothing to harm you or you family. And I'll take no action without your full agreement."

"Let's drink to that," Christian refilled Richard's glass and then partially missed his own, leaving a mulberry stain spreading across the table between them.

†

Richard considered Christian's news when he was back in his own room later on. It was indeed a huge opportunity. The cargo was worth nothing less than a fortune. Christian had not been able to resist placing a valuation on the weapons. The pistols and muskets were worth 40 shillings a piece, the crossbows 20 shillings each. There were thirty cases of muskets with fifty per case. Plus five cases of pistols with one hundred per case. The value of these alone was over seven thousand pounds; even if they sold for half of that, the total was still a staggering figure.

On top of that were seven cases of crossbows with thirty per case, Christian had a value on these of another six hundred pounds. These figures did not include the spare parts, powder holders, rods, bolts and moulds for shot that were also stored in Christian's warehouse. It was these extra cases that made the cargo so valuable. Anyone spending such an amount in munitions would want to know they could support them and that their investment would be a long term one.

Richard lay in the dark, listening to his brother snore in the other room. He was, for once, not jealous of Jack's ability to sleep. He had a puzzle, a challenge, but more importantly an opportunity; he would be damned if he was going to let this one go. If he could sell Christian's cargo it would provide enough gold, even when split between them, to make them both wealthy beyond imagining. His father and his bloody family name, he would then have little use for. If Mary died in childbirth then there was a good chance that England would fall to Elizabeth, if this happened he would not need to hide away. Richard cursed himself silently; he knew better than to indulge in wishful thinking: that was a fool's pastime. Mary was Queen and, until that changed, there was little point dwelling on what the future might or might not hold.

†

The next day Richard left the meeting with Fairfax with a list of instructions to carry out and, more importantly, a date. He needed to contact the captain of the Dutch Flower and request safe passage for six additional passengers. The Lady Elizabeth would be accompanied by a lady of their choosing to attend to her needs and four others to ensure her safety on the journey.

Richard had also requested that he also be included in the group taking passage on the ship. He had easily convinced the group that he too would like the opportunity to escape a Catholic England. The only real objection had come from Thomas Cresswell who had suspected Richard of trying to claim a free passage at their expense. However, when he had assured them that he would be financing his own crossing it had been agreed that he could join the group.

Richard had further offered to help on the night of the fire and attach himself to the group hoping to steal Elizabeth away; however Fairfax declined his offer, feeling he would rather use just his own trusted men. Fairfax however told him he would send word to Richard when they were ready to go to the Dutch Flower so he could join the party going to the ship. Richard reasoned that if they did indeed manage to acquire Elizabeth then at least he would be included in the group taking her to the Dutch Flower, from there he might be able to ensure her safety and frustrate their plans.

The Captain was Hugo Drego; as Christian Carter had indicated, he was as solid and reliable as the ship he ran. The carriage of additional passengers wishing to escape the Catholic threats was not a problem. Drego, a Protestant himself, was sympathetic to their plight and the fare to Holland was a reasonable sum. Drego showed Richard the two cabins on board that they would have full use of for the passage; one was his own, which he was happy to vacate. Both were clean, adequately furnished and comfortable enough for the crossing.

He had the dates on which the Dutch Flower proposed to be in London during the next two months, plus he knew where to find Hugo when the ship was berthed. Fairfax was happy with the passage fee. It was agreed that after the Lady had been rescued from her enforced captivity, they would arrange for her to be taken quickly to the ship. All Richard had to do was to book the passage now that they had finalised a date.

Richard returned from the meeting and cast his cloak over a chair, moving to stand in front of the fire where Jack was sitting warmed by the flames.

"I was most wholly wrong; they do intend to go ahead but not soon. They have a date of March 7th," Richard said in response to Jack's enquiring look.

"That's nearly six weeks away," Jack straightened in his chair. "What are we going to do until then? I thought you said they would need to act soon before Elizabeth was taken back to Court?"

"I did think so. Fairfax has friends at Court and he firmly believes plans have been put in place to move the Lady's household back to Court, but not until the end of March. They don't want to leave it any longer as they fear that Phillip will take Elizabeth to Court. If he does, there is not a chance of them ever getting anywhere near her," Richard conceded. "And on that point they might be right. Phillip has four months to wait to see if he will have the answer to the succession, in that time it would be wise for him to keep Elizabeth close."

"In case someone else decided to take a controlling hand in her affairs," Jack supplied helpfully.

"Indeed. I am just surprised that they have not done this already. Our best hope would be that they do move her household to Court before the 7th, but I fear time is not going to be on our side," Richard mused.

Chapter Ten

Durham Place was the most easterly of the houses along the east side of the Strand. Dating back to 1220 and built by the incumbent Bishop of Salisbury, it had been a royal palace for the Prince Bishops. Edward VI, in fulfilling his father's will, had granted it to his sister, Elizabeth, in early 1549 and it had been hers ever since.

The house was built around three sides of an extensive courtyard. A red brick front housed two stories and glistened with no fewer than thirty windows. The fourth side housed the entrance and gatehouse and, at the back, a short garden sloped gently to the Thames. A siding cut into the river meant the house had a private jetty and immediate access to the river. Fairfax's townhouse stood next along the Strand, elegant and spacious, yet dwarfed by the huge sprawl of Elizabeth's manor.

Jack felt out of place. He elbowed Richard as they rode side-by-side along the road. "Isn't that Somerset House?" he asked, inclining his head in the direction of the most impressive house they had passed yet.

"It is," confirmed Richard. "I can remember when it was open fields and we used to ride there." Pointing, he added, "over there were three inns and the Church of the Nativity of Our Lady. As Lord Protector, he didn't have difficulty acquiring them and levelling them to build this. It's said the altar steps are still under the dais in the great hall."

"It didn't do him much good did it? It can't have even been finished when Mary sent him to the block," Jack commented, shaking his head.

"Barely finished," agreed Richard.

"So who owns is it now?" Jack asked.

Richard smiled, "Thomas Tresham."

Jack groaned inwardly, "And Tresham is...?"

"Grand Prior in England, of the Knights of St John," Richard replied.

"That lot! Supposed to be bound by vows of chastity and poverty. I'm not seeing anyone living in there being particularly poor." Jack scoffed.

"Nothing to stop you joining them," Richard commented.

"There are just two problems with that. Firstly I don't need to take a vow of poverty, it's a permanent state which I am unhappily well acquainted with. And secondly, I am not making my life worse by taking a vow of chastity to mire it even further," Jack replied. "You'd like it though. Poverty, chastity and an overwhelming sense of self-importance; you'd get on with them fine."

Richard shot him a sideways look and pushed his horse on a little faster.

Jack caught up quickly; he hadn't finished. "Harry's cousin is in the Order. Remind me, what is it say they say about arrogance?"

"Arrogance diminishes wisdom." Richard replied darkly.

"No, not that one. Ah, I remember," Jack grinned. "It's only arrogance if you are wrong."

"Are you trying to annoy me?" Richard responded tersely.

"Hardly," Jack goaded. "When were you ever wrong?"

"Can we leave this until later? I know you are not happy with what I am trying to do," Richard was trying to remain calm.

"When I was drunk it sounded like a good idea," Jack continued to annoy Richard. "Maybe I just need another drink or two."

"Everything sounds like a good idea to you when you're drunk," Richard retorted. "I accept that you have let me know your true feelings. Now either help me, or shut up. Those are your choices."

"Oh, I'll help," Jack leaned from the saddle so he was closer to Richard. "Just remember, I'll be right there to remind you."

Before he could sit back up, Richard grabbed his arm and pulled him closer. "Just remember where you were a scant eight weeks ago." He let go quickly, Jack struggled to retain his balance.

"Alright, I'll say not a word more," Jack snapped. They continued the journey in silence, travelling twice more down the Strand passing Elizabeth's house, Durham Place.

Richard broke the silence as they rode back to their lodgings, "What did you see?"

"Not much to see; if they are lucky and the smoke blows over the wall then there is only one exit, that's from the gatehouse at the side, then down to the Strand. It's a wide street and there are no paths off it for a hundred yards at least. So if they are lucky - and they'd bloody well need to be - and the smoke comes from Fairfax's house in the direction God demands, then they'd leave through the gatehouse and go left down the Strand. If they have men in the street then they will undoubtedly meet her." Jack summarised.

"A fair assessment," Richard agreed. "Any other ways out that you saw?"

"None," Jack was wary, suspecting a trap.

"Alright, any other ways out that you can think of?" Richard said with exaggerated patience.

"You're doing it again," Jack complained.

"Doing what?" Richard said innocently.

"Treating me like you treat everyone else," Jack retorted. "Like a bloody idiot."

"Alright. A vice, I'm sure." Richard admitted his palms open.

Jack glowered at him before he continued. "At the back of the house it will connect with the river, there'll be moorings and also it will have its own private barge."

Richard smiled. Jack continued, "The back of the house will be dark, the river darker still. If we were to tether a boat to the bank someway upstream it's unlikely to be noticed: if you want to get someone out of the house that's the way we go. We go backward, rather than forward, away from Fairfax and his mob." Jack paused and looked at Richard's face. "But you've already thought this through. Already have a boat in place, I would guess. Am I right?"

"Probably," Richard conceded.

"Why do you bother asking my opinion when your course is already set? It is, Richard, bloody annoying. So you plan to take her out down the river?" Jack finished.

"If we enter the back of the house, we can wait to see if Fairfax's orchard sets alight. If it does then we can be helpful neighbours perhaps and guide the ladies to safety," Richard outlined the action they could take.

"Sounds too easy; why would they come with us?" Jack was suspicious.

"The lady knows me, remember," Richard reminded him.

"In most scenarios that should set her in the opposite direction if she has any bloody sense about her," Jack scoffed. "Then where do we take her?"

"Either back into the keeping of Travers, or very soon after the fire starts the Queen's men will also arrive and we can safely deliver her to them," Richard ignored Jack's remark.

"Well let's hope it goes well," Jack said, having a feeling that it probably wouldn't.

✝

They returned to Richard's lodgings. Jack opened the door and an unfamiliar tang met his nose. "What's that smell?" Jack recoiled on the threshold.

"Clean, that's what that smell is." Lizbet stood in the room, skirts kirtled up, hair tied in a neat pile on her head, sleeves tucked up to her elbows, a brush in one hand and a cloth in the other. "Not that you would ever be acquainted with it," Lizbet prodded Jack in the chest.

"For God's sake woman, open a window!" Richard exclaimed, wholly in agreement with his brother. "It smells like an apothecary's den in here."

"It's a bit of rosemary and rue that's all. I've scrubbed the floors and the table as well; it's clean, and it's stopping that way. There are fresh rushes, new candles, the bedding has gone to be washed and here"- Lizbet delved into her pocket, - "is your change." Lizbet reached down and taking Jack's hand, opened it and let four coins slide neatly from her hand onto Jack's palm. Then she tapped him under the chin. "Close that or you'll be catching flies." With that she left, banging the door closed behind her with a swing of her hips.

Richard laughed. "That is something you didn't see coming! Where did you leave your money for her to find?"

"I didn't," Jack pulled out his purse and inspected the contents. "Cheeky wench, one of her many talents. Richard watch your pockets with that one."

"It's a rare day when you meet a pickpocket and then get some of it back," Richard laughed. "I think Lizbet is after more permanent employment," he added, casting his eyes around the room.

"I'll not complain I admit it looks better. I might even invite a woman back here myself now," Jack contemplated. Picking up the cards and seating himself, he idly began shuffling the deck.

"And what would Lizbet say about that?" Richard asked, pulling up a chair to the table to join Jack. The wood was paler, freshly scoured and smooth. He ran his palms appreciatively over the cool wood.

"She'll not mind, she'll be out now turning a trick on the side," Jack began to deal out the cards between them, setting the remainder of the deck down with a heavy thump.

"Meaning?" Richard looked up from the cards. Jack had taken his hand, but Richard's cards lay still scattered in front of him where Jack had dealt them.

Jack met his eyes, having heard the edge in Richard's voice. "I meant she's only a..."

"Don't," warned Richard, "don't finish that sentence."

Jack stood suddenly, cards tumbling to the floor. Grabbing his brother's jacket he hauled him close. Richard felt Jack's breath on his face; he didn't pull away but matched his brother's stare. Their eyes locked, grey and blue, angry and haunted. It was Jack who spoke first. "So, now you're Lizbet's champion are you?"

Richard wrenched himself free. "I'm nobody's champion. You are a bastard, Jack. Do you think of yourself as such? I'm an outcast, a traitor, do I think of myself as such?"

"I'm not a bastard!" retorted Jack, banging his fist on the table, sending the suits to dance.

"Exactly!" Richard shouted back. "I'm not a traitor and Lizbet is not..." with effort he lowered his voice, "a whore."

"For God's sake!" Jack pushed his hands through his hair. "You never waste a chance do you? To show me the difference between us."

"Difference?" Richard was genuinely perplexed. "What difference?"

"You got everything I never got," Jack retorted, "Everything! Servants, an education, the best horses, the best clothes. What did I get? A bloody straw bed, sometimes, food maybe and my backside kicked from breakfast time to evensong, that's what I got. And now you start bloody lecturing me with your bloody humanist principles."

"It took a long time coming, you've been looking for a fight all day. I'm glad we got there in the end," Richard moved a pace or two backward from Jack.

"What do you mean, in the end?" Jack was shouting now, his anger barely contained.

"You think you are hamstrung because of your start in life. It's not your fault; the fault lies with the world," Richard said sarcastically.

"I'd be a bloody sight better off if I'd had your shoes." Jack's hand swept across the table, the abrupt angry gesture clearing it of what few cards remained following his previous outburst.

"Really? Why, what have I got that you haven't?" Richard's temper was barely in check.

"I've told you," Jack growled.

Richard retook his chair. "Sit down!"

Jack didn't move.

"Sit down! We'll weigh the scales, shall we?" Richard held his brother's eyes with his own leaden stare.

Jack grudgingly sat.

"So, I got the feather bed, the education, a comfy and untroubled life, so you think," Richard supplied. Jack didn't reply; he just glowered at his brother. "And you, what did you get?"

"Bloody nothing," Jack half-shouted.

"Really?" Richard's expression was incredulous. "I've rarely seen a man better than you with a sword. I've seen few who could best you on a horse. You read and write English well, Latin passably so, but don't like anyone to know." Richard opened his hands. "So how did you not get opportunities as well? Or did this all happen by some accident?"

"Aye, I got to attend classes with Harry, as his bloody whipping boy. I learnt at the hands of my Masters, believe me they were cruel hands," Jack stormed.

"Our father was no better to me. I'll not compete with you Jack. Life has not been easy for either of us. Can we not draw a truce?"

"But you still got..."

Richard cut him off, exasperated, "For pity's sake! I got what? What do you really feel you are missing? Tell me! Tell me and I shall get it for you?"

"You got an education. If I see you talking with the lawyers' apprentices in the taproom, I can't join you, can I?" Jack spat back.

"Why not? Do you not have a mind of your own?" Richard retorted.

"I wouldn't know where to bloody start," Jack knew it sounded poor and petulant.

"If you must know, I got one year at Trinity in Cambridge; that was it, one bloody year. Then our father decided it was an expense he could do without." Jack heard bitterness in his voice; Richard rarely opened a window into his soul. "I've leant more by my own enquiry. You've got an able mind, Jack. Use it. Maybe you can free it of some of the prejudices that you harbour there."

"Prejudices?" Jack shouted. "How dare you accuse me of such!"

"Jack, just ask yourself how you see Lizbet? She's a whore; you can't see past that, can you? It colours the way you talk to her, the way you treat her. That's her rung on the ladder of life and there she'll remain in your mind. Clement might be a piece of snivelling filth that would be better crushed in the gutter, but in your ordered little world, brother, he's far ahead of Lizbet on that ladder, isn't he?" Richard tried to keep his voice level but Jack heard the anger behind it. "So who is the better person? The one who tried to have you killed and used his letters and learning to get you into Marshalsea, or the one who wiped your arse for you and holds you when you scream in the night?"

There was horror on Jack's face.

"I can hardly not hear you can I? She'll not let me near you, she wishes to save you the shame. So who is the better person in your badly-ordered bloody mind? It is still Clement, isn't it?" Richard pushed his chair back and it toppled and banged heavily on the floor. "Isn't it?"

Jack was on his feet, his face white with anger.

"How can you say that?" Jack accused, "I hate Clement, he's..."

"That's not what I said. It isn't how you feel about him, it's how you regard him. He's lettered, he's a lawyer, he's better than Lizbet, better than Roddy who runs the taproom down there. His rank makes him better than any of the men who rode with you: better than Dan, better than Froggy, better than Mat."

Jack pressed his hands into his eyes. "What are you trying to do?" he yelled.

"I'm trying to make you bloody well think, Jack. Is that so very hard?" Richard was infuriated. "If you had, you might not have ended in Marshalsea."

It was too much. Jack couldn't stop himself. "The fault of that was yours. You bloody well left me!"

"For God's sake Jack, I was half dead with the last rites ringing in my ears. What would you have had me do?" Richard knew that they had finally reached the argument Jack wanted to have.

"You'd already left me, for her," Jack delivered the accusation quietly, his anger white-hot. "Her and the damned Reformist cause."

Richard's face darkened.

Jack couldn't stop, nor did he want to, his words sharpened by the cold pain of . "And when you could, you came back here, to London, for her. You left me. Damn you to Hell for that. Damn you to Hell!" Jack swung his fist at Richard; it was a blow he had wanted to deliver for a long time. Richard, seeing it coming, trapped Jack's wrist before the fist made contact. Then he dragged Jack forwards, pulling him off-balance. An arm locked around his neck and he had Jack kneeling before him, caught in a hold he could not escape.

"And that, little brother, I didn't learn at university," he released Jack, roughly pushing him away.

Jack wasn't finished. Richard thought he was about to speak, but instead, catlike, he sprang. Jack brought all his weight to bear down on the other man, bringing them both sprawling to the floor. On top, an arm jammed across Richard's throat - Jack had the upper hand. Richard fought back but Jack's brutal hold kept him down.

Releasing his grasp on Richard's arm for a second, Jack grabbed his brother's wrist in a vice-like grip, he forced his arm back towards the floor and onto the outstretched leg of the chair. Jack knew what he meant to do. Press the arm against the raised wooden rail, then push it on harder until the bone snapped. Richard realised as well as soon as he felt the pressure of the square leg in the back of his arm, then he began to fight back with every ounce of strength he had.

Jack's hold was a savage one, his arm across his brother's neck was restricting his breathing. Richard realised he was going to lose consciousness before the bone broke. Silently he congratulated himself on doing such a good job of raising the bigger man's temper. Then there a scream; at first he didn't realise it was his own.

Jack released him as if he had just been burnt. Richard had screamed and then stopped suddenly as he blacked out. Jack's face was wet; he smeared away the angry tears, breathing raggedly.

That was how Lizbet found them as she sailed through the door, a song on her lips abruptly dying.

"Oh my God! What's happened?" The basket she held dropped to the floor. Falling to her knees at Richard's side, a quick glance between the prone man and Jack kneeling next to him gave her the answer. "For the Lord's sake, have you killed him?" Lizbet slapped Richard's face and was rewarded with a groan. "Thank the Lord for that." She slapped him four or five more times until his eyes unwillingly opened and focused on her face.

"Lizbet, stop please," Richard croaked.

"Help him up, you bloody dolt." Lizbet shoved Jack hard to revive his attention.

Jack moved automatically to help; grasping hold of Richard's jacket, he pulled him to a sitting position.

"Can you stand?" Lizbet asked, receiving no reply. "Jack, get him under one arm and I'll get the other, we'll put him on my bed over there."

Jack lifted him easily; he was surprised by how light his brother was until he remembered Richard telling him of the weeks of illness he'd suffered. Jack realised shamefully that he was not the only one to have been so unwell. Richard also had still had not fully recovered. Through his clothing he felt bones with little flesh on them and something else as well. Laying him down on the bed, he pulled open Richard's doublet and saw what he had felt: blood. That was why Richard had screamed; the hold he'd had on him had torn open the sword wound and blood was trickling down his arm.

Lizbet was on her feet, panic on her face. Had Jack used a knife on his brother? "I'll get Lucy right away, you stop here."

"Stop, Lizbet, please, help me get this off him." Jack was pulling the doublet from over the bleeding arm and Lizbet helped, holding the inert body up while Jack pulled the material free. "Get me a knife." Lizbet looked at him askance as he met her eyes. "I need to cut this linen free."

The cloth removed, Jack viewed the extent of the wound. The flesh hadn't knitted together properly and the wound was a raw purple colour, swollen and angry.

"Let me get Lucy, please?" Lizbet pleaded, moving already towards the door.

"Alright lass, you get her, but before you go get me some water, needle and thread." The wound was a mess, but Jack's assessing gaze was already working out how he could piece it back together.

"You can't touch him; what are you going to do? What do you know about healing?" Lizbet protested.

"I've not stitched men back together, but I've healed up many horses in my time. I don't care what the Church says, they are skin, flesh and blood on the inside, same as we are."

Jack, bent to his task, didn't see Lucy Sharp watching him from the doorway. The flesh was swollen and it was hard to see where the cut needed to mend. The gap closed as he working along the wound, drawing the soft edges together with the thread. Eventually, all that was left was a neat line of black stitch marks.

"I'll not be letting you loose with my mending, lad, but that's not too bad," Lucy commented when he rocked back on his heels, the job done.

Jack rubbed his bloody hands over his tired face. "You want to try doing that when there's a hoof at one end and a set of teeth at the other, set on paring you to the bone. Then it's not so easy."

"You get out of the way. Lizbet fetch me that onion and hazel balm we used on this big lout, will you. I'm sure there's some left," Lucy instructed, Lizbet all the time eying Jack suspiciously.

When Lucy was gone, Lizbet took his arm in a surprisingly tight hold. The relationship she had with the elder brother was entirely different from that she had with Richard. "What the hell have you done to him?" she demanded.

"Let me be." Jack roughly pulled his arm from her hold. Lizbet swore as two of her nails bent painfully backwards.

"I'll not. He's had you cared for, I saw how he was when he thought you were dead. What did you do that to him for?" Lizbet was not going to be put off. "You could have killed him; it looks like you tried."

"I didn't mean to," Jack had the heels of his palms pressed into his eyes.

"Christ, well I'd not like to see you when you mean to then!" Lizbet picked up one of the still wet, red-stained cloths Lucy had used and threw it in his face.

It was too much for Jack to bear and he caught Lizbet's arm in a vice-like grip. Jack saw the fear on her face. He released her, realising what he had been about to do. Turning his back on her, he left her alone with his brother.

✝

Lizbet sat back on the edge of the bed and admired her friend's work. Lucy had wrapped the wound in linen layered with a poultice to draw out any poison. Then she put half a spoon of dwale in some warm wine. He slept silently now, his head on the pillow turned away from the injured shoulder.

About to draw the cover up over his chest, she stopped. Lizbet was, quite properly, wary of him: he'd hit her twice and she knew he'd think nothing of doing it a third time. He demanded obedience and she had learned her lesson. His body, like Jack's, spoke of a violent past. When Jack had stripped him she'd seen his back crisscrossed with the imprint left by a whip. She had been shocked; some of the tacks deeply marked the skin while others were just fine white lines. There was another old scar tracing a white line over his breast up to his collarbone - a sword or knife cut she guessed.

Awake she would not dare, but drugged and sleeping was a different matter and her curious hand couldn't help itself. It hovered, indecisive only for a moment, before she gently drew her fingers along the line of the scar. The ridge, where the thickened skin had healed, led her hand across his collarbone and onto his shoulder; once it had been a deep cut. Lifting her hand away, she made to raise the blanket over his chilling body.

"Don't stop."

"Oh Jesus Christ," Lizbet gasped under her breath.

"Be quiet, don't stop," was all he said.

Lizbet hesitated, her breath caught in her throat, heart hammering in her chest; she couldn't have been more afraid if she'd been caught stealing.

"I said, don't stop," the voice was barely audible.

A shaking hand resumed her delicate exploration of his body. She heard his breath escape, recognised the senses behind it and realised he didn't intend to hurt her. Careful still, Lizbet increased the pressure at her fingertips as they travelled over his skin. Confidence growing, she raised her fingers so now her nails gently raked his skin, their passage releasing a ragged gasp from his lips. With his good arm he reached up, his eyes still closed, found her neck and drew her to him, kissing her softly, gently caressing the side of her face and neck with his hand.

Lizbet's body was as taut as that of a startled cat. She sorely wished he would let her go.

"You're kissing me but thinking of another," Lizbet whispered. Maybe her words would break the spell.

"Be quiet..." An arm around her shoulders, he pulled her face to his neck. Her long hair lay across his chest and as she brought her lips to kiss him, she was rewarded with a sharp intake of breath. Nervously she continued, sometimes kissing, sometimes caressing, breathing just hard enough for his skin to sense the passage of her breath.

She heard the step on the stairs outside the room and sat back up with a look of pure relief on her face, pulling the rough blanket over him. He was quiet and his breathing shallow and even; perhaps now he was asleep. Lizbet knew the medicine he needed and resolved to get it for him - she'd rather not have to get that close to him again. Feeling very much like she had just had a lucky escape she left him, hoping the dwale would keep his memories from him.

Chapter Eleven

Gardiner did not like Phillip. He hid his dislike behind an austere mask of deference and bowed low. "You wanted to see me, Your Majesty?"

"Yes I did, come and walk with me," Phillip replied. Gardiner gratefully straightened and joined Phillip in the long gallery overlooking the wet and misty gardens. The wide corridor, with its marble diamond floor and tapestry-hung walls provided an indoor space when the weather outside was inclement. Windows running from floor to ceiling every few paces admitted the poor winter's light, the fires set in the walls warmed the air.

Gardiner knew better than to speak, he walked silently next to Phillip waiting for him to break the silence. He was slight man who burned with nervous energy. His confinement within Mary's palaces, whilst waiting to see if his Queen could secure the throne with an heir, was nothing short of a prison sentence. His father, Charles, had been heir to three of Europe's leading dynasties: among his titles were King of Spain, Holy Roman Emperor and Duke of

Burgundy. A lifetime of struggle and dynamic rule had left his father a hollow shell.

Dispatches between Spain and England passed and re-passed as the lines of communication between Phillip and his father remained open. The earnest wish his father had once held, that they add England to the empire Phillip would inherit, was now lessening. The distance between Spain and England was too great and his father was failing.

The last letter Phillip had read with both excitement and shock: his father wished to abdicate. Phillip longed to be at his father's side. His father was world-weary; Phillip knew his place now should be in Spain. There were others waiting and Phillip greatly feared that his father's brother, Ferdinand, may move to take his titles. Phillip lay awake night after night; it could not have been more painful if he had been chained to this miserable damp country.

There was now too much at stake. It was known amongst Phillip's nobles that he would return to Spain as soon as the issue of the child was finalised. Mary and Phillip both counted the weeks and days, but for very different reasons. Politics were now the daily bread of the Spanish at Mary's Court and it was becoming increasingly obvious that the custody of Mary's sister was a key issue. Phillip's own father had mentioned that if Mary remained childless then Phillip should bring Elizabeth back to the Spanish Court. There he could look to secure the lady a good Catholic husband, but in reality it would mean that they held the English heir to the throne, should the need arise. It had been mentioned more than once that Phillip marry the younger sister.

"My Lord Bishop," Phillip spoke at last - they had already travelled one full length of the corridor in silence. "Her Majesty will go into confinement soon and I've a mind to bring the Lady's sister, Elizabeth, to Court. I am informed you are in charge of her household?"

"Her Majesty did leave me with the task of organising her household, I believe I have done as she asked," Gardiner said a little guardedly, wondering where this was going.

"Indeed, I am sure all is correct. I am aware that you have been taking time to educate the lady on spiritual matters as well?" Phillip questioned.

"I have, Your Majesty." Gardiner was wary indeed now: he had no idea how much Phillip knew of Elizabeth's reformist views.

Phillip smiled, detecting the note in Gardiner's voice. "I am aware that there are," he paused before continuing, "difficulties between the ladies; however is this not always the case with sisters?"

Gardiner declined to answer. He saw the religious divide between them as more than mere 'difficulties', but he inclined his head anyway in acceptance of Phillip's words.

"I have only met with the Lady a few times and then, you understand, they were high state occasions. Soon she will come to Court when Her Majesty goes into confinement and I would like to meet with Elizabeth before then." Phillip concluded.

Gardiner wondered what this had to do with him. "I'm sure the Princess Elizabeth would be honoured."

"I'm sure she would be," Phillip accepted, then continued to the reason for Gardiner's summons. "However Her Majesty does not think it is such a good idea. I thought that, as one of her foremost advisors, you could ensure that the Lady looks favourably on the idea."

Gardiner grimaced inwardly, but knew he could say nothing against the suggestion. "I will indeed raise this with Her Majesty."

His request placed, Phillip had little more use for Gardiner and he found himself swiftly dismissed. Making his way back through the myriad of corridors of Hampton Court Gardiner bleakly considered how he was going to carry out Phillip's request. Mary, he knew, had been at pains to keep her new husband away from Elizabeth; it had been a tactic he had wholeheartedly agreed with. This change of heart was going to be a difficult one to convey to Mary.

He continued to grumble under his breath as he made his way back to the boat moored on the Thames that would transport him back to his own lodgings. Mist clung to the banks and the water; soon it began to penetrate the folds of his clothes to add physical discomfort to the mental one he was already suffering.

✝

Richard could never be sure whether he made a conscious decision to enter the Church or not; walking down Charterhouse Street he'd slowed, his feet had turned towards the great wooden door. St Etheldreda's, dedicated to the Anglo-Saxon saint, was one of the oldest religious houses in London. Wide and open inside, the wooden-beamed roof was supported by the wall buttresses, keeping the church itself clear of towering columns. Wherever a man sat he would be able to see the stained-glass windows behind the altar depicting St Etheldreda's ascent to heaven.

The smell of incense was still heavy inside the chapel; the smoke was supposed to represent the prayers rising to Heaven. A slight smile crept across his face as he absently wondered if the lingering aroma was attached to those prayers that had failed to inspire the Lord and were still stuck beneath the wooden roof. Indeed, was there such a thing as a poor prayer? Probably one made without conviction, he concluded, how many of those was he himself guilty of placing before the Almighty? Quite a few.

Richard took three more steps into the church when he felt it, or more rather became aware of it. Later, he'd tell himself it was from his loss of blood and the fight with his brother, but then, when he stood before the altar, winter light casting curious shadows from the arched glass windows, he'd felt his strength pouring from him, draining towards the stone flags on the floor. The muscles in his thighs and calves ached and he'd had to put out a hand and take hold of a pew to steady him. The feeling had continued and he knew if he had not sat down quickly he would have pitched forwards onto the floor, unable to stand.

Sitting with his head bent forwards, consciously trying to stabilise his ragged breathing, he honestly thought someone was going to find him in a heap on the church floor in the morning. Straightening his back, he took a long breath, the air thick and heavy. His heart was beating too fast as if he'd run a long way. Closing his eyes, he could almost hear sadness echoing from the church walls.

St Etheldreda's monks, devout and esteemed, had been Cromwell's first victims when he'd sought to make Henry Head of the Church to solve the King's Great Matter. If they would accept him as Head of the Church then many others would follow but they steadfastly refused choosing instead a traitor's end. He remembered reading Thomas More's words, written after he had watched them go to their deaths. From More's own cell in the Tower where he awaited his own end, he had described them as "merry bridegrooms." How could anyone face the horror of a traitor's end with calm acceptance? Hanged by their necks then cut down alive, the monks had then faced the slow agony of disembowelment. Richard had witnessed it: if the executioner was good with the crowd on his side, it could last an hour. What it must be to have that kind of faith! There was much to recommend it.

He heard a voice from his childhood in his head, Father Stephen – "the remedy for doubt is faith, boy," As a boy he had laughed and earned himself a thrashing for it. Still, the absurdity of the argument lit his face with a slight smile. Father Stephen had read the word of the Lord, Romans 10.17 - he could still remember it well - accompanied by an acute memory of a painful backside where Stephen had taken a rod to it. Richard rested his head back against the wooden pew and pondered Stephen's lecture again.

"How then will they call on him in whom they have not believed? And how are they to believe in him of whom they have never heard? Faith comes from hearing and hearing through the word of Christ."

Words, written words, can they ever be strong enough to banish doubt? That had been the question he had put to Father Stephen at the end of his lecture, a question that had earned him another thrashing and two days without any food. He had learned not to pose questions relating to theology after that experience. Since then he supposed his were the prayers that sank like mist and failed to make it beyond the church roof, his own words lacking any soaring conviction and his thoughts always so very full of doubt.

His shoulder was starting to throb painfully, reminding him of why. Jack, damn him! Why did he have to be so hot-headed! After the fight at Burton, his bloody last conscious act had been for Jack. He had begged Jamie to pass a message to Dan, he'd pressed his ring into the priest's hands and he knew it had been delivered as it had been amongst Jack's possessions redeemed from Marshalsea. He had left Jack in Dan's care, or so he had thought. He moved on the pew and pain resonated along his arm. Fixing his eyes on the gilded cross atop the altar, he spoke quietly: "Maybe you can persuade Jack to judge me by my actions, for I bloody well can't."

✝

Jack had awoken to find Richard had gone. There was the briefest of notes on the table stating bluntly that he'd be away a few days. Jack balled the paper and sent it to the back of the fire Lizbet had just lit. He wasn't going to get to talk to him any time soon, it appeared. Lizbet was relieved; if Jack had not been so preoccupied with his own misery he would have seen her face and asked her why.

Richard was gone for just over a week; on his return he found Jack toasting his feet in front of the fire, eyes closed with a half-eaten plate of food next to him. Lizbet was seated on the floor next to him, darning a sock.

"So it's been hard without me," Richard dropped a bag on the table. "But you managed?"

Lizbet pushed herself back into the shadows, unsure yet how he was going to react to her after he'd caught her hands stealing caresses from his body.

"Fighting does not determine who is right, only who is left; on this occasion that was you," Richard hitched himself onto the edge of the table, a half-smile on his face.

Jack didn't want to smile, but he couldn't help himself. As intended, Richard's words axed the tension between them.

"We've been repeating the same mistakes in life for so long now, I think I'm going to start regarding them as a family tradition," Jack replied. This time Richard smiled, genuinely amused.

"Before you say any more, I'm sorry," Richard held out his hands in a gesture of supplication. "I said things I should never have said."

Jack's face darkened. "Anything in particular?" He pronounced the words quietly and precisely.

"Some things I said were untrue," Richard continued.

"Go on," Jack's blue eyes were fastened on Richard's.

"Dixi tibi Latina fuit in invium, suus 'non tarn acerbitatem," stated Richard in Latin.

"What!" Lizbet clamped her hand across her mouth, she'd not meant to speak.

"He said," Jack translated without looked at her, "My Latin isn't passable it's terrible." He continued "Paenitet me temptatis quia sit e ipsum bene factus,"

Richard met Lizbet's eyes for a moment - she saw no malice in them - and indeed the corner of his mouth twitched into a smile. Lizbet let out a long breath; it seemed he had no argument with her at least. Then he translated for her this time. "He said that if I was trying to apologise that I was doing a very bad job of it." Richard pulled his cloak from his back and draped it over the table. "I've a thirst on me, I'm going downstairs; join me if you like." And with that Jack and Lizbet found themselves alone again.

Jack found Richard where he sat in the snug in the taproom.

"I am sorry, Jack, I did say something that was unfair," Richard moved along the bench so Jack could slide in next to him.

"I can live with you having slandered my Latin," Jack said sarcastically.

"I know Marshalsea was terrible," Richard admitted quietly, "I let Lizbet go to you when you scream because I don't know what to say. I had no right to shame you like I did."

Jack looked away. "Sometimes I actually think I was in Hell." Jack faced his brother once more, saying, "And I had no right to beat you, but you goad me so. One of these days..."

Richard cut him off, "Paenitet enim me."

"No, that's not quite right, you very well might *not* live to regret it," Jack advised darkly. "I meant what I said, look at me." Richard raised his face, meeting Jack's eyes. "You shouldn't have left me, I wouldn't have left you; ever. And..." Jack paused, "I should not have done what I did. Christ, the pain I felt when I thought you were dead, I just wanted to hurt you as badly as you hurt me. I couldn't stop myself," Jack dropped his eyes from Richard's, "I am sorry, truly."

Richard reached over and clapped him on the arm, "I know it. Because of our father we don't have a past together. I know that is hard; for both of us."

The corner of Jack's mouth twitched to a smile. "We are terrible apart, and even worse together."

Richard grinned as well, and grasping his brother's wrist, repeated Jack's words, "terrible apart, and even worse together – that would make us a fine family moto. Et mirabilia absque peius."

That was not how Jack had meant the words, but he nodded in agreement, and then said simply, "I am glad we are not apart. And I hope you know you have my eternal thanks for getting me out of Marshalsea."

"Aye, and I am sorry I did not find you before then," Richard said; Jack knew he meant it.

After a few minutes silence Jack, changing the subject, asked, "Been anywhere nice?"

"A village called Wittlesea, three days ride from here, if you must know," Richard supplied, "I'm trying to find Dan and some of the other men. Do you not think of them sometimes?"

Jack's guilty look was answer enough.

"Well they left Burton only days after you did - Jamie confirmed as much - and while you went north, they went south. I knew Dan had family at Wittlesea, a sister living still in his father's house, so I went to see if he had been there."

"Did you find trace of them?" Jack asked; he thought it would be good to see them again.

"Indeed, but months ago. He'd come by with Mat and Froggy but stopped for only a few days; he'd spoken of going to France, so his sister said." Richard answered, his face thoughtful, "I'm not sure why they would think that a good destination though."

"So they are still together - they could be anywhere. I'd be surprised if Froggy went to France again: he bloody well hated it last time!" Jack mused. "Convinced they were all talking French just to bloody well confuse him."

"Sometimes it doesn't take much to confuse Froggy," agreed Richard. "Dan's sister will pass a message on if she hears from him again, but I think it unlikely, so I'm not sure where to look next."

Lizbet appeared and demanded a seat, squeezing herself between the pair, oblivious to the fact she was not that welcome. "Come on, Jack, shift over," Lizbet wedged herself in next to Jack.

"Yes come on, Jack, make space for Erato," Richard sighed resignedly.

Lizbet looked to Jack for an explanation. "He means you are my muse," Jack supplied, then when her expression remained blank, "A muse? Actually what he probably means is that you're not very inspirational or I lack the wit to be inspired, one or the other."

"Probably both," Richard moved along the bench to make space for the newcomer.

"Thanks," Jack found himself on the edge of the bench, "Good God, girl, how much space do you want?"

Lizbet offended, gave him a shove which nearly sent him reeling onto the floor. "Hardly any, you cheeky beggar, I'm only small."

"There's nothing small about your backside, woman," Jack placed a hand on the wall to prevent his descent to the floor.

"I've not heard any complaints," she said tartly hoisting an arm around Jack's neck.

Richard leant back against the wall. Lizbet, for all her faults, was good for Jack in her own way. As he listened to them continue to trade insults, he smiled; the girl gave as good as she got. It was her hands that had coaxed Jack back to the living world. She'd heard him scream, seen him weep in the night, washed and cleaned him and yet she kept those memories to herself. The past to Lizbet had no value and, although it was never spoken, his brother knew she would never break that trust; Lizbet lived for now. Absently he considered that she probably *was* a muse, not one of poetry or music, but one that had helped to inspire a wounded and crushed spirit to live.

Lizbet's shout, too close to his ear, broke his thoughts and he jumped involuntarily. "Daisy!" Lizbet waved over a girl from the other side of the taproom.

Daisy smiled at Lizbet. Flecks of summer sun glinted in seemingly depthless eyes, lusciously lashed and the colour of hazel. Her hair had the deep shining lustre of a freshly cracked chestnut, the long tresses holding every possible shade of brown, all highlighted with the hues of autumn. Her nose was small and pink and gave her face an inquisitive and beseeching look.

"Daisy, Daisy." Then Lizbet turning to Richard continued, "I don't know why I'm shouting at her, I always do, even though the poor lass is deaf and dumb."

Daisy made her way through the labyrinth of tables and stools to Lizbet, who was smiling broadly as she spoke, looking directly at Daisy. Richard guessed the girl could read lips. "Daisy love, these are my boys I've been telling you about."

Jack - whose attention was wholly on the lass - was quietly disgruntled when Lizbet raised herself up and sat neatly on his knee, taking Daisy's arm she pulled the girl down to take the tight space she had just vacated. "There we go, my boy's will keep you warm." Lizbet, leaning forward, took Daisy's hand, placing it down gently on Richard's thigh. "You'll like Daisy, she's very quiet." She held his eye for a moment smiling nervously, suddenly feeling she had gone too far. Her voice shaking, she added, "And very gentle."

Five minutes later Richard left them, leading Daisy towards the door and to their rooms above. She was gentle and very quiet; in the darkness he forgot who she was. His kiss was tender and loving, and she felt he liked her. Afterwards, Daisy tried to snuggle up to him and he let her, keeping her warm in the crook of his arm.

✝

Mary clutched her belly and closed her eyes; her ladies all stared at Gardiner, but he held his ground.

"Your Majesty, it makes only sense that the Lady Elizabeth comes to Court during your confinement. I only made the humble suggestion that she should meet with your husband before then, when you yourself could also be present.

"She's met him before on several state occasions. Why should he see her now, in private?" Mary hissed.

Gardiner was on thin ice and he knew it. "Your Majesty, the Lady Elizabeth can be," he changed his words quickly, "could be, a problem. I might have failed, Your Majesty, to prove her allegiance to the Reformist cause, but she is known to sympathise with them. Would it not be wise to ensure that His Majesty - your husband - is fully aware of the danger Elizabeth could pose?" Gardiner pressed on hoping the woman's vanity would let him win the argument. "Your Majesty, your husband is a wise and intelligent man. Alerting His Majesty to the threat to your throne that Lady Elizabeth presents will encourage him to keep a particularly watchful eye on her during your confinement."

Gardiner had won the argument and it was a little over a week later when a very subdued Elizabeth was escorted into the long gallery at Hampton Court to meet with Phillip. The pretext to the summons was Elizabeth was to return to Court for the forthcoming birth of Mary's child. Phillip's -

and Spain's - interest in the red-headed heir to the English throne had heightened. If Mary had indeed lost the child and her ability to provide an English heir was called into question, then the political landscape shifted dramatically to one where the Princess Elizabeth featured prominently in the foreground.

Elizabeth, dressed soberly, head bowed, had answered Phillip's questions quietly and openly. He was finding her to be quite the reverse of the tempestuous redhead he had been led to believe her to be. It was perhaps an English myth that the child who bore Henry's likeness also bore his character traits.

Phillip had changed the subject to one for which Elizabeth had no liking; it was with difficulty she maintained a neutral expression. "So now that your dear sister is in confinement, I have the duty of ensuring your welfare befits your station as the Queen's sister." Phillip was surrounded by his Spanish nobles; she avoided their glances and raking eyes. "How old are you now?"

"Twenty-three Your Highness," Elizabeth knew exactly where this was going.

"Twenty-three. It surprises me that you have not been found a match before now. I shall have to give the matter some thought." Phillip mused, tugging at his beard. "Have you ever been to Spain my lady? I think you might like it: your complexion needs to be warmed by a proper sun, not this mellow one you have in England."

Elizabeth's eyes widened. Spain? She had never considered that there could be a move to send her to the Spanish Court. "I have never, Your Majesty, set a foot outside of England and I have no wish to."

Phillip's eyebrows raised a degree; finally the plain little creature had an opinion on something, "Why not? I could find you a most notable match." Smiling he gestured to his entourage. "Are my Spanish nobles not more alluring to a lady than your English men?" It was true that when it came to colour and flamboyance, the Spanish at Mary's Court seemed to spend a degree more time and money on their outward appearance than their comparatively dreary-looking English counterparts.

"I've been told, sir, never to judge a cock by his feathers," Elizabeth replied curtly meet his eyes for the first time.

Phillip smiled: so here was the temper he'd heard about. Hitching himself up on the edge of a table, he granted Elizabeth his full attention. "Surely a bird with beautiful feathers is preferable to a dour bird without any plumage?"

"Such plumage today may end up as a feather duster tomorrow. In England, we pluck the longest feathers to rid us of our pests." Elizabeth's eyes were fierce, shoulders square and she matched his stare.

Phillip's beamed broadly; indeed she was Henry's daughter. "I fear your tongue might pluck them of some of their finery, but it would be a fight worth watching." Phillip laughed and he was joined by the men around him. Elizabeth, her face red, was forced to stand and listen to them crow, her temper boiling beneath the surface.

Chapter Twelve

Richard and Jack spent the next month in London; they were idle weeks. It gave them both time to recover. Jack knew just from looking at his brother's face that there was, at last, more flesh on his bones than there had been since the fight at Burton. Jack knew his brother's shoulder was still healing and although he refused to talk to Jack about it, Richard had suffered Lucy Sharp to tend it. Letting her pick out the black stitches Jack had sewn in. Jack only knew this because Lucy had told Lizbet it had been the 'Devil's own work' to pry the black thread from the flesh. As she was pulling them free, there had been a great deal of cursing and even more when she had applied curative vinegar to the raw wound.

Jack knew he had lost his edge. In three months he had done little, and over his stomach there was a layer of soft flesh that had not previously been there. It worried him little; as soon as he had a horse and his feet back in a tilt yard then it would take but a short time for his skill and strength to return.

Jack had to admit that he had probably never eaten so well for such a long period of time. Lizbet, with Richard's money, provided some good fare for the table. There was a cooking pot over the fire from which steaming pottage would be produced, often with meat and bread came in daily from the bakery two streets away. Lizbet also seemed to know which of London's cook-shops to frequent, most of them clustered near the Thames and provided hot pies, fish pasties and cooked rabbits and poultry. Many of them would deal in rancid meat and offal disguised in pastry shells and the unwitting customer would get a lot more than a poor lunch when they were forced to eat such poor fare.

Eventually though some entertainment did arise. Jack, thankful at last for a diversion wholeheartedly agreed when Richard indicated that it was about time they paid the lawyer, Clement, a visit.

†

"Marcus, Marcus!" Clement yelled for the third time; where was that useless bastard? "MARCUS!"

The door began to open. At last the idiot was here, "Marcus I need..."

It wasn't Marcus. Clement rose from his chair.

"Marcus is a little... tied up at the moment," the man announced, strolling into the room to take a seat in the client's chair. "Sit, please. This is going to be unpleasant for only one of us, so you might as well be comfortable."

Clement lowered himself back into his chair and stared at the intruder. Well at least he knew now where Kettering's missing man was: he was right here, large as life and with a look of utter menace on his face.

The desk was piled high with cases. From where Jack sat, he could neither see Clement's hands nor the knife he slid out from between the case files. Clement jumped back up, knife in hand, pointing it directly at Jack's chest across the desk.

Jack just stared at him.

"Now the tables have turned," Clement sneered. "Stand sir."

"Really?" Jack responded, remaining seated, folding his arms comfortably.

"Stand, or I'll gut you like a pig," Clement squealed.

Jack shook his head and settled back in the chair. "I think not. Firstly, the width of the table is between us: you cannot make any strike from where you stand that would need worry me. Secondly, should you throw it, that stack of papers is in the way. You'd surely miss and then you would have just managed to disarm yourself. Thirdly, I'm not sure that the knife you hold could do much damage to a loaf of bread, let alone me. And finally, *finally...*" Jack raised his voice, "do you really think that you could ever best me?"

"I don't know if that has persuaded Clement, but I am convinced. Well put, Jack." Another man whom Clement didn't know entered the room.

"I thought so," Jack agreed.

Clement just stood, eyes wide, swinging the blade from one to the other.

"So, would you like to sit down," Jack invited again.

Clement's eyes flicked from Jack to the elegant man leaning against the door frame.

"Very well," Jack said wearily, "stand and keep the knife if you must. Now, I believe, I have you to thank for my recent stay in Marshalsea? Would I be right?"

Clement didn't say a word: his expression sufficed as an answer. Jack was out of his seat like a cat, the sea of papers on Clement's desk parted by the time the lawyer registered Jack's approach. Jack had an unbreakable grip on Clement's wrist that held the knife. The grasp was like iron.

"You're hurting me," Clement whined, his face contorted in pain.

Jack laughed. "Isn't that the general idea?" Jack squeezed the wrist tighter, forcing his thumb and forefinger into the gaps above the wrist bone. Clement howled and the knife clattered to the desk. Releasing his wrist, Jack thumped him in the chest with the flat of his hand, sending him flying back into this chair. "Have I made my point?" Jack asked, sitting down, smoothing out his doublet with exaggerated ease.

Clement's returned his gaze to the knife that lay between them on the desk.

"Obviously not," the cool voice from the door way stated.

Jack's voice was quiet and threatening, "If you pick that up, make no mistake, this time I will really hurt you."

"What do you want?" Clement managed.

"I want to know why I ended up in Marshalsea," Jack stated patiently.

"You've got enemies; someone wants rid of you that's why," Clement spat quickly. "People go into Marshalsea and they don't come back out."

"As you can see, I did come back out. Who wanted me in there?" Jack asked.

Clement remained silent.

"I think, master lawyer," Richard spoke from the doorway, "that he would prefer your silence." The threat was clear.

Jack stood, rubbing his hands over his face.

Richard folded his arms. He recognised that Jack was inviting attack and he looked on with interest.

Clement weighed his chances. With Jack standing he could indeed throw the knife true to the target. A scrawny hand reached for the knife and threw it end over end. The last time Clement had used a knife would have been thirty years ago. His throw lacked power, the flight was off-course and the delivery took so long Jack had ample time to lift a file from the desk to deflect the harmless blade.

"Oh dear," said an amused voice lightly from the doorway.

Clement made to scramble backwards but it was too late. Jack snatched the lawyer's throwing arm and slammed it forcefully on the desktop. Jack's other hand produced a knife of his own.

"This one," he twisted the blade in front of Clement's eyes, "is sharp."

Clement screamed.

"And my aim is a damn sight better than yours," Jack finished.

There was a sickening thump.

Clement's breath was coming in ragged gasps, but the scream wouldn't come.

"Oh look at that," Jack sounded annoyed, "I am losing my touch; that was meant to go through the middle."

The knife was impaled neatly in the desk between two of Clement's fingers. No serious damage was done but the blade had made two neat nicks in the fingers.

Jack grasped the hilt and pulled it free. Clement collapsed howling in his chair, the bleeding hand clutched against his chest.

"You do realise that this is going to take longer now and that the fault of this is your own," Jack advised wearily. "So tell me, who wanted me in Marshalsea?"

Clement looked at them mutinously, "You've hurt me! I'm bleeding to death, look!"

"Give me strength! It's perfectly alright for you to throw a knife at me but not the other way around, is that it?" Jack complained.

"You said I'd never have managed to hurt you, it wasn't fair, it wasn't fair," Clement sobbed, tears now coursing down his wrinkled cheeks.

Jack turned to Richard. "Can you actually believe this little weasel?"

Richard remained silent.

"I was only doing my job," wailed Clement at an even louder pitch.

"Alright, let's start there. Who was your client?" Jack asked.

Clement said nothing.

"I've just cleaned this." Jack held up the knife he'd used a few moments ago.

"Not on the russet, I hope." Jack chose to ignore Richard's remark.

"Do you want me to use it again on your other hand?" Jack started to stand up.

It was too much for Clement.

"Fitzwarren, Robert Fitzwarren. He's a client. I told him you'd been to see me and he wished for me to help you disappear. I arrange for people to go to Marshalsea from time to time. Nobody gets involved, they just disappear. People don't come out of Marshalsea again," Clement sniffed loudly.

"It was unfortunate for you that I did," Jack countered.

Richard moved into the room. "We now seem to have another problem."

Jack looked up to his brother's face and then back to Clement.

Clement saw the look they exchanged.

"Oh no, no, no, I'll not tell a soul I've seen you. I've already penned a message to Fitzwarren to say you died in Marshalsea. I want nothing more to do with this."

"I'm not sure your assurances are going to be enough," Jack replied. "Have you any idea what it is like in there? Have you?"

"Jack, settle yourself, of course he has no idea. As he said he was just doing his job," Richard moved forwards and placed a hand on Jack's shoulder.

"Whose bloody side are you on?" Jack snarled angrily.

"Yours, obviously." Richard said, then to the Clement, "There is something else as well that you might be able to help with." Richard held the lawyers moist eyes with his own, "I paid a good sum to release my brother, now where, master lawyer, do you think that money is now?"

"Kettering..." Clement stopped himself, the man staring at him across the desk was both dangerous and no fool.

"Go on," pressed Richard, "Kettering what?"

"He discharged the debt and sent the balance to me," Clement licked his lips.

Jack's temper had begun to rise. It was only Richard's steadying hand that kept him in his seat. "And this money, what did you do with it?"

Clement wisely had kept it close, unsure who might come looking for it. If Robert Fitzwarren found out about the debtors release at least he had reasoned he would be able to appease him with a hefty purse. If time went by and no-one asked then it would have been safe for Clement to add it to his pension. "I have it here," Clement offered quietly, then added, "locked away."

"Well, then. Let's unlock it. I would like my money back." Richard demanded.

Some minutes later Clement having unlocked a draw handed over the purse containing the eighty one pounds.

Richard hefted it in his hand, the coins chinked noisily. "Not so much is it the weight of a man's life?" He handed the purse to Jack, "that is most certainly yours. Now we just need to ensure master lawyer's silence one way," Richard smiled, "or the other."

"I'll not tell anyone, I swear."

Richard smiling, said. "So, master lawyer, we wish to become two of your newest clients."

✝

It was a week later when Richard glanced over the top of the cards he held at Jack's face; his brother had been staring fixedly at his hand now for a good while. That meant it was a poor hand and he could not decide whether to continue and hope for better cards, or fold. Retreat was not in Jack's nature.

Jack discarded a three of clubs and took the top card from the worn deck. He slid it securely in between his other cards and examined it carefully. A bloody five of spades, useless! A huff escaped his lips and Richard had to stifle a laugh.

"Can I not teach you anything?" Richard asked. He folded his cards together and put them face down on the table.

"What do you mean?" Jack smiling was using his cards to pull the coins on the table towards him.

"Never mind. We have a score to settle Jack, one which I think you'll like," Richard was watching his brother closely.

"Go on," Jack prompted, as he picked the coins up one by one from the table.

"Guess who is back and currently stopping with cousin Harry?" Richard knew exactly what reaction this was going to get from his brother.

"That bastard Robert," Jack slapped his cards down, Richard cast a finger over them to separate the hand to view the faces; he'd been right.

"Indeed. Shall we go and involve him in a little family reunion?" Richard suggested, scooping up all the scattered cards and reuniting the deck.

"I thought we were keeping out of sight?" Jack spoke warningly.

"We are, but if we time it right we'll be gone from London before they can find us," Richard assured, then added, "I think we both have scores to settle."

Jack met his eyes. "Just a few."

†

It had been Henry VIII who had cleared Southwalk of brothels: a royal proclamation in 1546 had closed all the bankside stewes and the prostitutes had scattered around the city. Many, like Lizbet, attached themselves to an inn where they worked as serving wenches, cooks, cleaners and, when the clientele so demanded, as whores. The licensed brothels, though, were gone, the Bishop of Winchester profited hugely from the arrangement, when the land occupied by the most notorious houses in Southwalk - The Bell, The Cat and The Gun - all passed into his grateful hands.

Henry's proclamation seemed to have overlooked a few of the wealthier houses who could afford to pay for their immunity. The Angel was one such establishment in Aldergate. From the outside, it gave off a look of Tudor respectability: white painted neat daub flanked the black oak beams, windows shuttered and closed, which kept both the noise and light inside from the street.

Richard must have had them followed, Jack assumed, for how he knew that Robert was at a brothel with Harry was otherwise beyond him.

Richard made for the door. Jack stopped, grabbing his arm. "I can't go in there," Jack blurted.

Richard stared at him. "Why not?"

"It's a brothel! it's a gentleman's house, not a bloody village inn, I can't go in there." Jack was obviously flustered.

"Jack, sometimes, you really do amaze me. Of course you can go in there." Richard was laughing, genuinely amused. Jack steadied himself. Why not indeed: he looked no lesser man than his brother.

An apologetic grin appeared on his face, "I'm still getting used to this."

Richard clapped him on the arm. "Let us go and entertain ourselves."

"I'll be perfectly fine when I find the bastard and starting beating the hell out of him. Just until then, well...," Jack left the sentence unfinished.

Richard knocked and the door opened almost straight away, they were met by a lady who took both of Richard's hands in her own and pulled him to her.

"My love, where have you been hiding yourself?" She spoke with genuine pleasure.

"Oh why doesn't this surprise me," Jack muttered under his breath.

"And your friend," she looked Jack up and down, a smile playing across her lips, "No wonder we have not seen you for so long when you have such a beautiful boy to yourself."

Jack gave her a perfect bow, then, looking sideways at Richard, "Did she just say what I think she said?"

"She did." Richard said tucking the ample lady's hand into the crook of his arm.

"Well tell her...," Jack said hotly.

"The lady has ears my beautiful boy, why don't you tell me yourself" she loosed Richard's arm and took Jack's instead. "My name is Nonny, come and tell me all about yourself."

Jack smiled back over his shoulder at Richard, left alone in the hall.

"My beautiful boy, do not worry, any friend of Richard's is a friend of mine." And she smiled widely. "Tonight the hospitality will be my own. So tell me, are you a friend?"

Jack hesitated.

Richard, drawing level with them supplied the answer. "Madam, he is my brother."

"Really!" She exclaimed, "And you let me insult him so; I am so sorry," she said with mock sincerity.

Richard bent his head to hers and spoke in a voice loud enough for Jack to hear, "He's a little nervous."

"Oh that's terrible. Well tonight," she patted Jack's arm, "you shall be my guest and I shall look after you." Clicking her fingers she beckoned over a girl. "You look like you need a little fire in your life. My little redheaded Maude will look after you." Maude attached herself dutifully to Jack's arm.

Jack looked at Richard. No words passed between them, but Jack sent his thanks. With the hostess attached to Richard, they set off.

There were four rooms on the ground floor and in the third one she showed them there were tables for cards, with several games in progress.

"I think I'd like to start with a game of cards," announced Jack; he had found his quarry.

"I agree, Nonny, can you introduce us to a game, there looks a likely table." Richard said steering her towards a small group of players in the corner.

Smiling she led them over, "Pray gentlemen I have two more to join you if you have space."

Robert Fitzwarren looked up. His eyes met those of Jack. At first there was no recognition, but the moment Richard turned from Nonny and stood next to his brother, his arms gently folded, Robert knew exactly who stood before him. Harry, lounging in a chair next to him, stared at Jack, his mouth not working but opening and closing nonetheless.

"Cards," Richard quipped, "the vice of the unwitting, the stupid and the deceived. Surprised to see me?" he asked his brother pleasantly.

There was little Robert could do: the room was full. This was not a place to start a fight and they both knew it.

Nonny raised a hand and a servant silently appeared from somewhere to place chairs for them. "There you go, my loves." She didn't leave but perched on the arm of Richard's chair, her arm lightly draped over his shoulders. "For luck," she whispered into his ear, a little too closely.

With her seated at the table, there was little anyone could say or do. Richard smiled broadly, slid his arm around her waist and gave her an intimate squeeze.

"Well then, Harry," Richard pronounced his name with malicious precision. "What's the game?"

"Primero," one of the other players provided when Harry failed to speak.

"Excellent," Jack noted that a small table had just appeared at his right hand, with wine and food laid out on it.

"You'll need your money," leaning her head next to Richard's, Nonny asked, "Shall I get it for you?"

Richard set his shoulders back in the chair. Holding Robert's stare, he replied, "Why not mademoiselle, we can play together."

Her hand slid across his chest and dipped inside his jacket, caressing his chest unnecessarily, before pulling out the leather purse, Richard kept his eyes on the players.

Nonny loosed the strings and peered inside, then smiled with approval. "Deal, gentlemen," she commanded.

The cards flew out across the table and she deftly collected Richard's, fanned them and held them for a moment for him to view before folding the cards away. Coins clattered on the table and she sent two of Richard's skittering to join them. Robert's hand shook as he threw his down to match them. Richard sent him a disapproving look.

"Harry, are you in?" One of the other players nudged Harry, who was transfixed, staring between Richard and Robert.

"Aye, here." He fumbled clumsily for coins.

The game ended when Jack, to his delighted surprise, won.

Robert stood, bowed to the Madam and left, Harry stumbling in his wake.

"Another game?" Nonny asked.

✝

"I thought he was dead," wailed Harry as they readied to leave.

"They both should be; if you'd not been such a coward on Harlsey Moor he would not have bloody well got away would he? Jack was your servant for God's sake!" snapped Robert.

"You said Richard was dead, you said he'd been found a traitor and tried for his crimes, you said..." A hard slap across the face from Robert stilled his tongue.

"Shut up, shut up," Robert spat, "let's get out of here."

Leaving the front door of The Angel they turned up the street walking briskly. Robert stopped suddenly; their way was impeded by two men.

"Going somewhere?" Richard enquired; to his side was Jack.

"How did you get out of there before us?" Robert said, disbelief in his voice.

"Robert, you've left us both for dead, if we can both manage an untimely resurrection, then getting out of the back door of brothel wasn't exactly going to be a challenge was it?" Richard pointed out conversationally.

"Get out of the way," Robert spat drawing his sword, "or we'll come through you."

"I don't think so, not this time," Richard didn't move. "You and that snivelling rat at your shoulder; are you sure?"

Jack closed in and stood ready, his sword drawn. Standing next to Richard, he leant his head close and said something Robert could not hear.

"You think that half-breed gutter whelp is going to back you up, do you? You might have dressed him in silks but he's still a baseborn piece of filth!" Robert shouted.

Jack made to step forward, but Richard grabbed his arm. "Not yet."

"Listen to your master," Robert addressed Jack, sneering. Jack's eyes narrowed and his breathing quickened as his temper rose.

"When was the last time your lackey raised a blade in earnest or yourself for that matter?" Richard asked, still holding Jack back.

Robert ignored him, seeing the effect his insult had on Jack he pressed on. "Has he told you what he'll do with you when he's finished with you? He'll dump you back in the gutter you came from, he has no care for you. How did you ever think you could be more than what you really are?"

Jack pulled himself roughly from Richard's hold. "Why don't you find out exactly what I am?"

"Robert's mine," Richard said angrily, making a grab for Jack's arm again to stop his advance.

"I'm not taking Harry, he's yours." Jack countered.

"We can't both take on Robert, that wouldn't be fair." Richard complained.

"Fair?" considered Jack for a moment, "When did fair come into this?"

Harry and Robert stared between the pair, neither able to believe they were arguing between themselves.

"Robert is mine," Jack stated again.

"No he's not," Richard countered hotly, "Bloody hell, I've waited years for this, out of my way."

There was a metallic crash as Jack slammed his sword back into the scabbard. Then he stepped forward and turned to face Richard, his back to Robert.

"You have to have everything, every time it's always the bloody same," Jack complained. Then turning to Robert, "See what I have to put up with?" Then looking back at Richard, "Well this time..." Richard gave a nod and Jack took the lead. He had closed the gap between them and Robert. When he stepped back and turned with lightening speed, his elbow smashed into the side of Robert's face. Robert's sword was lost to him, flying from his hand to clank and rattle noisily against the flagged street. In the same moment, Richard stepped past his brother and levelled the sword at Harry who, wide-eyed, dropped his own sword and raised his hands.

They stood looking at the pair: Robert with his hands to his blooded face and Harry, white as snow, staring at them, hands still raised in surrender.

Robert suddenly lunged for Jack, a knife aimed to slice between his undefended ribs, Richard repelled his advance, cannoning into Robert and sending him reeling backwards, off-balance.

"Come on, you churl." Robert had the knife in his right hand. Richard dropped his sword and pulled out his own poniard.

"You come here where I can see you." Jack grabbed hold of a handful of Harry's jacket and hauled him to stand in front of him. Pulling Harry's knife from his belt, Jack applied it to his ribs. "One move and this goes through your back."

Neither had engaged. Robert weighed the knife carefully in his hand, a sneer on his face. "The odds are in my favour, I think."

Richard said nothing but watched his brother carefully, waiting for his move. When it came, he threw his body along the arc prescribed by the knife, grabbing Robert's arm and pulling him forward. Lighter, but faster than his brother, he had the bigger man off-balance. He stamped his boot heel hard into the back of Robert's calf to ensure his descent into the mud. Robert knew he couldn't prevent his fall; he released a great howl, fastened his fist into Richard's sleeve and pulled him down with him. They landed heavily, Richard on top, but only for a moment, before Robert brought his greater strength to bare, reversing the positions and rolling away from Jack.

"Damn," Jack muttered, pushing Harry forward with the knife. Robert might not be aware of Richard's weakness, but Jack knew only too well that Richard was ill-prepared for a fight like this. Robert had only to pressure Richard in the wrong place and he would quickly know he had the advantage.

Richard still had his knife - the blade was between their bodies - but Robert also now had a hand on the hilt. Jack couldn't see which way the blade tip was pressing.

"Bloody hell." He deliberated for a second more, then he moved. Still holding Harry, he delivered as hard a kick in the side of the ribs as he could to Robert. It bought Richard the opening he needed and he was able to push Robert off him.

"Get up," Jack hissed under his breath. He shoved Harry to his left so that he could kick Richard's fallen sword back over to him.

As Richard stooped for it, Robert flung himself forward, aiming to land on top and take Richard face down into the street. The sword flashed in the moonlight, although the blade swung only inches from the surface of the road, it was high enough to catch Robert in the side of his thigh as he dived on top of his brother. There was a scream as he half-landed on Richard, who quickly pushed him away and was on his own feet in an instant, sword in his right hand and the injured left shoulder away from Robert.

Harry wailed and Jack shook him. "It's not you that's bleeding you idiot."

Robert had found the wall and was pulling himself upright, his right hand running with blood as he clutched it to the cut. "You'll bloody die for this, you bastard."

Richard sheathed the blade and stooped to retrieve his knife before walking over to Robert. Jack, trusting Robert not at all, forced Harry to follow at knife point.

"Hear me," Richard's voice was cold. "I'm going to take everything you have, I am going to take it slowly, it's going to be painful and in the end you will be stood with nothing."

"You'll take nothing from me," Robert retorted, breathing harshly.

"I can and I'm going to start right now," the point of Richard's knife pressuring Robert's chest. "Take off your jacket." Then to Jack, "Looks about your size would you say?"

"Aye, I even like the colour," Jack grinned.

Robert didn't move.

The pressure on the point increased, piercing the skin. "I can't bloody take it off with a knife in me, can I?" growled Robert, pressing himself against the wall and away from the knife.

Richard, inclining his head in agreement, took a careful step back. "The jacket, now please."

Robert complied and hurled it in Richard's face. It didn't meet its mark; Richard snatched it neatly from the air and hung it over his arm. A smile came to his lips. "Feels like it has full pockets as well." Then to Robert, "Now the hose."

Robert looked at him in disbelief.

"I said I was starting tonight and I am starting by taking your dignity." The knife point returned to his chest. "Now the hose if you please." Richard passed the doublet to Jack who held it up appreciatively before folding it over his own arm.

Robert leaned back against the wall. "I can't; can't you see I'm bleeding?" He had indeed gone quite pale.

"A point well made. You need some help? Harry, go and kneel down there and pull his boots off for him," Richard instructed Harry.

Jack chuckled and pushed Harry forwards with the knife that still pressured his back. Richard and Jack stood, shoulder-to-shoulder and watched as Harry knelt, pulled, tugged and whimpered as he removed Robert's boots.

"Bring them over here," Jack demanded, "they look a lot finer than mine, at a guess, I'd say about the right size as well."

Harry brought them over and Jack took them. Lifting one of his own boots, he measured the sole of Robert's against his own.

"A perfect match," Richard agreed grinning.

"I believe," Jack addressed Robert, "my brother said the hose as well. Come on, Harry, help him," Jack chuckled. "I think by the looks of this, Harry's helped you off with your clothes a time or two before hasn't he?" Then to Richard, "Do we stop here, or do we send them back to mademoiselle with their backsides out?"

"And the rest," Richard said, earning a broad grin from Jack. "Now, Harry, get yours off as well: I don't want Robert here covering his shame with your clothes."

In a few moments both men stood before them completely naked, shivering in the cold, Robert with blood running down his leg and leaning heavily against the wall.

"Now off you go back to The Angel," Jack laughing, watched the two flour-white backsides, lit by the moonlight, make their way back to the brothel.

Turning, he saw Richard was heading away from the brothel. "It's this way," Jack grasped Richard's arm.

"No, this way, come on follow me. We haven't finished yet." Richard set the pace and Jack hurried to keep up. Initially he had no idea where they were headed, but after ten minutes he realised they were setting their feet in the direction of the London Fitzwarren house.

Jack had suffered humiliation enough at William's hand already; he had no desire to be subjected to that scathing tongue again. He grabbed Richard's arm this time to stop him. "Not there again. I don't want to be reminded of just what I am by him."

Richard smiled, not at all put off. "This time will be different. Come on, we have an hour before Robert, in borrowed breeches, makes his sorry way back here, licking his wounds."

"You'd better be right, an hour is not long. If he arrives before we've gone, Robert will see us in Hell."

Richard laughed. "As Sybil found out, it is not the descent into Hades that is hard, it's the getting back that can prove tricky. We will get back out, have faith." He was walking backwards in front of Jack.

"You'd walk through Hell with a smile on your face," Jack's voice was resigned.

"Fortune favours the audacious," came the light reply.

"Oh well, in that case you'll be just fine on your own then, if audacious means stupid," Jack said tersely.

Richard was amused. "Robert and Harry are otherwise engaged, so come on: let's go and annoy the Devil."

They stopped shortly, outside the house.

"Front door, or back?" Richard asked, then before Jack could stop him or reply he announced, "Front I think."

"Oh God save us," Jack muttered under his breath.

"He won't, Jack." Richard had heard his words. "You'll save us, come on."

His knock was answered quickly; through the leaded panes both saw the torch bobbing as the servant made his way to the front door. He opened it a crack to see who was on the other side. Richard forced it open, bringing himself to stand in the passageway with the retainer backing from him.

"It's Charles, isn't it?" Richard, smiling broadly dropped his cloak onto the old man's arm. "Surely you remember me?" The look of fear on the man's face was answer enough. "Don't worry, Charles, my father is expecting me. I know the way; save your legs and we shall make our own way up."

With that, he mounted the stairs and set off, leaving Jack and Charles in the hall. Jack looked apologetically at Charles, added his own cloak to the old man's arm and bounded up the steps two at a time to catch up to his brother.

They met up outside the door to William's room. Richard silently lifted the latch and pushed it open. As before, the room was bathed in candlelight from the sconces and the fire, wrapping the sleeping man in the chair in a homely warm orange glow. Richard put his finger to his lips and closed the door quietly behind him.

Richard pulled Jack with a hard grasp on his sleeve until the two stood in front of the man sleeping in the chair. Jack longed to be anywhere else. Feeling the heat from the fire behind him, Jack wasn't sure if it was the flames or fear of the man before him that made him suddenly feel so uncomfortably hot.

Richard moved forward and kicked William's feet. Jack wanted to say under his breath: "Don't you'll wake him." But he managed to still the words.

William blinked and stared between them both, confusion apparent on his grizzled face.

Richard's shoulders slumped. "That's the last time I waste a dramatic entrance on you." He scooped the spectacles from the side table and carefully placed them over William's ears and nose. Satisfied, he stepped back once again and stood next to Jack.

William's eyes widened.

Richard smiled maliciously. "Hallelujah, what it is to be recognised! They say, do they not, that if no-one knows a man he shall cease to be?"

William was still recovering his senses, looking between the pair.

"And, of course, you've met Jack?" Richard continued. "He is, of course, your mistake, my trial, and he will be Robert's undoing." Jack reddened even further in the firelight.

William pulled himself up in the chair.

"I almost forgot." Richard picked up the side table and moved it just out of reach. "Now we have our happy reunion, what shall we do?"

William ignored Richard; he could sense the unease from the other man. "His idea was it, to drag you here? Humiliate you again so he can get what he wants? He only wants Robert's inheritance and then you'll be back in the gutter where you came from."

"Careful, Father, he has a temper I'm well acquainted with," Richard warned, then, considering what he had said, added "Pray continue."

William ignored him. "Association with him gets you nothing. It's only in his eyes you are not a gutter snipe. Look at you? He has you like a pet monkey - dressed to dance - but remember a monkey, remains nothing but a stinking animal, no matter..."

Jack cut William off. "Christ, still your words. I can see it is a family tradition to wound with rhetoric, but I prefer a poniard."

"A family tradition?" Richard repeated, raising his eyebrows.

The knife in Jack's hand glistened in the firelight.

"I'll not take your life, it's enough for me that age is robbing you of it very quickly." Jack's comment hit a wound and he saw it.

"Like you said, a family tradition," Richard remarked from where he had hitched himself up on the edge of a coffer.

"What do you want?" Spat William.

Jack looked expansively round the room. "All of this will do me fine."

Richard produced a sheaf of papers form his pocket. "I shall not bore you with the legal Latin, but this will, I am assured, stand up in the Court of Chancery. We need only your signature and then Jack will be named as your heir." Richard laid them flat, the last sheet he placed on top, the space for William's signature blank, an empty line awaiting his shaky handwriting.

"You sign, we leave. You can live out the last of your fetid days in that chair, then, on your death, Jack will claim his inheritance. We are prepared to wait. You doctor is Master Juris, am I right?" Richard asked.

"What right have you to see my doctor?" William was furious.

"I am your son. I have every right to worry about the failing health of my aged father." As Richard spoke, William became paler. "He tells me you have a tumour growing within you. Obviously he can't be certain, but he is confident you have one last Christmas in you."

William's nostrils flared and his mouth became a thin hard line.

"Juris is a fool," William spat.

Richard smiled maliciously. "Are we having a little difficulty dealing with our own mortality? Face the facts old man, age is creeping through your bones and it will not be long before they'll be sealing you in a shroud. We can wait."

William turned again to Jack. "You trust him?" he demanded.

Jack declined to answer, until a more familiar voice asked, "Well do you?"

"Aye, I trust him," Jack stated quietly and firmly, surprising both the other men in the room. "You laid the wrong bet. You know as well as I do what Robert is and where he came from. Mark me, he will lead your name into the gutter."

There was a silence in the room. Richard observed his brother closely.

William's eyes were fastened on his face. "That maybe, but I can feel nothing for you. Nothing, you hear?"

"Well then," said Jack without humour, "that is indeed something we have in common. Now sign that and we will leave you to what little peace you have left."

Richard offered the pen and William snatched it from his hand. He spoke to Jack as he signed the paper. "Having this will do you little good. No-one who matters will ever accept you."

Richard took the completed document back into his keeping. "Thank you for that." His eyes checked the signature before he stored the paper back inside his doublet. "If you have a conscience then maybe we have eased it a little for you." Then to Jack, "Time to go."

It was when he turned to leave that he saw her for the first time. He knew her name: Eleanor. While she had lived he had never set his eyes on her. It could be no other, he was sure. On the wall was a painting of her: long blonde hair strayed over her shoulders, at her feet a pair of black and white spaniels played and in her hand she held a goblet emblazoned with the Fitzwarren emblem. Her eyes, by some talent of the painter's trade, held his and seemed to look straight into his soul. Her face, faintly smiling, gazed at him and Jack stood transfixed. It took a hard shove in the back from Richard to set his feet moving back towards the door, such had been the shock.

✝

They walked back to their lodgings, Jack feeling better than he had for a long time. "So we are definitely leaving then?" he asked.

"After tonight we have little choice. We couldn't really strip Robert naked and expect to be able to remain in London. He will have every stone turned looking for us," Richard replied, kicking a pebble in the street.

"God, did you see Harry on his knees grunting, trying to pull his boots off," Jack laughed, "I'd say that we'd better be gone very soon as well. He'll be after more than our blood after that. I think there's a fair chance he'll give Clement a bloody hard time as well."

"And that bothers you?" Richard asked.

"Not at all, as long as Clement keeps his mouth shut," Jack replied.

"He will," Richard replied, "Firstly, because however much he fears Robert he knows that he is unlikely to kill him, whereas we on the other hand might just do that and secondly he scents a profit."

"Bloody lawyers. To say I actually went to him and trusted him." Jack shook his head. "If tonight is to be our last in London, then I am going out." Shrugging off his jacket and swapping it for the one of Robert's he had been carrying. Holding his arms out in front, he examined it. "Good fit: and what have we here?" Out of one of the pockets he pulled a purse and three cards. "The cheating bastard."

"I did wonder," Richard sounded amused.

"Knowing you as I do," Jack looked at the faces of the cards and then back at his brother, "you could probably tell me what they are?"

"One is certainly a seven of clubs," Richard said matter-of-factly. "The player to the left of Harry discarded it, it was obvious that you needed it and I would guess Robert picked it up along with his card."

"And the others?" Jack queried in disbelief.

"I needed a Queen, but you had the one I really needed..."

"How did you know that?" Jack blurted.

"Simple," Richard replied, smiling.

"How? I gave nothing away." Jack exclaimed.

"You didn't, but I asked Nonny to tell me what you held," Richard smiled. "Remember she filled your glass up for you and while she did..."

"She looked at my cards. Anyway stop changing the subject, what are these other two cards?" Jack pressed.

"I would say..."

"Yes..."

"I would say a three of diamonds and, let me see... yes I have it, a four of spades," Richard finished triumphantly.

"How did you do that?" Jack was looking at the three cards he held: the seven of clubs, three of diamonds and the four of spades.

"Ah, if I told you everything I'd never win again, would I?" Richard said.

"No come on tell me, we only played one hand, the deck was not even half way through so how could you know what that these three cards were going to be? I'll accept the seven of clubs, but the other two? How? Tell me?"

"Oh very well," spoke Richard patiently, as if he were talking to a child. "The three of diamonds was a card that Harry needed; he'd already picked up a four of diamonds and I had the two, so it was a fair bet he needed the three of diamonds. He was sitting next to Robert, who we know cheats, so it's more than a fair assumption that he looked at poor Harry's hand. The player on the left of Harry, however, was intent on spades, he'd picked up a three of spades. You held the five of spades, so the card he was missing was either the four of spades or the six of spades and Robert had the six, so then it had to be..."

"How could you know what was in Robert's hand, he was opposite you?" Jack complained.

"Does it matter? The fact remains that he held the six and so to frustrate his opponents hand he had palmed the four of spades off the table as well. It was obvious." Richard finished, a little too triumphantly.

The look on Jack's face clearly told Richard that he didn't think it was in any way obvious at all. "How do you do it?" he ran his hands through his hair, "I'm far from stupid, yet I have no grasp on how you do this, it's a great skill."

Richard saw the pain on Jack's face and for once relented. "Robert took his jacket off and what did he do with it?"

Jack looked confused.

"What did he do with his jacket, think?" Richard repeated.

"He flung it in your face," Jack replied.

"And then?" Richard asked.

"You handed it to me," Jack said cautiously.

Richard shook his head.

Jack looked at him blankly for a moment before the realisation dawned. "You bloody well looked in his pockets before you gave it to me!"

Richard grinned.

Still talking as they mounted the steps to the rented rooms. Neither noticed that the door was slightly open. Had they listened they might have heard the voices of the men in the room waiting for them. As it was they heard nothing and Jack, entering first, didn't even see the blow that felled him, sending him into an unconscious heap on the floor.

✝

Lizbet stopped at the bottom of the stairs, depositing the basket on the first step she paused to push back a coil of hair that had escaped from behind her ear. Later, she would curse herself for being so preoccupied, for if she had listened as she ascended the stairs, she would have heard the men's voices and the sounds of fists on flesh. As it was though, Lizbet expected nothing and, sailed through the door in her usual way, the scene before her stopping her in her tracks.

Jack lay face down on the floor, unmoving. Colan was seated at one end of the table and Richard was at the other. However, Richard had his face pressed against the wood, a man behind him holding him down. One eye was already closing to a bruise and there was blood and saliva trickling in a steady stream to pool on the table. The open eye met her horrified stare with an even cold gaze.

Lizbet swallowed hard and dropped the basket. It contained an earthenware flagon of gilly flower wine Lucy had made for Jack and a cloth-wrapped loaf of bread. The basket tipped and the wine rolled out across the floor, the vessel drumming noisily on the boards before it bumped to a stop against the table leg.

Colan smiled, reached down and picked up the bottle. "Ah Lizbet, you've even brought me a drink, lass."

Lizbet said nothing, her gaze swinging between Colan's beaming face and Richard's bleeding one.

"She's here now, you can ask her," Richard suggested. The man behind him banged Richard's head off the table again and he grunted at the impact; Lizbet gasped.

Colan's face soured.

Richard though, continued, "I told him that if he'd laid you right the first time then you wouldn't have minded him coming back for more." He stopped abruptly as his face was banged again into the table top, Richard spat out blood, "Obviously he's a lousy…" That earned him punch to the head.

"You can watch me in a minute and see what you think!" Colan announced, pulling the stopper from the earthenware jar with his teeth, he spat it across the room and sniffed the contents appreciably.

"Colan, he's just trying to fool with you, let him up," Lizbet gathered her wits. "I'll get a cup for that, it's too good to be drinking it from the jar," she added, moving carefully past him to where the cups stood on the top of the coffer. Returning she poured

Lucy's wine into the cup and put it down in front of him, the wine she put on the coffer.

"And you, lass, can come back with me," Colan give Lizbet's backside a painful squeeze and she smiled at him.

Colan drained the cup in two quick mouthfuls and licked his lips. "You don't mind a drop of the good stuff do you?" then holding the cup out to Lizbet, "Fill it woman." Lizbet returned it to his hands, full. Her eyes catching Richard's for a moment, she hoped he knew what she had done; he'd certainly been watching her carefully enough.

Colan eyed her, "And look at you," his eyes raked her up and down. "A white apron isn't going to make you what you're not." Reaching over, he grabbed the white front and ripped it from her waist.

Lizbet was not going to back down, "Now, Colan, that was new. Why did you do that?"

The man with his face against the table made a noise, it took a moment longer for Colan to realise that in fact he was laughing. Reaching across, his massive hand lifted Richard's head by the hair and he stared him fully in the face. "Go on, what's funny now?"

"Tes un chien et tu as l'intelligece d'un enfant de cinq ans." Richard seemed still amused.

"What's he saying, what's he said?" Colan demanded banging his fist off the table.

The man holding Richard down just shook his head and it was Lizbet who spoke, "I don't know a word of it. Let him up, Colan please, and we'll just go."

"You know what they say," the amused voice continued, "if you can't say something nice, then say it in French."

Colan's rage was starting to boil, his face reddening even further at the remark. "What did you say? Tell me, or by God I will make you suffer."

"I said you are a dog and a bloody idiot, shall we ask Lizbet for her opinion on that?" Richard suggested spitting out another mouthful of blood.

Colan stood up. About to send a fist at Richard's head, he suddenly stopped, his hand instead grasping at the collar of his jerkin. A great whooping gasp escaped his lungs, making him sit back down, eyes wide, and chest heaving with the effort of breathing.

"Colan, are you alright, Colan?" were the last words spoken by the man holding Richard down. Richard had retrieved the small knife from his boot unnoticed and he used it now slicing at the man's leg. The man staggered, holding the cut, blood pouring through his fingers as he backed against the wall, terror in his eyes as he saw what Richard meant to do. A brutally hard hand pressed against his mouth a moment later to silence him. The neat blade was first stabbed and then levered around, opening a gaping wound in his throat; air escaped with a sudden hiss, the blood bubbling from the incision. Lizbet's stomach convulsed and she staggered against the corner of the coffer, retching.

Colan just stared from where he sat.

Richard held the dead man upright. "Get a blanket, quickly." Lizbet hesitated until she suddenly realised why: blood pumped from the wound, soaking both men and soon it would pool on the floor and drip to the room beneath from between the planking. She appeared with two and the body was deposited onto the rough wool. The room suddenly had a sharp metallic, unpleasant smell.

Lizbet looked at Richard. There was blood from his neck to his waist. "Is any of that yours?"

Richard - shaking his head - retook the seat at the table. Colan's breathing came in shallow noisy gasps, his mouth hung open and saliva ran from it in a gloopy trail down his jacket. Richard met Lizbet's eyes and asked, "How much did you give him?"

Lizbet, her face still white, pulled the small bottle from her pocket and shook it. "All of it."

Richard returned his gaze to Colan, "As I said, an idiot." Colan looked like he was trying to speak, his mouth twitching in a drool-ridden mess, but if there were any words they were soundless ones. A moment later he pitched forward onto the table. After a convulsive shake that ran the length of his body he lay still, dead.

Lizbet put her hands to her mouth, staring at Richard. "Look at you, I am so sorry." Tears streamed down her face.

There was a groan from the floor and they both looked at Jack. Lizbet dropped to her knees. "Jack are you alright?"

Jack pushed himself up. "For God's sake what's happened?" Disbelief on his face as he absorbed the scene with two dead men and his brother covered in blood. He tried to push himself to his feet but Lizbet pressed him down. "It's done Jack, it's over."

Lizbet cried loudly, mumbling endless apologies, as she rocked back and forth, choking from sobs, her breathing irregular and ragged.

"Lizbet," Richard's voice was firm. "Look at me Lizbet!" Reluctantly, she raised her eyes to meet his. "You could have left with Colan, why didn't you?"

Lizbet rubbed her running nose across the back of her hand. "They were hurting you, I didn't want them to," she wailed, "I'm sorry, I really am."

"Colan wasn't going to hurt you was he?" Richard continued.

"No, I know how to sort Colan. It's easy to get on his good side, he's a bit rough but nothing I'm not used to," Lizbet agreed, still crying.

"So your choice was Colan who'd not hurt you much, or myself who certainly has hurt you quite a lot. Why Lizbet?" Richard asked quietly. She didn't answer. Quietly, he asked the question again. "Please Lizbet. Tell me why?"

"The apple, you bought me an apple." Lizbet buried her head in her hands and wept. Richard really couldn't blame her for crying; an apple was not very much to commit murder over.

✝

It was February and rumours were rife at Court. Quiet ones in corners, cautious words capped with the caveat: 'Don't tell anyone.' The news was such that it would not be contained and within days the whole Court had heard the elaborately embellished rumour that the Queen was no longer with child. Where the news came from no-one was quite certain. The truth of the matter was that Lady Jane Hardwich, attendant to Her Most Gracious Majesty Queen Mary, had seen a pile of blooded towels and sheets, replete with crimson lumps and what looked like the twisted wreckage of an incomplete baby.

Questions were asked. A desk was set up in an antechamber and one by one those closest to the Queen were interrogated. What had they seen? What had they heard? Jane Hardwich braced herself for the questions and answered them with smooth lies as she knew she must. She had seen nothing.

Her interview over, Jane breathed a little easier. There were others who knew, there had to be! The sheets, towels and the unformed child must have been seen by many. The Queen's closest ladies must have attended her. Jane couldn't understand: the child had died, it was not uncommon. Even Queen's were not immune to the fickle hand of God when it came to births. Why maintain that she was still with child?

Mary herself had been seldom seen, having now gone into confinement and closeted with only her ladies around her.

"So are these rumours true?" Phillip was exasperated. "The Lady tells me her doctors tell her she is still with child and give still May as the date it will be born. What am I to think? I can hardly press the Queen on the matter when she is in such a state."

"There is no clear path, Your Highness, I agree. It is hard to quantify what we cannot see, we are forced to rely on the Queen. If we don't we risk upsetting the whole English Court. They are already saying that the rumours regarding the Queen's condition were started by your servants as we all wish to be gone from this miserable isle," Alberto said gravely.

"I agree with that; I do wish to be gone. Yet I can't, not while we are in such limbo. Is there or is there not a child?" Phillip repeated.

"They say May, Your Grace. Will they be more specific on the date?" Alberto asked.

"Babes, apparently, can obey their own rules; sometimes it is early May, sometimes late in the month. My nerves are shredded with it, I tell you." Phillip said impatiently. He was indeed starting to feel like this country and this Queen, were making a mockery of him.

✝

Colan was found artfully posed in death the following morning, propped against a wall a street away from the inn. A blade was wedged between his ribs and another was grasped in his stiffened hand, his cousin lay dead across his feet. His head lay at an impossible angle with a gaping wound in his neck that the night time rats had already found an inviting opening. They were known to be a quarrelsome pair and their demise was the talk of the inn for some days.

Lizbet had been sombre, reluctant to join in the gossip and her friends assumed it was because she had known Colan, although they could not understand why as he had been a vicious man with a bad temper and fists he used too freely. After a week the subject was talked out and Lizbet breathed a sight more easily. Mercifully no-one had seen Colan and his cousin coming into the inn and making their way up to Richard's rooms and Colan, it seemed, had kept his grudge to himself. The knife that Richard had forced between his ribs before leaving the body in the side street had pierced his already stilled heart, and it was assumed that this was the cause of death, what had killed his cousin had been fairly obvious to all.

Chapter Thirteen

The 7th of March 1555 was a Saturday. The incessant wet weather had finally abated, but the air was still bitingly cold, despite the fact that it was no longer laden with icy droplets. The soil on the river bank had reached a soggy saturation where it could hold no more moisture; the surface like ice.

Both men found themselves on their knees more than once as they scrambled up the slope into the small ornamental garden. The palace was forward-facing and there were few windows at the rear; those that did overlook the garden were shuttered, offering no light to assist their passage through the regimented greenery. The small garden had wide gravelled paths leading around the low hedges of lavender and sage, the diamond shaped topiary designed to resemble green embroidery. Richard, knowing where the paths were, felt his feet tread on gravel. He was about to warn Jack when he heard the unmistakable sound of his brother tripping over the low hedging and pitching himself full-length into the ornamental design.

"Don't say a word." Jack, cursing under his breath, crouched down next to his brother.

"Would I?" Richard replied quietly, with difficulty stifling a laugh. "At least we were not trying to arrive unannounced!"

Jack shot him an angry look but swallowed the retort and settled down next to Richard to wait. It was cold, but Jack thought, thankfully, dry. Richard knew they were to time the fire to start just as dusk was starting to fall to ensure maximum confusion in the smoke and the dark. From where the pair waited, they could easily hear the noise of Fairfax's servants on the other side of the wall, trying to set alight to the woodpile. Fairfax's plan was going horrendously wrong. The green boughs that were cut and kept for the pyre were now too wet to set alight, following a winter piled against the low wall that separated the two properties.

They both exchanged exasperated looks: Fairfax's steward sent out for more tinder. There was a great deal of shuffling and swearing from the other side of the wall, but still the boughs would not catch.

"I think you were right, this isn't going to work. How much longer do we wait?" Jack asked quietly. He was cold and wet and didn't really want to remain in the garden any longer than he had to.

"Until they give in," came the quiet reply he had known he would receive.

"I can't think of a better place to spend an evening," Jack's word were heavy with sarcasm.

Night had now truly taken over. The only light was a faint glow from Fairfax's side of the wall where the Steward and his men continued to try and set the wood on fire. Suddenly, a dull thump heralded a yellow glow as whatever liquid they had doused the wood in ignited instantly at the torch's touch.

"I don't believe it, they are actually cheering, can you hear them?" said Jack in the darkness, utter disbelief in his voice.

"Trust me, I'm thinking of joining in. It's taken them nearly an hour to get that damned fire going." Richard replied sarcastically. "Indeed I might need to go and warm myself at it; I'm bloody frozen."

"You're not the only one," Jack was rubbing his arms in a vain attempt to keep warm.

"I'm guessing they have just poured Fairfax's entire supply of aqua vitae on it to get it to light," Richard watched the yellow flames dance above the wall in the dark.

"I could use a cupful myself to warm my insides, I can tell you," Jack replied, then hopefully, "the wood is so wet, there's a good chance the fire won't get hold. If we are lucky it will just burn the aqua vitae out without setting the wood on fire."

"We can only hope," agreed Richard, quietly rubbing his own hands together to keep them warm.

As they watched, the yellow flames fuelled by Fairfax's liquor began to change to orange as they dried the wood and then set it to burn. It was a still night and it could not have served them better; there was already a blanket of fog which had crept up from the Thames and the smoke seemed to be trapped between the land and the fog, clinging close to the ground.

"I think this is going to work, you know," Jack observed gloomily, then, "It looks like you might be wrong for once."

His brother ignored his remark, saying instead. "Wait here while I see what's happening," Richard pushed himself up and headed towards the house.

"Just hurry up, I'm bloody half frozen," Jack replied quickly as his brother disappeared into the night.

With Richard gone, Jack crouched down again to wait. The fog seemed to push the darkness back towards the ground. He could smell the aroma of woodsmoke on the air, masking the stale unpleasant tang given off by the river. Where was Richard? Jack's eyes searched the gloom of the gardens but he could discern neither movement nor the sound of his brother returning.

The back of the house was in complete darkness. The fog - thickened with smoke - had real substance, if there was moonlight in the sky, none was admitted through its smoky presence. The fog-riddled smoke had another effect; it seemed to have robbed the sound from his surroundings. There wasn't a bird call, the lap of the water on the river bank had gone and even the noise from Fairfax's men was now absent.

He stood up and turned about, casting eyes around for some point of reference. Jack's throat tightened. He felt sealed off from the world and, in the silence at the back of his mind, he heard a sudden mad cackle of laughter. Without warning, the sharp claw clamped onto his chest; he recognised it and cried out inwardly. *No, please, no...*

All thought of the night, his brother, why they were there started to leave him as the crawling, evil creature within spread its talons, it's incessant cruel laugh ringing in his ears. Jack tried to stop it. He hit out wildly at the wall he knew was to his left, feeling the pain as his knuckles left their skin on the stones. He hit out again and again, trying to feel the pain, to focus his mind on it and away from the creature in his mind, but the laughter just increased. Jack sank to the ground, his arms around his knees.

†

Richard ran back silently through the gardens, avoiding the low ornamental hedges and keeping his feet on the gravel paths more by memory than sight; it was now truly dark. Behind him, he heard the shouts of the servants raising the alarm in Durham Place as the smoke had begun to make its presence known.

"Come on, Jack, let's go," Richard had arrived back at the place where he knew Jack was waiting for him.

There was no reply.

"Jack?" Richard spoke a little louder this time.

Nothing.

He had to be here. Richard stopped motionless, closed his eyes and listened. The sound, when it finally came to him, was unnatural and directly in front of him. Moving forward carefully in the dark, he found Jack when his foot kicked something soft which moved.

"Jack?" Still no reply.

Richard knelt quickly. If they had found Jack in the darkness then there was no reason to suppose they would not find him and he hadn't exactly been quiet. Cursing his stupidity and as quietly as he could, he drew his knife, setting his senses to find Jack's assailant in the darkness. The only noise that met his ears was Jack's ragged breathing. Satisfied, after what seemed an age, that he was not about to be jumped in the darkness, Richard turned his attention to his brother.

He found his head. "Are you hurt?"

There was still no reply.

Richard ran his hands over Jack's body. There were no tell-tale sticky patches where a blade had entered, nothing seemed amiss. Jack was curled up, his head to his knees, breath coming in angry rasps.

"Jack, Jack, please speak to me," Richard had his hand on Jack's shoulder. He slid it down his arm and found his hands pulling his knees up to his chest.

"Jack, please." Urgently he grasped Jack's hand. As he took hold of it understanding caught up with him.

"No," his voice was as anguished as Jack's had been. As he'd found the trembling hand he realised what was wrong.

"I'm sorry," Richard said regretfully. Standing, he set off back across the garden, alone. He did not get as far as the house before realising he was never going to leave his brother. After taking three more slow false steps towards the house he stopped. Cursing under his breath, he turned on his heel and retraced the path to where he knew Jack was. Jack's rightful accusation ringing in his ears: 'Damn you to Hell you left me for her.'

"Come on, help me, Jack, don't make me do this all on my own," Richard tried to pull the prone man back to a sitting position. There was a wall to his left and he managed to get Jack propped against it. Still his head lolled in front of him and the harsh animal breathing never stopped.

"What do we do Jack? Why didn't you tell me? What do I need to do?" Richard asked desperately, shaking him. "Jack, tell me, what do I need to do?"

Jack's senses started to return to him sooner than was usual: the cackling laughter that haunted his mind was drowned out by another insistent noise. He couldn't understand it at first, but he recognised it and as he followed the sound of his brother's voice, it became clearer, as though he were climbing out of some cave back to the surface.

Richard, in his frustration, shook the unresponsive man violently again by the shoulders as he tried to break through and get Jack to listen to him, to hear him. "Jack, we need to go, Jack come on, come back to me. I'm here, for God's sake, Jack, talk to me." Richard kept on repeating the words, shaking him; he'd even slapped his face a good few times to try and elicit some response from him. He stopped and listened: he was rewarded with a calming in his brother's breathing. It was something.

Richard didn't know what to say, but his words, his voice seemed to have helped, so he continued. "This must be payment for when I pulled my shoulder out, do you remember? I have never known pain like it since. If I had a dozen knives thrust into me, it could not have hurt as much." Richard paused, sat down heavily next to Jack, put his arm around his brother and pulled his unresponsive body to slump against him

"You lifted me up. I never told you - I think when you did, I fainted with the pain - then I found myself helpless and supported up by you. God, I was furious. I'm not sure what hurt the most: the shoulder or my pride. Then you talked to me whilst I regained my senses, you never gave me an inkling of what you meant to do. God, it bloody hurt. I can't remember if I screamed, but I think I probably did. The next I knew was when I awoke on the hillside soaked with sweat and shivering like..." Richard paused, "shivering like you are now." Richard listened: Jack's breathing was now harsh but regular, so he continued. "I don't think I ever said thank you. You could have left me and I probably deserved that, but you didn't."

Jack's voice against his shoulder was barely audible. "Are you trying to say I am like a loyal hound?" There was a pause while he gasped in more air, "loyal and devoted but as thick..." He didn't finish as air choked in his throat.

"Jack, thank God." Richard felt control coming back to the lifeless body propped against him. "What do I need to do? Help me, help you."

"I'm sorry..."

"Later. What do I need to do now?" Richard asked firmly.

"I'll be alright in a minute..." Jack managed.

"You're about as alright as a hanged man," Richard countered. "Tell me, I need to know?"

"It comes on..." Jack started, then stopped: he couldn't say the word.

"Go on, it comes on when?" Richard prompted, holding Jack's shoulders tightly.

"In the dark, when it is quiet, when..."

"When you are alone?" Richard finished for him after Jack's words stopped.

"Yes, alone. It's what Marshalsea has done," Jack sobbed. Richard had to turn his head away.

Richard collected his thoughts quickly; he had to get his brother out of the garden. "Come on, get up. Take my arm." Jack did and clumsily, using the wall and his brother for support, he made it back to his feet.

Jack's arm over his shoulder, he began to guide him away from Durham Place, talking quietly all the time and hoping his words were helping. "None of us, Jack, are all solid and whole; we all have weaknesses." He shifted his grip on Jack's wrist to better manage his weight. "Christ man, how much has Lizbet been feeding you?"

"You don't have any," Jack managed in reply.

"I don't have any what?" Richard swayed slightly under the burden, focusing on keeping the pair of them upright and going in the right direction.

"Weaknesses," Jack managed, his voice shaking still.

"Oh no, we are not having that conversation now. I'm fairly sure you've pointed out mine to me on many occasions. And I think the scales are levelling up nicely. Now shift your bloody feet that way and keep on going," Richard acrimoniously retorted.

†

It was half an hour later when Richard shouldered the door open to their rooms.

"Lord, what have you done to him?" shrieked Lizbet, looking at Richard holding Jack up.

"Nothing. I'll be back later, I have to go," Richard said and with that he was gone, leaving Jack standing, holding onto the door frame.

"Jack, come in, sit." Lizbet pulled a chair out from the table and moved to take his arm. His skin was pale, there was blood all over his left hand and mud clung to his clothes. "What's happened to you Jack, have you been in a fight?"

"Leave me, woman, I need no help." Jack closed the door behind him and sat down heavily at the table, his head dropping into his hands.

"I want to know what's gone on," Lizbet demanded, pulling the cuff away from his hand to see the cuts better. "Oh God, they look sore, Jack, please tell me?"

"What's it got to do with you?" Jack's voice was weary.

"I'm charged with looking after you. So what happened?" Lizbet demanded none-to-kindly. "Look at you, you're covered in mud and blood."

"Bloody hell, what kind of man am I that needs a woman to look after him?" Jack buried his face in his hands once more.

"Will you tell me?" Lizbet demanded again sternly, her fingers on the buttons to his doublet. "Get this off, it's soaked."

When Jack didn't answer, she pushed his head back so she could look in his face. "You bloody fool." She released it with force. "What happened?"

Jack frowned unhappily in resignation, "We were just waiting, that was all, just waiting."

"In the dark?" Lizbet asked; she had recognised the haunted look on Jack's face all too well.

"In the dark," Jack repeated shakily. "Then Richard went to find out what was happening..." He couldn't bring himself to finish, or to say what had happened next.

"You haven't told him, have you?" Lizbet hissed, "God have mercy, you fool, why the hell not? I told you to tell him. How else is he going to look out for you, or himself?"

"I couldn't," Jack's voice was almost a whisper, "how could I tell him what makes me so afraid?"

"Oh well, at least he knows now." Lizbet stood next to Jack and wrapped her arms around him, pulling his head against her stomach.

"He knows now." Jack echoed with a painful breath, his eyes closed. He wound his arms around her waist and buried his face in the folds of her skirt, letting her rock him gently, as she would a child.

✝

"What are you doing?" came the shout from behind him.

"Please, Master, the Lady sent me back in for this?" Richard was holding aloft a delicate sewing box inlaid with mother-of-pearl.

"Bloody women! I told them the house was safe but nobody ever listens to me. It's just smoke. Happened last year and they've all gone screaming into the street." The man Richard had come across was Thomas Parry.

"Shall I tell them to come back in, Master?" Richard offered obediently.

"No, no, not until this smoke clears. The horses have been sent round and the ladies are going to York House tonight," Parry grumbled. "The place is full of bloody smoke, it'll take days to get rid of the smell. Bloody Fairfax will have a lot to answer for I can tell you."

"I'll go and take this out Master, if you'll not be needing me," Richard bowed and made a hasty retreat passed Parry and towards the gatehouse at the side of Durham Place where the doors stood open.

Outside in the Strand, the scene was one of chaos. God, it seemed, had indeed smiled on Fairfax's plan. No wonder Parry was hiding indoors. Servants holding aloft torches lit the way for their masters. Others carried valuables and boxes out of Durham Place and piled them in the street. There were several groups stood around and nobody seemed to be in control. A cart had been hastily brought around to transport the valuables away and it stood now outside the house. One of the horses, wide-eyed and kicking, had been released from the traces; a stable hand was holding it, trying to calm the beast. Its companion still stood attached to the cart, stamping angrily. There was no-one controlling it and the horse could smell the thick woodsmoke - a smell that instinctively bred panic in any animal.

Richard headed for the cluster of women standing near the cart; he recognised one of them. With a brown plait sneaking from under a white linen cap and a cloak over a nightgown, it was Catherine de Bernay standing in the torch lit gloom. He made his way straight for her.

"I've brought the box you asked for m'lady," stooping to put it next to her. As he stood, he placed a finger rapidly across her lips. She looked at him askance but obeyed the command.

"Where's Elizabeth?" he asked quickly.

"I've not seen her," Catherine replied, looking wildly about her, but she recognised nobody around her. Then, "What's happening? Where is the fire?"

Richard didn't answer; he was too busy looking around the Strand for Elizabeth. Away from the carriage on the other side of the street were a small group of men at arms and what looked like more of Elizabeth's household. As he set his foot toward them, the remaining horse still tethered to the carriage, reared.

Richard shouted a warning, then with all the strength he had, he rammed Catherine into the girl standing at her elbow. Both women staggered and he continued pushing. Catherine tried to push him away, her hands outstretched, but it was too late; she felt herself falling as her feet went from beneath her. She crashed heavily on the other girl and Richard landed on top of the pile. Both women were screaming.

The horse reared and, the cart only held by a horse on one side had tipped; when it reared a second time and there was enough momentum then for the cart to continue over onto its side, pulling the screaming horse still attached to the long wood shafts with it. The cart landed not two feet from where Catherine lay in a tangle of arms and legs, its impact sending out splatters of mud in all directions.

Richard was the first to stand, offering an arm, he pulled Catherine back to her feet. "Are you hurt?"

Catherine, her eyes bulging, gasped for air; the fall had knocked the air from her lungs. Richard held her tightly, realising what had happened, "it'll come back lass, it will, just be still."

She shook her head, panic in her eyes. She fought to breathe and couldn't.

"Just try and breathe in a little," Richard kept his voice even and level.

Catherine's face was the epitome of terror.

"It will. Lift your head up, here like this," Richard pushed her head backwards, her face to the night sky and heard the first whopping breath come back into her chest, followed by another angry gasp. Catherine's hands gripped hard; so tight was the hold she had on him, he felt her nails through his sleeve. Shaking, she began to sob. Richard pulled one arm around her shoulders Catherine buried her face against his chest.

"I'm so sorry. I have to go." Richard said firmly.

"Help me - there's two at least trapped under here," a man's voice shouted beside him.

Turning, Richard looked at the wreckage of the cart where he had stood only a moment before. A leg, running with crimson, protruded from the cracked planking.

"Catherine please." - Richard peeled Catherine's hands from him - "I need to help."

Catherine let go and Richard held her shoulders for the briefest of moments, "You're safe."

Turning, he moved to help pull apart the wreckage of the carriage.

"We need to free the horse, it's weighing it down," yelled Richard.

The panicking horse thrashed wildly, unable to right itself. Richard set to work cutting the leather traces that were securing the horse. The straps were pulled taut by the horses struggling weight and they were trying to lift the wagon against them. Using his knife quickly, he cut them away. As the last one was sliced, the tension released, the horse was free and the men trying to lift the wagon felt it.

Richard joined them. "If we pull now, it should come away." There were others there now, when he turned he saw that Catherine was one of them, all pulling at the broken carriage, trying to raise it enough so those trapped underneath could be pulled free.

"Higher, higher!" called one man; who was on his knees underneath the raised wagon bed, trying to reach those trapped. "Just a little more and we can pull them free. There, hold it there." Helping hands grasped three unconscious bodies and pulled them out from under the wooden trap.

"They're out, let go, lads!" It was a signal and those that had been straining to hold the cart side aloft let it go with an almighty crash. Richard caught Catherine's eye for a second before he turned and left them.

The group over the street had gone by the time Richard arrived. In the smoke that still emanated from the orchard, the street was cast into further gloom. There was indeed confusion, as predicted and the only light that punctuated the night came from those carrying lit torches aloft. One such man approached Richard at a run. Richard's foot caught his ankle and sent him falling headlong forwards. A hand gripped the back of his jerkin to stop him landing with full force and another neatly stripped him of his light before he even knew what had happened.

Torch in hand, Richard methodically searched the street. Every doorway, every turn, he found household servants out in the street agog at what was happening. He came across two men carrying a great chest between them in the dark; he could only guess that they had been sent to take it to safety, away from the fire. Fire made the hearts of Londoners run icy with fear. Its fickle fingers could in an evening take away a home, a business, a family, wealth, security - everything a man had.

Circling around the street twice again he could find no trace of any of Elizabeth's household, or of Kate. The pain of not knowing what had happened was almost physical. He'd arrived back too late. Elizabeth was gone; but to where he didn't know. He could only hope she had been forewarned and that she was safe with Kate; Travers men had hopefully taken her quickly to safety. The worry was that Fairfax's badly concocted plan had worked and that meant she was somewhere in London, waiting to be sent to the Dutch Flower. If this *was* the case, he needed to get back to his lodgings and wait for a messenger from Fairfax, requesting that he join the party going to the ship. It would be a long night and with luck the message would never arrive; he could only hope that Fairfax's men had failed to intercept her on the Strand. Extinguishing the torch in a trough, he turned back again towards the inn.

✝

 Jack looked up hopefully - but when his brother silently just dropped onto one of the chairs at the table opposite him, he knew better than to ask. Lizbet watched them both from where she sat quietly by the fire. Jack sat with his blond head bent, face buried in his hands. Richard had folded his arms on the table and his head lay on them, eyes open, staring at the wall. Whatever had happened to them tonight, Lizbet could only guess at.
 Both ignored her small movements and the noise she made as she placed four more pieces of wood on the fire, turning the embers with a poker so they would catch. The new wood was wet, but the fire was hot enough to burn it and suddenly the room was alive with the noise of it hissing and spitting as the moist life left the wood.
 Lizbet stood and wiped her damp hands on her apron. Leaving the pair to their thoughts, she quietly closed the door behind her. Neither man had moved when she returned carrying a basket and a tray. Her hands full, she closed it in her accustomed fashion: with her backside. She bumped the basket down on the table and lowered the tray, the two pewter beakers on it jangling together noisily.
 "Thanks for the help," she muttered.

Richard still stared silently at the wall. Without warning, a pair of eyes appeared in front of his face and he was forced to blink and change his focus.

"I don't care how clever you think you are, but you'll not find the answer on that wall, no matter how long you stare at it." Lizbet had an irritated edge to her voice.

"Leave me be," Richard commanded, his voice angry, his eyes full of temper.

"Aye, I will, soon enough." Lizbet rose and noisily filled both the cups and stood one in front of Richard's face. "And there's bread and cheese and ham. Now, get yourselves sorted out."

Neither man moved.

"I'm talking to you!" Lizbet slapped Richard on the back and gave Jack's shoulder a great shove forcing him to raise his head from his hands.

"Woman, you can't know what has happened, just leave us," Jack was angry now as well.

"I can't know, you're right, but I can see what's happening now. I'm ashamed. Both of you sitting there like children feeling sorry for themselves. It's not right." Lizbet banged down a loaf of bread on the boards between them making the cups rattle.

"Oh God, Lizbet, you're right." Richard pushed himself upright and ran his hands through his untidy hair.

"Drink this, eat some of that and sort yourselves out," Lizbet paused, then added, "Master."

Richard accepted the cup and pushed the other towards his brother. "Jack, things have been worse." Richard pulled off a chunk of bread, the smell of it reminding his stomach he was indeed hungry.

"When?" Jack asked, his hand scooping up the beaker.

"Often. I think the list too long to go through now, don't you?" Richard announced, "We can go through them all later. Here, have some of this," and he pushed the bread towards Jack.

Chapter Fourteen

That Fairfax's plan had worked owed a great deal to luck and in some measure also to the reduced household that Elizabeth had been provided with, paid for as it was by sister who kept an eye on the expenditure incurred by her. If there were more trained men on hand and if Travers had taken control of the situation, rather than hiding inside Durham Place, then the outcome might have been very different. They found out that the conspirators had managed to acquire Elizabeth from the street just as Lizbet was taking the empty pots back to the inn downstairs. Richard read the brief note and sat down heavily, the parchment still in his hand.

"Come on, tell me?" Jack was trying to read over Richard's shoulder. After an hour, all that remained now of the attack that had paralysed him, was a dull ache deep inside his head.

"Let me think." Richard screwed the paper up and sent it into the centre of the fire.

"What did it say?" Jack persisted, watching the white paper burst into flames.

"Shut up, Jack, I'm thinking," Jack sank back in his chair a dark look on his face. Jack began to wonder if his brother was ever going to speak whilst minutes dragged painfully on.

"Fairfax has Elizabeth. He wants me to get to the ship, ensure she is still good to sail in the morning and then meet back with Fairfax's group," Richard spoke thoughtfully. "There will be at least six of Fairfax's men with her and there are only two of us."

"Not good odds; and they'll be looking for trouble," Jack agreed solemnly.

"I agree. So we need to separate the group en route to the ship and improve the odds. Come on, we'll find somewhere on the way." Richard's chair scraped back and he was on his feet, heading for the door.

"I'm guessing I'm invited," Jack sighed under his breath. He followed Richard out of the door, pocketing bread and cheese from the table on his way.

†

The way to the docks was not far and London was quiet. In winter, the bells rang out for curfew at dusk which settled early still in March. A cramped and crowded city, with upper floors built out over the streets, light leaked round the edges of poorly fitting shutters and through oil cloth windows. The sky was clear and a cold cloudless night was lit by the white light from a moon that had only just begun to wane. Quickly and quietly, they made their way across the city. Only the main streets in London were paved and those, by necessity, they avoided. It was a gamble, but Richard took a route he hoped Fairfax's men would use when they took Elizabeth to the ship. After the curfew bell rang, those who remained in the streets were required to carry a torch with them and have a good reason for being outside - Richard had no intention of running into the night watch.

They went past a tavern, both men heard the voices and laughter from within and smelt the aromas - stale ale and food - that wafted into the street. Richard saw the barrels at the end of the tavern and held up his hand, signalling Jack to stop. They had been heading in a fairly straight line through the city to the river. A narrow alley cut across both sides of the street at the end of the tavern, and here were piled the empty barrels. Silently Richard pointed to where he wanted the barrels. The hogshead barrels they left - they were too heavy - but the firkins were half the size they could quietly heft them up the steep alley running alongside the tavern.

They couldn't roll them - the noise would have been too great - so they lifted the wooden casks and heaved them to a better position further up the steep alleyway. Four of them they moved and stood them neatly side by side; Jack was thankful when Richard seemed satisfied with the four repositioned casks.

He assumed that they were there to be rolled down the hill at an unsuspecting target, but, more than that, he could not even begin to guess at.

Richard touched his arm and it was the signal to set off again. Returning to the main street. Richard motioned Jack to wait near the other barrels. "Will you be alright for a few minutes?" Richard asked; his voice was not tinged with concern, he just needed to know the answer. Jack nodded, then scowled at his retreating back.

He was gone for only a few minutes and when Jack saw him return, he was walking backwards across the street carrying something. As he approached, Jack saw what he was doing; he held a coil of rope and he was laying it in a line across the street, taking the loose end up the narrow alley to where the firkins now rested. Then, as silently as he had arrived, he was gone again, but this time he returned almost straightaway: a pan in each hand filched from a stove top. Carefully - so the pans did not rattle together - he tied them to the rope and laid both next to each other on the ground at the side of the alley.

This time, when they set off, it was to the docks. It took them another twenty minutes to carefully pick their way through London to where the Dutch Flower sat on her moorings. She was a Fluyt, Dutch built and designed with one purpose: to transport cargo. Unlike her companions with which she shared her moorings the Fluyt was not constructed to allow conversion to a warship when needed. Her cargo sat low, well-packed and organised. Her wide beam meant she could carry twice as much as the other ships, a simple design meant she could be handled by a smaller crew. All of these details made the mechanisms of trade run economically smooth.

Jack eyed her for the first time from where Richard had bid him wait while he sought out the captain. She was lit with lamps and men were readying her for the morning tide. He thought her ugly, wide and flat the ship a fat appearance, not at all like the nimbler, taller English ships. Her shallow draft allowed her to get further upstream and the Fluyts were opening up trade routes never-before accessible. She stood out amongst the other ships and Jack knew he would easily know her if they came back to the docks again.

Richard soon came back and crouched down next to Jack. "They are ready."

"I thought you didn't want to bring her to the ship?" Jack had a confused look on his face, "I thought that was the whole point?"

"It is," Richard agreed, then added unnecessarily, "Things did not go exactly to plan this evening did they? So I'm hoping we don't end up back here later. But in case we do, I need to make sure there is a ship ready for us and not just an empty mooring."

"Sorry," Jack grumbled.

"We will head back now to where Fairfax's group are waiting and then hopefully they will take the route passed the tavern where we laid our traps, be sure you know where it is. I will meet with

Fairfax's men and hopefully they will take that route to the Dutch Flower. When we leave, get yourself in front of us and make it to the tavern, then wait for my signal. We need to split the group up." Richard grinning, slapped Jack on the shoulder. "And I'm sure we can."

Jack still had a pressing headache and wondered not for the first time where Richard got his enduring energy from. It had indeed, been a long day already and it looked like it was about to get even longer.

"What's the signal going to be?" Jack wanted to make sure this was going to go according to plan

"I don't know yet," Richard admitted. "I'll think of something."

"Bloody hell, that's helpful," Jack could see Richard's face lit by the moonlight, "You are actually enjoying this, aren't you?"

Jack saw him raise his brows. "And tell me you're not?"

Jack was about to reply to the contrary when he realised that actually that might be a lie. "Just make sure I hear your signal. There'll be at least six men, all nervous as hell and looking for trouble."

"You'll know it when it comes and with rope and barrel we will try and split the group in half. On the other side of that tavern is another narrow alley leading up to Moor Road and I'll go up there. If you go straight up as well we'll meet on the same street," Richard finished.

"Then hopefully there will only be three to deal with," Jack added, "or fewer if we are lucky."

"I hope so and if we are quick we can avoid the others before they realise we've gone." Richard completed the plan. "I'm sorry it's not much better than that."

Jack clapped him on the arm. "I'll be ready."

"Will you be alright, Jack?" Richard asked, a serious note in his voice.

"Aye, there's a fair moon, I'll not let you down," Jack managed, although he resented the reminder of his earlier incapacity.

"Good, let's set our feet on the path then," and the pair headed from the dock and the Dutch Flower.

†

Jack waited in the shadows at the address Fairfax had given Richard in his earlier message. He rubbed his hands up and down his arms to ward away the cold that was settling uncomfortably into his limbs and lifted numb feet to try and revive the stifled blood flow. *Come on Richard, I'm freezing my bloody backside off here.*

He had expected Richard to emerge with the group and set off to the docks sooner than this. Annoyance soon started to turn into worry.

Something's gone wrong. This is taking too long Richard, what is it you haven't thought of?

Jack was getting close to leaving his position and going in search of Richard when finally a side door to the house opened and figures emerged into the night.

Jack, relieved, set off silently on the route he knew they were going to take. As he made his way quickly to the tavern, the bells struck nine times. *Was that all it was?* A sense of time had left him tonight; it seemed almost a day ago that he had waited at the riverbank for Fairfax's men to light the fire.

Jack was soon in the alleyway, the firkins lined up in front of him and the rope ready in his hands, listening. He thought they would be closer behind him than they were, but then of course they would be moving at a woman's pace and that would slow them.

The signal, when it came was crude, simple and effective.

Jack had not heard them approach, but suddenly a voice in the night spoke, a voice he recognised.

"There, there's someone in the dark over there."

Very subtle thought Jack, a smile on his face.

Jack pulled on the rope and the pans clanked on the opposite side of the street.

"My God," a familiar voice spoke again, "they are coming towards us, I see them!"

"Poor bastards, having him on your side," Jack said under his breath and pushed the first of the four firkins down the alley. The last two had not even left the alleyway before Jack was running up the hill towards Moor Street. Behind him he heard a thud followed by a scream as one of the firkins found a mark and then another howl as a second cannoned into another man.

Now there's only four - Jack grinned; he was starting to feel much better.

Jack was making his way along the back of the tavern towards the alley he knew Richard would be coming up, when he heard the men moving towards him.

Keeping back in the shadows, he waited for them to draw level. Jack stepped out of the blackness, and Richard, seeing him, released his guiding hold on Elizabeth. The pair turned on the two men behind them.

†

One man drew his sword whilst the other hesitated. A mistake. Richard was upon the unarmed man in a moment. Jack's own sword whistled from the scabbard; both blades, not yet engaged, caught the moonlight. Jack could barely see his attacker and he had no measure at all of the man. Swordplay in the dark was a fool's game and he knew it.

A poniard in his left hand, sword held defensively in his right, he waited for the other to move. His attacker was shielded from the moonlight by the shadow of a building, apart from seeing the nightlight play along his blade for an instant Jack could see very little.

Bloody Hell! Jack swore silently. He knew the man saw him clearly and he had no idea where the attack was going to come from. When the blade came at him, it was a deadly swing aimed at his head. It was half training and half instinct that deflected it. The steel of his own blade squealed as it slid along the length of the other sword. The hilts rattled together bringing both men close, too close. Jack got a kick in first to the other's groin before he received one himself.

Two moves was all it had taken to tell Jack the man was a danger. The next attack when it came was a quick double flash of the blade designed to wrongfoot him and break through his defence. Jack, out of practice, almost got it wrong, his own blade too low, he was forced to slam the attacking blade back with his poniard; it saved him, but it was clumsy and his arm jarred painfully from the impact.

Breaking all his own rules he took two steps backwards, giving him time to get his blade back in front of him, but it informed his attacker he was on the defensive and it invited an attack. When the blade came at him again, it was a low swing designed to cut in to his legs. His own steel engaged just in time, sparking in the dark as it blocked the blade.

The fight was against him.

The next attack on his defence he did not see, but his ears heard the blade slice the air and his own met it just in time to deflect the lethal sharpened edge. Then another stroke came his way, high and from the right. He took the other's blade down the length of his and twisted his own away.

The moonlight was still in his aggressor's favour. He could see Jack faintly outlined by the light. But Jack's vision gave him almost nothing, the other man was still cloaked by the dark shadows. Jack was guessing, and he knew it.

The man who sought to kill him was well trained and he was making a deadly attack. Jack quickly dropped his sword and his blade met the other's as he attempted to hamstring him. Expecting now a blow to his right side, Jack spun left and tried to reverse his position with his attacker's.

The attack never came. There was a sudden dull thud, followed by something that sounded like a sack of grain falling and a series of light metallic tinkles as the blade his attacker had been holding rattled on the pebbled street.

Richard's face appeared before him. "That was either inspired or bloody good luck."

"Jesus! It was luck and it was about to run out on me. Thank you," Jack exhaled with relief as he slammed his blade back in the sheath. Next to the collapsed man in the street was the broken earthenware pot Richard had used to fell him.

They needed to put as much distance between themselves and Fairfax's men as possible. There were still three Jack guessed and from the noise he could tell they were perilously close. Richard had hold of Elizabeth's arm and even with a guiding hand on her elbow the woman was moving at a sorry pace, stumbling and making enough noise to wake the city.

They arrived at a junction; the narrow street opened onto a wider one well illuminated by the moon. It was hopeless to set off down it as they would be seen and caught up in moments.

"Over there," Richard indicated. Jack saw what he was pointing at: a dark passage between two buildings on the opposite side of the street.

Let's just pray it leads somewhere, said Jack silently.

It was narrow and crammed with debris which caught around ankles and clanked painfully into shins. Any hope of concealment was lost as soon as Elizabeth cried out. Their feet disturbed loose wood, a sleeping dog left the alleyway yelping after Richard trod on it and Jack, tripping on a broken cartwheel, cursed. Still they kept moving. Richard increased the pressure on her arm and propelled her even faster down the alley.

Throughout the city, there were inlets from the river; some of the cuttings were boat yards or moorings and all of a sudden the alley spat them out onto the edge of one. Jack made a grab for his brother's jacket as soon as he realised that the blackness in front of them was water. Richard had seen it as well and made a sudden stop, Elizabeth clumsily banging into him. If not for Jack's hold on his jacket he would have pitched forwards into the water.

"Which way?" Jack hissed, hearing their pursuers making equally hard work of coming down the narrow passage towards them.

"Over there," Richard pointed. It was tidal and the river was low and across the mouth of the inlet ran a narrow plank. It was set down a few feet from the bank, leading across the cutting to the other side.

Jack peered down at it dubiously. Even in the moonlight the growth of green algae was visible and he knew it would be as slippery as an eel's skin. "We can't go across that," Jack hissed.

"You haven't got a choice. Take the lady across, I'll delay them," Richard turned to go.

"I'm not damn well leaving you," Jack had hold of Richard's arm.

"The only way out is across the river. Get the lady across, Jack. For me, please. Go now, please." Richard pulled against the hold Jack had on his arm. "Let this be my bad plan alone."

"Damn her to Hell!" Jack, reading the plea on his brother's face reluctantly let him go.

"Go, please, now." Richard was already disappearing into the darkness back towards Fairfax's men. This was his cause, not Jack's - he'd be damned if he'd let Jack sacrifice himself for it. Richard just hoped he could give him the time he needed to get over the river.

"How do we get over that?" Elizabeth was staring at the wood that was beneath them.

"Carefully, how do you bloody think!" Jack retorted through gritted teeth.

Sitting on the bank, he swung his feet down to the plank and applied some pressure; it was lethally slippery. The river was easily ten feet below them - he couldn't see it, but he knew it was there, as black as Hell. Under his hands Jack felt the gravel on the bank, and quickly launched several handfuls along the length of the path they were going to have to take.

It's only ten paces. Ten slippery paces. Ten feet to the river.

Jack did not like the way this was all adding up. Then he heard the fight break out behind and knew he had no choice and no time. He flung two more handfuls of gravel rapidly along the slimy wood.

"Get on my back," Jack stood up on carefully on the wood.

"What!" the woman exclaimed.

"Get on, close your damned eyes, stay bloody still and I'll carry you over," Jack commanded.

She crouched down and sat on the edge of the bank where Jack had been and from there she reached two arms round his neck.

"Carefully," Jack warned. Pulling her skirts up, Jack passed his arms back and tucked them under her knees.

"Ready?" he asked. "Stay bloody still."

"I will," the woman's voice was near his ear.

"Here we go. Ten paces, that's all I've got to do," Jack was talking to himself. Carefully, lifting his foot he moved it along the wooden bridge. Putting it down, he felt some of the gravel beneath his boot and prayed it would help to stop him slipping. "Nine, more, only nine more. Come on Jack. There eight, only eight to go."

"Is this going to go on all the way over?" Elizabeth hissed in his ear.

"Don't bloody speak to me and don't bloody move," Jack silenced her.

Behind him he heard the fight; he wanted to go back, he didn't want to be doing this. Then there was a scream in the dark and Jack hesitated; he couldn't do this. He could still go backward to the bank.

Forcing his breathing to calm, he steadied his nerves.

Seven, six... the next two steps were not too bad and the gravel was helping hold his boots solid on the slippery perch. "Halfway, halfway, now come on. Four. Three. Jesus Christ..." his right foot slid on the wet wood and it took every ounce of his strength to stop the slide and regain his balance.

The bank on the opposite side and was only a few more paces away. Keeping his eyes fixed steadily on the grassy edge he took another step towards safety. It was then that he felt the plank beneath him give as someone else joined him on the slippery traverse.

Jack couldn't look back; he didn't know if it was his brother or not. He took the next two steps firmly and quickly. Reaching the edge and grasping the side, he bent his body over, allowing the woman to scramble off his back to safety and then he pulled himself up to the grass bank.

Looking back he saw it wasn't his brother who had followed him halfway over.

"Damn." There was a cold whistle in the night as Jack pulled his sword from its sheath. "Go back," he threatened.

The man's instinctive reaction was to back from the blade and that was his undoing. The movement cost him his balance and he screamed as he fell, then continued to scream as he fought to keep his head above the water.

"Come on, let's leave," Jack set off again away from the river and back into the London streets. He offered her a guiding hand and she was forced to run to keep up with him.

Jack stopped and signalled for her to be silent. He heard nothing. They weren't being followed any more; no-one else, it seemed, had tried to cross.

"Now what are we..."

"Shut up, I'm trying to think," Jack held his hand up to silence her.

Elizabeth's eyes widened, "I think..."

This time he put a finger across her lips.

Where now? What to do? He needed to find his brother and that meant...

Elizabeth slapped his hand away. Jack ignored her.

Think. Think!

If Richard was safe he would be looking for them and if he wasn't then...

"Right we are going back, the long way round," Jack spoke decisively.

"Why? You need to take me somewhere safe," she wailed grabbing his arm to stop him.

Jack wrenched his arm from her grasp, his face close to hers. "Know this, lady. I don't like you." Elizabeth stared in disbelief, "I need to find Richard. He knows I'll not leave him and that I'll go back for him, so that's where he'll be looking for me," Jack was pleased that he had a plan and one that made sense, if only in his own head. "It's not far, come on."

They indeed met Richard two streets away, running towards them. Elizabeth watched them silently as they exchanged a few words and then again she had Richard's guiding hand on her arm.

"Just a few more minutes and we will have you safe and arrange to get you back to York House," Richard reassured her.

Chapter Fifteen

They had to go somewhere quickly and it had been Jack who came up with the idea.

"Take her into the taproom at the inn and wait there," Jack suggested. His brother's face looked incredulous. He continued, "there are four ways out of there, everyone knows us and if we need to get out in a hurry it's as likely we'll get some help. And who is going to bother us if we take a lady in there? You said they'll likely be here for her in less than an hour. Sometimes it's safer to hide in plain sight."

"You might have a point," Richard conceded. His face betrayed that he didn't like the idea one bit. "Go on, you first."

Richard said something to Elizabeth; what it was Jack could not hear. Having already opened the door to the taproom all he could hear was the companionable banter of thirty voices on the other side. It was late but this was the student quarter so the inn closed when the last revellers left, fell asleep or ran out of money. Inside the smoky room there was laughter, music and a loud, familiar voice.

"Jack, come over here and sit down." Lizbet was already moving towards him. "Ah both my lads," she added seeing Richard behind him. "Come on over here, I'll clear a space for you. Eddie, shift your backside. Aye, go on move - my lads want to sit down and they've got coin, so off you get." The unfortunate Eddie was shoved from the bench as Lizbet made space for them. Then she yelled across the taproom, "Roddy, Roddy, send Patsy over with a jug and two." Then Lizbet saw the lady behind Richard. "Make that three cups." She yelled, her loud voice instantly gaining the landlord's attention.

Richard took a bench opposite Jack with Elizabeth sat next to him. Lizbet settled on Jack's knee, placing a proprietary arm around his shoulders.

"I'm fair pleased to see you back and looking a bit less sour, I have to say." She elbowed Jack playfully in the ribs.

"With such as you around me all day, woman, it's hard not to be sour!" Jack replied amicably and put his arm around her waist. Lizbet smiled broadly. She was relieved that their earlier quarrel was over, at least for the moment.

Ale arrived and Lizbet filled and passed out cups. "There you go, it's not the best, but it'll quench a thirst and turn a smile," she passed a cup to the lady sat next to Richard, one who was quite out of her place. *So where's Richard been hiding you then my lovely?*

Two musicians who had been taking a break returned to the middle of the inn and resumed their seats on the end of the central table; one held a battered lute and the other a whistle.

"He's good, got a fine voice on him," Lizbet confided to them, then turned and with two fingers in her mouth whistled loudly. "Give us Pastimes."

The lute player saluted her with his instrument. "For the lady, Pastime with Good Company." He bent his head to check the tune on the lute strings.

"I've not heard that for an age," Jack remarked. The song had been a popular one, especially with the students and apprentices in Henry's day. Written by the King himself shortly after his coronation, it spoke of a very different Henry to the one who had ended his days bedridden and bitter.

"Right then, a bit of quiet if I may..." The lute player raised his voice and the general hubbub died as he laid his fingers on the lute strings and began to play. "So here's one for good old King Hal, God rot, sorry God rest his soul." The patrons laughed and settled to listen to the players.

> *Pastime with good company*
> *I love and shall until I die*
> *Grudge who lust but none deny*
> *So God be please thus live will I*
> *For my pastance*
> *Hunt sing and dance*
> *All goodly sport*

> *For my comfort*
> *Who Shall me let*

There was a pause then Jack joined in with the second verse.

> *Youth must have some dalliance*
> *Of good or ill some pastance*
> *Company me thinks then best*
> *All thought and fancies to digest*
> *For idlenss*
> *Is chief mistress*
> *Of vices all*
> *Then who can say*
> *But mirth and play*
> *Is best of all*

The lute player nodded his approval and came over to sit on the end of Jack's table, his fingers still strumming the tune. "I'll leave the verse to you," and Jack sang alone, the closing part.

> *Is virtue vices to flee*
> *Company is good and ill*
> *But every man has his free will*
> *The best ensue*
> *The worst eschew*
> *My mind shall be*
> *Virtue to use*
> *Vice to refuse*
> *Thus shall I use me*

The lute player finished with a flourish of notes and bowed low to Jack, who, grinning, received the applause from the tap room. Lizbet, both hands on his shoulders, held him away from her, a look of pure delight on her face. "Well, my bonny boy, you'll never go hungry will you?" She regarded the woman sat next to Richard. "Have you ever heard better? I never knew he had such a voice in him." And then reproachfully to Richard, "You never told me he could sing so well."

"If I started to tell you about Jack's talents then we'd be here until Easter. It's best if you just discover them yourself, one at a time," Richard replied sarcastically.

Lizbet put her arm around Jack's shoulders protectively. "You're just jealous, I didn't hear you piping in." Then leaning across the table she said conspiratorially to Elizabeth, "He snores like fire pit bellows and I've always said a snorer can't hold a tune."

Jack in the middle of a mouthful of ale snorted so hard he had to clamp a hand to his face to stifle the ale that was pouring from his mouth and nose. Lizbet absently wiped his face on her sleeve, her own expression quite serious. Elizabeth's eyes were wide and the grey ones Richard turned on Lizbet were full of fury.

Lizbet just smiled widely, her own brown eyes twinkling with mirth. "Let's have a jig," she yelled over at the lute player, who had returned to his original table. Loosening her arm from Jack, Lizbet slid off the end of the bench. Kicking two fallen stools to one side, she cleared a space on the floor. "Come on, lads," she stood ready her hands on her hips.

"Name one, anyone you want," the whistle player asked the room in general.

"The old Grey Goose," someone piped up from across the room. "Do you know it?"

"Aye, we know that one," the lute player replied, then to Lizbet, "are you ready lass?"

"I am that." Lizbet hoisted her skirts to just below her knees revealing two badly shod feet. As soon as the first notes left the whistle she danced. The measure started at a slow pace and as the notes from the whistle began to increase in speed the patrons began to clap in time and smiling widely at her audience, she picked up the pace.

"She is quite good," Elizabeth leant towards Richard. The noise in the taproom was increasing as the drinkers clapped, banged the tables and shouted encouragement to Lizbet.

"Yes, I am sure Lizbet and Jack could join a touring troupe. Indeed I'll suggest it," Richard replied acidly.

Jack had heard his brother's comment and not about to be put down he joined in saying, "Maybe I could. I've got a few tricks with balance as well that I could add in, haven't I, my lady?"

Elizabeth laughed then. "And for that I am very grateful. You could become one of those tricksters walking on ropes across the river."

Had this bloody woman never met anyone who didn't like her? Jack supposed not. He leant a little closer, his voice was cold and his face unsmiling when he said. "Well, if I do and I need some practice and a lassie on my shoulders, I'll let you know. Can you swim?"

"The secret, I suppose, is not to look down." Elizabeth replied, her brown eyes holding his

"Ah now, that would be my problem and my undoing," Jack said, his blue eyes serious, holding hers. "I like a lass to look down onto."

Elizabeth blushed; Richard slammed his cup down on the table and Jack just laughed. Lizbet chose her moment well. Dropping her skirts, she held out both her hands in invitation to Elizabeth to join her in the reel.

"I can't," Elizabeth told Lizbet, but those were just words, her eyes said something else as she smiled at Lizbet.

Before Richard could complain Elizabeth had slid from the bench and was on her feet next to Lizbet, skirts held in ringed hands, revealing silk stockings on her ankles and a pair of Venetian calfskin shoes embroidered with small roses, the centre of each one glinting with a jewel, Lizbet gasped when she saw them, appreciation apparent on her face.

"Oh and to think I had those legs wrapped round me a while ago," Jack smirked at his brother.

Richard made to grab Jack's arm but his brother was faster and evaded him; there was a murderous edge in his voice. "She's not a bloody tavern wench; still your tongue. What did you do to her tonight?"

Jack regarded him levelly and wisely, for once, backed down. "Nothing. I had to carry her over the river, that was all."

The jig went on, Lizbet tucked her arm into Elizabeth's and the pair went round, side by side. As Elizabeth passed the opposite table, a hand came out and gave her backside an appreciative squeeze. "Get off her Roddy," Lizbet warned, sending one of her feet towards his shin.

Notes from the whistle fell one upon another as the pace became frenetic. Lizbet, releasing Elizabeth, took to the floor alone, her feet matching the quick notes. There was one long last note and Lizbet finished with a spin, her arms in the air. The inn cheered. Elizabeth clapped and Roddy, ignoring Lizbet's threats, went for another exploration of the silken behind not too far from his face; Elizabeth yelped. "Why don't they do that to you?"

Lizbet, breathing hard, swiped her hand across the back of Roddy's head, "They can see who I'm with, love, there's none in here that are stupid enough to pick a fight with Jack over a lass. You just need to show them you've declared and they'll sharp leave you alone," Lizbet explained.

"Declared?" Elizabeth was confused.

Lizbet couldn't resist, a smile on her face. "Here it's simple, I'll fix it for you." taking Elizabeth's hand she led her back to the table and there gave her a gentle push landing her on Richard's knee. Leaning forward so they could both hear she added, "Now they will sharp leave you alone, m'lady." And with that, Lizbet returned to sit again on Jack's knee. He didn't even look up as she settled herself back down.

Spinning around so she had her back to Richard and Elizabeth, an arm around Jack's neck, she pulled his head close to hers saying, "So who's the lady then?"

"Don't ask, Lizbet, just leave this one be, we'll not be here for long," Jack warned.

"Good. I don't think I can watch him suffer for much longer anyway," Lizbet chuckled.

"Suffer?" asked Jack his brows furrowed, confused, "He looks fine to me."

"Really? Lizbet exclaimed, then lowered her voice even further. "Look again."

"What are you on about, woman?" Jack was puzzled, seeing nothing at all.

"He's smitten and I'll bet his lady there doesn't even know it either," Lizbet announced.

"Are you serious?" Jack looked at the pair across the table from him with fresh eyes.

"Yes look. He's got his hands curled into fists so tight I'd wager his nails have drawn blood. And look every time she leans towards him he moves away. He can't bare the thought of touching her."

Jack, watching them closely now saw that Lizbet did indeed have a point.

Lizbet continued to talk quietly in his ear. "And look, her hair has caught on the button on his doublet. He wants to move it but he just can't allow himself to touch those red locks. He's as rigid as a statue and I'd wager if you hit him now he'd break into tiny pieces," Lizbet supplied and then added.

"Oh and he's never once looked in her face since you brought her in here. Anything else you need to know, just ask." Lizbet leant back from Jack, pinched his cheek and winked at him. Jack's face told her he still wasn't convinced. "You still don't believe me do you?" there was a hurt tone in her voice. "You just wait, I'll make him proper suffer for you then."

"What are you going to do?" Jack warned, holding her a little tighter

"Ah me, nowt, just watch." Lizbet whistled again and the lute player saluted her across the room. "Would you play for me a song I've not heard in a while?"

"Name it," he replied, strumming chords still from the lute.

"My love see's me not," she called back across the taproom. Then to Jack, "Do you know it?" Jack grunted an affirmative reply.

"Bit melancholy tonight aren't you?" he asked smiling, then grinning at Jack, "You not been treating the lassie right?"

"I want me man here to join you, he has a fair voice and I'd be hearing him sing it for me," Lizbet returned, giving Jack a sideways smile and a squeeze around his neck.

"I think, lad, that she's on to you and trying to tell you she knows you've got another woman," the whistle player joked. Jack ignored them.

The whistle player put down his instrument and picked up his beer while the lute player began; this was a piece for the strings alone.

"There's a tale, an old, old tale." He strummed the lute and three more chords drifted into the air, "When old King Hal went wooing for his new Queen." The gentle notes continued to fall like sprinkled water - "he wrote her a song and when she heard it," he paused making sure he had all of their attention, "she could do nothing other than fall in love with the King. Her heart broke when she heard his pledge of love, for none can love as truly or as faithfully," - there was a little rumble of laughter in the Inn - "as a King." His fingers crashed across the strings, the sudden noise raising all eyes to him. Then he began.

My love is lost, my love is gone
How ever will I live through a day
I see her with another man
She sees me not at all

My heart is lost and pledged for life
How ever will I live through the years
I see her love is another man's
She sees me not at all

Lizbet looked back over her shoulder at Richard, then quietly in Jack's ear, "Told you so." The lute player moved into the chorus joined by many in the inn.

The lady has all my love
The lady is my hearts desire
The lady cares not at all

Whether I shall live or die

The lute player strolled over and took his place again, leaning on the table between Richard and Jack. He inclined his head to Jack, indicating he should take the next verse as he finished the chorus.

In a voice that was surprisingly steady, Jack took up the song,

My desire is lost and gone from me
How ever will I live through my life
I see her happiness is another's
She sees me not at all

The lady has all my love
The lady is my hearts desire
The lady cares not at all
Whether I shall live or die

Jack held Richard's eyes for a moment as he sang; Lizbet could never have even guessed how close the words were to a truth. The look on his brother's face of open torment and pain was real; indeed he had gone quite pale. Jack signalled to the Lute player and handed him back his song. He left the table as he encouraged the patrons to join him in the chorus one more time.

The lady has all my love
The lady is my hearts desire
The lady cares not at all
Whether I shall live or die.

"Now then lets see if we can get the lassies to dance for us again," said the whistle player and the tone altered as his high pitched notes sparkled through the tavern.

"Oh I like this one." Lizbet was on her feet in a moment. "Come on." She'd taken hold of Elizabeth's hands again and pulled her from the seat on Richard's knee. It was obvious what Richard thought about Lizbet's actions, but to stop them would have meant taking hold of Elizabeth and pulling her back to his knee; he couldn't do that.

"We go back to back like this," Lizbet reversed into Elizabeth, "then forward four steps and both backward four."

Richard reached out blindly for a cup, knocking it over, ale pouring over the table top to drip between the planking to the floor.

"Here, have some more," Jack spoke with mock sincerity, raising the jug and pouring more into the empty cup. Jack put the jug down. "I thought so, look at that?" He smiled and held out his hand flat. Both men looked at it - the tremor was absent.

Richard laughed hoarsely, holding out his own right hand for a moment. "I think you've passed it to me!"

He picked up the ale cup and emptied it, gesturing for Jack to refill it straight away.

"Steady, we still have our charge remember and we are not out of this yet," Jack warned.

"Yes, pray God they are not long," Richard agreed. "Oh God, they are back."

Both women returned laughing and breathless from the dance and resumed their seats opposite each other on the brothers' knees.

"So are you Jack's wife?" Elizabeth was asking.

Lizbet laughed loudly, "Lord no, your man there'd not be letting his brother marry the likes of me."

"Brother?" Elizabeth swivelled round to face Richard.

"It is a long story. The details would most assuredly bore you, but it's true," Richard leaned away from her.

"But," Elizabeth looked between them, "you don't even look alike."

Jack spoke this time, catching Richard's eye, "I'm saddened he never thought to speak of me."

"The occasion never arose," Richard replied bitingly.

"I shall introduce myself then, John Fitzwarren, Richard's older brother. I would get up, but, as you can see, I've been pinned to the trestle by Lizbet's backside." He managed some kind of bow, seated as he was with a woman on his knee with her arm around him.

Richard had posted a look-out at the front door and the lad, half frozen from his hour in the street, dived through the door, his eyes casting about for Richard.

"That's us." Jack saw him before Richard did. Rising he deposited Lizbet neatly on the bench.

"I'm afraid we must leave. Parry is here and I'm sure you'd rather not be found with us," Richard was unable to bring himself to move, he was still seated with his knee employed as a chair.

"Lady." Jack held his hands out. She took them and rose. "Sit yourself next to Lizbet for a few moments please, while we" - Jack whipped his jacket from off the chair - "make our exit. And I think the best one is that one over there." He pointed behind Richard to the door through which they had entered.

†

Thomas Parry had followed the directions sent in the note. However unlikely they may be; he was a desperate man. He arrived with three liveried men and was more than a little surprised to find a distraught Elizabeth, who wanted nothing more than to return home. He could get little from her, only that she had become disorientated in the smoke and fog, that initially she had been with Kate and that somehow she had become separated from her as they walked the streets, becoming more and more lost as they went. A kindly lady it seemed had taken pity on her and had taken her to the inn and sent a message back at her direction.

Wrapped in Parry's own cloak and seated in front of him, he had been further scandalised when Elizabeth slipped off both her shoes and insisted they be taken to the lady who had been so kind to her.

Richard and Jack watched them leave from where they both stood in the shadows next to the inn, both breathed a sight more easily, even if it were for very different reasons.

"And us?" Jack asked. "We can't stay here now. Fairfax will be after your hide damned soon I would say."

"Agreed," Richard said, as they returned for the last time to the rooms over the inn. "Let's leave."

"Where to this time?" Jack asked.

Richard grinned. "Fairfax has paid for a passage for six to Holland; we may as well take advantage of the situation."

Jack smiled: Holland would be a damn sight safer then London.

"Come on then, it sails at seven. I doubt very much that they will go there to look for us," Richard supplied, then added, "wait here, I just need to pay Lizbet."

Jack let Richard go back downstairs alone into the inn. He didn't want to see her again, didn't want to say goodbye. The woman would make it hard he told himself and busied himself making sure he'd left nothing he needed.

†

The dawn was beginning to break through the dark night sky by the time they got back to the Dutch Flower. Hugo and his crew were already getting the Fluyt ready to take the tide. Richard showed Jack the small cabin they would share. It suddenly felt like the end of a very long journey. Jack sat down on the edge of the cabin bed and rubbed his palms over his face.

"Have you ever had a day without an end? This one surely has come close," Jack began to unbuckle the sword belt. "Do you need me?" he asked.

Richard clapped him on the arm. "Not at all. I won't be long. Stop in the cabin and stay out of sight, even if Fairfax's men come looking they don't know who you are so you will be safe."

Jack placed his sword on the floor next to the bed and slid his poniard under the pillow. He lay down and pulled the blanket over him. Richard, watching from the door, was sure that the other man was almost instantly asleep. About to leave, he stopped himself. There was a heavy brass gimble lamp on the table and, taking it, he left the cabin and came back a moment later with it lit and set it on the floor near the sleeping man, the glass closed on the lamp to preserve the flame.

†

Christian was asleep in bed when a servant knocked nervously on his bedchamber door. "Master, a visitor, he is most insistent,"

Christian was out of bed in a moment, a cloak hastily thrown over his linen shift; this could only be bad news. His friend, Mercher, had woken to find his warehouse picked clean by thieves and when he was directed by his own servants to the kitchen where the visitor was, he expected a messenger bearing this calamitous news. The terrible dread in his chest disappeared as soon as he laid eyes on the man in his kitchen - his warehouse was safe. Then another kind of worry set about his nerves. He shooed away the servant who stood behind him and quickly closed the door.

"Richard, what's happened?" Christian asked, his eyes taking in the state of the man before him. He looked tired. His clothes, usually so ordered and neat, were marked. There was a tear in the velvet at one shoulder and several buttons were missing. There's been a fight, Christian concluded.

Richard raised a hand. "Nothing you need worry about. I'd never bring trouble to your door, Christian." Then, "I'm leaving England and I want to take some of your cargo with me. I have a buyer in mind" - then he added grinning - "in Malta."

Christian pulled out a chair from the table, sat down heavily and listened. When he'd heard it all, he sat quietly. "They are dangerous people to deal with Richard, you know that, don't you?"

"Dangerous, I agree. However the Knights of St John are well financed and at the moment there are many parties who would prefer that they retain control over the Mediterranean. A large shipment, such as the one you keep in your warehouse, could be useful in keeping the Ottoman Empire to heel," Richard laughed. "And if they don't want it, then Suleiman certainly has the wealth to buy it."

Christian looked at him askance. "You wouldn't? Would you?" Then shaking his head, he added, "Keep those thoughts to yourself. If the Knights suspect you would do that should they turn you down you'll not be leaving Malta in one piece."

"Forgive me, it's been a long night," Richard sounded serious once again.

"How do you propose to do this? You can't take all the cargo to them; it's too much," Christian was drumming his fingers on the table thinking over the proposal carefully. "You'll need samples at a guess?"

Richard smiled. "Samples of everything." Then tapping his head with a forefinger he added, "I have your inventory in here. I told you, I would not act without your consent. I am asking for it now."

Christian eyes held Richard's steel-grey ones for a moment before he gave an almost imperceptible nod.

Richard smiled. "Thank you."

"I'm guessing you are leaving soon given your early morning visit?" Christian questioned.

"In an hour or so all being well, can you get me some sent to the Dutch Flower. I'll be leaving with her this morning."

"So you are the Protestant escaping persecution," Christian raised his brows enquiringly.

"Not quite, but the passage was paid for and I am, at the moment, looking for an open door to duck through, so this is as good as any," Richard smiled.

Christian laughed rising from the table, "Richard, you've spent your whole life looking for open doors. There is no time to waste. I will have what you need on the quay in an hour."

✝

Jack didn't know how long he'd slept, only that it wasn't long enough; his eyes felt as they were full of grit and his mouth was dry. He seemed to be surrounded by noise. The slap and suck of the water against the ships sides, the unnerving voice of the oak timbers as the Fluyt settled and twisted on the ever moving sea. Jack had never liked ships. His first voyage from England to France had been thankfully short and he'd made the passage drunk so he could remember little of it, adopting the same condition when he'd made the return journey. An irrational notion gripped him when he was at sea and he didn't like to dwell on the fathomless depths over which the wooden vessels hovered. Nor did he understand why they remained on the surface and were not sucked beneath by the ravages of the waves. There were voices outside as well, the accents foreign and guttural as they readied the ship to sail; then his ears picked out the shouting of one voice in particular.

"If you bloody drop that I'll piggin' skin you myself," Lizbet was yelling.

Jack was on his feet in a moment; the ship hadn't sailed. *Why? What had gone wrong? What the hell was Lizbet doing here!*

He made it at a run out of the cabin, buckling his sword back on as he went and exploded from the door onto the deck.

Lamps lit the Dutch Flower as they readied her to sail on the tide. There was a sneaking light from the east heralding a dark March morning, but the ship and the quay were still in the clutch of the night.

Drego was on deck. "Why didn't we sail? Where is Richard?" Jack stammered.

"Lad, we are about to; if he's not up the plank soon he'll miss his passage. We'll not delay. He had some extra boxes loaded on and then went back on foot. I did warn him we'd not wait," Drego exclaimed.

Jack looked and the coffer from Richard's rooms was being unsteadily carried up the loading planks by two of Drego's men and behind them, shouting unhelpful directions, was Lizbet.

Jack dived under a side rail and skidded down the loading plank to her. "Where's Richard?"

Lizbet shook her head. "I don't know, he told me to pack that up." She pointed at the coffer making its way now onto the deck. "And wait, these two cloth heads" - she waved a hand at one the Drego's men lugging the coffer onto the ship - "called for me about an hour ago and I came straight here."

"Jesus Christ!" Jack cast his eyes around the quay, but there was no sign of his brother. Pushing past Lizbet, he made it back onto the quay. Where the hell was Richard? Jack would be damned if he was going to sail without him.

Then he heard the noise.

Hoof beats. God's bones he'd gone back for his bloody horse!

The steel-shod hooves rang out getting closer. Something was wrong, the horse was coming at a gallop. A moment later Corracha's elegant head, main flying silver in the moonlight, flew round a corner into view and headed straight for the Fluyt.

On an ordinary day the horse would be led up the planks by hand. Not today.

Richard pulled the horse to a halt at the bottom of the loading planks and then, short reined, pushed him up the ramp. The Arab took three steps forwards. It's eyes bulged in panic as it felt the wood bend beneath it's weight and, snorting, it backed away, wheeling around on the quay.

There were more horses coming. Jack heard them approach, as his brother still battled to push the stallion to move up onto the Fluyt. The horse took two more steps and then, as the wood dipped, he reared.

"How many behind you," Jack shouted, ducking to avoid the flailing hooves.

"Four," Richard called back. His legs employed in exerting as much control over Corracha as he could. He had him a third of the way up, moving him sideways towards the level deck. Jack caught his bridle, adding a steadying hand and set to pull the horse swiftly up onto the deck.

The other riders were coming down the quay now. Jack could hear their shouts and also Drego yelling at Richard to get the horse off the loading ramp. The two front mooring ropes were already off and the Fluyt was nosing out into the Thames. Very soon the ramp would collapse into the river as the Dutch Flower pulled away from the Quay.

The horse's hind quarters were tense, his eyes wide and the hooves danced noisily on the wood. As he pulled his rider round again, Jack had to let go of the bridle, as he risked being pushed off the ramp into the river.

"Come on, damn you!" Richard shouted. The horse turned back towards the ramp and Richard pushed him on hard. Hooves clattered and slipped as the stallion reluctantly obeyed the commands and finally made it onto the ship, the loading plank swiftly withdrawn behind him.

Richard's pursuers made it a moment too late. They could almost reach out and touch the ship from where they were on the quay, but with the river tugging at her timbers she might as well have been a mile away. All they could do was shout.

Richard dropped from the saddle, holding tightly on to his horse; Jack had a firm grip on the bridle as well.

"Fairfax's men?" Jack asked and Richard nodded. "Bloody hell, you cut that a bit fine." And then nodding towards Lizbet. "And why is she coming?"

Richard grinned, "I can't look after you on my own all the time, can I?"

The coffer would share the hold in the Fluyt with three other large boxes, all provided by Christian Carter. Inside the boxes, wrapped in grease and oil cloth, were the Italian guns. The boxes were skilfully packed. Sea water and salt would be their enemy and the guns had been dipped in wax, then wrapped securely in swathes of linen cloth thick with noxious grease.

✝

Durham Place was cold. The fire had filled the rooms with smoke and all of the paned windows had been opened to the winter weather to dispel the acrid smell. Floors, furniture and stonework - everything within the house normally warmed by the blazing fires had cooled in the winter air. The fires, alive again, struggled to infuse the house with warmth. The solar was too big and airy and cold, so Elizabeth and Kate had retreated sensibly to Elizabeth's own bedroom. Small and well furnished, it was easier to heat. The walls were hung with tapestries depicting the nine daughters of Zeus. A depiction of Melpomene, the muse of tragedy, wringing her hands in front of a flaming house, hung near the fire. "At least she's warm," thought Elizabeth bitterly.

"Kate, it's so cold," Elizabeth complained.

"I know, we've had all the windows open for so long to get all the smoke out and it's let the winter weather in, the place is freezing. Here, put this over your knees." Kate passed her an embroidered shawl.

"What happened?" Kate asked.

"A lot, Kate, a lot. I met quite a man last night," Elizabeth smiled at the memory.

Kate's brow furrowed. "Who did you meet, do I know them?"

"I don't suppose so, did you know that Richard had a brother?" Elizabeth asked.

"Yes, Robert I think his name is," Kate supplied.

"He has another one called John," Elizabeth continued to stare in front of her, a smile lighting the corners of her mouth as she thought again about their perilous crossing of the river. He'd said he didn't like her, Elizabeth however, didn't believe him.

Epilogue

"They're going to kill it, Jack. They're going to kill the horse. Jack, where are you?"

Both men heard Lizbet before she'd even got up the stairs to the cabin and they all met in a jam on the steps. Lizbet flattened herself against the wood panelling and let them go down. Richard seemed to take all of them in two paces and Jack was hard on his heels.

Corracha, Richard's horse, was in a makeshift stable on the Fluyt. The crossing to Holland was to take only three days and, for a fee, they had agreed to take the animal. A makeshift stable had been rigged between two lots of packing cases and, with the crossing being so short, only a minimal amount of feed was needed. So far the Arabian had been happy with the stall and with the journey.

They heard constant pounding before they got there. Corracha was kicking out sometimes with both rear hooves and sometimes with one. The makeshift partition was open and the ship's cook, a burly Dutchman with a hatchet in one hand, was being goaded on by his shipmates, standing at a safe distance behind him

"Stop," Richard commanded, "You touch that animal and I'll put that blade between your eyes."

The Dutchman hefted the axe in his hand. "Then you do it. Leave it much longer and the damn thing will have holed the hull."

Corracha continued the incessant kicking. Iron clad hooves were indeed splintering the wood.

"That hull is a hand's width thick, a horse isn't going to kick it through," Richard moved swiftly between the horse and the axe. Jack moved even quicker and slipped between the pair. Richard heard him talking calmly to the stallion.

"Donny, get captain Drego now, he'll settle this. I'm not waking in the night up to me armpits in water," the Dutchman bellowed, shouting over his shoulder at the group of men. One of them ducked away and went in search of Drego.

The horse's eyes were wide, it's coat thick with sweat, as it continued to blindly kick at the wall behind it. Jack, his head against the horses cheek, smoothed his hand down it's neck. His voice level, calm and easy he spoke quietly to the animal. Twice it pushed him away, the first time hard into the wooden partition and the second time backwards out of the stall, sending him reeling into Richard. Both times he went back the third time he wound his hand round the head collar, firmly pulling Corracha's head down to meet his. All the time he kept talking in a level voice, the hooves missed a beat. The arguing outside the stable stopped as the deafening crashing halted. He kicked out again, just once more, but with less conviction. When Jack's hand hard on his head-collar he allowed him to turn him in a tight circle in the stall. He neighed and stamped but the kicking, the incessant kicking, had stopped. The Dutchman dropped the hatchet to his side and a cheer went up from the men standing behind him.

A Request from the Author

This has been a difficult journey for both Richard and Jack; finally they are beginning to understand one another. As Richard points out they lack a shared past, their father has denied them this. From now on though, they will fight side by side and back to back; they are indeed terrible apart and even worse together.

Can I beg a moment of your time and respectfully ask you to leave even a few brief words on Amazon as a review.

Excerpt from A Queen's Mercenary

Book 3

"This is the best I can do, so don't go complaining at me," Lizbet said as she backed into the room, opening he door with her rear, her hands carrying a laden tray. "It's some sort of bread, God knows what they make it from, it's tougher than boot leather."

Richard looked up from the table where he was seated, "Jack, is he awake?"

Lizbet's brows raised, "I'd have thought you'd know better than to ask that. The lot of them went to bed when the larks got up, kept us awake half the night with their drunken laughter." Lizbet had slept on the floor at the back of the inn with the other staff in a communal room.

"I know, you weren't the only one to suffer it," Richard said, then smiling, "Lizbet, could you get me a bucket of water?"

Lizbet read what he meant to do on his face, "really? I'll make sure it's bloody cold," with that and still grumbling under breath she left to find a pail.

Richard kicked open the door, the smell of sweated beer fumes wrinkled his nostrils. His sudden entry had not breached the sleep of any of those within. Froggy, sat on the floor his head resting on the end of the bed, one boot on and one off, he looked as if he had succumbed in the act of trying to remove the second. Dan was sprawled face down, head pillowed on his arms and Jack had made it to the bed where he lay flat on his back, open mouthed and snoring. Richard considered them all for a moment, before taking a firm hold of the bottom of the bucket and threw half of it over Dan and the other half square in Froggy's face; Jack he spared.

✝

Dan stared mutinously at Richard over a cup of restorative ale. "Aye, it did get late quick." He said by way of apology. Mat was still asleep on the floor where he had landed after he had slid from his perch on the table during the night, Froggy was trying to dry himself, and Jack remained blissfully unaware asleep still.

"The happy reunion over with, do you want to tell me what happened after I left?" Richard said equably.

"After you left?" Dan said dismayed, "you hardly left, we all thought you were dead."

"Well, as you can happily see, that did not come to pass. I sent word to you via Jamie did I not? To stay with Jack," Richard said, his eyes holding Dan's until the other was forced to shamefully look away.

"You did, but you don't know what he was like? I tried to help him, it wasn't easy." Dan said, and he knew his words sounded poor.

"No-one would ever accuse Jack of being easy, nevertheless he ended up in London on his own, why did you leave him?" Richard asked, his voice still level.

"He chose to go his own way, I couldn't stop him could I?" Dan said quietly.

"He ended up in Marshalsea Dan in just a few weeks, and you could have stopped that. I left him with you, he was in your charge," Richard said, his voice hard now.

"Why does that not surprise me," Dan said shaking his head. "And you think I could have stopped him gambling his way into gaol do you?"

Richard slammed his fist down hard on the table making Dan jump, "my family put him in Marshalsea, not his own actions. Had you been there it might not have happened. I didn't leave him alone. I left him, so I thought in your care, and what did you do?"

Dan staring firmly at the table chose not to answer.

"Tell me, why?" Richard demanded again.

Dan looked up, and met his eyes, "Because you were dead and he's not you. I couldn't make him into something he's not could I?"

Both men stared at each other, the silence was broken by a women's voice.

"Shift your elbows otherwise I've nowhere to put the plates," said Lizbet, Richard sat back and removed his arms from table ignoring her, and Dan did the same as a plate of cheese was placed between then and then a moment later another topped with bread, Dan scowled at her. The loud noise from the clanking plates grating inside his painful head. Lizbet held his eyes as she loudly banged down another pitcher of beer between them. Turning on her heel she left them Dan muttering swear words at her retreating back.

"If I may continue," Richard said drawing Dan's angry gaze back from where it rested on the serving girls back.

Dan nodded, he did not particularly though want Richard to continue. He had tried to help Jack, but he'd been shown he door, more than once, he'd not wanted anyone's help. Finally he said, "I tried, I truly did, but there was no persuading him."

"There is never any persuading Jack when he has a temper on him, and you know that." Richard said coldly, "you should have followed him."

The words hung between them. Dan knew he should have followed him, but he'd had his own grief and he'd not wanted to deal with Jack. Jack reminded him too much of Richard, and Jack had been making a mockery out of everything he had been left. Dan realised he was going to have to say something, as poor as it may sound. "I should have," then he added, "I'll not make the mistake a second time." And then, "are you going to tell me what happened to you both?"

Richard looked at him with cold eyes, "I got Jack out of Marshalsea, but I didn't save him from it, he's not the same Dan. He'll never be the same."

"Looks fine to me," Dan retorted.

"Now you are back, you make sure stays that way," Richard said with finality.

Printed in Great Britain
by Amazon